Her Scottish Scoundrel

Diamonds
in the Rough

SOPHIE BARNES

HER SCOTTISH SCOUNDREL
Diamonds in the Rough

Copyright © 2021 by Sophie Barnes

Cover Design and Interior Format

© THE KILLION GROUP, INC.

ALSO BY SOPHIE BARNES

The Summersbys
The Secret Life of Lady Lucinda
There's Something About Lady Mary
Lady Alexandra's Excellent Adventure

Standalone Titles
The Girl Who Stepped Into The Past
How Miss Rutherford Got Her Groove Back

Novellas

The Townsbridges
An Unexpected Temptation
A Duke for Miss Townsbridge
Falling for Mr. Townsbridge
Lady Abigail's Perfect Match
When Love Leads To Scandal
Once Upon a Townsbridge Story

The Honorable Scoundrels
The Duke Who Came To Town
The Earl Who Loved Her
The Governess Who Captured His Heart

Standalone Titles
The Secrets of Colchester Hall
Mistletoe Magic (from Five Golden Rings: A
Christmas Collection)
Miss Compton's Christmas Romance

CHAPTER ONE

London
July, 1821

BLAYNE MACNEIL PICKED up his glass of Madeira and saluted his host. Nothing improved his mood as much as a meal at Windham House. The duke and duchess, Valentine Sterling and his wife Regina, had an incredible chef whose skill in the kitchen was second to none. Considerably different from what the two men had known in their nearly two-decade friendship in St Giles. But now that Val, once known as Carlton Guthrie, the Scoundrel of St. Giles, had taken his rightful place as Duke of Windham, he denied his new wife nothing, including incomparable food.

The sweet wine slid down Blayne's throat, sending a warmth through his stomach. Truth was, sometimes he missed the old Guthrie—and the brutal force he and his friend had used to vanquish the vermin of the world. Now he himself was a businessman with a respectable tavern to run...well, a tavern, at any rate. And Guthrie still made sure justice was served, but it was done with more discretion now that he was a duke, and by accepting help from the authorities.

"I have been toying with the idea of hosting a ball," Regina said. She glanced at her brother, Marcus, who also resided at Windham House, and then at Blayne. "If I do, I shall expect you both to attend so you can dance with some of the ladies the marriage mart has to offer."

The comment was jovial – teasing even – yet it still caused Blayne's lungs to strain against his next intake of breath.

Marcus snorted. "As if any well-bred woman would dare."

Blayne met Marcus's gaze and slowly exhaled. His insides eased and he forced a wry smile. "Even if one of the lasses cared to, I'm sure her parents would quickly step in to prevent it."

"I could coerce them into compliance," Guthrie murmured, a twinkle in his cat-like eyes.

"And into marriage, I'm sure," Marcus said with a grin.

"Good lord," Regina murmured.

"Without a doubt," Guthrie told Marcus. "Shall I?"

"No." Regina gave her husband a firm look. "There will be no coercing. I merely thought it might be nice to offer Blayne and Marcus the means by which to attend a social function."

"To the horror and despair of the *ton*," Blayne said right before he spooned more shortcake into his mouth. "I thank ye for yer thoughtfulness, Regina, but I think yer ball would be better served if I stayed away."

"Nonsense," she said. "You are a handsome man, Blayne. Kind, too, and hardworking."

"Not exactly the qualities upper-class parents seek in their future son-in-law." Blayne took another bite of his dessert. It truly was exceptionally good. "A yearly income close to five thousand pounds and un-calloused hands would be more desirable. Preferably a title or two as well. My income is modest though, my hands as rough as tree bark, and I've nae title to speak of."

More importantly, he had a past he couldn't in good conscience chain another person to. And he sure as hell couldn't confide it in any woman. So if he did wed, his marriage would be a sham. He took another sip of Madeira.

"My situation is similar," Marcus said. "Worse than Blayne's, in a sense, seeing as I had a title and lost it because of our father. No man in his right mind would allow his daughter to be seen with me, Regina."

The duchess huffed a breath. "In my opinion, a man's character – his very own actions – ought to be of greater value than what a relation of his might have done."

"I don't think any of us disagrees with you there," Guthrie said. He gave Blayne and Marcus a pensive look. "Perhaps I can help?"

"Thank ye, but no." Guthrie had offered to give Blayne a handsome sum once before, and Blayne had turned him down then as well. He didn't want handouts, not even from a friend who wished to disguise it as overdue wages.

"There is something to be said for earning one's own living."

"I'm of a like mind," Marcus said. "Although I might appreciate a loan for the sake of acquiring a profession."

"Indeed?" Regina regarded her brother with a pensive mien. "And what profession do you have in mind, Marcus?"

"Well." Marcus cleared his throat. "Medicine would be an interesting field of study. Certainly more so than law."

"I think that would be marvelous," Regina said with a smile. "Don't you agree, Guthrie?"

Guthrie nodded. "I would be happy to provide you with the necessary funds, Marcus."

"As a loan," Marcus reiterated.

Blayne hid a chuckle behind his last spoonful of dessert. It was clear Marcus did not want to feel beholden to Guthrie any more than he did.

"Of course," Guthrie said. He turned his assessing gaze on Blayne. "What about you? If you accept a loan you'll be able to purchase that property you want a lot sooner than otherwise."

"What property?" Regina asked.

"I've been of a mind to get away from London for a while now," Blayne said. "With my interest in plants, I'd like to have a spot of land to cultivate, maybe with a wee house on it. I dinnae require much in the way of a home, but a sizeable piece of property would be grand." It would provide him with the freedom he'd started to crave since Guthrie had left The Black Swan. Blayne ran the St. Giles tavern on his own now and saved every hard-earned penny, but the place was different without his friend there, and with every passing day Blayne could feel himself getting older. It was time to move on and settle down to a quieter way of life.

"Then I hope you shall soon be able to acquire it," Regina said. She raised her glass. "To Marcus's medical aspirations and to Blayne's countryside acquisition."

Blayne drank and breathed a sigh of relief when the conversation turned to the recent coronation of George IV.

It appeared Regina's idea of a ball had been forgotten for now, for which he was grateful. Aside from the obvious reasons he had for not wanting to attend, there was the more dreaded prospect of being recognized. As unlikely as it might be after twenty years in hiding, one couldn't be too careful.

Least of all when one was on the run for murder.

Apprehension filled Charlotte Russell's veins whenever she had to visit Carlisle & Co. Located on the east side of London, the publisher wasn't in the worst possible neighborhood, but it certainly wasn't in the finest one either. Poverty was still rife here, especially if one ventured near Dorset Street where filth and suffering appeared to be on the rise. Toxic fumes from industries such as tanning and dyeing permeated the air with a poisonous scent while the cries from unhappy children made her heart clench.

Dressed in the simplest gown she owned, Charlotte hoped to blend in with the people who lived and worked here while she visited her friend, Avery Carlisle. The pair had known each other since adolescence when a birthday party had brought them together. They'd looked forward to promising futures back then with dreams of marrying suitable gentlemen and settling down to the lives their parents envisioned.

Goodness, how quickly one's situation could change. Avery's mother had one day realized she'd rather sail the world with a roguish captain. When the couple ran off together, it plunged Avery's father into a state so severe he'd eventually shot himself. The scandal had ruined Avery's prospects completely, but at least she and her younger brother had been remembered in the will. Enough to start their own business.

As for Charlotte, she'd made her debut at the age of eighteen, but rather than succeed at snatching up an eligible gentleman for herself, she'd managed to pair them all off with other ladies. It had been, as her mother, Viscountess Elkins, had called it, an absolute disaster. But the truth was, Charlotte had longed for more than an untitled lord who only viewed her as his entrance to the peerage, an aging gentleman looking to snatch up a young bride, or a penniless fop whose only interest in her was based on her monetary value.

Instead, Charlotte had dreamed of adventure, of impassioned glances and stolen kisses. She'd wanted more than bland conversation and politely reserved conduct. What she'd sought was love – true love – the kind to spark jealousy in the hearts of those who'd chosen to marry for other reasons. She'd wanted a husband whose eyes would burn with desire whenever he saw her, who yearned for her as fervently as she yearned for him. And when she'd realized she sought the impossible, she'd given up trying to find it.

Eventually, desperate to make some progress, Charlotte's mother had given her attention to Charlotte's younger sisters, Melanie and Edwina. Both were now respectably married; Melanie to Sir Nichols, whom she'd wed a couple of years ago, and Edwina, to Mr. Henshaw, last month. Neither appeared to be the least bit besotted with their spouse, but then, they also hadn't had the same romantic notions as Charlotte. With Melanie now residing in Yorkshire and Edwina tucked away in Devon, she had no expectation of seeing them more than once a year at most from now on.

Presently, at the advanced age of seven and twenty, Charlotte knew she was firmly on the shelf. She no longer dreamt of the happily-ever-after she'd wanted when she'd been presented at court. Instead, she lived vicariously through the characters in her stories. Her goal now was of an entirely different nature. It involved a quiet countryside cottage where she would be free to commit her imagination to paper. An independent life completely her own. One with no room for a husband at all.

"This third book of yours is utterly splendid," Avery said. "There's still the humor and excitement readers became familiar with in the first two novels, but this one has an added degree of maturity to it. Your writing is stronger and the plot... Well, I could scarcely turn the pages fast enough."

"I'm glad you like it," Charlotte said. "I wasn't sure if the murder was convincing enough."

"On the contrary, I thought that part worked really well. What I think you may need to look at is Lady Gertrude's characterization. I fear some readers will find her too brazen when she and the marquess are first introduced. It seems a bit unrealistic."

"You think I should soften her up."

"Yes. If she grows more from experience, then the scene where she must overcome her fear of heights in order to help the hero would be so much stronger."

"Hmm..."

"I have some notes." Avery handed over a couple of pages for Charlotte to look at. "There are a few other minor details as well, like the inconsistent color of the marquess's eyes and the elapsed number of years since Mrs. Verdanne, the victim, first arrived in London, along with the number of guests present at the dinner party she was attending when the crime was committed."

"I see." Charlotte scanned the notes and saw there was more than that. Several parts of the manuscript would have to be re-written, but she was used to this by now. Apparently, no matter how perfect she thought her story to be when she handed it over to Avery, there were plenty of mistakes to be found.

"With all of this taken into consideration, how long do you suppose it would take for you to review, revise, and return the corrected work?" Leaning forward, Avery met Charlotte's gaze. "I ask because I think it would be wonderful if we could get the book into shops before Christmas."

"Would a month be too long?"

"No. I think a month would be fine, but not a day more or it will have to wait to be printed until next year, in which case we miss out on the extra sales we ought to acquire during the holiday season. And since we will be aiming to move quickly on this, I should like to prepare the front and back matter for the book, which brings me to the title. Have you decided on one?"

Charlotte nodded. "What do you think of *The Marquess's Unresolved Mysteries*?"

"Oh! It's perfect, Charlotte. Completely in keeping with the previous titles and with a nod to the three old cases Lady Gertrude helps the marquess crack."

"In that case, I shall leave you to sort out the front and back matter while I take care of the edits." Retrieving her manuscript, Charlotte placed Avery's notes on top and slid the stack of papers inside the folio she'd brought with her and stood.

"On another subject," Avery said. Having also risen, she rounded her desk and faced Charlotte.

"I think my brother, Albert, is quite besotted with you. He would most likely die if he learned I'd said anything, but is there a chance you might be willing to accept his attentions?"

"I'm afraid not," Charlotte said. She gave her friend a pleasant smile. "My pursuits have changed. I no longer wish to marry but rather to avoid it."

"He would support your writing, Charlotte."

"He would also make demands on my time and besides, you know my position. I would want passion and with Albert there's never been one single spark. I'm sorry, Avery, but it's not going to happen."

"No matter," Avery said, "but I could not resist asking."

Appreciating her friend's honesty, Charlotte left her office and stepped into the publisher's antechamber where Albert sat behind a wide reception desk. He immediately stood, his cheeks flushing a bright shade of pink the moment he saw her.

Charlotte smiled politely and with the hope of not adding any encouragement. "Mr. Carlisle."

"Miss Russell," he replied, and rushed toward her. "I trust your meeting with Avery went well."

"Oh yes. Thank you."

"Please. Allow me to walk you to your carriage."

Unwilling to let him think she might be remotely interested, Charlotte shook her head. "There's really no need."

"Oh, but I insist." He reached for her folio.

Charlotte sidestepped him. "You're ever so kind but I do think you ought to stay here in case other clients show up."

"Right. Um. Will you be back again soon?"

"In a month or so. I shall see you then." She turned away and moved toward the door leading out to the foyer.

"Indeed you shall," Albert called after her. "Without fail."

Charlotte winced in response to his eager tone as she pushed through the doors and made her escape. Turning right, she continued out into the street and scanned it for the hackney she'd hired in order to come here. She'd asked the coachman to wait, insisting she wouldn't be more than fifteen minutes at most. More like half an hour or more. Apparently the coachman had thought this too long and had driven off.

Muttering a curse, Charlotte commenced walking. Whitechapel Road wasn't far. She'd find another hackney there, no problem. With one hand on the pistol she carried in her skirt pocket whenever she went out, she set off. But when she turned left several minutes later, someone caught her from behind, his firm hand snaking around her person to trap her in place. The sharp metal edge of a blade pressed into her throat.

"Scream, an' it'll be the last sound you make," a gruff voice said.

Charlotte curled her fingers around her pistol's grip. If only she could get some leeway – spin around – threaten the villain in return. Unfortunately, her current position allowed for no such thing. "All right."

"Did I say you could speak?" The blade pressed deeper. One hand latched onto her reticule "I'll just take this an' be on my way."

Charlotte closed her eyes and prayed. She'd never felt more helpless. And she hated it. But what choice did she have? She couldn't ask one of her parents' footmen to join her on her excursions. Their loyalty lay with her parents so they could not be trusted with Charlotte's secret while Daisy, the maid who'd been meant to accompany Charlotte, had been sent on an errand by Charlotte's mother at the last minute, leaving Charlotte with no other option than to set off alone if she was to keep her appointment.

Swallowing, Charlotte tried to steady her breathing – to not panic while the thief grabbed her reticule. It contained more money than usual – three months' worth of royalties in the amount of two hundred and eighty pounds.

Harsh laughter filled her ears. "I like the weight of this. Now stay still and count to twenty."

Charlotte started to do as she was told, but the moment the blade left her throat, she drew her pistol from within the folds of her skirt and whipped around, only to learn that the thief had waited for just the right moment to flee. A group of children were now approaching the spot where she stood, blocking her line of fire as the thief raced away behind them. Charlotte's hand shook in response to the shocking encounter. She lowered her arm and took a tremulous breath.

This really wouldn't do. If she was to keep on coming here, she would have to ensure her own safety.

Intent on solving the problem as soon as possible, Charlotte set off the following morning after breakfast, this time with Daisy in tow. She was convinced she'd achieve her goal without much hardship. All it would take was a day – one week at most.

But after spending the next month visiting various tea-shops, scouring the parks, and taking luncheon at some of the more reputable inns, she was forced to acknowledge that finding the sort of man who could blend in on the streets of Mayfair and scare the devil out of a villain was no simple task.

Now, with her next meeting at Carlisle & Co. approaching fast, she decided to make one last desperate attempt at engaging the capable sort she required.

"Are you sure we ought to risk coming to this part of Town, miss?" Daisy's voice conveyed a healthy dose of nervousness as she glanced out the window of the hackney they'd hired a short while earlier. "Doesn't it contradict what you're trying to achieve?"

It did, but after failing to find a suitable candidate for the position elsewhere, Charlotte had decided to try another option –The Black Swan tavern. An acquaintance of hers, Regina Sterling, the Duchess of Windham, had met her husband there, and while the duke was not con-sidered the least bit respectable, he was precisely the sort of man Charlotte needed – one capable of instilling fear in any thug who threatened her safety.

"I realize it's not ideal, Daisy, but I cannot walk into Gentleman Jackson's and offer employment to one of its patrons." Only upper-class gentle-men and peers frequented the high-end boxing establishment, and although Charlotte was cer-tain several would be capable of warding off a thief, she could not trust them not to tell her family of her exploits.

What Charlotte needed was an individual who answered solely to her – a man who needed the coin she offered and knew he wouldn't receive it if he betrayed her.

"I suppose not, miss, but I still don't like our being here. Even with the window closed, it stinks worse than a chamber pot. If you'll for-give me saying so."

Charlotte scrunched her nose. She'd noticed the putrid stench the moment they'd turned down Drury Lane. "The place shouldn't be far from here. I believe we'll reach it soon."

The carriage turned onto Parker's Lane with a bounce brought on by the uneven paving. A startled gasp sprang from Charlotte's throat in response to the scene before her – of a woman sitting on the doorstep of a dilapidated build-ing. Dressed in filthy rags, she cradled a sobbing infant while two older children, both barefoot, splashed in a nearby puddle. A little way past them, a one-legged man hobbled along with the use of a crutch.

Cast in shades of grey, the street held no resemblance to any Charlotte had seen before. This was much worse than what she'd witnessed in the East End. This was true squalor painted in bleakness and utter despair.

The carriage passed as if blind to the suffering before it rolled to a halt in front of a crooked building built from black timber frame-work. It looked like it was about to fall into the street.

"Goodness," Charlotte muttered. She knew she shouldn't be surprised, but really, the tavern did not appear the least bit sturdy. Certainly not for a place renowned for its bare-knuckle fights. Setting her jaw in preparation for what she would find inside, Charlotte turned to Daisy. "You should stay here."

"And let you go in there alone? I can't possibly."

"I absolutely insist on this point." Charlotte had spent a great deal of time deliberating over it. The last time she'd taken a hackney, the blasted vehicle had driven off before she'd returned. She'd be damned if the same thing would happen again. Least of all in a place such as this.

"It's not seemly," Daisy protested. She jutted her chin toward another building – one located just beyond The Black Swan.

Charlotte considered it for a moment. *Amourette's.* She frowned. The name was familiar though she couldn't quite—

She sucked in a breath as realization struck.

This was the brothel where the Earl of Fielding's new wife had been hiding until he'd accidentally outed her. As the daughter of an accused traitor, their relationship had been mired in scandal until they'd managed to prove her father's innocence. The incident had served as excellent inspiration for Charlotte's latest adventure novel.

She stared at the brothel. A lady of her class ought to blush and avert her gaze. Instead, Charlotte absorbed every detail, ferreting it away for later use when she returned home and took her seat at her desk. She'd be much better equipped to describe back alleys and places of ill repute now. Which clearly meant a few extra scenes from *The Marquess's Unresolved Mysteries* would have to be re-written.

Pleased with the prospect of being able to improve upon her work, she offered Daisy a wry smile. "Between the two, I wonder that it is the brothel you're most concerned with."

"It's your reputation, miss."

"Which won't be any better off if someone I know sees me sitting right here in a carriage located on this very street. Now, Daisy, do try to relax and please make sure the driver waits for me. This could take a while."

"But—"

Deciding to end the discussion, Charlotte opened the door, stepped down, and swept inside The Black Swan. The interior was surprisingly neat and tidy – not at all what she'd expected. Round tables were placed with an appropriate amount of space between them. Several were occupied by men who clearly worked the docks or breweries and had chosen to come for a bite to eat. They stared at her in baffled silence.

Charlotte cleared her throat. "Gentlemen. I'm looking to employ a trustworthy individual who's strong and capable of providing me with protection. If you would like to apply for this position, you may come speak with me at your convenience."

Conscious of having all eyes upon her, Charlotte took a seat at the nearest table and pulled out a small notebook and pencil. Ten minutes later, after receiving a glass of decent wine from a barmaid, she was interviewing a skinny fellow who probably wouldn't be able to fight off a knife-wielding thief no matter how eager he was to prove his worth.

Charlotte politely turned him away and he thanked her for her time.

"I'm afraid you're not what I'm looking for," Charlotte informed the next man who approached her – a mister Robbie Jones. He was a scruffy sort with one tooth missing. Charlotte almost feared the repercussion of being spotted with him more than she feared the danger of venturing out alone.

"'Ow's that?" Mr. Jones asked. He scratched his ear until one finger disappeared inside it. "Ya said ya need protection and I'm big an' strong. I'll make sure no one even looks at ya wrong."

Charlotte watched him retrieve his finger. He studied it for a moment and then proceeded to wipe it on his trousers. Mr. Jones clearly wouldn't do, even if he was large enough to frighten away an assailant with nary one glance.

"As much as I appreciate that," she said while thinking up some way in which to dismiss him without causing too much offense, "I'm not sure you would fare well amid high society."

"'Igh society?'"

"Well, yes. I might require your escort to the occasional soiree and ball."

"Blimey." He began fiddling with his other ear. "Don't think I'd like that. Mingling with toffs aint one of my strengths."

Charlotte did what she could to hide her amusement and breathed an inward sigh of relief. "I see."

Mr. Jones gave a respectful nod. "Sorry to 'ave wasted ya time, miss."

"Don't be," Charlotte assured him. He might be scruffy and he might not know not to pick his ears in public, but he was making an effort to be polite and that in itself deserved her appreciation. "It's been a pleasure meeting you, Mr. Jones."

He smiled broadly in response to her comment, made an awkward bow, and strode away. Another man soon took his place and then another and another. None fit the neat appearance she had in mind. Good lord, whatever had she been thinking to suppose an individual with the sense of style inherent to footmen would ever be found in a place such as this?

Prepared to declare defeat, Charlotte thanked the last man with whom she'd spoken and started gathering her things. Perhaps she could place an advertisement in the paper for an actual footman? Would such a man accept not being part of a household? Of not wearing livery and of simply meeting her when she requested his aid?

There was only one way to find out, she decided as she prepared to stand. But before she was able to get up out of her seat, a stout fellow dropped into the chair directly beside her and placed his hand on her thigh.

"Hello, luv." His oily voice dripped with disturbing lewdness while his fingers curled into her flesh. "I hear you is lookin' for some protection. Thought I'd come right over and offer me services."

There was no question about the sort of services he hoped to provide her with, and since Charlotte knew a delayed reaction on her part would only make him bolder, she didn't waste a single moment. Without thinking twice, she turned in her seat while slipping her hand discreetly inside her skirt pocket and retrieved her pistol. One second later, she had the barrel pressed up against the man's ribs.

"You were saying?" she asked with deliberate sweetness.

The man, whom she now had a much better view of, looked like he was at least twice her age. With thinning hair already showing hints of grey, he had a wide face with a bulbous nose, hard eyes, and a mouth that had opened wide enough to reveal several blackened teeth.

"You can't shoot me," he hissed with contempt.

Without even blinking, Charlotte pulled back the hammer on her pistol. "Care to bet on that?"

"You'll 'ang for murder."

"My solicitor would disagree with you there." She pressed the pistol more roughly against him. "Now please remove your hand from my person before you wind up dead."

He gulped. "You is mad."

"Quite," she agreed. The madder he thought her the better since that made her unpredictable and far more dangerous than a woman who had no intention of causing him harm.

Scrambling out of his chair, the man almost stumbled to the floor in his haste to escape her proximity. He threw her a hasty backward glance as if to make sure she wouldn't pursue him and ran out the door. Charlotte expelled a breath, allowed herself a moment to gather her wits, then disarmed her weapon and carefully returned it to her pocket.

Well, at least she had more fodder for her novels, even if the excursion itself had proven a waste of time. She stood, turned, and immediately froze at the sight of another man standing not too far away, his gaze fixed upon her with interest as he approached. Compared with everyone else she'd met that afternoon, however, this particular man showed promise. Tall, broad shouldered, and with the sort of lean body that spoke of an active lifestyle, his chiseled features, intelligent eyes, and perfectly curved mouth suggested he'd be handsome as sin once he got a good shave and a decent haircut.

Pleased with this discovery, Charlotte allowed a smile.

"How did ye..." His words trailed off as he gestured toward the door through which the other man had so hastily departed.

Her smile widened in response to his bafflement. She liked being able to surprise people on occasion – to not always be the perfectly turned out lady they all expected. "I never leave home without my pistol. Knowing I'm able to defend myself against questionable characters eases my mind."

"So would keeping to safer parts of Town, ye ken," he told her with an immediate scowl.

She tilted her head and proceeded to study him in greater detail. His height was truly impressive. Now that he was closer, she almost felt dwarfed by his much greater size. He was the sort of man who demanded attention, who'd easily instill a degree of wariness in others. And while he did speak with a Scottish burr that lent a gruffness to his voice, there was an unmistakable degree of charm to it.

Charlotte almost grinned. "Do you know. I think you'd be perfect."

His eyes narrowed. "For what?"

"For the position I'm trying to fill."

He crossed his arms in a show of defiance. "I already have a job."

She leaned forward, more determined than ever to enlist his help now that she'd set her mind to it. A rich musky scent filled her nostrils, the appeal of it momentarily startling in this place where every other scent she'd encountered had more or less repelled her. Charlotte forced herself to ignore it so she could focus on tempting her quarry. "It pays exceedingly well. Five pounds per week."

It was a large sum – huge in fact for what she required – considering the fifteen pound yearly salary indispensable servants received. She certainly hadn't planned on offering anywhere near as much when she'd first arrived, but now that she'd found the man she wanted, she'd no intention of letting him walk away when she could afford to lure him with an attractive wage.

As expected, his mouth dropped open. Caramel-colored eyes turned a darker shade of chocolate. The frown he'd been wearing since she'd suggested hiring him deepened. "What the devil do ye want me to do, lass? Kidnap someone and hold them hostage?"

"Don't be silly." She chuckled, dismissing his suggestion with a wave of her hand. Should she be concerned that this was where his mind had gone? She decided not to let it affect her. "What I need is much simpler than that. Less taxing too, I imagine."

The pause that followed was so long it almost caused Charlotte to lose her nerve. Until he suddenly asked, "How so?"

She squared her shoulders and straightened her spine to hide her discomfort. "What I need is an escort who can ensure my safety."

A smirk tugged at his lips, affording him with

a roguish sort of charisma that did something odd to her insides. "Ye seem quite capable of protecting yerself."

"Nevertheless, having a strong and capable man accompany me when I travel about the City would be the sensible thing to do."

He studied her, allowing his gaze to sweep the length of her body with unabashed interest. "How long would ye need me for?"

"Oh." Charlotte's heart jolted. If he was asking her this, then he must be thinking of accepting her offer. The very idea sent a thrill through her veins. "I don't know. What if I hire you on a monthly basis?"

He tilted his head, appeared to ponder the suggestion, and finally stuck out his hand. "Very well. Ye have yerself a new employee. When would ye like me to start?"

She clasped his hand while doing her best not to look too relieved. Warmth wrapped itself around her skin at his touch, forcing an almost inaudible gasp from her lips. Desperate to add some distance, Charlotte cleared her throat and promptly released his hand.

She took a step back. "Tomorrow. Shall we say ten o'clock at Number Two Berkley Square?"

"Indeed, Miss…"

"Russell." She raised her chin. "And you are?"

"Mr. Blayne MacNeil."

She forced herself to hold his gaze while allowing that piece of information to settle. Good lord, she'd heard of this man. He'd been Windham's lieutenant before the duke had been domesticated. A strained smile stretched the muscles in her cheeks while she fought for composure. This was the man who'd be coming into her home tomorrow – the man she would have to introduce as her newly employed servant?

"A pleasure," she said while doing her best not to wonder about the number of men he'd possibly tortured and killed over the years. No backing out now. She'd rather die than show him an ounce of fear or weakness. Instead, Charlotte turned and rushed out the door, eager to depart before she saw reason and ended their arrangement before it had even begun.

What the hell had he just agreed to?

Walking into Mayfair like a bloody idiot, that's what.

Blayne stared at the door through which Miss Russell had vanished. Slight of build with glossy black hair peeking out from beneath the brim of her bonnet, a pair of piercing green eyes, and the prettiest mouth he'd ever seen, she'd been like a tiny package of dynamite, exhibiting the sort of authoritative command one might expect from a general.

Christ have mercy.

He swiped one hand across his brow. The only reason he'd even considered her offer was because the ridiculous sum of money she'd mentioned would let him start over somewhere else a lot quicker. But the truth was he should have turned her down. He *would* turn her down. Tomorrow, when he went to meet with her, he'd apologize, offer his deepest regrets, and leave before he got more involved with a woman he had no business associating with.

By God. Just the memory of her sweet fragrance when she'd leaned toward him was more than enough to make him wish he'd demanded something extra from her as payment. A kiss, perhaps? He shook his head. No, she would not have allowed such a thing anymore than she would an unwelcome touch to her thigh. Blayne's hands clenched at the memory. He'd been prepared to intervene the moment he'd seen what was going on. Indeed, he'd had a brief vision of cutting off Mr. Evans's hand so he'd never do something like that again, only to watch him flee seconds later as if he'd encountered a ghoul.

Damned if Blayne hadn't been proud of Miss Russell for handling herself so well, even if her coming here to begin with had been remarkably foolish. This neighborhood wasn't safe. Certainly not for an upper-class lady dripping with wealth and prestige. He'd have to have a word with her about that when he called on her. It was the least he could do to ease his own conscience before putting an end to their brief acquaintance.

"What the devil are you doing?"

Blayne started. "What?"

Claus, a much shorter and younger man whom Guthrie had hired a few years earlier and who now helped Blayne run The Black Swan, studied him with open curiosity. "You've been standing here staring at that door for the past five minutes." A cheeky smile curved the edge of his lips. "Something to do with that fine piece of muslin you were cozying up to?"

"Bugger off," Blayne muttered. He stepped around Claus and headed toward the back of the building. Surely some accounts needed settling – anything to distract him from the nightmare he was presently living. He'd have to deal with it tomorrow, but for now, he'd no desire to think of the reason why he couldn't help Miss Russell.

"She's quite pretty," Claus said, following Blayne into the office. "And I was very impressed with how she handled Mr. Evans. Scared the hell out of him with that pistol of hers."

"Ye saw that, did ye?" Blayne dropped into the armchair behind his desk and pretended indifference by busying himself with some of the papers he'd left there.

"Aye." Claus folded his arms and leaned one shoulder against the doorjamb. "She's a rare find, Blayne. If you don't ask her to marry you, I surely will."

Blayne snapped to attention. "What?"

Claus grinned. "Christ. She really made an impression on you, didn't she?"

"Ye've got scrambled eggs for brains," Blayne muttered. He found a ledger and opened it with a frown. "Now get out so I can get on with my work."

"All right, all right." Clause straightened. "No need to get your unmentionables in a twist."

Without even thinking, Blayne snatched up an empty coffee cup and hurled it directly at Claus's head. Claus caught the projectile with ease, his ensuing laughter so raucous it stayed in the air for a good while after he'd taken his leave.

"Idiot," Blayne muttered, only to wonder if the word might not be better suited to himself when he glanced at the clock an hour later and realized he'd just been sitting there, unable to focus on his work because of the female who'd taken up residence in his head.

All the more reason to end their arrangement before it began in earnest. Today he'd been taken off guard, which was something he never allowed to happen. But damn if the feisty little vixen hadn't convinced him to agree to something he would have walked away from right away if he'd been given a moment to think. Tomorrow he'd be more prepared because he'd know what to expect. And there was no way in hell he'd let her talk him into keeping the job he'd accepted.

No, it was time to show Miss Russell exactly who she was dealing with. Not some Mayfair dandy she could talk circles around until he submitted to her way of thinking, but a hardened criminal who'd watched the life seep out of men's eyes while he shoved a blade through their hearts.

CHAPTER TWO

WHEN CHARLOTTE ARRIVED at break-fast the following morning, the tension filling the air was thick, like an early morning fog. She glanced around. Nothing was out of place, but her parents weren't exchanging a single word with each other. Not that they were especially chatty in general, but Papa would often remark on the news he read in the paper while Mama made non-committal responses.

Today they silently watched Charlotte's every move as she entered the room and proceeded toward the table. Reaching her chair, she offered her parents a smile and took a seat. "Good morning."

Her father, Viscount Elkins, tapped the top of his soft-boiled egg with his spoon while pressing his lips together as if to hide a wide grin. "Did you sleep well?"

"Yes."

"Good. I'm glad. Very pleased to hear it." Papa cleared his throat. He cast a glance at his wife and...

Was that a flicker of eager anticipation Charlotte spied in his eyes? She frowned. As the sort of man who'd always prided himself on his stoic self-control, few things caused him to give away any hint of emotion.

Nerves on instant alert, Charlotte poured herself a cup of tea. She had a dreadful feeling she'd need the soothing drink to calm herself very soon.

"You do look well rested," Charlotte's mother said. "Which is wonderful to see."

Charlotte narrowed her eyes. "Mama?"

"Yes, dear?"

"What's going on?"

"Well. Um." Her mother's lips almost trembled with the effort it seemed to take for her not to break into a wide grin. "It's just that I'm sure your fresh-faced appearance is bound to please Mr. Cooper."

Certain her morning was about to take an immediate descent into hell, Charlotte took a deep breath and said, "Whoever this Mr. Cooper may happen to be, I don't see why his opinion of me ought to matter."

"Oh," Mama said with a start. Her eyes twinkled. "I'm so sorry, Charlotte, but it seems my excitement has gotten away from me. You see, Mr. Cooper is an American businessman, the owner of the steelworks company your father has been investing in for the past three years, and—"

"Mr. Cooper and I have been enjoying an interesting correspondence of late," Papa said, taking over. "In fact, I'd like to say we've become good friends. He's truly a remarkable man. Fine fellow. Wealthy of course, with an excellent head for business on his shoulders. *And he just happens to be in the market for a wife.*"

"Oh no," Charlotte murmured.

"Naturally I mentioned you since Americans do seem to find prestige in marrying into the British peerage. As a viscount's daughter, you'd be the perfect fit."

Charlotte groaned. "Perhaps if I were seven years younger."

"A minor detail," Mama said with the widest grin Charlotte had ever seen on her face. "The thing of note is that Mr. Cooper is presently on his way here to meet you."

"According to the letter we received from him this morning," Papa declared as if he were handing out a prize, "he ought to arrive on Tuesday."

"Isn't it exciting?" Mama was almost bouncing in her seat like a toddler about to be served her favorite dessert. "Just when we thought you'd never marry, a potential suitor fills us with hope. I can scarcely believe your luck."

Neither could Charlotte. She'd had everything worked out – her entire future planned in her head. She'd pursue her writing, amass a small fortune, buy a home for herself in the countryside, and create a retreat for likeminded women who wished to avoid the bonds of marriage in favor of enriching their lives with art and culture. Not once had any of her imaginings included a husband. Indeed, a husband would ruin everything.

"He'll want me to go to America with him," she said, horrified by the notion.

"Naturally, my dear," Mama said without any hint of remorse over having to send her daughter halfway across the world.

Charlotte's mind whirled, frantically seeking a way to escape what was rapidly turning into a real catastrophe. "You should have consulted me first."

"We wanted it to be a surprise," Papa said in a far more characteristic no-nonsense tone than he'd applied thus far.

"And it most certainly is," Charlotte said. She reached for her tea. The time for soothing her nerves had come. "Though not a welcome one."

Her mother's mouth dropped open. "How can you say such a thing?"

"You are seven-and-twenty years of age, Charlotte," her father announced as if she needed reminding. "The fact that a man like Mr. Cooper might be prepared to offer for you is a bloody miracle, my girl."

"Lord Elkins," Mama gasped.

"I beg your pardon, my dear," Papa said, "but expletives are sometimes necessary when under-lining a point."

Mama leaned forward in her seat and regarded Charlotte as if she were a madwoman who ought to be carted away at once. "You cannot possibly want to become an eccentric woman, pitied by society, and suffering the emptiness you'll surely endure without a family of your own."

"You certainly paint an uplifting picture of

Aunt Florence's bohemian way of living," Charlotte said. Annoyance trickled through her, prompting her to fill her plate to capacity.

"My sister is an anomaly," Mama said with a sniff. "And since she never received an offer of marriage, her situation is also completely beside the point."

Given the fact that Charlotte hoped to follow in her aunt's footsteps, she couldn't quite agree with her mother's statement. Especially since she knew her aunt was exceedingly happy with the freedom she'd managed to acquire for herself.

"Nevertheless," Charlotte said. She took a few bites of bacon and allowed herself a moment to savor the smoked flavor. "I see no issue with becoming a permanent spinster."

Mama gasped.

Papa tensed so much his shoulders almost grew level with his ears. "You will meet Mr. Cooper when he arrives. More than that, you will make every possible effort to impress him. Is that clear?"

Charlotte stared at her father. His face was turning a rather alarming shade of red. In fact, she couldn't recall a time when she'd seen him quite so angry. And yet, for the sake of her own future, she knew she could not afford to cower. So she straightened her spine and spoke a distinct, "No."

"What?" he blustered.

"I appreciate the effort you've gone to on my behalf. Truly, I do. But I cannot accept Mr. Cooper's attentions."

"Why the devil not?" Papa exploded while his wife began fanning herself with her napkin.

"Because I am already spoken for."

Silence.

Charlotte's parents gaped at her in dumbfounded shock. Which was rather fortuitous since it gave Charlotte a much needed moment to come to grips with her impromptu announcement.

"By whom?" Papa asked once he'd managed to find his tongue.

"Hmm?" Charlotte wracked her brain for an answer while shoving more food in her mouth. As long as she was eating, she wouldn't have to speak.

"*Who* has asked for your hand in marriage, Charlotte, and why in blazes hasn't he come to me first?" Papa glared at her as if she were an enemy combatant he'd like to skewer with his bayonet.

"Language, dear," Mama murmured. She patted her husband's hand before telling Charlotte, "I wonder why you haven't mentioned this gentleman before. And where on earth could you possibly have met him? You've not attended a ball in ages. So that can only mean you must have encountered him during one of your many walks. Which is highly inappropriate and doesn't speak well of your intended. I mean, what sort of man would think to approach an unmarried lady with whom he's not acquainted. Unless of course—"

"Well?" Papa raised an eyebrow and waited

while Charlotte swallowed her food. "Answer your mother."

Drat it all. She'd have to say something now.

"That's exactly it." Charlotte decided to latch onto the explanation her mother had just provided. By incorporating her recent experience in the East End, she hoped her story would sound credible. "Mr. Wright...er...came to my aid a couple of months ago when a thief stole my reticule."

Charlotte's mother paled. "You never said."

"I didn't want to worry you."

"Where did this happen?" Papa asked.

"In the park," Charlotte said, deliberately meeting his gaze for the purpose of selling the lie. "The thief came out of nowhere. He threatened me with a knife."

"Good grief," Mama gasped.

"I could have been seriously injured, or worse, had Mr. Wright not come to my rescue." There was no turning back now. Not unless she planned on getting married to Mr. Cooper, which she most certainly did not. And just like that, whatever guilt she felt about being dishonest died in the face of what her parents had planned for her – marriage to a stranger who might very easily be short, fat, and balding. Not that there was anything wrong with that, but—

"Where on earth was Daisy during all of this?" Papa asked.

"Ah..." Charlotte would have to hunt her maid down before her parents got the chance to do so and beg her to back up the lie that was now expanding like foam in a poorly filled glass of champagne. "She was helping a child who'd fallen and scraped his knee."

"What child?" Mama wanted to know.

"A small one," Charlotte said. She took a hasty sip of her tea. "He'd broken away from his group, I think, and tripped over a stone or something. Honestly, I was too distracted by the thief to notice."

"And Mr. Wright gave chase, I suppose?" Mama asked, her brow knit with concern.

"Indeed," Charlotte said. She returned her cup to its saucer. "He caught the scoundrel and returned my reticule to me." Fiction was so much more pleasant than real life. "Since then, I've happened upon him a few times. We've talked at great length on a number of subjects, and then yesterday quite out of the blue, he proposed."

"Did he really?" Papa didn't sound entirely convinced.

"Considering my dwindling chance of getting married, I leapt at the opportunity and accepted right away. I was intending to mention it to you this morning since you were both out last night at the theatre." Thank God or Charlotte wasn't sure how she'd have explained the delayed declaration of her upcoming nuptials, no matter how fictional they might be.

"Considering I've never heard of this Mr. Wright, he cannot be a member of the peerage or the aristocracy, which means he must be a bloody nobody," Papa stated.

"I believe he's a Scottish entrepreneur," Charlotte said.

"I...see." Charlotte's mother blinked a few times and eventually reached for her tea.

"Have you completely lost your mind?" Papa thundered.

Charlotte stared back at his outraged expression. She wanted to yell at him for assuming she'd fall in line like her sisters and give up her hopes and dreams for a future she no longer wanted. Except doing so would undermine her attempt at pretending she'd already gotten engaged. So she pushed down her anger and schooled her features. "If that is how you define falling in love, Papa, then I suppose I must have."

He threw up his hands. "Unbelievable."

"You've no idea," Charlotte muttered.

"What was that?" Papa demanded.

"Nothing," Charlotte assured him with a fixed smile while taking another sip of her tea.

"Well." He glanced at his wife, then back at Charlotte. "I want to meet this Mr. Wright no later than tomorrow."

"You won't have to wait that long since he's due to arrive here in roughly one hour." She began eating as quickly as she could. There was much to be done before Mr. MacNeil came to call. She had to speak with Daisy. A bouquet of flowers would have to be purchased. Somehow, she'd have to convince her newly employed guard to play along. Her heart began racing with uneven beats.

"Excellent." Papa stood, whatever fatherly

affection he'd shown toward her earlier was now completely buried behind a façade cut from granite. "And just so we're clear, I'd better approve of him, because if I don't, you'll be marrying Mr. Cooper the moment he sets foot in England."

Charlotte sank back against her chair while her father marched from the room. She couldn't understand his reasoning. What did it matter if she didn't marry the man he'd selected for her? The only thing she could think was that her father would be embarrassed by wasting Mr. Cooper's time. Unless there was something else she wasn't aware of.

"Charlotte?"

Expelling a deep breath, Charlotte met her mother's inquisitive gaze. "I suppose I should go and prepare myself for my fiancé's arrival."

"Your father and I value honesty, Charlotte." It was clear Mama wasn't completely convinced by the story either. "Armed robbery in the park while there were at least three other people nearby? Honestly, dear. We don't appreciate being lied to. Especially not by one of our daughters."

"And I don't appreciate being manipulated into something I do not want."

"We're only trying to safeguard your future."

"I know." Perhaps if she'd confided in them from the very beginning, she wouldn't be in this mess. But no, her parents would never support her writing or her desire to be independent and different. They wanted her to adhere to a model they understood, and that involved getting married and having children. The end.

Which meant there was only one thing for it. She'd simply have to convince them Mr. MacNeil was Mr. Wright and make sure they approved of him so they'd not force her to break off her imaginary engagement. Which Mr. MacNeil still knew nothing about. How hard could it possibly be?

Determined to succeed, she refused to answer that question, finished her toast, and excused herself from the table, then rushed to find Daisy.

"Has Papa questioned you about a Mr. Wright?" Charlotte asked, just to be sure. The maid was in Charlotte's bedchamber, putting away some freshly laundered clothes.

"No, miss. I've not seen your father today." Daisy frowned. "Who's Mr. Wright?"

Charlotte took a deep breath. "You may want to sit for a moment while I explain."

Ten minutes later, Daisy was gaping at Charlotte as if she'd materialized from thin air. "Are you mad?"

"No. Just desperate."

"This plan of yours is destined to fail, miss, and then what'll you do?" The maid had been with Charlotte for so many years the two were more like friends than mistress and servant. As such, Daisy often spoke her mind, which was something Charlotte valued.

"Not marry Mr. Cooper," Charlotte muttered. "I'll fight with whatever weapons I have at my disposal."

"Which clearly includes an overactive imagination," Daisy said. Her eyes softened as she regarded Charlotte. "You haven't even met Mr. Cooper. Maybe he's not so bad. From what I hear, Americans can be more relaxed when it comes to the freedom of women than we Brits tend to be. Maybe he'll support you in your endeavors?"

"Maybe. But how will I find the time to pursue them if I'm to be a wife and mother? There will be a home to manage and children to see to. If Mr. Cooper is indeed the wealthy businessman Papa professes him to be, he'll probably have a large mansion with dozens of staff awaiting attention from their future mistress. It will be exhausting – a full job in and of itself. And that is without considering social functions I'll no doubt have to attend and dinner parties I'll need to host. Honestly, Daisy. All I want to do is write."

"Well then." Daisy pressed her lips firmly together. "In that case we'd better prepare."

"Mr. MacNeil will be here within half an hour if he's punctual."

"Then I should go and see about those flowers so he fits the part you've created for him."

"What if he refuses to play along?" The details had been easy enough to come up with when she'd been desperate to ruin her father's plans. Now, it seemed unlikely any sane man would willingly let himself get tangled up in her mess.

"No sense in worrying over that before it's happened." Daisy went to the door. "I'm sure it'll all work out exactly how it's supposed to."

Charlotte had her doubts but chose not to argue. Instead she offered a smile and a nod while Daisy slipped from the room. How on earth had it come to this? Yesterday, when she'd hired Mr. MacNeil, she'd felt like she was in control of her destiny. Now, she found herself at his mercy. All she could do was pray he'd be more forgiving and kind than his reputation suggested. Because if he wasn't, there would be hell to pay for her deception, not just from her father, but from a notorious St. Giles criminal.

CHAPTER THREE

SINCE HE'D MADE up his mind to cut ties with Miss Russell, Blayne didn't bother much with his appearance before heading over to Number Two Berkley Square. Unshaved and with a thick mass of dark brown hair falling in haphazard locks around his face, he ignored the knocker. Instead he gave the front door a succession of hard thumps with his fist.

What he expected was for a condescending butler to open the door and question his purpose, upon which he'd simply tell the man to give Miss Russell his regrets and then leave. Instead, the door was opened by the lady herself.

Blayne stared, his intention to quit her presence with immediate haste abandoning him on account of her hair which was now completely visible since she wasn't wearing a bonnet. He'd known it would be black and glossy, but judging from the voluminous pile at the nape of her neck, it was also unfashionably long and thick. Dazed, he took a step forward, following her into the foyer. The door closed with a gentle thud, prompting Blayne to blink.

Hell and damnation, she'd managed to get him inside.

He cleared his throat, more determined than ever to set things straight.

"Mr. MacNeil." The welcoming smile she'd initially worn when she'd greeted him had been transformed into a flat line. "I appreciate you keeping our appointment although I had thought you'd make a bit more effort with your appearance when keeping in mind the nature of your job. After all, you shall be escorting me around Town."

"About that—"

"But you're here now and that's what truly matters." She frowned at him, not with displeasure but with a calculated degree of thoughtfulness that instantly put him on edge.

"Miss Russell, I really dinnae—"

"Don't what?"

"Er..." Somehow, she'd made his mind go completely blank.

She huffed a small breath and quickly glanced about as if to ensure they were quite alone before saying, "Unfortunately, there's been a bit of a snag."

Instinct tightened his muscles. "What sort of snag?"

And why was he even asking when his intention was to quit the job before he began?

"One that requires you to add faux fiancé to your job description."

"What?" The word was more of a croak.

"There really isn't a choice. It's completely out

of my hands."

"Out of yer hands?" Good God, he was starting to sound like an imbecile. He cleared his throat. "Miss Russell, I came to inform ye that I've changed my mind about accepting the job ye offered. And that was before ye added this new stipulation."

"Naturally, the salary shall be increased according to the extra requirement," she said as if she were deaf to his protest. "I'll add another five pounds per week for the inconvenience."

Ten pounds per week for however long Miss Russell required his help would be a splendid addition to what he'd managed to stow away so far, but playing fiancé to an upper-crust lady was further than he was willing to go for any amount.

Not because he didn't think himself capable of pulling it off. Not even because the people he'd have to mingle with intimidated him in some way. Rather, it was because the very last thing he needed after keeping his head down for nineteen years to avoid a good hanging was making the headlines in every paper published within the British realm. No matter what, his height, looks, and Scottish heritage would be noted and that alone might prompt his uncle to hunt him down.

Blayne shuddered. He could not under any circumstance let that happen.

"Your imposing size and handsome features are an excellent start and..." She waved her hand as if hoping to grab the necessary words from the air around her. "I'll simply have to think of a good excuse as to why you haven't managed to groom yourself lately. Come along."

She marched off, disappearing through an open doorway and leaving Blayne with little choice but to follow. Which he finally managed to do once his brain had finished processing what she'd just said about him being handsome. Christ above, it almost felt like he'd been clubbed on the head. Hell, no woman had ever told him any such thing. They just commented on his size and the pleasure he gave them in bed. And since he'd never entertained the sort of woman with whom he'd consider building a future, he hadn't cared what they thought of his looks as long as they satisfied him in return.

Shoving away those thoughts, he sought out Miss Russell amid the dainty furniture neatly positioned throughout the parlor he'd just walked into. She'd taken a seat on one of the sofas. Blayne moved toward her, intent on saying his piece, when he realized they weren't alone. Another woman of a similar age to Miss Russell sat in the far corner, examining him with the pinched expression people tended to use when they came across a piece of refuse.

He scowled at her and she instantly drew back as if seeking shelter against the backrest.

"Daisy, would you please be so kind as to tell Mama and Papa Mr. Wright has arrived?"

Only the briefest hesitation conveyed Daisy's disapproval of this request before she stood, spoke a quick, "Right away, miss," and departed.

Blayne waited until he could no longer hear her retreating steps before he raised an eyebrow. "Mr. Wright?"

"Yes." Miss Russell folded her hands in her lap. "That is your name from now on."

He actually laughed, dismayed by her audacity. The situation was more ridiculous than he'd supposed, and it was high time he up and left before she decided to do something truly horrendous like tell her parents he'd gotten her with child. A surge of panic went through him on that thought. He studied her calmly composed features.

Dear merciful God, he'd not put it past her. Which prompted him to march forward, lean over, and ask, "Are ye demented?"

She clenched her jaw. Sparks danced within the emerald green of her eyes until they blazed with righteous indignation. Unable to move, Blayne stared back at her while doing his damnedest to fight the effect she was having on him. Lord, she was a passionate creature and he couldn't quite help but wonder what it might be like to encourage this fiery streak of hers in other more interesting ways.

"Keep your voice down," she hissed. "And no, I am not. But I cannot very well introduce you as Mr. MacNeil. Can I? Since even I know who you are I'm sure Mama and Papa must have heard of you too, which would not be to my advantage at all. Besides, I hardly see the issue with you employing a different name when bearing in mind the exorbitant price I've agreed to pay you."

Mentioning their deal helped banish the inappropriate thoughts attempting to gain a foothold in his brain. He shoved his hands in his pockets and straightened his posture until he was truly towering over her. "Ye're making an excellent effort to force my hand, Miss Russell, for which I must give ye credit. Unfortunately, I have nae come here to start work or to let myself be bamboozled into deceiving yer parents or whoever else ye may have in mind. Indeed, I've come to inform ye that ye must find someone else to fill the position."

She blinked and proceeded to smooth out her skirt. Blayne watched as she swallowed and took a few breaths. It was almost as if he'd finally managed to knock the wind out of her sails, and for some peculiar reason, he hated the result.

"I'm sorry if you feel as though I've attempted to trick you in some way. No doubt I'd imagine the same if I were in your position, hired to do one thing and promptly asked to do another." The sincerity with which she spoke surprised him. Until now, she'd been the very image of cool self-assurance, forging ahead with the sort of manipulative expertise the swindlers of London could learn a great deal from. A hint of uncertainty and remorse softened her features. She bit her lip. "My situation has changed a great deal since yesterday."

"That may well be, but I'm afraid ye will have to ask someone else for help."

"But…" She stood with hasty resolve. Her

brows drew together above a pair of imploring green eyes. "I need you, Mr. MacNeil. Please. Don't go."

Blayne's gut twisted in response to the urgency in her tone. He deliberately hardened his features in order to bury the inconvenient sensation beneath the annoyance he ought to be feeling. "I'm sure ye think so, but whatever yer reason for wanting a fake fiancé, the truth is ye ought to steer clear of men like me. In fact, I'd advise ye never to venture into St. Giles again. It was downright foolish of ye to go there to begin with." Anger rose at the memory of Mr. Evans pawing her thigh. "What happens if ye're attacked by a group of thugs working together? What will ye do when they hold ye down and force themselves on ye?"

"My intention was to avoid such a scenario by employing you," she muttered.

"Except ye're also asking me to attend social functions with ye now, are ye not?"

She shrugged one shoulder. "Perhaps one or two."

"During which I'd be introduced as the man ye mean to marry." He snorted. "Forgive me, but I've nae intention of letting such a rumor attach itself to my name."

"But it wouldn't be *your* name. It would be—" She clamped her mouth shut and smiled at a spot behind him, all traces of her distress carefully stowed away beneath a composed exterior. "Mama. Papa. Allow me to introduce Mr. Wright. Mr. Wright, these are my parents, Viscount and Viscountess Elkins."

Blayne wanted to gnash his teeth together. He'd no intention of continuing this charade for one more second. In fact, he was tempted to say he was not the man Miss Russell claimed him to be, storm out of the town house, and get himself as far away from her as possible. Except when he turned and saw her parents regarding him with a mixture of shock, disapproval, and downright disbelief, the devil sitting upon his shoulder tempted him with an almost perverse desire to needle them.

So rather than walking away from what was without doubt the worst decision ever, Blayne ignored the instinct he'd always relied on and stuck out his hand. "It's a pleasure to finally make yer acquaintance. Yer daughter has told me so much about ye."

Lady Elkins, a thin woman with sharp features who clearly favored bright colors judging from her orange gown, sucked in a breath while her eyes seemed to double in size. "Good heavens. He's not just unkempt, he also speaks like a hoodlum."

"Mama," Miss Russell admonished. "I did mention him being Scottish."

"It's quite all right…darling. As ye ken, I must look the part I'm requested to play." Blayne gave his supposed fiancée a devilish smile before returning his attention to her mother. "An explanation is certainly in order."

"It is?" Miss Russell squeaked.

"Indeed." Blayne allowed himself an inward

grin and promptly reached for Lady Elkins's hand. Executing a perfect bow, he kissed the air immediately above her knuckles, then straightened and deliberately faced the viscount. "My undercover work for the Home Office forces me to remain in character at all times. In case I happen upon the men I've spent the last year trying to bring to justice."

"I was led to believe you were an entrepreneur," Lord Elkins said with eyes too sharp for Blayne's liking. "At least, that is what our daughter told us."

"I see. Well…um…I also have a business," Blayne said. "I suppose it would make more sense to mention that."

"Oh look, Mama," Miss Russell said in an obvious attempt to distract her parents from his blunder. "He brought flowers for each of us." She produced two bouquets consisting of cream colored roses and other blooms in various shades of blue, pink, and yellow.

Startled, Blayne watched as she handed one to her mother. When he caught a skeptical look from Lord Elkins, he did his best to school his features and act like the flowers were as expected as his presence in their parlor and his intention to marry their daughter. "I wasnae sure what yer preference might be so I do hope ye like them."

"They're stunning," Lady Elkins declared with the sort of surprise that informed Blayne she'd not believed him capable of locating a hothouse. "And very expensive looking."

The added jibe rankled more than it ought to

have done. He'd never cared much for prestige or wealth. Hell, he'd given both up a lifetime ago and hadn't missed either since. But standing here in this parlor, being judged by people who'd not even bothered to get to know him yet, caused every muscle within him to tighten and strain with resentful irritation. Rather than let it show, he offered Lord Elkins his hand and proceeded to lie through his teeth. "I'm glad we're finally able to meet face to face, my lord."

The viscount, a man quite a bit shorter than Blayne, stared back at him through narrowed eyes. Time stretched, until the stern looking fellow finally chose to accept the handshake. "Neither my wife nor I knew of your existence until this morning, so you'll have to forgive us for being a bit astonished by your arrival."

Ah. So they'd suspected their daughter of lying about his existence. Miss Russell's desperation to earn his collaboration was starting to make more sense although he'd yet to discover why she'd made him up in the first place.

"And um…" Lady Elkins appeared to struggle with finding the right words while examining him from head to toe. Eventually, she made an exasperated sound in the back of her throat and said, "We are curious to know how you plan on supporting Charlotte?"

"Mama," Miss Russell exclaimed with a theatrical dose of outrage.

Blayne silently thanked the viscountess for supplying him with his supposed fiancée's name since that was something he probably ought to know. The lady, however, ignored her daughter's note of warning and took a step forward. "You will have to forgive me, Mr. Wright, but you do not strike me as a man of means."

"Dear lord," Miss Russell said. "Please accept my sincerest apologies, Mr. Wright."

"Your mother is quite correct," Lord Elkins said. "We need to know precisely who Mr. Wright is."

"Perhaps we should sit?" Miss Russell said in a weary tone that suggested she might be losing her nerve. "I'm sure we could all do with refreshment."

"I for one will not permit my daughter to marry just anyone," Lord Elkins said.

"Papa..." Miss Russell said with a longing glance at the sofa. "Mr. Wright is the man I've fallen in love with."

Love? Blayne almost choked on the air he was breathing. Did she really have to drag that particular emotion into this mess? He tried not to flinch beneath the weight of it but the truth was he wasn't sure if his acting skills were up to par with her requirements.

She sidled close to him until he was left with no choice but to put his arm around her waist. To his surprise, she fit against him perfectly. Hmm.

Lord Elkins gave the ceiling a brief perusal before returning a hard and assessing stare to Blayne and Miss Russell. "Love will not put food on the table nor a roof over your head. It is the least important factor when making life-altering decisions. Trust me, Charlotte, Mr. Cooper will make a far better choice than this...individual. I'm sure of it."

Years of keeping a cool head under Guthrie's command allowed Blayne to let the insult slide so he could focus on the bit Lord Elkins had said about Mr. Cooper. Another piece of the puzzle fell into place. Obviously Miss Russell's parents had selected her husband and as a result she'd created Mr. Wright.

"And who is Mr. Cooper?" he asked, deciding to take the opportunity to learn a thing or two about his opponent. Although why in God's name he was making the effort he wasn't quite sure. Something about the viscount and viscountess's condescension and the manner in which they were trying to dictate their daughter's life made him want to put these people in their place.

"Nobody," Miss Russell muttered.

"An American steelworks manufacturer," her father supplied with a satisfied smirk. "He's made quite a fortune for himself, owns several estates, and is presently on his way here with every intention of courting Charlotte. And since I'm the one who encouraged him to make the long journey, I'd hate for her to be otherwise engaged during his visit."

The request for Blayne to walk away immediately was clear.

He ought to leap at the chance to escape this debacle. After all, that was what he'd been planning to do when he'd first arrived. But after seeing the hope in Miss Russell's eyes when she'd pleaded with him for help, a strange urge to save her had taken over.

Ignore it you idiot.

Leave before it's too late.

"Unfortunately," Blayne said while pulling her closer, "I have nae intention of giving Charlotte up without a fight."

"You don't?" Miss Russell asked. She was gazing at him as if he were some sort of Arthurian knight intent on championing her cause no matter the danger.

The desire to set aside his own concerns in order to help her was suddenly overwhelming. "Of course not, darling." Deciding the time had come for him to put on the best performance yet, he dropped his gaze to hers. "Meeting ye was the best thing that ever happened to me. The very idea of having to give ye up would shatter my heart and destroy my soul. Ye're everything I've ever wished for, Charlotte, and knowing ye feel the same about me makes me the luckiest man alive."

"I...um...really?" she half sighed, half stammered.

"If it's money you're after," Lord Elkins remarked, "I'm happy to come to some sort of agreement."

Every cell in Blayne's body drew tight, like a twig being bowed to the point of snapping. He felt Miss Russell flinch and heard her sharp intake of breath. Heat radiated up his spine, settling at the base of his skull where it started to throb. And yet, somehow, by some bloody miracle, he managed to calmly say, "Thank ye, but that willnae be necessary. I'm perfectly capable of supporting Charlotte without yer help. Shall we sit?"

He didn't wait for a response. Merely guided Miss Russell toward the sofa she'd been eyeing for the past ten minutes. Standing about like this with one proverbial foot out the door was getting ridiculous anyway. It was time to let her parents know he was staying. Indefinitely.

Was he though?

Apparently, yes. He certainly wasn't about to let them run roughshod over his pride or treat Miss Russell as though she was undeserving of seeking whatever happiness she desired for herself. Mr. Cooper clearly wasn't the answer and forcing her to tie herself to him for life seemed unnaturally cruel.

That's the way of the ton.

You know this.

He certainly did, but he'd be damned if such foolishness broke Miss Russell's spirit. She'd been like a blazing diamond when she'd approached him at The Black Swan. Faced with her parents' disapproval, however, she'd lost some of her sparkle, and that in itself made Blayne want to hit something.

"But..." Lady Elkins followed them over to the seating arrangement and lowered herself to one of the armchairs.

She waited for her husband to join them while Blayne adjusted his position. The delicate piece of furniture creaked beneath his weight as he did his best to get comfortable in the snug space. He'd apparently failed to consider the sofa's narrowness, which was suddenly near impossible to ignore since it forced his thigh to press against Miss Russell's.

"Not to sound unappreciative of our daughter's fine qualities," Lady Elkins continued once her husband had claimed the other armchair, "but she spent six years on the marriage mart without acquiring a single suitor and now, all of a sudden, she has two." The woman wore a perplexed expression. "Mr. Cooper makes sense of course. He's acquainted with my husband and believes the match would be beneficial to both families, but you...I mean, what exactly are you hoping to gain from marrying her? If it is her dowry you're after, you ought to know it will be withdrawn if her father and I disapprove of the match."

"My dear Lady Elkins," Blayne said in the same tone he'd used to intimidate cutthroats in the past. He clasped Miss Russell's hand, anchoring himself to her so he wouldn't leap out of his seat and strangle her mother right then and there. "As we've already established, I have no interest in yer money, or yer daughter's for that matter. In fact, the only thing I care about is her and her happiness, or did ye miss the part where I told ye I love her?"

"I don't—"

"Here's what matters," Blayne said, cutting Lord Elkins off. "I will continue to court yer daughter until she and I have decided upon a date for the wedding. Once we do, ye're welcome to participate in the planning of said event, if ye wish. Should ye choose not to, ye'll simply receive an invitation – one I hope ye will choose to accept since I'm sure yer daughter would like ye to. Now, as far as my ability to provide for Miss Russell goes, my annual income of three hundred pounds may not be as much as ye'd hoped for, but I doubt it's as little as ye feared."

"It's certainly not in the same league as Mr. Cooper's fortune," Lord Elkins muttered, "but you're right. It's not as bad as I would have guessed based on..." He made a gesture with his hand as if to indicate Blayne's overall appearance.

"As I've explained, my current work forces me to dress a certain way in order to blend in. However, I do believe that will soon change as I'm getting closer to finding the proof required to bring these men to justice."

"I see," Lord Elkins said.

"So with all of this taken into account, will you give us your blessing?" Miss Russell asked with renewed forcefulness to her voice.

Her hand, warm and delicate, was still wrapped in Blayne's and for some absurd reason, he was reluctant to let go.

"Not yet," Lord Elkins said after a moment's reflection. "I absolutely must insist you give Mr. Cooper a chance, Charlotte."

Miss Russell stiffened. "Papa, I cannot pretend an interest where there is none."

"I am not asking you to," Lord Elkins said, "but I will be damned if I convince a man to cross the Atlantic for you just to have you snub him before he's even arrived."

Blayne had to admit the man had a point.

"Honestly, I don't see why I should have to suffer the repercussion of your mistake," Miss Russell told her father.

Apparently, she'd found her inner warrior again. Blayne was almost tempted to cheer. Instead, he decided to end this discussion before the viscount became more difficult. "Ye must-nae fault yer father for doing what he believes would be in yer best interest, lass."

"Hmm?"

Blayne chuckled lightly on account of Miss Russell's confused expression. There was something immensely satisfying about surprising her for a change. "Being courteous toward Mr. Cooper and making him feel welcome after he's travelled halfway around the world to meet ye ought not be too much to ask."

"He might be awful," Miss Russell muttered.

"I'm sure yer father wouldnae want such a man for a son-in-law," Blayne told her, but just to be certain, he eyed Lord Elkins. "I trust ye've met him?"

"Of course. I'd never invest in a business without having met its owner."

Interesting how that sentence said nothing about never thinking of asking the fellow to marry his daughter without having seen him first.

"And?" Miss Russell asked. Apparently she'd been so overwrought by the mere idea of marrying a stranger she'd forgotten to ask a few pertinent questions.

"He's a little taller than you, though not as tall as Mr. Wright. His build is slimmer and I'd peg him at roughly thirty years of age."

Miss Russell blew out a breath. "Fine. I shall give Mr. Cooper the chance he deserves. But only if Mr. Wright is given the same consideration."

Blayne blinked. What the hell was she trying to accomplish now?

"In other words," Miss Russell continued, "if you invite Mr. Cooper for dinner, you must invite Mr. Wright as well. The same goes for balls and soirees. If any such events must be attended, I want Mr. Wright there with me."

"Um… Balls and soirees are nae really my thing," Blayne said with rising dread. In her dogged attempt to thwart her parents Miss Russell was dragging him further into a situation he had to avoid at all cost. And he, imbecile that he was, had enabled her to do so because of some misplaced desire he had to help her. It had to stop now.

"I completely agree with you, Charlotte," Lord Elkins said with a smirk. "Mr. Wright must be included in all our coming arrangements. After all, it's only fair he be given a chance to prove his own worth. An equal advantage, so to speak."

Without needing to look at Miss Russell, Blayne sensed her unease. It was the sort he'd encountered dozens of times before when someone had been backed into a corner of their own making. He stared at her father. The cunning man was clearly hoping to make a fool out of Blayne, to prove to his daughter that he wouldn't do as her husband. Judging from his satisfied expression, he already envisioned Mr. Cooper behaving with elegant grace while Blayne stumbled his way through social etiquette.

A struggle ensued within Blayne. On one hand he knew what he had to do if he wished to stay hidden, but on the other, he'd love nothing more than to put Lord Elkins in his place.

Helping Miss Russell avoid the bonds of marriage would also be damn rewarding. Not only because he believed every person deserved the right to choose their own fate, but because he genuinely liked her. In spite of her somewhat underhanded method, he admired her for trying to forge her own path – for her willingness to openly oppose her parents' wishes in her own little battle for justice. In his estimation, most young ladies would have lacked the strength to try. Besides, her initial reason for hiring him had been for the sake of protection. Perhaps then, this was how he ought to assist – by stepping up and keeping her safe not only from thugs when she travelled the City, but also from those who wished to control her.

He considered Lady Elkins for a moment. The woman was watching him with a knowing gleam in her eyes. Like her husband, she expected him to back away from the challenge they'd issued. His gut clenched as it always did at the thought of stepping out of the shadows and walking into the light. After all, he'd been hiding for nineteen years – so long he barely recalled who he'd been before that. And while he knew being introduced at *ton* events would make him look over his shoulder, the truth was the risk of discovery was minimal. Especially since he would be using yet another assumed name.

"Thank ye, Lord Elkins. I appreciate the consideration." Blayne raised Miss Russell's hand to his lips for a kiss. "Attending a few events with my future wife will be an absolute pleasure."

"Your future... Um... Mr. Wright," Lord Elkins sputtered, his face an amusing shade of red. "I really wasn't—"

"Papa." Miss Russell's voice was stern. "I believe we've reached an agreement."

"I'm not sure that's true," her father said. "In fact, there's one more stipulation I'd like to add."

"If you do, I'll have no choice but to remind you that I am seven and twenty years old with every right to marry whomever I choose. The only reason we're even having this discussion is out of respect to you and Mama, mostly so you won't be embarrassed when Mr. Cooper arrives and learns I'm already attached. But if you push me too far, I will leave."

"And go where?" Lord Elkins asked.

"To one of my sisters. I'm sure I can count on Melanie or Edwina to set me up until I find a place of my own. Now, if we're done here," she stood, so Blayne did as well, "I should like to take a turn about the garden with Mr. Wright before he leaves. Daisy will serve as chaperone."

Before her parents could voice a protest, Miss Russell pulled Blayne out of the parlor and marched him toward the back of the house while Daisy trailed behind.

CHAPTER FOUR

MORTIFICATION SEARED CHAR-
LOTTE'S skin. How could her parents be
so awful? She'd always considered them pleasant
and easy to get along with. Today, however, she'd
been faced with two people she barely recognized.

"I'm so sorry," she told Mr. MacNeil once
they'd stepped out onto the terrace. "I never
imagined they'd treat you unkindly."

"It's all right, lass." He linked his arm with
hers, drawing her closer to his side as they
walked. The heat of his body was soothing. It
allowed the tension within her to ease. "After all,
it's not like we're really angling to get ourselves
hitched, so what does their approval really matter? And can ye honestly blame them for being
dismayed? As far as they know, their daughter's
decided to marry a man who doesnae ken how
to use a pair of shears."

"Because you're apparently working undercover for the home office." She'd had to fight
not to roll her eyes when he'd started concocting
that far-fetched story. "I'm not sure they bought

any of that. Least of all since I'd told them you were an entrepreneur."

"Yes. Well. I wasnae aware of that since ye failed to fill me in on the details of yer fib. I'm sorry if I mucked things up but I couldnae think of any other explanation short of telling them the truth."

"I'm sorry I didn't have more time to explain the situation before introducing you to them. And I am extremely grateful to you for your willingness to collaborate." She considered that before asking, "You won't back out now, will you?"

"I dinnae suppose I will." He dropped a mischievous look at her. "I'm actually looking forward to watching yer parents suffer through having their daughter romanced by a Scottish brute. I reckon it'll be amusing."

Charlotte's heart squeezed in response to his self-deprecation. She glanced at him, at the unruly locks falling over his jacket collar and the scruffy beard lining his jaw. A pair of warm brown eyes met hers and she almost stumbled. When he'd kissed her hand earlier, a fuzzy sensation had spread through her limbs. The same happened now, only this time her stomach had chosen to do a cartwheel as well, which was not only inconvenient but also incredibly silly.

"You're not a brute." Why on earth did her voice sound so faint? She cleared her throat and squared her shoulders. "Considering my lack of forthrightness with you from the beginning followed by all the thinly veiled insults you just received and your ability to refrain from smashing a vase before quitting my presence for good, I'd say you're something of a saint."

"I did consider it, ye ken. In fact, I had every intention of breaking off our arrangement this morning when I arrived."

She'd suspected as much. "Why didn't you then?"

He chuckled, a lovely full-bodied rumble that vibrated through her before sinking into her toes. Goodness, she liked that sound. "Because ye wouldnae listen and barely let me get a word in before yer parents were upon us. After that, I suppose I decided I'd like to get the better of them."

"Poking the bear will eventually cause him to bite," she muttered.

"So I'm a bear now?" he asked with a hint of amusement while they strolled toward the rose bushes.

"In a way. And just so you know, I'm very fond of bears." She'd said the last part because she didn't want him taking offense, only it sounded so much better in her head than it did out loud. In fact, she very much feared Mr. Mac-Neil might think she was flirting with him now. Which she most certainly was not.

"Hmm..." He gave her a thoughtful look. Oh God, he *absolutely* believed she was flirting with him. Charlotte's heart started to race, her mind struggled for something to say. Only he beat her to it, saving her by avoiding the comment completely by saying, "We need to make a clear outline of our arrangement so we're prepared for what's to come. And ye have to be more open with me. No more surprises. Is that clear?"

"Of course."

Drawing her to a halt, he turned and met her gaze with unwavering directness. "I mean it, Miss Russell. If I so much as suspect ye of trying to pull the wool over my eyes, I'll leave ye to find yer own way out of whatever mess ye've created."

Charlotte swallowed and did her best not to shrink away from the very imposing man she faced. Instead, she stiffened her spine and stared back into his dark eyes. "I understand."

He studied her with sharp precision, as if attempting to read her mind. Eventually, he gave a swift nod. "Good."

Charlotte's heart thumped. She accepted his escort once more and allowed him to lead her toward a stone bench set beneath a frothy cascade of wisteria. Taking a seat, she glanced toward Daisy, who appeared to be studying the cherry tree in minute detail.

Mr. MacNeil lowered himself to the spot next to Charlotte and angled toward her in such a way that their knees bumped together.

A shock of awareness swept through her. Instinct urged her to move aside, to add some distance. And so she would have if he hadn't leaned in and whispered against her ear. "Stay."

One word, breezing across her skin, sinking deep until it buzzed through her veins and did funny things to her insides. She drew a sharp breath and forced herself to remain where she was, to relax her muscles and not shy away from the contact.

"Yer parents dinnae fully believe we're in love. So if ye want to convince them, we must act the part." He tucked a stray lock of hair behind her ear. The gesture caused his fingers to scrape her cheek, which in turn produced a shiver. "Now, why dinnae ye share the details of our relationship with me so I dinnae muck this up. How did we meet, for example?"

"I was feeding the ducks in Hyde Park a couple of months ago when a thief approached, threatened me with a knife, and made off with my reticule while my maid was distracted by an injured child. You witnessed the act and chased down the culprit. We've been meeting regularly ever since."

He chuckled lightly. His hand fell away, leaving a cool spot in its place. "Ye've quite the imagination, Miss Russell."

"You've no idea," she murmured, so low she doubted he heard her.

"Now look at me." She did as he asked and was instantly snared by the force of his gaze. "Think of something that makes ye happy – yer favorite thing in the world. That's it. If yer parents are watching us now, they'll believe ye're incredibly fond of me. Will ye tell me what's on yer mind?"

She'd never shared her greatest pleasure with anyone. "Perhaps some other time."

Disappointment dimmed his eyes for a second before he smiled back as if she were the sun, the moon, and the stars in his own private universe. It was enough to make her forget who he really was – a criminal—and that this whole thing was only pretend.

"Give me something else then. If we've known each other as long as ye say, then we need to become more familiar. Let's start with yer favorite color."

She shook herself and forced herself to concentrate. "Red. What about yours?"

"Green," he told her. "The exact same shade as yer eyes."

Heavens.

If she didn't know any better she'd think he was genuinely trying to win her heart. She glanced away, steeling herself against the appreciative warmth with which his words filled her. It was important she stay focused. "I favor daffodils to other flowers and wish they would bloom all year round. My favorite food is pancakes, either with raspberry jam or with sugar and lemon."

"Pancakes aren't really a food. They're a desert, wouldnae ye say?" She frowned at him and he grinned. "Very well. Yer favorite food is pancakes. What else?"

"I don't like spiders or insects in general. When I was little I fell off a swing and broke my arm. I've always wanted a dog but Mama won't allow animals into the house so I'll have to wait with that. Unlike most young ladies, I'd rather engage in shooting contests and archery than embroidery or painting."

He gave a low chuckle. "Why is that?"

"Aside from the fact that it's much more fun?" When he nodded she said, "My father's a military man, or was, until he retired a few years ago. When he realized he'd only have daughters, he chose to raise me, the oldest, as he would have done a son."

"And now he demands ye transform into the perfect young lady." MacNeil snorted and shook his head. "Foolish man."

"I thought he and Mama had abandoned the idea of getting me married," Charlotte told him. "I hadn't even heard of Mr. Cooper until this morning when they decided to mention him over breakfast."

"Jesus."

"I believe they thought I'd be thrilled, but…" She scrunched her nose.

He took her hand and held it lightly within his own. "Ye weren't. Because they tried to remove yer choices?"

"In a way, I suppose. Truth is, I've no wish to marry anyone."

"Not ever?"

She shrugged. "The idea of tying myself to a man I don't love for the sole purpose of appeasing someone else's dream feels wrong. I'd much rather be the master of my own fate, live by my own rules, and be independent."

"What about children?"

"My sisters are sure to produce enough for me to dote on without me having to deal with all the challenges motherhood poses."

He began threading their fingers together,

distracting her briefly with the sight of his much larger palm enveloping hers. A raised line spanned his knuckles, prompting her to wonder how he'd received the scar and how many others he had on his body.

"So ye will become a spinster, living alone somewhere in seclusion. Is that yer goal?"

"I'd invite other likeminded women to live with me," she said, her voice a tad harsher than she intended. Becoming defensive only increased her irritation, mostly with herself, but drat it all, the way he was speaking suggested he thought her a dimwitted fool.

"Ye dinnae ken what ye'd be giving up, lass."

"Then so much the better since I shan't know what I'm missing."

"Oh, ye'll know all right, when ye're lying in yer empty bed. Yer brain may not want to admit it, but yer body's sure to do so eventually."

"What are you talking about?" She was certain she shouldn't be asking this question and yet it popped out, before she was able to stop it.

Mr. MacNeil raised her hand to his lips, abrading her with the hair from his beard. As he gazed deep into her eyes, he said, "Ye're a passionate woman, Miss Russell. 'Twould be a shame if ye didnae allow yerself to experience the joys of lovemaking."

Charlotte gasped. She didn't think of herself as a prudish miss who was easily shocked by indelicate words or blunt remarks, but having a practical stranger speak to her so brazenly was enough to make her ears burn.

"I think we've talked enough about me. Let's discuss your association with Carlton Guthrie instead, shall we?"

By God, he'd not expected the woman to challenge him so directly, though why the hell not, he'd no idea. In spite of the brief vulnerability she'd revealed when her parents had tried to lay down the law, she was impressively brave.

Deciding to reward her with nothing less than complete honesty, he said, "I've known him for almost two decades – since before he became the Scoundrel of St. Giles. Now that he's walked away from that life, I've taken over the running of The Black Swan. And while I do keep my ear to the ground and make sure the worst kind of scum are dealt with, the need to vanquish crime with violence has been diminished significantly. As the Duke of Windham, Guthrie's influence is greater than ever. Bow Street listens to him now in ways they never did before. So for the most part, I simply point them in the right direction and let them handle the monsters."

"And the rest of the time?"

Blayne stared at her. "Ye want to know if I'm capable of bloodshed. Is that it?"

She sighed as if he'd just tripped over his own feet and banged his head. "If you recall, my initial reason for hiring you was for protection, so it's only reasonable for me to ask if you're used to fighting off thugs."

"Um…" It was his turn to gape at her as if she were daft. "Have ye seen what I look like?"

"Yes. You are impressively large." She knit her brow. "What is it? Why are you laughing?"

He coughed and did his best to swallow the crass rejoinder that landed upon the tip of his tongue. "It's nothing. Do continue."

She gave him a look to suggest she was sure she'd missed something, which of course she had, though he'd be damned if he was about to give her an explanation.

"My point is," she said, sounding a little disgruntled, "I'd like to know what you're capable of. As a form of reference, per se."

"Very well. I've engaged in countless fights, Miss Russell. One doesnae survive a place like St. Giles without having done so. While working for Guthrie I helped him track down the most despicable people London had to offer, and when I saw what they'd done to helpless women and children, I took great pleasure in making them suffer. So yes, I've hurt people. I've also killed, though never unless I had to."

A lie.

He had murdered someone once in cold blood. Nausea tightened his throat.

He tried to take a calm breath. Did his best to tamp down the guilt and self-loathing.

"Thank you for being honest."

He hadn't been. Not completely. If Miss Russell knew his darkest secret she'd run from him without second thought. The rest was apparently something she could accept, which meant they'd be seeing more of each other.

"And just so you know, it doesn't frighten me

in the least." She gave him the sort of smile that would have knocked him on his arse if he'd been standing. "What are your hobbies?"

"My what?"

Her smile widened into a mischievous grin. "You know, those things one does for pure enjoyment? As I've mentioned, I like to shoot and you like to…"

He flattened his mouth, withdrew his hand from hers and crossed his arms so he could serve her the scowl she deserved. "Plants and books."

Dismay captured her features. "Truly?"

"I like watching things grow." Nurturing a seedling until it thrived was more rewarding than anything else in the world. Realizing she was studying him as if he belonged behind glass in some collection of the bizarre, he hastily added, "And reading has always been a great pleasure of mine. I've got hundreds of books."

Sparkling green eyes held him captive. "If you were forced to give them all away, save one, which would you keep?"

A thought-provoking question, so different from any other he'd ever been asked. Yet another thing he liked about her. This woman wouldn't bore him with inane conversation pertaining to fashion or the weather. "I suppose I'd have to base my selection not only on my appreciation for the author's skill as a writer, but on the content's ability to entertain me each time I read it. With that in mind, I think I'd choose *The Earl's Secret Escapades* by Charles Cunningham."

Miss Russell stared at him in an odd sort of

way until he almost wished he'd mentioned something else. *The Works of Aristotle*, perhaps? Or Benjamin Franklin's memoires? But the truth was he liked the adventurous story about an aristocrat spy. It was clever, filled with action, amusing banter, and danger.

"I, um…" Her cheeks pinkened. She fidgeted with her skirt. "I am familiar with it."

His respect for her continued to grow, not so much because she'd read the book but because she'd admitted it to him. After all, it did contain a few risqué scenes consisting of passionate kisses between the earl and his paramour.

"And what are your thoughts on the story?" he asked while doing his best to hide the amusement he found with Miss Russell's discomfiture.

She cleared her throat. "It's wonderfully entertaining."

"I particularly like the part where the earl is chasing the villain across the rooftops. The ensuing struggle when he catches him and they nearly fall to their deaths is thrilling."

Her face lit up. "I think so too." The shy smile teasing her lips was so enchanting he was almost tempted to reach up and trace his finger across the dimple it formed at the edge of her mouth. "It might not be very realistic but one of my favorite scenes is where the earl is fighting off ten men in an alley."

"Ye're right. They should have been able to overpower him by sheer number, but I do agree that it was exciting to read."

"Do you…" She bit her lip, seemed to hesitate

briefly, before she finally asked, "Do you think the story could have done with less romance?"

"Maybe, but I certainly didnae mind it. In fact, including some romance should make the book appeal to both sexes. As I dare say we've just established."

She gave a thoughtful nod. "It's my reason for liking the story. Not the romance, I mean, but the balance between the romance and the rest of it. I find it appealing."

A comfortable moment of silence followed without either one of them saying a word. They just sat side by side on the bench, enjoying the sunshine, the soft twitter of birds, and the beauty the garden offered. Blayne inhaled deeply. He could remain here all day if he didn't have other tasks to attend to. It would be a pleasure for him to enjoy the peaceful retreat while letting himself relax in Miss Russell's company.

He'd already stayed much longer than he'd intended. It was time for him to take his leave. "If ye dinnae require me for the rest of the day, I'd like to get back to The Black Swan. When I left, I meant to return within the hour so I didnae give my colleagues instructions on how to deal with the ale delivery we're expecting."

"Of course." Miss Russell stood and shook out her skirts. "Make the necessary arrangements today so you can be free tomorrow. There's an errand I have to run in the East End, so I'd like to have your escort."

"What time do ye want me to call on ye?" Blayne asked as soon as he'd risen.

"We'll meet at the corner of Oxford Street and Tottenham Court Road since your coming here will only result in unnecessary questions." When he remained silent she added, "My parents have busy schedules. The only reason they were here this morning was for the sake of meeting you. Otherwise, they're both out of the house by nine, but there are the servants to consider. I wouldn't trust any of them besides Daisy not to inform my parents that I've gone out with you for the day."

"Duly noted."

"There's something else. My father may have given you the impression that I'm not good for the ten pounds I've offered to pay every week for your service. If this concerns you, I am willing to provide you with an advance."

"That willnae be necessary. Ye've given yer word, and that's good enough for me. Besides, ye seem like the practical sort so it wouldnae surprise me to learn ye've been setting aside some pin money for when ye need it." He offered his arm and she took it, instilling in him a deep sense of satisfaction. She knew he was dangerous and yet, she seemed to trust him completely. It was only fair of him to return the favor.

Water streaked down the window, smudging the view of the street. Comfortably dry inside the carriage she'd hired, Charlotte waited patiently for Mr. MacNeil's arrival. Daisy sat beside her, tapping her foot in time to the rapid beat of the rain.

"He's going to be late," the maid said. She'd been checking her pocket watch every minute since their arrival. "Honestly, miss, I think we ought to leave."

"He'll come," Charlotte assured her with every bit of confidence she felt. "Mr. MacNeil is a man of his word."

At the very least he'd been clear about wanting to thwart her parents. She also sensed he needed the money, though for what exactly she'd no idea.

Perhaps she'd ask.

As a woman who valued her privacy, it wasn't her nature to pry into other people's affairs. But if doing so would result in another interesting conversation with a man who intrigued her more and more with each word he spoke, it might be worth defying her own principles for the time it would take to pose the question.

"I think you should find someone else," Daisy said. "Your parents would have a fit if they learned you were seein' him again today. They clearly don't approve."

"Which is why they'll never find out," Charlotte told her sternly. "Just as they'll never know I'm not really attending book clubs or poetry discussions."

"Of course, miss. I didn't mean to imply I'd betray you. I'd never do that. It's just Mr. Mac-Neil isn't really the sort of man a woman like you should be seen with."

"He's not a bad sort, Daisy. In fact I'm inclined to think higher of him than I would most upper class gentlemen."

Daisy gasped. "How can you say that when you know he's connected to Carlton Guthrie?"

"An association he himself confessed to," Charlotte snapped. Honestly, she was starting to lose her patience. "As far as people go, Mr. Mac-Neil is proving himself to be more forthright than anyone else I've known."

"That doesn't change the fact that—"

The carriage door was thrust open, allowing a damp wind to sweep inside the cabin. Mr. MacNeil climbed inside and pulled the door shut before claiming the opposite bench. Water soaked his hair, the droplets dripping over his forehead and shoulders. A puddle formed around his booted feet. "A pity ye didnae pick yesterday for yer outing, Miss Russell. Today's a wee bit soggy." He wiped his palms on his brown breeches. "Shall we be off then?"

"Indeed," Charlotte said and knocked on the ceiling. She hadn't meant to notice his thighs but it had been deuced hard not to with his hand movements drawing attention. Swallowing, she forced her gaze out the window and tried not to think of the scandalous display of wet fabric clinging to solid muscle.

"He arrived on the dot," Daisy whispered as the conveyance took off, dragging Charlotte's thoughts back to a more appropriate subject.

"I've always prided myself on punctuality," Mr. MacNeil said with a wry twist of his lips, not bothering to pretend he hadn't overheard the comment. "Being late is inconsiderate."

"You could have been early," Charlotte said with levity. "I was."

He leaned back and crossed his arms, his eyes snaring hers. "I'd rather set a standard I'm able to keep. No sense in giving ye false expectations, is there?"

"I suppose not," she said, appreciating his candor.

"So where are we going?"

Charlotte wished she didn't have to tell him. She'd kept her secret life hidden for so long the idea of letting someone besides Daisy into her confidence rather unnerved her. But she'd hired Mr. MacNeil for the purpose of escorting her about and seeing to her safety. Attempting to keep him in the dark would be foolhardy. Besides, he'd see where they were heading soon enough, so she might as well let him know.

Still, she wasn't about to reveal more than absolutely necessary. "To Carlisle & Co."

Mr. MacNeil's blank expression made it clear he'd not heard of the business.

"It's a small publishing house," Charlotte informed him, in response to which he arched a brow. "When we spoke yesterday, I mentioned a few of my interests."

"Archery, for example."

"Yes."

"And shooting."

"Right. Well." Charlotte tried not to grin. While Mr. MacNeil's tone was dry as desert sand, his eyes shone with unabashed humor. Perhaps he doubted her competence? A sudden desire to prove herself to him assailed her, but first... "I also dabble in story writing."

"Really?" He stared at her with narrowed eyes. It didn't look like he believed her.

"It started as a hobby, but once I'd been doing it for a while I thought I'd make an attempt at publication. My parents don't know and I have no intention of telling them until I'm sure I will be a success."

"You dinnae want them to think ye a failure?"

"Something like that," Charlotte said. She clasped her hands in her lap. The truth was a bit more scandal inducing. "Anyway, we're going to drop off my latest work with my editor."

MacNeil's eyebrows rose. "Ye have an editor?"

"Yes. Anyone who publishes anything has one."

"So ye're already published?" He leaned forward, pinning her with interest. "Anything I might have heard of or read?"

Charlotte's heart went straight from a steady beat into a near gallop. While she had no desire to lie, she wasn't ready to tell him the truth. Not with regard to this. So she took a deep breath and tightened her grip on the leather folio she'd brought with her. It contained the corrections Avery had requested to her manuscript. "I seriously doubt it. Unless you have a penchant for observational train of thought musings."

His expression suggested he didn't, but then he said, "If they're written by ye, I just might."

Well, thank God she was sitting down or her legs might have given way beneath her. The intimacy of his voice, the low timbre an almost velvety caress against her skin even though they were several feet apart, was enough to turn her brain to mush.

She shook herself. This was the utmost of preposterousness. He was a man with a criminal past – her newly hired employee for heaven's sake. She absolutely could not allow herself to *feel things* in his presence.

"I value the compliment." Thankfully, her voice was both strong and firm. She angled herself in such a way where she would be looking more directly at Daisy and less so at Mr. Mac-Neil. "I've been thinking we could buy some purple ribbons tomorrow, Daisy. The color would liven up that white muslin gown I don't care for."

"An excellent idea," Daisy said. "If you agree, I could add some crystal beadwork as well so it shimmers a little."

"Yes. I think that would work rather nicely."

Happy to have found a subject Mr. MacNeil would not participate in, Charlotte avoided hearing his deep masculine voice for the remainder of the journey and thus managed to steady her riotous nerves by the time they arrived at Carlisle & Co.

Observational train of thought musings? Blayne reckoned it was a while since he'd heard such a load of absolute horse shite. Did she think he was daft? Here was a woman who'd scared the bejesus out of a lecherous scoundrel two days ago with her pistol, and now she expected him to believe she was publishing something that lacked one ounce of excitement? If she'd been serious about her other hobbies, he rather suspected her writing to be edgy and possibly even improper. That would certainly match the character of a woman who'd hastily turned him into a fake fiancé in order to thwart her parents' attempts at matchmaking.

Keeping this thought to himself, Blayne stayed quiet for the remainder of the journey while Miss Russell prattled on about ribbons and beads and lord knew what else. Whatever she was up to, it wasn't his business. She'd merely hired him to protect her, even if the terms of their initial agreement might have been stretched a bit further than planned since their first encounter. Still, she was entitled to her privacy.

Except, damn it all, she'd piqued his curiosity like nothing else ever had, and now he wanted to figure her out. He wanted to know how good a markswoman she truly was, and he definitely wanted to know what she'd really written. After all, she'd confessed to reading and liking *The Earl's Secret Escapades*. Surely her own writing would reflect the penchant she clearly had for adventure. It had to. Didn't it?

The carriage rolled to a halt and Blayne glanced out. The buildings on this side of town were more squat and dilapidated than the ones Mayfair had to offer. In fact, he'd think he was back in St. Giles if it weren't for them having a touch more color. And to think Miss Russell had come here alone did not sit well with him in the least.

An uncomfortable notion sprang to mind. "Why did ye suddenly feel the need to hire protection, Miss Russell?" When she didn't respond, he swung his gaze toward her and caught her fidgeting with the oiled umbrella she'd brought along. "Something happened. Didn't it?"

She raised her chin, affecting an arrogant air so ill-suited to her he almost laughed. "It was nothing."

"It was enough to give ye a fright," he countered.

A frustrated sigh escaped her. "If you really must know, the carriage I'd hired to take me here last time didn't wait, so when I left, I was forced to walk for a while. A man followed me and... Well, the truth of it is I was robbed."

"Bloody hell." Every muscle inside Blayne tightened, the very idea of Miss Russell in danger twisting his gut with unexpected force. He turned to Daisy. "And where were ye while this was happening?"

"Running an errand on behalf of the viscountess," the maid said in a small voice. "Her own lady's maid was indisposed that day, so she turned to me for assistance."

"Leaving yer mistress without any, it would seem." Blayne jerked his gaze back to Miss Russell. "Why in God's name would ye not postpone yer meeting? Surely it wasnae worth risking yer safety over."

"Hindsight does make one more susceptible

to judgment." Miss Russell looked him squarely in the eye. "Since I'd been here before without incident, I didn't imagine I'd be in danger as long as I went by carriage. Naturally, it never occurred to me that the driver would choose not to wait."

"And yer pistol?"

"If you really must know, I did not have the chance to use it until it was too late."

He considered her for a moment, then asked, "Did the thief threaten ye with a weapon?"

She gave a curt nod. "He had a knife."

Blayne had no choice but to gape at her while this information sank in. So this was where she'd gotten the inspiration for the story she'd told her parents about how they'd met. Of course, the problem was he'd not minded the tale when he'd thought it a work of fiction. Now, aware of the danger she'd been in, he was almost tempted to shake her.

"And yet ye have no compunction about coming back here?" he ground out.

"I've taken precautions this time by hiring you."

He blinked. While he appreciated her faith in his ability to fight off a thug, he was starting to worry she might be deranged. "We shouldnae be here. It clearly isnae safe, and risking yer wellbeing for a chance to publish whatever scribblings ye've produced would be the utmost of stupidity. Surely there must be a Mayfair publisher ye can use instead?"

Miss Russell's face tightened. Her mouth,

which had been pleasantly soft mere seconds ago, transformed into a hard line. A dark red hue tinged her cheeks while the green of her eyes glowed bright with displeasure. "You are welcome to stay here and wait for my return if you wish. I'm sure Daisy would value the company since I'll be leaving her here to make sure the carriage waits this time. I, however, have an appointment to keep."

Miss Russell leapt out into the pouring rain before Blayne could stop her, and in her haste, she'd forgotten her umbrella.

"Devil take it," Blayne muttered. With a hastily spoken apology directed at the maid, he grabbed Miss Russell's umbrella and stormed after her. The rain hadn't eased one bit. It pelted down and almost rendered him blind. Swiping the water from his eyes, he marched forward and grabbed the front door of the nearest building before it managed to swing shut. "Miss Russell!"

She didn't stop to wait for him. Hell, he barely caught a glimpse of her retreating back before she vanished around a corner. Biting back yet another curse, he went in pursuit. His longer strides ate up the distance between them until he was able to grab her elbow and pull her to a swift halt.

"What's wrong with ye?" he growled.

She gave her arm a hard yank and he released her. "You are in my employ, Mr. MacNeil. I'm not paying you to offer an opinion on my writing. Least of all when you haven't read it."

He fought the urge to roll his eyes. "Forgive

me. I know I can be a touch brash at times. My intention was merely to point out the risk ye're taking and to try and make ye see reason. If ye were robbed in this part of town, it makes sense not to come back, wouldnae ye say?" When she continued to glare at him he sighed. "I'm sorry I referred to yer work as scribblings."

"I put a lot of time and effort into my writing. It's not just a hobby to me."

The seriousness with which she spoke suggested her work was part of who she was and that taking it from her would somehow lead to her downfall. The notion was so odd he struggled to grasp it. And yet in a way it made perfect sense. Miss Russell had found a purpose. Whatever it was, it mattered enough to risk her reputation and safety. And that was without pondering what in God's name she'd told her parents she was up to.

"May I see it?"

"May you see what?' she hedged while inching her way past a potted plant and continuing toward a desk behind which a young man, clearly a clerk, was seated. He glanced up and beamed the moment he spotted Miss Russell.

Blayne ignored the blatant interest gleaming in the clerk's eyes along with the unpleasant surge of irritation he felt in response. "Yer writing?"

"No." She quickened her pace, practically sprinting toward the young man and away from Blayne. "Mr. Carlisle. It's a pleasure to see you again."

Blayne traipsed up behind her and gave *Mr.*

Carlisle a quick head to toe perusal. He didn't look older than twenty although he probably was. Slim with elegant features, he was Blayne's direct opposite with his head of blonde hair, a clean shaven jaw, and a pair of dazzling blue eyes.

"Your presence is a delight as always, Miss Russell," Mr. Carlisle said, his eyes twinkling as if he were gazing straight at the sun.

To Blayne's annoyance, a flushed shade of pink crept into Miss Russell's cheeks. "Thank you. You're much too kind. May I present Mr. Wright? Mr. Wright, this is Mr. Carlisle."

Mr. Carlisle gave his attention to Blayne and even managed a polite greeting, but it didn't escape Blayne's notice that his smile was forced and the words a touch insincere. Hmm. Clearly Mr. Carlisle objected to his presence. Out of jealousy perhaps?

The name suddenly struck. "Are ye the owner then?"

"Partially, though I'm afraid all credit for the business must be given to my sister, Miss Avery Carlisle. She was the one who thought to invest the money our father left us when he passed a few years ago." He returned his attention to Miss Russell. "Avery did ask to send you in straight away when you arrived. Shall we go in together...*Charlotte*?"

Blayne grimaced. By God, he wanted to knock the young pup's block off for being so overly familiar with Miss Russell. Blayne didn't care how long he might have known her, but it was clear he was trying to stake a claim by engaging in some sort of ridiculous pissing contest.

Unwilling to participate, Blayne allowed the clerk to escort Miss Russell while he took up the rear. Until she suddenly turned back to face him. "I'd like for you to stay here."

"Are ye sure that's wise?" Blayne didn't like the idea of her disappearing into another part of the building with this fellow. He was too bloody young and eager to make a conquest for Blayne's comfort.

"Quite," Miss Russell informed him. "I need to speak with Avery alone."

In other words, she wanted him to bugger off. Right. Message received.

"Fine." He shouldn't give a toss since he was nothing to her but an overpaid servant and she no more to him than a means to an end, but the dismissal still rankled. Determined to put that aside so he could focus on his job, he lowered his voice and quietly asked, "Do ye have yer pistol?"

Her eyes widened. "Of course. But I shan't need it here."

"Perhaps not," he agreed, "but I'm more comfortable knowing ye're not unarmed. Just in case."

She gave him a perplexed look, shook her head, and turned away. Mr. Carlisle sent Blayne a smirk over her shoulder while ushering her through a door. They disappeared into a hallway while Blayne wished the little weasel would be his next opponent at one of The Black Swan boxing matches. Unfortunately, such an outcome was unlikely. And since Mr. Carlisle hadn't really done anything wrong, he probably didn't deserve ending up in the hospital just because Blayne didn't like him panting after Miss Russell.

And why the hell should he care anyway? Miss Russell had been all smiles when she'd greeted Mr. Carlisle. Perhaps she fancied him a bit. He'd made her blush for heaven's sake.

So did I.

The amount of pleasure he found in the memory was cause for serious concern. She shouldn't matter to him. Not in a possessive way at least. And she didn't. It was ludicrous to think she might after such a brief acquaintance. But since he liked her and she was paying him to keep her safe, it was only natural that he should consider all manner of danger – even that which included a potentially unwelcome suitor.

Satisfied with his reasoning and the fact that Miss Russell was most likely right about being safe inside this building, he allowed himself to relax in a chair until she returned.

She did so half an hour later. To Blayne's annoyance, Mr. Carlisle, who'd returned to his front desk duties in the meantime, leapt to his feet and rushed to offer her his arm. "Allow me to escort you back to your carriage, Charlotte."

Blayne bristled. This really was too much.

"Thank you, *Mr. Carlisle*," Miss Russell said, "but I'm sure Mr. Wright can manage."

"I'm sure he can, but it would give me tremendous pleasure if you would allow me," Mr. Carlisle said while beaming at Miss Russell like a dog chasing a treat.

When he made to take her by the arm, she swiftly moved from within his reach. An awkward pause followed before she managed to force a smile and say, "I fear I may have neglected to introduce you and Mr. Wright properly. He is my fiancé, Mr. Carlisle, and as such, I would like for him to escort me."

"Indeed," Blayne murmured. It took every ounce of self-control he possessed not to preen like an arrogant bastard or to give Mr. Carlisle the same sort of smirk he'd received from him earlier. Instead, he did his best to behave with civility and even managed to bid the young and now disgruntled man farewell with decorum.

"He's overly eager," Blayne told Miss Russell while escorting her back to the front of the building.

"Yes."

When she said nothing more, he asked, "Were ye able to conclude yer business to yer satisfaction?"

"Yes."

"So yer editor liked what ye've written?"

"She did."

"Wonderful." Blayne stepped out into the street and opened the umbrella for her. The carriage wasn't far — just a pavement width away — but it was still pouring, and while Miss Russell had gotten significantly damp earlier on her way inside, there was no sense in getting more soaked or risking a bout of influenza. Clutching her folio, she stared at him with surprising wariness before stepping forward.

Instinctively, Blayne wrapped one arm around her and pulled her close to his side so she would be better covered. She made a squeaky sound which he ignored, and then he hurried her toward their conveyance. It took but a couple of seconds, but they were long enough for him to consider how good she felt tucked against him. She was petite without being scrawny, and his hand was able to make out the gentle flare of her hip.

His imagination stirred, bringing to life a curvaceous figure clad in nothing at all.

Enough of that, you cad.

He flung the carriage door open and offered his arm for support. She accepted his assistance and allowed him to help her up, after which he climbed in behind her.

"I'll let you know when I need your help next," she said when they stopped a while later to drop him off.

Blayne considered her inscrutable expression. While she'd chatted softly with Daisy during the return ride, she hadn't spared him one glance until now. It was clear she'd not yet forgiven him for the comment he'd made earlier, and while he supposed it had been a bit harsh, he wasn't going to apologize any more than he already had when his point had been valid.

"Ye can send me a note."

Jaw clenched, she gave a tight nod.

Blayne fought the chuckle that threatened to rise up his throat. He dipped his head to hide his smile and leapt out into the rain. Pausing there on the street corner for a moment, he watched the carriage drive off. Miss Russell had a delightful temper, and while he knew he probably ought to feel some remorse over riling her, he couldn't muster the effort.

Turning down Bambridge Street, he made his way back to The Black Swan. She was the most compelling woman he'd ever met – prim and proper on the outside, with passion brimming beneath the surface. It was enough to stir a man's fantasies in the most wicked way imaginable.

CHAPTER FIVE

CHARLOTTE'S INITIAL PLAN had been to ask for Mr. MacNeil's escort the following day when she went to buy ribbons. Not because she feared for her safety on Bond Street, but rather because it made sense to enlist his help as often as possible while he was in her employ.

Except then he'd gone and put his arm around her while holding the umbrella.

She'd been shocked by the forwardness even though there had been a practical reason for it. He'd only meant to shelter her from the rain. Only she could still feel the press of his hand against the side of her waist four days later. With a firm grip, he'd held her so tightly she'd become overwhelmed by the physical strength he'd exuded, his powerful body a solid wall of pure muscle next to her smaller frame. It was the closest she'd been to him yet – closer than on the sofa in her parents' parlor or on the bench in the garden – and the scandalous proximity had made her incredibly aware of him as a man.

The incident had lasted no more than a couple of seconds, yet in that space of time she'd wanted to press her nose against his person and inhale the most alluring aroma of bergamot mixed with coffee, wet wool, and leather. Clearly, she was an idiot. But the shock it had given her had been enough to prevent her from seeking his company the following day. She needed to recover and gather her wits before she saw him again. In the meantime, she could only hope he'd think she was keeping her distance from him on account of the quarrel they'd had.

His comment had certainly been more direct than most. She'd taken offense because she took her writing seriously and didn't believe it deserved to be degraded to scribblings. But Mr. MacNeil didn't know that. And besides, even if he did, he'd just been trying to make a point. An understandable one considering he'd been hired to protect her.

Charlotte sighed and blotted the page she'd just finished. The argument had only led to a brief upset. It was Blayne MacNeil himself who gave cause for reflection. *He* was the true reason she'd needed distance. If only to figure out what her response to him meant.

Not that the past four days had offered any enlightenment whatsoever.

She'd just gotten more confused.

A knock at the door sounded and Charlotte hastily tucked the paper she'd been working on into her desk drawer and pulled out her diary. "Come in!"

It was her father, his bearing as stiff as always, his expression typically guarded like a castle behind its fortifications. "I've just received word of Mr. Cooper's arrival."

Charlotte sucked in a breath. Her stomach tightened with unease. And yet she managed a smile. "Wonderful."

Her father nodded in that approving manner of his. "I mean to invite him for dinner tomorrow evening and since I did agree not to favor him over Mr. Wright—" he spoke the name as if it possessed a bitter taste "—you may ask him to join us as well."

"Thank you, Papa."

"Hmpf. I'll do what I can to rid your head of any fanciful notions you have regarding that man. Having met Mr. Cooper myself, I've no doubt you'll agree he'll make a better match."

Charlotte bristled. "I very much doubt it."

She didn't want a match of any sort. All she desired was independence. And her most recent meeting with Avery had reconfirmed her ability to acquire such. Her earnings were good – excellent really – enough for her to view the theft of her previous royalty payment as nothing more than a brief annoyance. If she could just keep a ring off her finger until she published her next book, she ought to have saved enough to afford a small cottage somewhere.

"Have it your way then," her father said. "You may tell Mr. Wright to be here at seven."

Charlotte narrowed her gaze. "Dinner usually starts at seven."

"Indeed," her father agreed. He was already halfway out the door.

"Drinks are generally served at six."

"Right you are. My mistake. I'd quite forgotten."

The devil he had, Charlotte thought while sending his back an angry glare. The door closed and she slumped back in her chair. Her father was used to crafting plans of attack. He'd specialized in covert operations, sending spies into enemy terrain, and undermining every attempt made by his opponents.

Drumming her fingers against her desk, Charlotte came to a swift conclusion. If she was to beat her father at his own game, she'd have to be equally cunning. And that would mean making use of Mr. MacNeil's full potential.

Shoving her diary aside, she retrieved a fresh sheet of paper and penned a few words. Sealing the missive with a blob of crimson wax, she collected three pounds, and called for Daisy to join her.

"It's vital this reaches The Black Swan today without any of the money going missing. Can you think of a way to make that happen?"

Daisy considered briefly, then nodded. "One of the grooms owes me a favor. He'll get the job done."

"Thank you, Daisy."

The maid departed, letter in hand, and Charlotte tried her best to relax. All she could do now was hope for Mr. MacNeil to do his part.

Weary from the boxing match he'd just engaged in, Blayne kicked off his shoes and padded across the floor to the washbasin. Since parting ways with Miss Russell, he'd put his energy into training the bare-knuckle fighters The Black Swan kept on its payroll. The exercise stopped his mind from getting bogged down by thoughts of the raven-haired beauty. As he'd predicted, envisioning Mr. Carlisle as his opponent helped him deliver more powerful punches.

He soaked a cloth in his washbasin and used it to clean away all remnants of his exertion before drying up and donning a clean shirt. A sideways glance brought the letter Miss Russell had sent into focus. It sat on his desk, inviting him to tear it open and read its contents.

He would resist for another few minutes.

After she'd kept him waiting four full days, he'd not rush to respond. Instead, he'd take a moment to care for his plants. The seedlings he'd brought to life in the spring were maturing. Collecting his watering can, he moistened the soil. His garlic was sprouting remarkably well in their clay pots on the window sill. So were the chives, mint, and parsley. Blayne studied the two empty pots at the end where tomatoes were meant to grow. But nothing appeared to be happening there yet.

He set his watering can aside, poured himself a drink, and snatched up the letter that taunted him almost as much as the woman who'd penned it. Christ above, she'd even begun invading his dreams, luring him into dark corners, then vanishing right before he managed to catch her.

Dropping into the only armchair he owned –

a hideous thing clad in orange velvet he'd once picked up from a furniture shop going out of business – he tore the seal and unfolded the crisp white paper. The script was neat and perfectly straight with no hint whatsoever of belonging to someone who painted outside the lines. Blayne snorted and sipped his drink. It was absurd to think he knew her better than her own family, and yet he was starting to suspect that might be the case. In any event, she'd allowed him a glimpse behind the façade.

Granted, she'd felt cornered at the time – threatened by the imminent arrival of a man her parents hoped she'd marry, which was what had prompted her to make up the whole hodge-podge story about him being her fiancé in the first place. And then there was the tale about train of thought musings which didn't make an ounce of sense when considering everything else he'd learned. Having admitted to hating needle-work and water colors while favoring archery and shooting, imagining her in a quiet corner transcribing her opinion on the movement of clouds — or some such nonsense — to paper, was ludicrous.

He shook his head and proceeded to read.

Dear Mr. MacNeil,

Mr. Cooper has arrived and shall be joining me and my family for dinner tomorrow evening. In keeping with the agreement I made with my parents, you are invited as well, starting with drinks at six p.m. sharp. It is clear Papa means to champion Mr. Cooper and prove his superiority by making you blunder. Of course

I shall help you as best as I am able, but since a great deal of weight will be placed on appearance alone, I am hoping you will accept the three pounds I've included and spend it on a new set of clothes.

Please don't take offense to this request. I am merely arming my weapons.

Regards,

Charlotte Russell

Blayne set the letter aside and frowned. He ought to send his regrets. And yet the idea of letting her suffer some strange man's attention – to leave her unguarded and alone – caused his heart to contract. Miss Russell deserved the chance to escape her cage and be free. No one, not even her parents, had the right to tie her down and stomp on her dreams.

Expelling a breath, he made his decision. It was just a dinner after all. He'd attend, take his leave, no harm done. His gut tightened with a twinge of guilt. In spite of her fibs and her ploy to place him squarely in the middle of her fight for independence, Miss Russell seemed to be a good person. She certainly didn't deserve to get involved with a scoundrel, never mind a man who was guilty of murder. Which meant he had to keep his distance from her at all cost. He could not, for any reason, allow himself to forget the role he was meant to play in her life or that they were merely play acting.

Right.

He snatched up the coins she'd included and jangled them loosely in the palm of his hand. It was time for him to pay Guthrie a visit. He'd know exactly where Blayne could find some more fashionable clothes on short notice, and Blayne was not too proud to realize he needed his help.

"What the bloody hell is wrong with you?" Guthrie asked roughly one hour later while staring at Blayne as if he'd just set his house on fire.

It took a great deal for anything or anyone to catch the former crime lord by surprise, so Blayne silently congratulated himself before responding. "The blunt Miss Russell is paying will help increase my savings faster than if I didnae accept the job. And besides, I'm nae sure I'd trust anyone else to protect her as well as I can."

Guthrie stared at him, aghast. "I was referring to the part about you pretending to be her bloody fiancé! How the devil she managed to lure you into that trap I've no idea. I just can't believe you of all people let it happen." He leaned forward in his chair and pinned Blayne with a hard look. "Are you angling to get under her skirts? Is that it?"

Blayne held Guthrie's gaze with unflinching determination while he did his best not to let the disparaging comment rile him. "Miss Russell is a lady. For ye to even suggest I've such a motive is utterly disgusting. I would have hoped yer opinion of me was higher than that, Guthrie."

Maintaining a serious mien, Guthrie settled into his seat. "You're a man, for Christ sake. Allowing yourself to hope for a bit of bed sport in exchange for the favor you're dealing her would not be completely amiss. Least of all since it's the only thing that makes sense to me. I mean, you must have considered what helping her like this would mean. Dinner tonight is just the beginning, my friend. I can promise you that."

"Let's take one hurdle at a time, shall we?"

Guthrie snorted. "If you wish. Naturally, I'll help you."

"Excellent, because I'll need yer influence with the Home Office."

"What?"

"I may have suggested to Miss Russell's parents that I work there as an undercover agent."

"Why the hell would you do that?"

Blayne shrugged. "I needed to explain my appearance."

"And that was the best you could come up with?" Guthrie shook his head. "This is madness, Blayne – a recipe for disaster. In my opinion, you should let me give you the funds you need to buy whatever land you're after so you can cut ties with Miss Russell before things get out of hand. If you don't want to feel indebted, we can call it a loan. Just give me the word and I'll speak with the bank."

"Thank ye. I appreciate the offer, but I prefer to make my own way."

"Why?"

"I reckon the sense of accomplishment will be greater if I dinnae accept any handouts or loans." What he didn't mention was the fact that he wasn't quite ready to walk away from Miss Russell. That would only confirm Guthrie's theory regarding him wanting her in ways he shouldn't. Which he did. He might be able to lie to Guthrie about it, but he couldn't lie to himself. Not when Miss Russell plagued him with increasingly primitive yearnings.

"Nevertheless, the offer remains. In the event you change your mind." Guthrie held Blayne's gaze a moment before relaxing his posture. "In the meantime, you're getting a proper haircut and a shave. My valet will see to that. And once you look presentable, I'll take you over to The Gentleman's Emporium where I'm sure we'll find some appropriate clothes."

"Is the shave really necessary?" Blayne asked. He'd gotten used to the facial hair and wasn't sure he wanted to part with it.

For the first time since this meeting had begun, Guthrie grinned. "Oh yes. By the time you arrive at Miss Russell's home tomorrow evening, you'll be so dashing her father will not have a single bad thing to say about you. Unless of course you muck it all up the moment you open your mouth. I trust you can still remember a thing or two about proper speech and etiquette. From before?"

They never discussed the before. In the nearly two decades they'd known each other, their pasts had been mentioned only once, right after Blayne had saved Guthrie's life.

The stab wound Guthrie had been dealt on that long ago winter's day had left him in a fitful state. Later, while Blayne nursed him back to health, he'd revealed things in his fevered sleep. When he'd recovered and Blayne had questioned him, the truth had gradually seeped out. In exchange, Blayne had allowed Guthrie a glimpse of his own story, and in so doing, had forged an unbreakable bond.

Blayne answered the question with a nod. He'd attended Eton as a boy for the purpose of, as his Da had put it, forging lifelong connections within the peerage and learning how to fit in with the Brits. In Blayne's opinion, it had been more about prestige than anything else, but the teachers had certainly done their part to beat the 'uncouthness' out of him. As a consequence, he'd learned to pronounce his words with proper diction within a fortnight.

"What about dancing?"

"There'll be nae dancing."

"Are you sure about that?"

"Quite."

"Very well." Guthrie didn't sound the least bit convinced, but at least he'd agreed to drop the subject. "Let's get on with it then. Shall we?"

Dressed in a gown of turquoise silk and with crystal-tipped pins adorning her hair, Charlotte descended the stairs to the foyer. Her white satin gloves stretched past her elbows, leaving only an inch of bare flesh on display between them and the edge of her puff sleeves. Not that this should disappoint a man hoping to see more skin. The décolletage was low enough to satisfy any wandering gaze. It was fashionable, of course, but to Charlotte's way of thinking it did seem odd that women could put most of their bosom on public display while it was considered improper to show off an ankle.

She paused in front of the hallway mirror. Perhaps she should have worn a fichu? Not so much for Mr. MacNeil's sake, but rather because she wasn't too keen on Mr. Cooper ogling her the entire evening. It certainly wasn't with him in mind that she'd picked out the dress. On the contrary, an unkempt Scotsman had prompted that decision.

Which was perfectly stupid.

In fact, wanting to look her best for him – *no, that wasn't quite right* — wanting him to find her attractive was possibly the most idiotic notion she'd ever had. But it was the truth. She couldn't deny it. For some absurd reason, Mr. MacNeil had stirred a need within her, a need to be seen as more than a spinster, a need to be desired. And heaven help her, she wanted to affect him as he'd affected her the other day in the rain.

Continuing toward the parlor, she glanced at the hallway clock. It was ten to six. The guests would be arriving soon. Her stomach tightened into a knot of anticipation and then she entered the room where her parents had already gathered together with—

Charlotte stopped. Mr. Cooper was already here? She'd not heard him arrive, which meant he must have done so quite a while ago. Stiffening her spine, she clenched her jaw and tried not to let her annoyance show. She'd hoped Mr. MacNeil would show up first and offer support, but clearly that was not to be.

Don't worry. He'll be here soon.

"Charlotte, my dear." Her mother's voice drifted toward her with musical gaiety. "Come meet our guest."

The man with whom her parents had been conversing stood and turned. Remaining where she was, Charlotte allowed herself three full seconds in which to assess him. At roughly the same height as she, Mr. Cooper appeared to be…not nearly as hideous as she would have liked. In fact, one might even say he was handsome, if one was being honest.

Blue-eyed and fair with chiseled features, the fortunate man also possessed a lean body. Dressed from head to toe in expensive evening attire, Mr. Cooper cut a striking figure. And with his fortune taken into account, Charlotte believed him capable of making most women sigh with pleasure and flutter their eyelashes while in his presence.

Of course, his Achilles' heel here in England would be his profession. The *ton* did not take kindly to men who engaged in trade. No, it was far more desirable for a peer to marry his daughter off to someone who chose to while away his hours at his club doing absolutely nothing at all. But for a spinster with no marital prospects, Mr. Cooper would be considered a catch.

Charlotte squared her shoulders and did her best to school her features. In her estimation, Mr. Cooper had just become an even bigger problem. One that would take much more effort to be rid of since no sane woman in her position would refuse him marriage in the event he proposed. Her parents would never understand or forgive her. They'd probably have her committed for being mad. Especially if she kept insisting she'd rather have Mr. MacNeil.

Of course she wanted neither, but that was beside the point.

Forcing a smile, she approached Mr. Cooper. "It's a pleasure to make your acquaintance, sir."

"Indeed," he murmured with a twinkle in his eyes and a smile of appreciation upon his lips, "the pleasure's entirely mine, Miss Russell."

Executing a perfect bow, he reached for her hand, raised it, and kissed the air immediately above her knuckles. Kindness emanated from his gaze as he straightened and offered his arm. With no choice but to accept his escort unless she wished to be rude, Charlotte placed her hand in the crook of his elbow and let him guide her to one of the seats.

"You're quite a jewel," he murmured, his breath breezing across the side of her neck in a manner that should have produced a sensual shiver if she'd been remotely attracted to him.

Instead, she felt nothing. Not one iota of pleasure or any desire for added closeness. On the contrary, she was relieved when he released her and she could add distance between them. "Thank you," she said while lowering herself to the armchair. "I trust your journey to England went well?"

"It was pretty uneventful. The weather was

good for most of the crossing, and my cabin so comfortable I hardly needed to venture beyond it."

"You did not stroll about the deck?" While Charlotte had never been aboard a ship, she imagined it would be an adventure. She'd want to savor the endless view of the ocean, the chance to meet other travelers, and all the unfamiliar sights, sounds, and smells.

"Lord no. That would have meant running into other passengers, many of whom would have recognized me, which would have led to unwanted conversation while distracting me from my work."

"So you remained in your cabin for three weeks?" Charlotte asked, incredulous. "Without getting any fresh air or exercise?"

"There was a window," he said with a touch of defensiveness seeping into his words. "And one needn't wander about in order to get some exercise, Miss Russell. In fact, with a bit of creativity one needn't much space. Besides, it was only for three weeks and now that I am here, I fully intend to ride and fence and visit that Gentleman Jackson place I've heard so much about."

"But—"

"Charlotte," Papa said with an arched brow, "I daresay the subject has been exhausted. Perhaps we can move onto something else? Like Mr. Wright's apparent tardiness?"

Charlotte glanced at the clock on the fireplace mantle. It wasn't quite six o'clock yet. There were still a couple of minutes to go.

"You must forgive our daughter," Mama said, addressing Mr. Cooper. "She's invited a *friend* – a rather...um...interesting fellow. Not the sort of person we'd generally associate with and certainly no one of consequence, but she does have a soft heart and being charitable toward others is—"

"Mama," Charlotte hissed without any attempt to act civil or to hide the sudden, almost explosive anger, building inside her. "Mr. Wright is my fiancé. I've told you as much so I'd very much like it if you wouldn't treat him like dirt beneath your dainty slippers."

"That's quite enough," Charlotte's father growled. "Apologize to your mother at once."

Charlotte had no intention of doing any such thing. She'd stand behind her opinion even if she did regret the hurt in her mother's eyes.

Mr. Cooper looked dismayed. "You're already engaged?"

"Nonsense," Charlotte's mother gasped, finding her voice amid the tension now filling the room. "A misunderstanding, my dear Mr. Cooper, I assure you. Charlotte has not yet been spoken for and is consequently looking forward to a potential courtship."

"Hmm..." was Mr. Cooper's response. He studied Charlotte with quiet interest, much like she imagined he'd ponder a new investment opportunity.

Increasingly vexed, Charlotte glared at her mother. If she'd been a main course, she would have been force fed to Mr. Cooper by now.

What a sickening thing to acknowledge of one's own parent.

"Mr. Wright has arrived," Everet, the butler, intoned from the doorway.

The mere mention of that one particular name caused a leap of delight within Charlotte's breast. She straightened her posture, then spoke to the servant before her mother or father did something horrid like ask Everet to turn Mr. MacNeil away – an option she wouldn't put past them. "Do show him in."

Six o'clock on the dot, she noted while sending her father a smug look of satisfaction. Lord Elkins scowled with distinct displeasure and Charlotte returned her attention to the door. One moment later, the handsomest man she'd ever laid eyes on appeared. Her mouth fell open. She carefully rose to her feet while clutching the armrest. Good heavens. It couldn't be. And yet it most certainly was. Clean shaven and with his hair trimmed in a manner that still left a few stray locks falling over his brow with roguish abandon, he didn't look the least bit out of place in the parlor.

Unlike Charlotte's father and Mr. Cooper, who both wore evening black, Mr. MacNeil had elected to wear a midnight blue jacket with trousers to match, and a beige waistcoat. In Charlotte's opinion, he looked divine.

"Mr. Wright." His name whispered past her lips in pure astonishment. The transformation he'd made was nothing short of remarkable. Not that she'd been averse to his more rugged looks, but this...this was something so much...*more*.

"Lady Elkins. Lord Elkins." Mr. MacNeil's voice carried in even tones with only a hint of the brogue she'd become so accustomed to. "It's a pleasure to see you again. And you must be Mr. Cooper?" He gave Mr. Cooper a swift once over before allowing his warm gaze to settle on Charlotte. The edge of his mouth curved in an almost secretive sort of way that sent tiny tingles scattering over her skin. "Miss Russell."

Striding toward her as if it were just the two of them in the room, as if she were the only woman to ever capture his interest, he closed the distance between them and presented the flowers he'd brought. With her heart beating wildly against her breast, Charlotte accepted the offering — a lovely and most untraditional collection of fragrant pink peonies, blue hydrangeas and bright yellow sunflowers.

"Too much?" Mr. MacNeil murmured so low only she would hear.

"Not at all," she whispered back, her voice more shaky than she would have liked. "It's perfect. Thank you."

His smile widened until she felt slightly giddy. And then he winked, leaving her in a state so wobbly she had no choice but to sink back onto her seat. She took a deep breath while Mr. MacNeil addressed Mr. Cooper. "I gather you're in the steel business?"

"May I offer you a drink, sir?" Everet inquired, breaking into the midst of the conversation with almost invisible delicacy.

"A brandy would be nice," Mr. MacNeil responded. He kept his attention on Mr. Cooper while Everet saw to his request. "With the high cost of blister steel production taken into account, I'll assume you're using puddling furnaces rather than cementation?"

Charlotte blinked. Who was this person and what on earth was he going on about? She glanced at her parents who appeared equally baffled.

Mr. Cooper however responded with undeniable pleasure. "Sounds like you know a thing or two about the industry."

Accepting his drink from Everet with a distinct, "Thank you," Mr. MacNeil took a quick sip and smiled. "I like to stay abreast of important matters."

"I must say, I applaud you," Mr. Cooper said. "Tell me, what do you do for a living?"

Lady Elkins coughed while Lord Elkins made some sort of non-distinct sound. Charlotte simply grinned. Oh, this was good. An outspoken American ignorant of the conversational subjects taboo amid the upper classes, and a tavern owner she'd paid to play her fiancé. The evening was certainly off to an excellent start.

"I'm in the alcohol business," Mr. MacNeil explained. "Beer and wine mostly."

"When we last met you told us you worked for the home office." Papa narrowed his gaze like a jungle cat ready to move in for the kill.

"If you'll recall," Mr. MacNeil said, "I also mentioned being an entrepreneur. The Home

Office venture is only an occasional stint, and with my most recent assignment now completed, I am once again free to be myself."

"Really?" Papa did not look the least bit convinced. Or pleased.

"How exciting," Mr. Cooper said. "I can't wait to hear more about the two different lives you lead, Mr. Wright."

Charlotte bit her lip. Perhaps she should go find a maid who could put her flowers in water before she ruined everything by erupting in a fit of laughter. Rising, she tested her legs, and finding them sturdy enough, she exited the room while Mr. MacNeil began delving into soil compositions and how this affected the flavor of grapes. By the time she returned, the incredible man had even managed to engage her mother by explaining to her why the port she preferred was sweeter than wine.

"If you please," Everet intoned when a moment of silence arose in the conversation, "dinner is ready."

"Shall we?" Charlotte's father suggested. He'd already risen and was gesturing toward the door leading into the dining room.

Everyone else got up as well and Mr. MacNeil, the sneaky fellow, was swiftly by Charlotte's side. He offered his arm with the gallantry one would expect from a duke. "Allow me to escort you, Miss Russell."

Swallowing, she ignored her mother's frown and the fact that it might be wrong to openly favor one gentleman over the other, but dash it all, she wanted the nearness, the contact and the feel of that sturdy forearm beneath her gloved hand. Without a moment's hesitation, she complied, and was instantly overcome by a fluttery feeling deep in her belly.

Careful now.

This isn't real.

It's only pretend.

He didn't want her any more than she wanted him. She couldn't afford to lose sight of her goal. To do so would be disastrous, but for a teensy tiny fraction of a second, she would allow herself to be swept away on the feeling of being desired by the most refined man in the world.

Contorting his mouth around each perfectly enunciated word made Blayne's jaw ache. It was exhausting, this business of pretending he was the same well-bred person his mother had raised him to be with the speech pattern drilled into him by Eton. He'd gotten so used to speaking without finesse, he struggled to get his well-polished phrases to slide off his tongue with ease.

And he missed his beard.

Frankly, he felt underdressed without it – naked, even. It was most peculiar.

But the glow of appreciation in Miss Russell's eyes when he'd entered the parlor, and the absolute shock on her parents' faces, was worth every effort. He held back a grin. If only they knew who he really was. Lord Elkins would probably march him straight outside and have him shot.

"A toast," the viscount said once everyone had

been seated and their glasses filled. "Mr. Cooper, we welcome you to England and hope your future happiness will be settled while you're here."

"Thank you," Mr. Cooper said. He'd been placed next to Miss Russell with Blayne and Lady Elkins directly opposite. "Your hospitality is much appreciated."

Lord Elkins inclined his head and drank, upon which everyone else followed suit. The first course was brought in – a pastry cup filled with tuna–fish mousse. A discussion about the sights and events London offered ensued with Lady Elkins insisting Mr. Cooper see Vauxhall Gardens while he appeared more inclined to visit Parliament.

"From what I gather, it's different from our Senate and House of Representatives," Mr. Cooper said, "and older too."

"Indeed, we Brits do pride ourselves on our history," Lord Elkins said. "As a member of the House of Lords, I would be delighted to give you a tour."

"Thank you." Mr. Cooper glanced at Blayne. "Perhaps you'd like to join us?"

It was hard not to like the man. Blayne held his gaze. He saw no hint of malice, jealousy, or haughty superiority in his eyes, but rather a sense of enthusiasm he seemed most eager to share. If it weren't for Miss Russell's aversion to the idea of marriage, Blayne reckoned he'd push her in Mr. Cooper's direction himself. Rich, yet down to earth, the American was certainly a finer catch for her than that Carlisle fellow. In fact, Blayne rather liked him, which was quite surprising since he'd not have thought he'd like anyone Lord Elkins might recommend.

"I don't believe Mr. Wright has a seat." Lord Elkins's snide remark was delivered on cue.

"Neither does Mr. Cooper," Miss Russell said, "so I see no reason why that should prevent him from going with you. Provided he would like to do so, of course."

Lord Elkins frowned while taking another bite of his food.

Blayne met Miss Russell's gaze and offered her an appreciative smile. "Unfortunately, business must come first and since this is a busy time of year for me, I fear I must decline."

"Perhaps I can see it one day?" Mr. Cooper asked.

"See what?" Lady Elkins inquired.

"Mr. Wright's company," Mr. Cooper clarified.

Blayne nearly forgot to breathe and although his attention was no longer on Miss Russell, he knew she was having a similar problem. He reached for his wine, took a sip, allowed a moment to pass...

"I will do my best to find a suitable day for it," Blayne replied. To his relief, his voice flowed with the smoothness of a trained liar. God help him. This situation was getting completely out of hand. He fought the urge to glance at Miss Russell and tried to focus his mind on the money he earned by helping her out. Inspired, he turned to Lord Elkins. "You're welcome too, my lord."

Lord Elkins made a gruff non-committal sound and nodded. Plates were cleared and the main course arrived. It consisted of suckling pig with baby potatoes, steamed asparagus, and mushrooms in a creamy sauce. There was no need for Blayne to look at Miss Russell for him to feel her eyes upon him. He could sense her willing his gaze in her direction, no doubt with every intention of serving him a silent reprimand for not turning Mr. Cooper down flat.

In Blayne's estimation, doing so would have been a mistake. If anything, it would only have piqued Lord Elkins's suspicions. Grateful to Lady Elkins for bringing up a new exhibit at the British Museum, Blayne kept quiet and ate his food. He'd have to have another word with Guthrie so there would be a respectable business for him to show off in case things went completely sideways. Lord, he dreaded that conversation already.

"Miss Russell," Mr. Cooper said when a lull arose in the conversation, "I wonder what your interests might be."

"Oh, Charlotte loves to paint and embroider," Lady Elkins said.

A snort escaped Blayne's throat. He coughed to mask the insult. "Forgive me."

"Commendable activities for a young lady," Mr. Cooper said, "though I would like to hear *her* speak of them."

Blayne almost cheered and suggested a toast in

Mr. Cooper's honor.

"Oh. Of course," Lady Elkins said with prim indignation.

"To be honest," Miss Russell said, "I loathe painting and embroidery."

"What do you like then?" Mr. Cooper asked.

"Shooting and archery, along with reading and writing."

Lady Elkins groaned.

"Mr. Cooper." Lord Elkins grinned in an apologetic manner. "What Charlotte means to say is that she's a skilled markswoman with a penchant for literature."

"Ah." Mr. Cooper nodded. "We've something in common then since I also enjoy shooting for sport. Which books do you favor?"

Miss Russell scowled with distinct displeasure, forcing Blayne to press his lips together in order to keep from laughing. It did seem as though Mr. Cooper was far more agreeable and better suited to her than she'd expected.

"There's a new author," Miss Russell said, her voice tight with defiance. "His name is Charles Cunningham."

Lady Elkins gasped while Lord Elkins spoke his daughter's name in warning.

Mr. Cooper ignored them both. "The novelist who writes outrageous adventure novels?"

"You've heard of him?" Miss Russell asked while Blayne raised his eyebrows in equal surprise. The books were fairly new. He'd not have thought they'd have made it across the Atlantic yet.

"An acquaintance of mine was in London last year. He picked up a copy of... *The Earl's*... um..."

"*The Earl's Secret Escapades,*" Miss Russell supplied.

"Yes. That's the one," Mr. Cooper said. "Strange book. Very little made sense."

"Unfortunately, the author seems to pride himself on shocking people," Lady Elkins said.

"Have you even read one of his books, Mama?" Miss Russell stared at her mother with abject displeasure.

"No, and I do not need to in order to know his books do not belong in respectable households."

"I enjoy them," Blayne said, deciding to defend his favorite author and Miss Russell's shared appreciation for his work. "They're marvelously entertaining."

"But completely illogical," Mr. Cooper argued. "I mean, the very idea of a man dangling from a roof by his fingertips for a full minute is utterly preposterous."

"I'm guessing he had very strong fingers," Blayne muttered.

The plates were removed and dessert brought in.

Mr. Cooper waited for the footmen to retreat to their positions by the wall before saying, "I prefer something more relatable – grounded in reality – not to mention less provocative."

"Provocative?" Lord Elkins asked.

"The story is not designed to be realistic," Miss Russell said with surprising passion for someone who simply enjoyed Mr. Cunningham's style. She'd clearly turned this discussion into a crusade meant to push Mr. Cooper out of her life forever. "It is only meant to entertain."

"The banter between the characters is hilarious," Blayne said, deciding to offer additional support.

"I found it...silly, for lack of a better word," Mr. Cooper said with a shrug.

"Silly?" Miss Russell squeaked.

Blayne spooned a piece of chocolate cake into his mouth. His appreciation for the American was now in swift decline. Judging from Miss Russell's expression, she'd like to hit him over the head with something.

"I'd still like to know what you meant by provocative," Lord Elkins said.

"Well," Mr. Cooper said, "there are several impassioned embraces between the main character and his lover."

"Good grief," Lady Elkins gasped. "I'd no idea."

"They kiss with heated fervor," Mr. Cooper continued, "and it is mentioned, if I'm not mistaken, that they have a rambunctious time together in bed."

Blayne wasn't sure what to say to that. The man wasn't wrong, only Blayne hadn't really thought twice about that particular scene. After all, the book was penned by a man and featured a hero who, as a bachelor, would naturally have a paramour.

Lord Elkins, however, did not look like he

would ever share this opinion. His face was turning a deep shade of crimson, and his eyes, which had been hard to begin with, were now like a pair of lethal spears. "Had I known, I never would have permitted you to read such rubbish, Charlotte."

"Papa—"

"You will bring me whatever books you have by this author so they can be gotten rid of. Is that clear?"

"My lord," Blayne began without really knowing what to say next. "I don't believe Mr. Cunningham's writing is as inappropriate as Mr. Cooper suggests. Perhaps you should read one of them first before passing judgment."

"Thank you, Mr. Wright, but I see no reason to dismiss Mr. Cooper's opinion whereas yours clearly leaves a great deal to be desired. Not that I'm surprised, mind you. The Scots have always been more lenient than we Brits with regard to propriety." Lord Elkins scoffed. "A country that facilitates marriage over an anvil at no more than a moment's notice is not to be trusted."

Blayne studied the viscount's neck and wondered how long it might take to wring it.

"My apologies," he said, infusing each word with the thickest brogue he could manage. "I wasnae aware a man could be judged by the country in which he was born, though I do thank ye, Lord Elkins, for bringing the notion to my attention."

"What's he saying?" Mr. Cooper whispered to Miss Russell. "I don't understand the half of it."

Blayne ignored him in favor of raising his glass. "To Lord and Lady Elkins, whose hospitality this evening has been incomparable."

The viscount narrowed his gaze on Blayne, but said nothing else. Instead, he silently drank while everyone else did the same.

"Come, Charlotte," Lady Elkins said once dessert was over, "let us remove ourselves to the parlor so the gentlemen can have their brandy in peace."

Blayne dearly wished he could go with them. Suffering through another half hour or more in Lord Elkins's company did not appeal in the least. But, protocol was protocol and on the heels of his latest argument with the viscount, he probably ought to try and make a better impression.

Catching Miss Russell's eye as she left the table, he gave her a reassuring smile. She'd employed him to save her, not to make matters worse. It was time he swallowed his pride and got down to business.

CHAPTER SIX

CHARLOTTE MET MR. MacNeil the following day in much the same way she had when he'd escorted her to Carlisle & Co. This time, however, they were headed for the bank so she could deposit the latest royalty payment she'd gotten from Avery.

"I'm sorry about last night," Mr. MacNeil said as soon as he sat down across from her in the hackney. "I have a tendency to say what I think instead of what others might need to hear."

"And yet, by some miracle, Papa had only good things to say about you this morning."

"Perhaps on account of me telling him I voiced my support for yer choice in literature not because I approve, but because women like to believe they are given the freedom to do as they please."

Charlotte sat up straighter. "You did not."

His eyes gleamed with amusement. "I explained to him that in my experience, independent minded females must be allowed to believe they have a say and are getting their way. Naturally, in the end, a wise man will know how to steer them in the right direction."

"You presented it like a tactical campaign."

"Lord Elkins is a former field marshal, is he not?"

"Good lord." His manipulative skill was most impressive. Until a thought struck. She frowned back at him. "Was any of it true?"

"Of course not," he told her gently. "I merely sought to gain his approval."

"In that case, I do believe you met with success."

A smile teased the edge of Mr. MacNeil's mouth until Charlotte's stomach began to tie itself into knots. He held her gaze. "Did he follow up on his threat and confiscate yer books?"

Charlotte did her best to tamp down the rage she'd experienced after the guests had taken their leave. It wasn't easy. "He tossed them into the fire."

Her throat worked with the effort it took to hold back her tears. It wasn't so much the harsh words her father had spoken that pained her, or even his act of destroying something she valued, but rather his rejection of her as a person. She'd labored for months over those books, poured every piece of her heart and soul into them. If he ever discovered she'd not only read them but that she had penned them, he'd probably have her thrown out of the house.

As for Mr. Cooper, his opinion of her work only underscored her need to avoid marriage. He'd never approve of her writing such *nonsense*, as he'd put it.

"I'm sorry," Mr. MacNeil said. His gaze was truly conciliatory. "If ye like, ye can borrow my copy. Or we can stop by a bookshop so ye can purchase another."

Warmed by his kindness and understanding, Charlotte gave him a smile. "Thank you. I appreciate the offer and the suggestion, but the thing is, Mr. MacNeil, I only gave Papa one of each book. There are duplicates under my bed."

His grin was instantaneous. "Ye scheming minx."

She savored the light camaraderie she felt in his company. So when they were done with her errand and he suggested they stop for a walk in the park, she agreed.

Anything to prolong their time together and delay her return home.

Not wise.

She didn't care.

"Do ye ever wonder why we were put on this earth or what our purpose might be?" Mr. MacNeil asked while they walked with Daisy following at a respectable distance.

"Sometimes. More so when I was younger, I think."

"And did ye ever figure it out?"

She laughed in response to his teasing tone. "I believe I decided it had to be for the sake of the puppeteers."

He gave her a curious look. "The puppeteers?"

"Yes. All those people who want to dictate the lives of others."

"Like yer parents?"

"For example," she agreed with a small shrug. "Of course they never planned on resistance – on some of the puppets having wills of their own."

"Hmm… I've recently been reading Descartes' *Discourse on the Method*."

"Ah, *je pense, donc je suis*. I think therefore I am."

"Ye're familiar with it?"

"Not especially. Just with that one saying. My sister, Edwina, dabbles in philosophy. At one point this particular idea was all she cared to discuss."

"It is an interesting observation. If one can call it that."

"And hard to dispute, although I must confess some surprise at hearing you mention it. *Discourse on the Method* has very little in common with *The Earl's Secret Escapades,* which you've already claimed to be your favorite book." She gave him a playful nudge with her elbow.

"Am I not permitted to have a broad interest?" When she failed to answer quickly enough he said, "One enriches my mind, the other offers escape. They're as different as…pork roast and ice cream. One doesnae have to exclude the other. They're just differently suited."

"Hmm. An interesting point."

In fact, everything about Mr. MacNeil was interesting. He fascinated her and left her wondering long after they'd parted ways. Each time she saw him during the course of the next eleven days, he'd say something surprising – something that didn't fit with the sort of man who just ran a

St. Giles tavern. Even with his history as Carlton Guthrie's lieutenant taken into account, something didn't add up. He was too skilled at sliding into the role she'd asked him to play. To the point where she was starting to forget he wasn't who he pretended to be.

As for Mr. Cooper...

While he was nice enough and not nearly as terrible as she'd expected, he bored her to tears with his constant talk of steel production and furnaces and the factories he'd built and the businessmen he associated with and how he'd once visited Mr. Astor. It just seemed to go on and on with no end in sight.

So she wasn't unhappy when he chose to cancel his visit one sunny Wednesday morning on account of a last minute business meeting he'd managed to set up. Intent on using her free time to catch up on the writing she'd been neglecting for the last week and a half, Charlotte called for some tea to be brought to her bedchamber and went to work.

She was three pages into her newest scene when Daisy arrived with a letter from Avery.

Dear Charlotte,

I scarcely know how to begin since I know the impact this letter is bound to have on you.

My offices were robbed last night and while it pains me to inform you of this, I have no choice but to let you know that I cannot locate your most recent work anywhere. Indeed, I fear the thieves may have taken it.

Please come see me as soon as you are able.

Your friend,

Avery Carlisle

Charlotte clasped the letter between her hands and read it again. It felt like the air she'd inhaled was wedged in her throat. She couldn't breathe.

"What is it?" Daisy asked. "What's happened?"

Hot little pin pricks climbed Charlotte's back, spreading their way across her shoulders and up the nape of her neck. She had notes, but only one copy existed of the completed work. It was irreplaceable. Several months' worth of effort was gone, just like that – vanished into thin air.

Tamping down the anger building inside her, Charlotte stood, folded the letter, and carefully placed it in her desk drawer. She wanted to scream, to throw a vase against the wall, to punch something.

Instead, she smoothed the skirt of her gown and raised her chin in defiance. "We're going out, Daisy. Right now."

Half an hour later, Charlotte entered The Black Swan as if she were on a mission from hell. "Where can I find Mr. MacNeil?" she asked a young man who was carrying a tray filled with tankards of beer.

"We shouldn't be here, miss," Daisy had warned when she'd realized their destination. "It isn't safe."

"It's not as dangerous as you think," Charlotte had countered. "Least of all in broad daylight. But if you're concerned for yourself you may wait for me in the carriage."

It was what she'd chosen to do the last time Charlotte had come here. This time, however, the maid decided to try and be just as brave as her mistress.

The young man Charlotte had stopped gave her a quick head to toe perusal. "He won't like that you've come here, Miss Russell."

Ignoring the fact that this man knew who she was for the sake of efficiency, Charlotte gave him her boldest stare. "I wouldn't have done so unless it was very important. Now if you'd please point me in the right direction, I'd be much obliged."

He hesitated briefly, then glanced at a nearby table before returning his attention to Charlotte. "Wait one second and I'll take you to him myself."

She remained where she was while he served a few men, conscious of the fact that the tavern had gone completely silent. Everyone stared at her as if she were some anomaly that defied explanation.

"This isn't a good idea," Daisy whispered.

"We're going to Carlisle & Co. from here," Charlotte explained. "So we need Mr. Mac-Neil's escort."

"Of course. I just think a note would have worked as well while saving you from taking risks."

"This is quicker."

Thankfully, Daisy refrained from saying anything else. Charlotte wasn't sure her patience could be stretched much further without her snapping, and Daisy didn't deserve being subjected to an angry outburst.

"This way," the young man said when he

returned. He led them farther into the tavern, through the taproom, and toward a door at the back. Pushing it open, he stepped outside, and held the door for them. Charlotte followed him into what turned out to be a large courtyard. She hadn't realized how big The Black Swan actually was until now when she saw that the structure was shaped like a U with an external walkway linking the second floor rooms. The wing opposite the one she'd exited was comprised of stalls. She wasn't sure what the smaller one to her right contained. Perhaps the kitchen and an office?

"That's it. Now come at me again."

The familiar voice drew her attention toward her right. It must have drawn Daisy's as well because she gasped while all Charlotte could do was stare. Two men, both half-naked, confronted each other, their fists raised, until one of them dealt the other a series of punches to the chest.

Charlotte's eyes widened.

"Ach, Richard, ye can do better," Mr. Mac-Neil told his opponent with a cheerful grin. The other man struck Mr. MacNeil in the jaw. "Aye, like that, but damn ye, I did say to spare my face."

"Sorry," Richard shouted as he bounced away, dodging a blow from Mr. MacNeil only to stumble a moment later when one of Mr. Mac-Neil's large fists made contact with his shoulder.

Charlotte could not look away. Indeed, if someone had tried to drag her from the scene she would have resisted. Because she didn't want to miss a thing, not one single glimpse of Mr. MacNeil's bare chest, of the muscles rippling over his broad shoulders and down his arms with each move he made.

The sun danced off his skin, reflected in the sheen of sweat coating his torso. Charlotte's stomach tightened. Heat gripped her veins as her pulse leapt with furious excitement and something more – something so primal it made her want to reach out and touch him.

The desire to run her fingers over each exposed inch of flesh, to feel the flex and pull of his tendons while breathing in the pure male fragrance she knew he'd exude, was nearly irresistible.

She swallowed. How could this be? Mr. Mac-Neil had clearly been training for quite a while. Shouldn't she find him disgusting until after he'd bathed? If so, she didn't. In fact, she'd never been more drawn to him – to the point where she almost wanted to drag him off to some secret location for her own private exploration. Maybe she just wasn't normal. After all, she was different from other women in almost every other regard.

"MacNeil," shouted the young man who'd escorted Charlotte and Daisy.

"Give me a minute, Claus," Mr. MacNeil responded. "I'm almost done."

"That's what you think." Richard grinned.

"Aye, it is." He seemed to predict the ensuing attacks Richard made, sidestepping every blow until Charlotte realized the ones that had made contact with him earlier had done so only because he'd allowed it. And then, with remarkable swiftness he suddenly turned, catching Richard off guard with a punch to his left shoulder.

The man fell back, landing in a sprawl on the packed dirt ground. Mr. MacNeil stepped forward and offered his hand. "Looks like ye've yet to learn a few tricks."

Richard accepted his assistance with a wry smile, spitting on the ground as he stood.

"Oh my," Daisy murmured. "This is most uncivilized, miss."

It certainly was, Charlotte silently agreed, but it was also incredibly thrilling and excellent fodder for the book she was currently writing. She started forward. Mr. MacNeil turned, his gaze landing on her with remarkable force.

A delicious spine-tingling sense of awareness swept through her.

He frowned and then his eyes darkened to midnight black. "What in hell and tarnation are ye doing here, lass?"

Oh, he could sound as angry as he liked. Her body still delighted in the sound of his voice. Unafraid, she moved closer, until he was well within her reach. He stood stock still with his hands on his hips, eyeing her as she drew to a halt. With brazen disregard for what might be proper, Charlotte allowed herself a moment to simply admire his gorgeous physique. After all, how often did a woman like her have a chance like this?

The opportunity was too perfect to pass up,

so she let her gaze wander across the hard planes of Mr. MacNeil's exposed chest and toward the muscular ridges bellow. Her eyes shamelessly followed the faint dusting of hair that ran from his naval and over his lower stomach before disappearing beneath the waistband of his breeches. Good God. He was beautiful. And while she didn't mean to drop her gaze any lower, she did, absorbing each inch of perfection until—

"Lass?" Mr. MacNeil's voice was both hoarse and strained. "I can strip bare if that would help ye with yer assessment."

Charlotte's cheeks flamed in response to his words. Good heavens. She'd quite forgotten herself and he, scoundrel that he was, had called her on it. Her chin jerked up and she took a sharp breath. With her heart knocking wildly against her breast she retreated a step, almost stumbling as she did so due to the fierce intensity burning within his gaze. Jaw clenched, he watched her with the quiet scrutiny of an experienced predator on the prowl.

"Thank you," she rasped. "That won't be necessary."

He raised one eyebrow. "Are ye sure?"

"Quite," she squeaked. "I'm here because I need your help."

"Really?"

She gave a firm nod and tried to focus on why she'd come. "There's been a theft at Carlisle & Co. My most recent work has been stolen. I must go there at once."

Whatever roguishness he'd allowed was

quickly replaced with a businesslike mien. "Let me clean up a bit and get changed. Claus, please serve these ladies some tea while they wait. I won't be long. Ten minutes at most."

Grabbing his discarded shirt, he marched toward some exterior wooden stairs. He took the steps two at a time and quickly arrived on the overhead walkway. One second later, he'd disappeared from Charlotte's sight.

They arrived at the publishers twenty minutes after leaving The Black Swan, following what Blayne could only describe as the most awkward carriage ride he'd ever experienced. Miss Russell, with whom he'd believed he'd developed a friendship of sorts during the course of the last week and a half, had refused to look at him. A problem she hadn't lacked in the least when she'd faced him after his training session with Richard.

Reminded of the appreciative gleam in her eyes while she'd let her gaze wander across his bare skin, he forced back the devilish smirk that threatened while he helped her alight. Covered in sweat, he should have offended her senses. Instead, she'd looked at him with the sort of interest that had sent blood rushing straight to his groin. God help him, he'd tried to pretend he was made of stone while she looked her fill – to not respond in any way. But of course that had been utterly impossible. As soon as her gaze had dipped below his waistband, arousal had spiked through him with such intense fierceness his only recourse had been to force her gaze away from that area before it turned into a bigger and far more obvious problem.

Between the day he'd first met her and now, he had to acknowledge an increased attraction toward her. It was deuced inconvenient of course, but he wasn't about to deny its existence. Hell, seeing her in that gown she'd worn when he'd dined at her home – the way that silk had hugged her gorgeous figure and allowed him a more daring glimpse of her breasts than ever before – had fed his nightly dreams ever since. At the time, it had also instilled in him a sense of possessiveness he ought not allow himself to feel. It had made him want to cement his position as her fiancé. Even though he wasn't. Even though he had no right. Even though it was all a charade.

And yet, while he'd begun to suspect a reciprocal pull on her part, he'd not been completely certain until today. Charade or not, Miss Russell desired him, and while that certainly made his whole body hum with delicious expectation, he couldn't ignore the danger of it. His job was first and foremost to protect her, and since he always took his work seriously, he intended to do precisely that. Which meant he would never be able to act on his baser urges with her. He'd have to guard her against his past, against the demons that chased him wherever he went, and against the darkness that gripped his soul.

An unbidden memory flickered to life before he was able to shut it out. Pain-stricken eyes wide with fear stared back into his. Hands – his hands – gripping the base of a candelabra. His father's enraged words and his uncle's shocked voice immediately after. "Christ have mercy on yer soul, James Callanach. Ye'll hang for this."

He blinked in response to a softer tone and realized Miss Russell was staring at him, her expression puzzled. "Are you all right?"

A nod was all he could manage just then.

She tilted her head. "Where did you go?"

Air. He sucked it into his lungs and expelled it while keeping his eyes trained on her, anchoring himself in the present. "Nowhere important."

Was that disappointment he saw on her face? The look was gone before he could figure it out, but at least she wasn't ignoring him anymore. She tugged on her hand and he realized that he still clasped it while Daisy waited impatiently for them to move so she could get out of the carriage as well.

Muttering an apology, Blayne turned to assist the maid. Moments later, the three of them entered Carlisle & Co. where shattered glass, upended furniture, and scattered items gave evidence of the break-in that had occurred. A blonde woman Blayne hadn't seen before was crouched in the middle of an office, picking papers up off the floor while Mr. Carlisle offered assistance.

Miss Russell rushed forward.

"Avery," she exclaimed, drawing the blonde woman's attention. "I came as quickly as I could."

Recalling Mr. Carlisle's mention of his sister's given name being Avery, Blayne realized this was the woman who'd started the business.

Miss Carlisle stood and accepted the fierce embrace Miss Russell gave her. "I'm so sorry, Charlotte. I should have taken your manuscript home with me. I should have—"

"It's not your fault," Miss Russell said with a hasty glance in Blayne's direction. Turning her back on him, she lowered her voice to a whisper and told Miss Carlisle something he couldn't hear.

Another secret perhaps? Interesting how Miss Carlisle had referenced Miss Russell's work as a manuscript. If the raven-haired beauty merely dabbled in observational train of thought musings, wouldn't they be considered collections?

Deciding not to question the accuracy of Miss Carlisle's phrasing, he addressed Mr. Carlisle. "Any idea when the break-in took place?

The young man tore his gaze away from Miss Russell with unmistakable irritation. "I left the building yesterday evening at roughly seven o'clock and returned here this morning with my sister at eight, so it must have occurred at some point during that time."

"Ye were here alone last night?" Blayne asked.

"Of course," Mr. Carlisle said.

"And yer reason for being the one to close up was..?"

Mr. Carlisle glared at Blayne. "I always do so. It's part of my job."

"Hmm... Well, the thief made quite a mess."

Blayne glanced about. It looked like he'd been rummaging around for something specific. "What else did he take besides Miss Russell's manuscript?"

Miss Russell gave him a startled look – the sort that confirmed she'd been hoping he might not have picked up on that particular word. He almost grinned. Spotting inconsistencies, noticing things that weren't as they should be, was part of who he was. It was what had kept him alive in St. Giles all these years – the reason he'd always gotten the better of those who'd attempted to bring him down instead of the other way around.

So he'd been right to doubt Miss Russell's attempt at convincing him she had a penchant for boring prose. If he were to place a bet, he'd wager she'd written a novel or two. Most likely containing plots she didn't want anyone knowing she had concocted. His fascination with her increased.

"The lock box containing our petty cash has been pilfered along with the work belonging to several authors. Two other clients stopped by right before you arrived. Neither one was pleased to learn of the robbery." Miss Carlisle sank into the nearest chair. She looked close to tears. "I've notified Bow Street, of course. Hopefully, they'll launch an investigation that leads to the culprit's arrest."

"And until then?" Miss Russell asked with a nervous look in her eyes.

"I'm sorry," Miss Carlisle muttered. "You'll

receive the payments owed to you for the books we've already published. But you know how this works. Considering the small size of my business I cannot afford to invest in any author ahead of time."

"In other words, I may never earn a penny from my most recent book," Miss Russell said. Her tremulous voice and troubled gaze conveyed her distress. "It took me half a year to write it, Avery. Surely, you must be insured against this sort of thing. There must be a way in which to—"

"Miss Russell." It was Mr. Carlisle who spoke this time. "If I may, I would like to remind you of your contract. Unfortunately, the only thing you're entitled to right now is voiding any demand we might have had on your next manuscript. You can in fact choose to take your future books elsewhere."

"But…"

"Come, Miss Russell." Blayne took her gently by the arm. "There's nothing more for us to do here. If anything, I believe we're getting in the way."

"But," she muttered once more while glancing around in desperation. "Maybe it's just been misplaced. I'm happy to help you look."

"Thank you," Miss Carlisle said with a note of defeat, "but I'd rather go through everything on my own, and besides, I'm expecting a constable any moment. Please rest assured I will send word straight away if it reappears."

It didn't sound as though she believed there

was any chance of that happening. Blayne gave Miss Russell's arm a gentle tug and was glad when she finally started moving her feet. Seeing her so lost and upset did something savage to him. It made him want to catch whoever had done this and tear the blighter limb from limb. By God, if there was a chance in hell of finding the damned thing Miss Russell had written, he'd do it.

"I'll put a crew on this right away," he said once they were back in the carriage. "See if they can find out who was behind this."

"You did mention Miss Carlisle informing Bow Street," Daisy said when Miss Russell failed to respond. "I'm sure they'll figure everything out. Wouldn't you agree, miss?"

Miss Russell stared stiffly out the window. The faraway look in her eyes made her appear so vulnerable – so unlike the woman Blayne knew her to be. And it made him want to do whatever he could to ease her concerns, if only to have her true self returned.

"Bow Street is an excellent start," Blayne said while keeping his gaze firmly fixed on the woman who'd somehow started mattering to him. "But if there's a thief, I'd trust my men to find him first. It would help if ye could tell me exactly what to look for."

Daisy glanced at her mistress with marked concern. "Miss?"

"It's a novel," Miss Russell said with a weary sigh. She turned away from the window and locked her gaze with Blayne's. "As of right now, it consists of four hundred hand written pages entitled *Book Three* by Anonymous."

So it was a novel. He'd been right in his deduction thus far. "What's it about?"

"You'll know if you find it."

"Hmm…" So she wasn't willing to let him in on that particular secret yet. He pondered the out of the way publisher she'd decided to use, the mess the office had been in, and what had been taken. Something didn't add up. He angled his head in contemplation. "Not to disparage yer writing, but why on earth would a thief steal an unpublished book?"

"More than one, according to what Avery told us."

Blayne nodded. Yes, there had been at least two other clients. "What could he possibly hope to accomplish?"

"I'm sure I don't know," Miss Russell said. "Maybe he likes to read."

"Books aren't cheap," Daisy added.

No. They weren't. But if the unpublished books had been the thief's main goal, then why not rob a bookshop instead? Unless it was a very particular manuscript he was after.

Deciding to file that piece of logic away for later, Blayne leaned back against the squabs and gave Miss Russell a smile. "Whatever his reason, I'll do my best to track him down."

"Thank you, Mr. MacNeil. I'm glad to know I have your assistance."

Her dismal attempt at looking happy almost broke his heart, but her words made him feel like a king.

The incredulous stare he received from Guthrie later that day when he mentioned the extra problems he faced had the opposite effect. "Please remind me, Blayne. Did I not advise you to avoid getting involved with her?"

"Ye did, but I dinnae regret doing it."

"No?" Guthrie studied him for a long moment before saying, "What if I refuse to help?"

"Then I suppose Miss Russell will lose credibility with her parents, be labeled a liar, suffer potential ruination, and possibly get shipped off to America if Mr. Cooper still wants her after all that." Not something Blayne would allow to happen if he had anything to say about it.

"Why the hell did she have to say you were an entrepreneur and why in all that is holy did you feel inclined to invite this American person to visit your place of business together with her father of all people? Blayne, the situation with the Home Office aside, this is madness, and cleaning up your mess along with hers is beginning to require a dedicated team of people."

"I'm sorry, Guthrie. I realize the situation has worsened."

"Devil take it, Blayne. If you were anyone else I'd toss you out on your arse and let the both of you suffer the consequence of your idiocy."

"Except ye can't. Can ye?"

Guthrie blew out a frustrated breath and grabbed his brandy. He took a long sip and set the glass aside. "Unfortunately, my conscience will not permit it. And you probably deserve a thousand curses for counting on that."

Blayne couldn't deny it. He knew Guthrie would always feel indebted to him. It was something he could have taken advantage of repeatedly during the time they'd known each other, but he hadn't. Not until now. "I'm sorry."

"Christ. I know what it's like to be smitten. I just don't want to see you give up on everything you've worked so hard to achieve, that's all."

"Thank ye, but after all this time, getting recognized is unlikely."

"But not impossible," Guthrie warned.

The sound advice stayed with Blayne long after he returned home that evening.

CHAPTER SEVEN

TEN DAYS LATER, the case of the missing novel was still unresolved. No one, not even Mr. MacNeil, had been able to figure out who the thief was or where he'd gone.

For all Charlotte knew, her manuscript could be in Scotland by now.

Choosing not to think about that at the moment, she glanced around the crowded room where London's elite mixed and mingled beneath the glow of two gilded chandeliers.

"You look especially lovely this evening," Mr. Cooper said. "Quite exquisite."

He handed her a glass of lemonade intended to offer refreshment after the reel they'd just danced together. Thanking him, Charlotte sipped the cool drink with quiet relief while allowing her gaze to wander the room. It was an age since she'd last attended a ball and while she hadn't missed doing so, she couldn't help but admire the splendor of this particular one. The Duke and Duchess of Coventry's spacious mansion lent itself perfectly to large gatherings with plenty of space to allow for proper air circulation.

Every member of Society must have been invited. There were hundreds of people, all dressed in their finest evening attire. Ladies garbed in shimmering silks and adorned with glittering jewels sparkled beneath the two luminous chandeliers while the gentlemen cast more elegant silhouettes in their simple evening black.

"You don't think it's too much?" Charlotte asked Mr. Cooper.

"Of course not."

When he said nothing else Charlotte tried to locate two of her cousins among the crowd. Rose and Violet had assured her they would join her as soon as they'd finished greeting some of their friends. Their presence would surely help with the strained atmosphere Charlotte felt when she was alone with Mr. Cooper – this constant effort to think of something to say and never being satisfied with whatever came out of her mouth. She rose up onto her tiptoes, hoping to get a better look, but the effort made no difference. She was so short she couldn't even hope to spot a tall Scotsman with dark brown hair if he should appear.

"Maybe we can go for a walk on the patio," Mr. Cooper suggested.

Charlotte tried not to roll her eyes or sigh with obvious exasperation. Since meeting him for the first time three weeks earlier, she'd been alone with him – or as alone as an unmarried woman could be with a gentleman – a total of seven times. Twice her parents had managed to get her to go on a carriage ride with him in Hyde Park and on five occasions she'd entertained him for tea. On neither of those instances did she or Mr. Cooper have much to say to one another. Not after he'd made his displeasure of her reading preference clear.

"I'd rather stay here." At least then she could busy herself with watching other people.

"You're searching for *him*, aren't you?"

She hadn't been. She'd been looking for her cousins.

Liar.

"I've no idea to whom you might be referring."

Mr. Cooper chuckled. "Really, Miss Russell. I'm not blind or stupid you know. Look, it's obvious you'd rather talk to Mr. Wright, but the fact of the matter is he's not here. I am. And if you'd just give me a chance to prove myself, you'd realize I'm not as awful as you might like to think."

Horrified by her transparency, Charlotte swung round to face him only to be caught off guard by the spark of humor in his eyes when what she'd expected was disapproval. "I'm so sorry. It is just…"

The edge of his mouth curved. "I understand." He glanced askance for a second. "Or at least I think I do. Your parents arranged for me to come here without discussing the matter with you, and in the meantime, you met someone else – an option who makes your heart soar. And now you feel trapped between obligation and desire."

"Mr. Cooper. You should not—"

"Say such things?" He grinned. "If there's one thing I'll never understand about you Brits, it's your inclination to keep the truth neatly tucked away behind all that pretense. Isn't honesty better?"

She stared at him for a long moment. "Do you know, I think that's the first compelling thing you've ever asked me."

"You see? I'm not so bad after all."

Charlotte supposed he might have a point. Perhaps she had been biased against him right from the start and hadn't allowed him the chance he deserved.

No. That wasn't quite it.

The truth was, he didn't fill her breast with eager fluttering or draw her into conversations that stirred her mind. Whenever she'd tried to steer their conversation toward a subject of her own interest, he'd invariably directed them back to steel. The man didn't seem to consist of anything else. He'd married his work.

"Mr. Cooper," Charlotte said. "Since we are being honest with one another, I must inform you that I have no intention of wedding anyone."

His eyes narrowed ever so briefly, just enough to convey his frustration. But then he smiled and offered his arm. "Come, Miss Russell. Some fresh air will do us both good. And besides, there's a matter I'd like to discuss with you in private."

He watched her with the same degree of focus

she imagined him giving a business contract. And then his gaze dropped, ever so fleetingly to her breasts, and whatever appreciation she'd felt in response to the levity he'd displayed a moment ago was swept away by aversion. Mr. Cooper could be pleasant, jovial even, but the idea of letting him touch her in all those places a husband would have every right to made her recoil.

"I really don't think—"

"Miss Russell." A smooth voice near her left shoulder rumbled through her in low tones.

Charlotte sucked in a breath and turned. Every tightly strung nerve within her relaxed while a rush of heat bathed her skin. "Mr. Wright."

He bowed, his warm gaze snaring hers until it was almost as though they'd been swept away to some private corner where only the two of them existed. Her heart beat with frantic anticipation as he raised her hand to his lips for a kiss. His mouth pressed down over the back of her white satin glove, completely destroying the one inch distance etiquette deemed appropriate. Charlotte's stomach became a jumbled chaos that nearly erupted into a blaze of fire the moment she felt his teeth scrape against her.

It was over before she could fully comprehend what had happened. To anyone watching it would have looked like nothing more than a thoughtless show of interest on his part, but to her, it had been like a lightning bolt to every sensitive part of her body.

"Mr. Cooper," Mr. MacNeil said as if he'd not

just turned her legs to jelly. "It's good to see you again."

"Likewise," Mr. Cooper said with a forced smile suggesting he didn't agree with what he was saying. "We were just talking about you. I was ready to bet you wouldn't show."

"And yet," Mr. MacNeil said while meeting the other man's gaze head on. "Here I am."

"So you are," Mr. Cooper murmured while taking a sip from the champagne he'd just snatched off a passing tray. "What a relief."

"I actually think you might believe it is in a moment," Mr. MacNeil said. "You see, I've just learned there are talks of building a cast-iron arch bridge across the river Severn in Gloucestershire. The tender will be announced next week, but I was thinking you might want to—"

"Who's in charge of the project?"

"You'll want to speak with Mr. Hugh Lewis. Are you familiar with him?"

"We've met." Mr. Cooper glanced about. "In fact, I saw him only an hour ago when I arrived, but then…"

To his credit, he stopped himself from suggesting Charlotte had gotten in the way of what could be a lucrative deal for him. Not that she cared. If she had to choose between writing her next novel and spending time with Mr. Cooper, she would choose work as well. With Mr. MacNeil however, the decision wasn't as easy to make. In fact, she was starting to fear he might have the power to lure her away from the one thing that filled her with purpose and joy. He might even be able to make her forget that the only reason he was here right now was because she was paying him to attend.

And yet, she was more than eager to lose herself in the pretense if only for a night. The future she had planned would not include him or any other man for that matter. Her chance to savor this feeling of being desired was fleeting. Even if it was just an illusion, Charlotte had no wish to squander a single second.

With this in mind, she addressed Mr. Cooper. "Perhaps you would like to go find him?"

"I probably shouldn't leave you alone."

With Mr. MacNeil.

The unspoken words were implied by the uncertain look he sent the large Scotsman.

"It's all right," Charlotte said. "There are plenty of other guests about and my cousins did say they would find me as soon as they'd spoken with some of their friends."

Mr. Cooper gave her a pensive look. Eventually he nodded. "Please don't go anywhere. I won't be long and when I return I'd like to escort you to supper."

"Of course." Charlotte added a sweet smile and waited.

Mr. Cooper turned to Mr. MacNeil. "I'm still hoping you'll find time to show me your company. Perhaps we can agree on a day and time later this evening?"

Mr. MacNeil answered with a tight smile. "Of course."

Seemingly satisfied with this response, Mr.

Cooper turned and walked away with a clipped stride. Charlotte breathed a sigh of relief.

"I thought he'd never leave," Mr. MacNeil said, echoing her unspoken thoughts.

She glanced at him. "I was starting to doubt you would show. After all, you've always been punctual before."

"I'm sorry if I gave you reason to worry." The soft murmur of his voice added a sense of intimacy to his words even though he'd dropped the brogue for the evening.

"I wasn't worried." To suppose such a thing would mean she cared. *Oh, but you do.* She'd never admit it. "Merely surprised."

"So…you didn't miss me at all?"

"Not in the least." Why on earth did she sound so breathy? "Your absence was more of an inconvenience really."

"Is that so?" A hint of mirth clung to a throaty growl.

Goodness.

His voice alone filled her head with the sort of imaginings no unmarried lady ought to be capable of having. Combined with the spicy sent of bergamot he exuded and her knowledge of what he looked like without his perfectly tailored clothes, he'd managed to turn her into a mess of riotous emotion and indefinable yearning. Somehow, with each additional second spent in his company, her body craved something more – something new and unfamiliar, yet so incredibly basic it felt essential to her existence.

"Have you learned anything new about

the Avery Carlisle theft since the last time we spoke?" She had to drag her mind away from her inappropriate musings. Only danger lurked in that direction, not to mention the risk of humiliation when Mr. MacNeil explained he'd just been playing a part and that she was wrong to have read any more into it than that. After all, she had practically coerced him into pretending he loved her.

Unfortunately, her father still insisted she marry Mr. Cooper. It was as if the earl had gotten a fixed idea in his head and refused to be swayed from it no matter what. Not even Mr. MacNeil's success at ingratiating himself had made her father relent.

Not that it mattered. As soon as Mr. Cooper was gone she'd break things off with Mr. MacNeil and...

No. She still needed another one hundred pounds to afford the property she wished to purchase. One hundred and forty if she took into account the money she'd have to pay Mr. MacNeil next week. Gazing at the man whose help she'd come to rely on more than she'd ever expected, she prayed he'd offer some hope with regard to her missing novel, no matter how small.

"Unfortunately, I've not had a great deal of time to learn more since yesterday morning when we last spoke." He'd accompanied her to Mrs. Lowell's charity event at St. Agatha's Hospital while her father and Mr. Cooper visited Parliament.

"I see."

"But I've done some additional thinking." He gazed at her intensely. "The crime makes no sense unless the thief was after a very specific piece of work. Now, I had a man stop by Carlisle & Co. to ask for a list of the stolen properties and what their anticipated worth would be, but Mr. Carlisle, with whom the man met, was less than helpful. He refused to offer up any information about the authors."

"And rightfully so," Charlotte said. "That sort of thing is confidential. If he were to hand it out to anyone who asks and word about it got out, any author published by Carlisle & Co. would lose faith in the company. Surely you can see that."

"As a matter of fact, I can. Indeed, I must confess to respecting Mr. Carlisle more for proving to be a man of principal, but it doesn't help me in any way. As it is, I believe the culprit must have been someone in their employ."

Charlotte shook her head. "The door was forced open. Things were scattered about in disarray as if someone unfamiliar with the place had been searching for something in haste."

"Indeed they were. In fact, I'm inclined to believe the entire thing was staged for the sole purpose of making us think it was simply a random break-in. But it wasn't. I'm certain of that. Which means we must figure out who, besides the employees, might have known you and the other authors had work lying about the office during the time of the robbery. Because the thief wasn't after the money, Miss Russell. That much I can guarantee."

"In that case we probably ought to visit Miss Carlisle and her brother again. They're our best chance of getting the answers we seek, and if I come along I believe we've a bigger chance of learning more." She would speak with Avery alone and find out which stolen work was of greatest value, even though she already feared she might know the answer.

"We can meet at the same place as usual," Mr. MacNeil suggested. The corner of Oxford Street and Tottenham Court Road had become their designated spot whenever Charlotte had errands requiring Mr. MacNeil's escort. It had prevented him from coming by the house too often and her parents growing suspicious.

"I'll pick you up at ten if—"

"There you are, Charlotte." Her mother's voice prompted her to turn and discover she wasn't alone. Indeed, she was accompanied by the odious Countess of Warwick. Why the two had to be friends, Charlotte would never comprehend. "We've been looking everywhere for you, but it's such a crush it's near impossible to find anyone who's not immediately at one's side. Lady Warwick, if you recall, knows everyone there is to know so when I mentioned your Mr. Wright and she told me she'd never met anyone by that name, I naturally insisted upon an introduction. Thus, here we are."

Cold unease wrapped itself tightly around Charlotte's body. Notorious for being a gossip who thrived on discovering scandals, Lady War-wick's penetrating stare was cause for concern.

"I'm honored to make your acquaintance, my lady," Mr. MacNeil said with a reassuring gentleness that soothed Charlotte's nerves.

Lady Warwick swung her eagle-eyed gaze toward him and gave him a proper look. Her eyes narrowed and something akin to confusion assailed her features. "You look awfully familiar. Have we met before?"

"Unlikely," he said, his voice a notch tighter. "I rarely attend social functions."

"Hmm..." Lady Warwick scrutinized him until Charlotte felt the need to shift with discomfort. Mr. MacNeil on the other hand didn't so much as flinch. The countess tapped her fan against her hand in thought. "It will come to me. Yes. I've definitely seen you somewhere else though I do think it was a long time ago."

"As I've already implied," Mr. MacNeil said, "you must be mistaken."

"No...no... I'm never wrong about this sort of thing."

Mr. MacNeil turned to Charlotte, his face a mask of inscrutability. "Miss Russell. I do believe our set is about to begin."

"It is?" She blinked and then mentally kicked herself for not realizing his intent sooner. It was just that when his focus was on her all intelligent thought abandoned her. She rushed to gather her wits. "Ah yes. So it is. If you'll please excuse us, Mama. Lady Warwick. We'd rather not miss the um...waltz?"

Good heavens. *That* was what they'd be dancing?

Charlotte braced herself for the very real prospect of soon being held by Mr. MacNeil. She took the arm he offered and started moving away.

"I've got it," Lady Warwick exclaimed with delight.

Everything about Mr. MacNeil slowed and hardened. Muscles strained beneath Charlotte's fingertips and the air around him shifted as if in preparation for some sort of battle. She glanced at his handsome face and was shocked by what she saw there – an emotion so powerful it gripped her heart and threatened to tear it in two.

He, the strongest most confident man she'd ever known – a man who'd confessed to killing those who'd threated his life – was scared. And something about that terrified Charlotte. But it also instilled in her the need to protect him as he'd protected her.

So she said the only thing she believed might be helpful. "I trust Mr. Wright implicitly, Lady Warwick. If he insists he has never met you before, then I believe he must be correct and that you must be entirely mistaken."

"Charlotte!" Her mother stared at her in absolute outrage

"I'm sorry, Mama. But this is my future happiness at stake. I shan't allow anyone to ruin it with attempts to disparage the man I intend to marry." Thank goodness Mr. MacNeil was as strong as he was for she was gripping his arm as if it were the only thing that could save her from falling right now.

"I was only going to say that he bears a striking resemblance to someone I knew in my youth," Lady Warwick said with a disgruntled sniff. "He was Scottish too, you know."

"A lot of people are," Mr. MacNeil murmured. "Come Miss Russell or we'll miss our dance."

"Who was it?" Charlotte heard her mother ask while Mr. MacNeil began drawing her away through the crowd.

"Mr. Bruce Calla—"

Music and chatter swallowed the rest as Mr. MacNeil led Charlotte further away.

"Where are we going?" she asked, almost stumbling as he pulled her through the crowd. "The dance floor is over there."

He didn't respond. He just kept on going at a clipped pace until they burst through the French doors and onto the terrace.

The only thought on Blayne's mind was escape. He needed to get away from that awful woman, away from all these people and their prying eyes, and away from the walls closing in around him. Without slowing his pace, he strode out onto the terrace, and down the steps leading into the garden.

Turning onto a paved path, he inhaled a lungful of crisp clean air. His heartbeats slowed and he finally drew to a halt. But it wasn't until he heard a feint yelp that he glanced down and saw Miss Russell was with him. Most likely because he was clutching her wrist like a vice.

He unclamped his hand and took a step back. "Forgive me, lass. I didnae realize."

She rubbed the spot where he'd held her, but rather than look annoyed or hurt, her eyes filled with concern. "What happened back there?"

Clenching his jaw, he stared at her in silence.

A sigh of exasperation filled the air. "You're obviously keeping something from me."

He crossed his arms in defiance. "I think I have a right to do so. After all, we're not really engaged. I'm just yer employee, which means I dinnae owe ye an explanation."

"You do if it threatens my reputation."

He laughed. "Lass, every moment ye spend in my company threatens yer reputation. Ye dinnae ken that by now?"

"Because you're not really a gentleman who's made a fortune for himself in wine and beer?"

That wasn't what he'd been referring to, but her suggestion was equally valid. "Ye hired a St. Giles thug, Miss Russell."

"One who knows how to fit in among the elite." Even in the darkness surrounding them, he was aware of the curious gaze with which she assessed him. "How is such a thing even possible?"

His heart knocked wildly against his ribs. "I'm a very skilled actor."

"That's what I kept telling myself all this time."

"And it's the truth. The only truth."

There was a long pause, and then she quietly said, "I don't believe that. In fact, your reaction just now suggests the opposite. It suggests you have a secret – that you're keeping something important from me and—"

"What?" Tension coiled around every limb. His chest squeezed tight against his lungs. Fists clenched, he stalked toward her. "It's not as if ye're nae doing the same."

"I don't know what you mean."

Irritation clutched at his stomach. "Ye're lying."

"I'm n—"

"There's something about ye and yer stories, Miss Russell, something ye're desperate to hide." He loomed over her. "Care to tell me what it is?"

She shook her head. "No. I can't."

Unexpected disappointment cooled his blood. "Well then. In that case I hope ye can understand if I may have my own reasons for wanting privacy."

"Yes. Of course. I'm sorry. It's just…"

"Just what?"

She swallowed and looked away. Blayne moved a bit closer – so close he could smell her tempting perfume, an intoxicating scent of chamomile and honey with an added hint of citrus. "If there's something you fear and I'm able to help, I want you to come to me in the same way I came to you."

Undone by her offer, Blayne gazed at her in wonder. Every restriction he'd placed on his heart through the years came undone. He felt it swell with the sort of fondness he'd not thought he'd ever be capable of again. "Sweet lass, ye've already done so much just by placing yer trust in me. And the set-down ye gave Lady Warwick was extraordinary."

"I had to say something."

"Nae, ye didnae have to say a single thing, which is what made it all the more impressive." Without even thinking he reached up and brushed his thumb along the edge of her jawline. A tremulous sigh escaped her, the sound a jolt to the need she'd instilled in him since the moment they'd met. "Why did ye do it?"

"Because I couldn't stand to see you hurt."

Her honesty broke him. Raw emotion overtook all reason and before he had a chance to contemplate what he was doing, he'd pulled her into his arms and captured her mouth in a kiss he hoped would impart what his words could never convey.

You matter to me as well.

More than you should.

I want you.

I need you.

I have to have at least this.

As if in agreement, she arched against him and parted her lips. Rogue that he was, he took advantage, tasting her as if she were the sweetest confection he'd ever been served. He lowered his hand to the flare of her hips and shamelessly drew her flush up against him. She gasped, but did not pull away, thank God. Instead, she clung to him even more, answering each of his movements with ones of her own while letting him savor the fruity flavor of rich champagne still lingering on her tongue. His hand stroked over her spine, then lower toward the curve of her bottom.

Shifting her slightly...just so...he moved into the space between her thighs and kissed a path along her jaw, then down the side of her neck. A soft moan filled the air, the sound so rewarding it almost brought him to his knees.

His fingers tugged at the delicate sleeve of her gown, pulling it down, bringing it lower, his only aim to free her just a little bit more so he could—

A cough broke through his lust-filled haze. Blayne stilled, every muscle and nerve ending drawing tight with apprehension while he paused to listen.

And then, "I think it's time for my next dance."

Miss Russell squeaked in response to Mr. Cooper's stiff voice.

Shite.

Blayne pressed a kiss to her shoulder for reassurance — *this wasn't a meaningless dalliance, lass* — then put her sleeve back in order, straightened himself, and took a step back. Turning toward the other man, he waited to be admonished for his actions — to have the threat of immediate marriage thrust upon him.

Instead, Mr. Cooper calmly extended his hand toward Miss Russell and waited.

She glanced at Blayne and he realized she'd turned to him for guidance.

"Ye should go with him," he said.

A frown appeared on her brow — just a couple

of barely visible lines in the darkness. "All right."

The confusion in her voice made him feel like he'd just stolen something pure and precious from her, only to stomp on it with muddied boots. He cursed as she started moving away. This wasn't what he'd wanted, it wasn't how it was meant to be. Miss Russell belonged with *him*, damn it.

No.

She can't.

She deserves better than you.

And yet, Blayne could not stand the thought of her in the arms of another man. Not after what they'd just shared – not after the way she'd responded to his caress. Christ above, he knew he wasn't a well-polished gentleman suitable for a lady like her. He was rough and crude, forged from the sort of experience nightmares were made of. She deserved better. And yet, he feared there was no walking away from her now. Somehow, that kiss – that moment of pure surrender – had bound them together with unbreakable force.

He could feel it in his bones.

"Miss Russell," he said, even as she moved further away. "I dinnae regret what just happened between us. I'll nae apologize for it."

She was gone then, back to the ballroom with Mr. Cooper.

Blayne wished he could go in pursuit but doing so in his current state would be highly inappropriate. So he blew out a breath and forced himself to consider the ramifications of his actions. Miss Russell would want a declaration of sorts. She'd expect him to make her an offer now. But would she accept him if he did and, more to the point, could a man like him even hope for her acceptance?

He wasn't the least bit sure. After all, she'd hired him to play her fiancé so she could avoid marriage, not launch herself straight at the altar. And what the hell was he doing anyway, contemplating domestic bliss with Miss Russell as though he were free to do as he pleased? His chest tightened. He couldn't dismiss his past and he certainly couldn't marry a woman without confiding his sins.

To do so would be wrong.

Plain and simple.

Although...

Almost two decades had passed since that awful night at Merkland Manor. He'd never forgive himself for what he'd done, but maybe he could allow a bit of light into his life. After looking over his shoulder all these years, ever fearful he'd be clapped in chains and either transported or hung by the neck, nothing had happened.

Until tonight when Lady Warwick had pointed out his familiarity.

Blayne bristled.

If he cared for Miss Russell, he'd walk away now before she discovered the truth.

He stared up at the brightly lit windows behind which she danced with Mr. Cooper. If only he could erase the past so he wouldn't be forced to let the one woman he'd ever felt more than a passing interest in slip between his fingers.

CHAPTER EIGHT

"HAVE MY PARENTS gone out yet?" Charlotte asked Daisy when she came to help her with her toilette the following morning.

"Yes. Your mother's embroidery group is working on a quilt for the charity auction next week, so she'll probably be absent until some point this afternoon."

"And Papa?"

"He left right after the viscountess, but I've no idea where he's gone."

Charlotte stifled a yawn with her hand and proceeded to dress. "Probably to meet with Mr. Cooper with whom he's become annoyingly friendly. Help me with these buttons please. I'll have a quick breakfast and then we'll head out as well."

One hour later, Charlotte was back at The Black Swan, much to Daisy's disapproval. Not that Charlotte cared one whit. She needed to see Mr. MacNeil. *Blayne.* After what had transpired between them last night in the Coventry garden, it seemed silly not to use his given name.

Moving through the dining area, Charlotte let

her gaze roam. The tavern was mostly empty at this hour, save for one lone man enjoying a cup of coffee along with a plate of surprisingly tasty looking eggs and bacon. A scraping sound farther back in the taproom caught her attention. She approached until the same young man she'd met here before came into view. If memory served, and she believed it did, his name was Claus.

"Miss," Daisy hissed. "Maybe we should—"

"Excuse me," Charlotte said. She waited until Claus turned. His eyes widened with surprise and he suddenly looked like he might drop the broom he was holding. Charlotte added a smile. "I would like to speak with Mr. MacNeil please."

"He's not here, miss."

The excitement that had gotten Charlotte out of bed with haste and propelled her to call on a man she shouldn't like half as much as she did, in a tavern located in what most would call an unseemly part of Town, dimmed. "I see. And when do you think he might return?"

Claus shrugged one shoulder. "Hard to say. Although he usually likes to be here when the fighters arrive for training. With a match taking place tomorrow evening, he'll want to spend as much time with them today as possible seeing as he hasn't…um…"

"Hasn't what?" Charlotte prompted.

Claus averted his gaze. "It's nothing, miss. I'm sure he'll be back any moment. You can wait for him in his office if you like."

"Thank you. That would be much appreciated." Charlotte followed Claus while Daisy traipsed behind. She had a niggling suspicion Claus had meant to suggest Blayne hadn't been spending as much time on his work here at The Black Swan as he ought to have done since she'd swept into his life.

Charlotte frowned. She didn't like knowing she'd upended Blayne's life, but of course that was what she'd done the moment she'd turned a job that required only his occasional help into one that demanded he sacrifice evenings as well. Selfishly, she'd even asked him to accompany her on errands that didn't pose any danger to her. After all, it was highly unlikely she would be robbed between her carriage and the front door of St. Agatha's Hospital when she went there for her charity meetings. And yet, she'd asked Blayne to join her simply because she'd begun enjoying his company. Not to mention the way he made her feel – vibrant, alive, desirable.

Heaven help her, she was awful.

"I'll fetch some tea for both of you," Claus said once he'd shown her into a large room that seemed to serve as both study and library. He smiled at Daisy who instantly turned a deep shade of red.

Interesting.

Thanking him, Charlotte waited until he was gone before giving the room her full attention. There was a wide desk with a single chair on one side, upholstered in burgundy velvet. Two simi-lar chairs intended for visitors faced it. Ignoring them for now, she wandered across to one of the massive bookcases lining the walls. Not a hint of dust could be seen on any of the polished shelves. Instead, neatly arranged collections of reading material seemingly organized first by category, then by author, greeted her gaze. In between, as if to break the monotony, was a potted plant – a violet here and a jasmine there.

"It looks like Mr. MacNeil enjoys the same kind of stories as you," Daisy said.

Turning away from the fragrant white flowers she'd just discovered, Charlotte noted the book Daisy held up for her to see. Unlike the rest of the books she'd spotted so far, this one appeared to be very well used. Removing her gloves, she took it from Daisy and ran her fingers across the worn leather binding. The title which had adorned the front and spine in gold lettering was scarcely visible anymore.

The Earl's Secret Escapades.

A smile pulled at Charlotte's lips as she turned back the cover and found Blayne's name inscribed to mark his ownership. The pages, which would have been crisp when the book was new, were now slightly wavy along the edges and even creased in the occasional spot.

He hadn't lied when he'd told her this was his favorite book. Indeed, his love for it was plain to see. The man must have read it at least a hundred times – a thought that filled her heart with tremendous joy. She shook her head. How silly of her to feel such happiness just because he enjoyed her writing.

She set it aside and instinctively searched

the shelves for its sequel. Considering Blayne's appreciation for Mr. Cunningham's writing, it wouldn't surprise her if he'd already purchased a copy of her latest release. And read it ten times.

She grinned.

"Daisy, can you please help me find *The Viscount's Clandestine Meetings*?"

It had to be here somewhere...

"I havenae managed to acquire it yet," a deep voice said. Charlotte gasped with the startled jumpiness of being caught doing something she shouldn't, along with the sensual effect Blayne's rumbling brogue wrought on her nerves. Her pulse leapt while tiny embers scattered across the exposed skin at the nape of her neck.

Straightening, she turned. And promptly forgot how to speak the moment her gaze collided with his. All she could do was stare back into his smoldering eyes while butterflies fluttered around in her stomach. She'd kissed that gorgeous mouth of his last night, had discovered what the firm lower lip felt like beneath her own, hoped there would be a chance for additional exploration.

"Good morning," he murmured when she continued to moon over him like a brainless ninny. He added a nod of acknowledgement in Daisy's direction. "Claus says ye've only recently arrived. He'll be in with the tea he promised ye in a moment."

"We'll take it in the taproom," Charlotte blurted.

Daisy spun toward her. "In the taproom,

miss?"

"Yes," Charlotte confirmed with a resolute nod. "That's what I said. You should go wait for Claus there. I'll join you in just a moment."

"You'll what?" Daisy looked positively flabbergasted. As if Charlotte had just suggested running naked through the streets.

"There's something I wish to discuss with Mr. MacNeil in private," Charlotte said with a pointed look she hoped Daisy wouldn't dispute. "I'll see you as soon as I'm done."

Daisy's eyes grew impossibly large. "I can't let you be alone with him, miss. It's not proper."

"I promise not to ravish her in yer absence," Blayne said.

Charlotte attempted the most serene expression she could manage after that comment. "It's a business matter, Daisy. A rather delicate one if you don't mind."

"Very well," Daisy grumbled. "I'll wait for you in the taproom then."

Of course she deliberately left the door open.

Blayne glanced at it and raised a questioning eyebrow. "Should I..?"

"Yes," Charlotte said. "Absolutely."

He crossed the small distance, shut the door and, she noticed, turned the key in the lock before giving her his full attention. "Now then, lass. What is it ye wish to discuss?"

"I don't want to get married." Perhaps if she said it out loud she'd be able to hold on to this conviction. She couldn't allow herself to lose sight of her dreams.

"I know," he said with gentle reassurance. "Neither do I."

Her breath caught. She'd not expected him to say that. The words dealt an unexpected stab to her heart. Which made no sense at all. She shouldn't care. After all, she'd just told him she didn't want a future with him either. But to know he felt the same, hurt. More than she ever would have expected.

Determined to stay her course, she told him, "I've built an entire web of lies in order to avoid having to do so."

"Yet another reason why I shouldnae have kissed ye."

"Another?"

He chuckled lightly, easing the tension between them a little. "There's also the fact that it's frowned upon for an employee to take liberties with his employer."

Swallowing, Charlotte took a step forward. "What if the employer didn't mind?" She watched his chest rise and fall with heavier movements. His eyes darkened a fraction. She stepped closer still. "What if she actually liked it?"

"Lass…" His voice was gruff, his expression uncertain, but he did not back away.

Reaching him, she flattened her palm against the spot right over his heart. "What if she's hoping he'll do it again?"

"This isnae a good idea."

The firmness with which he spoke made her second guess herself for a moment. She wasn't this woman – this brazen temptress skilled in the art of seduction. That role was better suited to a character in a Charles Cunningham novel.

"You're right."

What on earth was she thinking? That she could become someone else for a few weeks and have an adventure with a brawny Scotsman? Live a little before she got too old to bother trying?

Yes, that was precisely what she'd subconsciously hoped for. Which made her an idiot – the sort who ought to retrieve her maid and return to the respectable life she was used to before it was too late.

"I'm sorry, Mr. MacNeil." It seemed like the most appropriate thing to say. "Would you like to end our arrangement?"

"Not on yer life," he growled as he swept one arm around her and pulled her against him.

His mouth met hers and she forgot how to think.

All she could do now was feel: his hardness and his strength. Just him. He was every bit as intoxicating as he'd been last night. Lord, how she'd dreaded getting chastised by Mr. Cooper, of having to explain herself to him and possibly to her parents as well. But when he'd failed to address what he'd seen, it had almost started to feel like the kiss had never happened.

Until now.

Charlotte raked her fingers through Blayne's hair and clasped him to her. His teeth nipped her flesh and she instinctively parted her lips, inviting him in. Lord, he tasted good and the feel of him, so intimately caressing her in a way no one else ever had, flooded her body with liquid heat.

Clutching his thick upper arm for support, she kissed him back with equal fervor. Desperation for more tore through her. A dull thud sounded as her back connected with one of the bookcases. Blayne pushed her against it, his large hands gripping her hips as he pressed up against her with greater insistence.

Heavens, this was indecent and wicked and oh so good.

Sharing such closeness with him felt incredible, like a culmination of everything she'd ever wanted without even being aware. "Blayne..."

"Aye. I'm here, lass." He kissed his way across her cheek while allowing one hand free reign to explore. It stroked over every curve, increasing her need and her pleasure.

His teeth scraped the side of her neck as he pressed himself to her, and as his kiss deepened, she felt more alive than ever before. He was staking a claim, linking them with a shared experience she would never forget. His hands gripped her more roughly. Urgent and fierce, he kissed her with a primal sort of possessiveness, and rather than fill her with dread or the need to add distance, it filled a place in her heart she'd not even known was empty.

Before she was ready, he tore his mouth away and gazed down at her with stormy eyes. "This is madness."

"I know." Her breaths were as ragged as his.

"Christ, Charlotte." He kissed her again, more gently this time.

She kissed him right back.

This is where I want to be.

I wish I could stay here forever.

With a sigh of contentment she leaned against him, embracing his much larger body as best as she could. He stiffened for a second before relaxing once more.

His lips grazed her temple. "Ye're like a dessert I cannae get enough of."

"So are you," she murmured, breathing in that now-so-familiar scent of bergamot, coffee, and something uniquely him. "Thank you for showing me what I've been missing."

His chest rumbled slightly beneath her ear while his hand stroked her back. "There's no need for that, lass. Indeed, it was my pleasure. And an honor."

She smiled against the wool of his jacket. Heavens, this man would be easy to love.

Closing her eyes on that thought, she allowed herself another deep breath before pulling away. "We ought to find Daisy before she gets worried."

"Go ahead." He unlocked the door and stepped aside. "I'll join ye in a moment."

"But…" She searched his face. The strain in his features concerned her. "Are you all right?"

"I just need to make myself a wee bit more presentable."

Charlotte held his gaze. "You look perfectly fine to—"

"Charlotte." His voice was firm and slightly hoarse. "Ye need to go now. I'll see ye in a minute."

Deciding it might be best not to press him further, Charlotte made her way back to the taproom where she expected to find her maid sitting quietly at a table, drinking her tea. Instead, to Charlotte's shock and dismay, she arrived just in time to see Daisy raise her arm and hurl something through the air while Claus cheered her on. Even more astounding, the generally quiet maid squealed with delight and shouted, "I did it," before she flung her arms around Claus's neck and allowed him to swing her about.

"Daisy?" How could this be the same prim woman who always reminded her of propriety and decorum?

Daisy stumbled slightly in Claus's arms before finding her balance. Straightening, she stared back at Charlotte. "Sorry, miss." She cleared her throat. "The tea's ready. Would you like some? It's really good and there are some tasty shortbread biscuits to go with it."

"What were you doing?" Charlotte asked, her gaze shifting from Daisy to Claus and back again as she approached.

"Um..."

When Charlotte raised an eyebrow, Claus stepped forward. "I was teaching Daisy how to throw knives."

The very idea was so outrageous Charlotte was forced to press her lips together to keep from laughing. Until a thought struck her. "Can

I have a go?"

"Of course." Clause went to retrieve the knife Daisy had thrown.

"I probably ought to dissuade you," Daisy said with a smile so bright it lit her face. "But it's great fun. You'll see. But I warn you, it's not as easy as it looks."

"All right." Charlotte accepted the knife Claus handed her and paid close attention while he showed her how to hold it and the exact angle at which to throw it. Standing behind a white chalk line ten feet from a post marked by hundreds of other attempts, Charlotte gave it her best.

The blade flew through the air, struck the post with a muted *clack* before tumbling onto the floor. Well, that was disappointing. As an expert shot she'd rather thought this skill would come naturally to her. "I'd like to try again."

"It took me at least thirty turns before I got it right," Daisy told her encouragingly when Charlotte still failed to make the blade stick.

"Don't pacify me," Charlotte told her, trying to focus on holding the knife by its handle just so with her palm flat against the blade and...

It bounced off the post and landed on top of a table.

"Here," Blayne's deep voice spoke near her left shoulder. "Allow me to show ye how it's done."

He took the knife from Claus and waited for him to get out of the way before placing the knife in Charlotte's hand. "The first thing ye need to do is change yer stance and learn how to move. Now then…" He patted her left hip as if doing so was perfectly normal. "Angle yerself so the target's slightly to yer side. Lean back on yer right leg as if ye're mid-stride, just a wee bit more. Aye, like that. That's perfect. Now raise the knife in yer hand." He curled her fingers around the lower part of the handle, positioning her index finger along the top of the blade. "Make sure it's horizontal with yer target throughout the throw, take a big step forward with yer right foot, and throw the knife as hard as ye can. Like this."

Releasing her, he stepped to the side and gave her a quick demonstration of what he meant. "It's important to follow through and to make yer movement as fluid as possible. Ready?"

She gave him a nod and positioned herself as he had instructed. After testing the movement a couple of times, she released the knife with a forceful throw and watched it splice the air with arrow sharp precision before sinking into the wood.

A laugh bubbled up inside her. Daisy clapped and Claus whooped while Blayne pulled her into his arms and kissed her. Right there for all the world to see. And Charlotte didn't mind it one bit.

"Well done, lass." Blayne grinned at her with something that looked a lot like pride mixed with some sort of feeling she couldn't quite place. Before she had a chance to discern it, he withdrew and went to collect the knife. "I knew ye had it in ye. Now practice a few more times and then we'll have a wee competition."

Charlotte's throws improved with each attempt she made, but the blade didn't always stick the way it seemed to do for Claus and Blayne. In the end, the two men were declared the victors while Charlotte came second just one point ahead of Daisy.

"I think I'm going to set up a throwing range in the garden as soon as we get home," Charlotte told Daisy while they enjoyed the tea and shortbread biscuits they'd forgotten to have earlier. "We'll work on honing our skills at this sport together."

"That'd be fun, miss."

Charlotte sipped her tea while following Blayne with her eyes. He'd been called to the front of the tavern a few minutes earlier in order to handle a fresh delivery of wine. Claus had gone with him and along with a few other Black Swan employees, they unloaded crates from a cart and carried them to the store room.

"We'll beat them next time. Won't we, Daisy?"

"Next time?"

Charlotte gave her maid a broad smile and jutted her chin in Claus's direction. "There must be a next time. Don't you think?"

Daisy's cheeks began turning pink. "I'd like that, miss."

"Even though it's not very proper and we really shouldn't be here," Charlotte teased.

"I'm a terrible chaperone, miss. Your father would have my head if he knew what I let you get up to."

"In that case, we'll have to make sure he never finds out. Won't we?"

If Daisy gave an answer, Charlotte failed to hear it with Blayne now making his way back over, his eyes fixed directly upon her.

"How's the tea?" he asked once he'd reached the corner in which they sat.

"Excellent."

He gave her a slow smile – the sort that turned her bones to jelly. "Good."

"I'll just, um…" Daisy slid out of her seat and wandered toward the front where Claus was quick to intercept her. Charlotte was glad. Daisy was young and deserved to experience a bit of romance, which wasn't something servants had much time for.

Blayne dropped into the vacant chair behind her and scooted closer. His hand came around her shoulders and then his mouth was suddenly on her neck, just as brazenly as when he'd kissed her earlier in front of Claus and Daisy. Sparks ignited in Charlotte's belly, fanning outward until desire sprang to life once more.

"You shouldn't," she gasped even as she leaned a bit closer and angled herself to give him more access.

"I know, but I cannae seem to stop myself. Ye're temptation incarnate, Charlotte, and…" He pressed a deep kiss to the spot where her neck met her shoulder and slowly leaned back. "That Charles Cunningham novel ye mentioned earlier – the sequel to *The Earl's Secret Escapades*. I was thinking we could go and buy it together.

As long as ye dinnae have to rush home yet."

"What about the fighters? Claus said you'd want to—"

"It's nothing that cannae wait, lass."

"Blayne. I…" She wasn't sure what to say. Especially not with him looking at her with such hope in his eyes. "Haven't I taken enough of your time already? You're busy and I've made too many demands of you as it is."

"This wouldnae be a demand, lass."

No. It would be yet another chance for them to bond – to form a closer attachment by sharing a common interest. Much like the knife throwing, it would be an experience uniquely theirs, so different from the standard walks and social functions that generally served as backdrops for *ton* courtships.

Charlotte straightened and turned to face him. "I've told you I don't want marriage."

The words didn't sound nearly as convincing as they once had.

He gave her a queer look. "I know. Several times. Most recently before ye seduced the hell out of me in my office."

She couldn't help but grin in response to his teasing tone even as her skin began burning. "*I* seduced *you*? I rather think it was the other way around."

"Hmm…" His eyes darkened while his hand found her thigh underneath the table.

Charlotte sucked in a breath when he gently squeezed her. "What are you doing?"

"Putting ye slightly off balance while savoring

yer responsiveness." He chuckled and withdrew his hand. "It's just a trip to the shops. Nothing more."

"All right," she said, even though she feared she was making the wrong decision. Not because she didn't want to spend time with Blayne, but because of how much she wanted to stay in his company. Somehow, he'd started mattering to her. And she was beginning to worry that walking away from him wouldn't be nearly as easy as she would need it to be.

CHAPTER NINE

H E SHOULDN'T HAVE kissed her last night
at the ball and he definitely shouldn't have
kissed her today in his office. Blayne acknowledged this fact while escorting Charlotte along
Borough High Street a little over half an hour
later. They'd taken a hackney to the south side
of the Thames where his favorite bookshop was
located, and had chosen to get out and walk
when the traffic had slowed to a crawl. From the
looks of it, a top-heavy cart transporting barrels
had toppled over and was now blocking part of
the street. Silver herring-like fish poured out of
several damaged barrels, creating a slippery mess
for any carriage wanting to pass.

Blayne drew Charlotte against his side, not
caring one whit about whether or not it was
proper to do so. Somehow, between that first
day when she'd shown up at The Black Swan
and now, he'd developed a constant craving for
her. It wasn't just sexual. For although he wanted
nothing more than to strip her naked and swive
her until she forgot her own name, there was
something more – a need to simply be near her.

He wanted to learn her expressions, savor her smiles and each of her laughs. He liked knowing he was allowed to touch her. Just the gentle press of his hand to her back or the brush of his fingers against her hand was enough to make him feel closer to her than he'd ever felt to anyone before.

And then…

And then there was the passion. Hell, she muddled his brain and lit him on fire in ways he'd not have thought possible until now. Whether she realized it yet or not, the kisses they'd shared so far were forging a bond that could not be broken or forgotten. It had also made him realize that by forcing a deeper connection between them he risked complicating both of their lives. For as she'd said, she didn't want marriage. And while he'd not been completely honest about his own thoughts on the matter, he knew he could never have her in that way. Which pretty much meant there was no point in allowing such dreams. Instead, he'd focus on what was possible – an oasis in time for them both to look back on later with fondness. As fleeting as it would be, he'd best make every second count. Because he knew she'd be gone from his life again before he was ready.

With this in mind, he led her into Lee & Jones and held the door wide until Daisy had entered as well. The owners of the small shop had chosen to fill it not only with books but with odd bits of furniture too. The effect was charming. It almost felt like one was sitting in a cozy parlor owned by some sort of eccentric artist.

"What do ye think?" Blayne asked with more eagerness than he'd intended.

Charlotte beamed and his heart swelled in gratitude. "It's absolutely lovely. If only I'd discovered it sooner."

"Ye're here now." With him. Squirrelled away in a small private corner of London. "Come. Let's see if they've got the novel we're after."

Taking her by the arm, he steered her toward the bookcases where the literary fiction was kept in alphabetical order. Before they reached them however, a man Blayne instantly recognized as one of the owners came to greet them.

"It's a pleasure to see you again, sir," the man said. "And you've brought a friend along with you this time."

"Miss Russell," Blayne said. "Allow me to introduce ye to Mr. Lee. He and his partner took the run-down building this used to be and turned it into the marvelous retreat it is today."

"I'm impressed," Charlotte said. "And it's a pleasure to meet you, Mr. Lee."

"Indeed. The pleasure is all mine," Mr. Lee assured her. "Is there something I can help you find?"

"We're actually looking for the latest Charles Cunningham novel," Blayne told him. "The one with the viscount."

"It's *The Viscount's Clandestine Meetings*," Charlotte supplied.

"Oh yes. Popular story, that one. It's right over here." Turning away, Mr. Lee led them over to a display table where a pyramid of books had been arranged. "This is where we put the latest arrivals. As you can see, Cunningham has another addition. *The Marquess's Unsolved Mysteries* came in yesterday and has almost sold out completely since then. We've only one copy left."

"How marvelous for us. We thought we'd be snatching up one new release and instead there are two." Blayne gave his attention back to Charlotte, only to have the joy knocked out of him when he noticed her pallor. Concerned, he dipped his head and whispered near her ear. "What's the matter?"

"I... I don't understand." She sounded more than a little confused. Clearly something had upset her greatly.

"I'll be over there by the counter in case you need me," Mr. Lee said. He'd apparently picked up on the increased tension and the need to offer some privacy.

"Thank ye." Blayne waited until he'd moved away before turning back to Charlotte. "What don't ye understand?"

"It's not possible." She stared down at the book she held between her hands – *The Marquess's Unsolved Mysteries* – and slowly shook her head. "It just can't be."

"Would ye like to sit down for a wee bit, lass? Ye're not looking so well." Indeed, she seemed to be on the verge of tears. Troubled by her sudden shift in mood, Blayne eased her away from the table and toward a comfortable looking armchair. "I'll just fetch Daisy for ye. It willnae take a moment."

Hurrying over to where the books on sewing, knitting, and needlepoint were kept, he located the maid. "There's something wrong with Charlotte. I think she needs yer help."

Without hesitation Daisy handed him the book she'd been leafing through and rushed to Charlotte's side. Blayne watched from a distance while she attempted to ease her mistress's troubles. It bothered him that he couldn't discern the cause behind Charlotte's sudden distress. It also vexed him that she wouldn't explain it.

"She'd like to go home," Daisy came to inform him a few seconds later. "Immediately."

"What happened?" When Daisy made to turn away without providing an answer, he stayed her with his hand. "Tell me."

"I can't," Daisy said with a pained look in her eyes. "I'm sorry."

Not good enough.

He cared too much about Charlotte and her well-being to let her or her maid brush him off when she clearly required assistance. Hell, she'd hired him to protect her. And now... Well, now there were all sorts of confusing feelings whirling around inside him. They'd kissed, damn it. Twice. That had to mean he was more to her than a passing fancy.

Without second guessing himself even once, he stormed past Daisy and sank into a crouching position in front of Charlotte. "Ye ken ye can trust me."

Her gaze seemed to focus on his. She blinked, and finally nodded.

Good.

He reached for her hand and gently held it. "Tell me what this is about."

Instead of confiding as he had hoped, she gave her head a small shake and closed her eyes.

"Please," he begged. "Whatever it is, let me help ye sort it out."

She bit her lip and indecision filled her eyes. She wanted to confide in him but something was holding her back.

He squeezed her hand and spoke the only words that mattered. "Ye must realize by now that ye're more to me than a mere employer." The truth might end things between them sooner than he would have liked. But if it didn't – if she stayed with him and faced what they were becoming instead of running away – it might give her the courage to open up and be completely honest. "I want ye to forget the agreement we made and the money ye offered to pay me."

"But—"

"No, just listen. This is no longer a job to me, lass. It's a hell of a lot more. And right now, seeing ye like this is killing me inside. Do ye understand what I'm saying?"

"I think so."

"Right." He held her gaze a while longer, then carefully retrieved the Cunningham book from between her fingers. No sense in pressing her further. "I'll purchase this along with the other two books, then we'll find a hackney so ye can go home."

"I'd like to stop by Temple Gardens first," Charlotte said when Blayne gave the driver instructions a short while later. The small park was on their way but more importantly, it was never very crowded. "It's a warm day. Perfect for a walk if you're able to spare the time."

"Of course I can," he said as he handed her up.

Swallowing, Charlotte lowered herself to the forward facing bench. Daisy climbed in immediately after and sat down beside her while Blayne chose the opposite seat. His steady gaze never left Charlotte's. It stayed on her for the duration of the ride, reminding her of his friendship and support, as well as the *so much more* that still filled her heart to overflowing.

He mattered to her as well, but she wasn't sure she was ready to face the extent of her feelings for him just yet. Besides, there were other things for them to discuss. Something of greater importance right now than the recent shift in their relationship.

The carriage slowed and came to a halt. Charlotte waited until Blayne had stepped down before she turned to Daisy. "I wish to speak with him alone. Can you wait for us here, please?"

"Are you sure this is wise, miss?"

"No. Not in the least."

Daisy smiled at her with quiet understanding. "He's a good man. I know it's not my place to say this, miss, but maybe you should reconsider what you want."

"You think I should try for a future with him?"

"All I know is that he makes you happy."

But would that be enough for her to alter her course? For years, she'd wanted to realize her dream of owning a writer's retreat and of living a life devoid of a husband's command. Independence was her goal. Could she truly consider giving that up for a man she'd known only one month? A man who'd told her that very morning he didn't want marriage either?

She wasn't the least bit sure, but the conversation she was about to have with him would hopefully offer some guidance. So without saying anything further, she accepted his hand and climbed down onto the pavement. He offered his arm and she took it. The park was almost deserted save for a small group of people strolling along at the opposite side. Charlotte tried to gather her thoughts. She wasn't sure how to tell Blayne what he wanted to know and her jittery nerves weren't helping.

"What's yer greatest concern?" he asked when they'd walked for a while in silence.

"That you won't approve of what I'm about to tell you."

"I'm flattered, lass."

Surprised, she glanced at him and caught him giving her a playful smile. "You are?"

He drew her closer to his side and stopped as if to point out some flowers. Instead, he leaned in and spoke in a low drawl. "It must mean ye care for my opinion – perhaps a wee bit for me as well." He chuckled low. "A man can only hope."

His voice alone was enough to melt her bones. Add to that his masculine scent and the feel of his breath breezing over her skin with each word he spoke, and it became a struggle to form coherent thoughts. Her heart raced.

"Of course I care for you," she whispered. "I could never kiss you as I've done and not feel anything."

He was silent a moment before he said, "Ye mustnae trouble yerself, lass. There's nothing ye can tell me that would make me think any less of ye. Not when ye've been able to accept the things I've done without shying away."

She resumed walking and he fell into step beside her. "I don't write observational train of thought musings."

"I ken." When she met his gaze with surprise he said, "Figured that out almost right away. Ye're much too interesting not to write something more creative in nature."

"Oh." She blushed in response to the compliment "Thank you."

"And then of course, Miss Carlisle did mention yer missing manuscript when we went to check on the theft. So if I were to guess, I'd say ye're a novelist."

Charlotte's stomach started spinning like an out of control top. "Your deductive skills are admirable."

He grinned. "I've had enough time to observe ye and draw conclusions based on various things ye've said as well as reactions ye've had. I also have an inkling of who ye might be based on what happened in that bookshop today, but I cannae be completely sure until ye tell me."

"Not even Daisy knows. She's aware I've written a couple of novels, but I've never told her what they're about or that I'm published under a different name. I'm sure she believes I'm quite unsuccessful."

"But ye're not. Are ye, lass?"

"No." She dipped her head, avoiding the intensity of his gaze while taking courage. "I'm not just Charlotte Russell. I'm also Charles Cunningham, author of *The Earl's Secret Escapades* and—."

His arm swept around her, pulling her into a fierce embrace. She gasped, and then his mouth captured hers in the sort of kiss that would make a courtesan blush. It was deep and rough, executed with a plundering possessiveness that made her wish, if only for a brief moment, that they could have a future together.

But to wish for that would be as unrealistic as the stories she wrote. They came from two different worlds and even if that weren't enough, he'd told her he didn't want marriage. And neither did she. Or so she kept telling herself. But the truth was it was getting increasingly easy for her to envision Blayne in a far more permanent role than the one he currently held. Pure stupidity on her part. They had a working relationship as employer and employee, which now involved an intimate sort of friendship.

Eventually it would end. It would have to. And she would walk away knowing what it was like to feel desired. There would be no regrets, only wonderful memories to look back on.

A bird chirped, reminding Charlotte of where they were. She pulled away and pressed her hand to her mouth. "Heavens. What if someone saw us?"

They were in a public park and that kiss... Good lord, it hadn't merely been scandalous it had been ruinous. She glanced around, frantically searching for possible witnesses.

Blayne brushed his thumb along the side of her jaw. "The other people who were here left a few moments ago while ye were talking. There's no one here besides us."

She blew out a shuddering breath and forced herself to meet his dark gaze. "I hope you don't misunderstand the reason for my concern. I'd never be embarrassed to be seen with you like that, it's just that we're not really engaged, and even if we were that display would have given fodder to serious gossip. I've still my reputation to consider and—"

"Charlotte." His voice was both firm and calming. "Ye're the most remarkable woman I know. Brave, bold, and beautiful. The books ye've written are impressive – the best I've ever read. Ye ought to be proud of them, not ashamed."

"And so I am," she told him as they continued along the path that skirted the edge of the park. "But you have to agree that they contain several outrageously inappropriate scenes."

"How many books have ye sold?" he asked, seemingly ignoring her comment.

"Somewhere in the vicinity of four thousand

copies."

He produced a low whistle. "Seems to me there are people who like those outrageously inappropriate scenes."

"My parents would be horrified if they learned what I've written, not to mention that I'd be ruined if word got out. People will think I'm a wanton."

"Hence the pseudonym branding ye a man." When she gave a swift nod, he said, "In my opinion, those scenes ye're referring to add an extra layer of excitement to the plot while making it more realistic. After all, yer hero's a rakehell spy. It makes sense that he'll bestow a few passionate kisses here and there throughout the story."

"Naturally, that was my reasoning behind it, but the depiction of said kisses is slightly more descriptive than what can be found in other novels."

"Certainly. But it's not nearly as provocative as in say...*Fanny Hill*."

"I should think not," Charlotte choked. "That book has a great deal more than passionate kissing in it."

"Ah. So ye've read it." He gave her a teasing nudge.

Her cheeks flamed. "Considering my age and the path I'm currently on, I do think I've earned the right to read whatever I want."

"Touché." They continued on in silence for a while before he said, "So if ye're Charles Cunningham, I gather the reason ye got so upset when ye saw *The Marquess's Unsolved Mysteries* was because ye didn't expect to find it in a book-shop?"

"Whoever stole my manuscript published it without my knowledge," she told him bitterly. "They're making money off my work and name."

"Aye. We're dealing with a really dishonorable scoundrel, but we should be able to track him down now without too much trouble. The name of the publisher will be listed inside the book. We'll pay them a visit, tell them what's happened, and ask them to put us in touch with whoever delivered the manuscript to them."

Charlotte blinked. "Of course." She'd been so distraught she'd not thought of the fact that in publishing the book, the thief would have left a trail for them to follow. The despair that had gripped her when she'd seen *The Marquess's Unsolved Mysteries* for sale dissipated. "We've a real chance of catching the culprit now."

"Indeed we do. Meet me at our usual spot at nine o'clock tomorrow and we'll head over to the publisher together."

They were almost back at the carriage. Charlotte slowed her steps, forcing him to do the same. "Thank you for helping me. It means a great deal."

The words encompassed more than she could express. Having his support, knowing he was there for her to lean on, sharing her most guarded secret with him and realizing he wouldn't walk away over it, added a level of unity she'd never had with anyone else. Blayne knew her. He accepted her for who she was and even praised her for her achievements. No one had ever made her feel more appreciated. She almost believed she could take on any challenge as long as she had him by her side.

And perhaps she could.

What the bloody hell did he think he was doing?

Blayne glared at the plants still refusing to grow. But his mind wasn't on them. It was on the petite raven-haired beauty who'd gradually slipped beneath his skin and found a place for herself in his heart.

Damn.

He raked his fingers through his hair.

She was Charles Cunningham, the author who'd written his favorite book, and while he'd begun suspecting as much, hearing her say it – having her place her unfailing trust in him – made him feel like he'd just won a thousand pounds. Discomfort gnawed its way through him until he acknowledged the guilt. It had been steadily growing since her confession.

He'd pushed her to tell him her secret, but could he ever share his?

Chest rising heavily, he expelled a deep breath, set the watering can aside, and went to pour himself a glass of brandy. He took a long gulp and savored the burn as the liquid slid down his throat. Charlotte wasn't the only one with two identities. But there was a hell of a difference between a woman secretly writing successful novels under a man's name, and a callous murderer posing as a tavern keep.

He was dangerous. More so than Charlotte realized, in spite of her knowing about his history with Guthrie. There was a time before St. Giles, a time Blayne had been trying to flee for almost two decades.

Those terrified eyes he'd struggled so hard to forget filled his mind with unforgiving insistence. *Look here*, they seemed to say. *Remember what you've done.* He could still recall in painful detail the feel of the candelabra connecting with bone, could still hear the choking gasps his mother made while his father collapsed to the floor.

He downed the rest of his drink.

In truth, he had no right to Charlotte Russell. And yet, the very idea of walking away from her caused his heart to ache. God, she was incredible. He'd regretted having to take her home because he'd wanted to spend more time in her company. If it were up to him, he'd never leave her side again.

He closed his eyes and shook his head.

Wake up, you fool.

As much as he wanted to change her mind about marriage and build a life with her, she didn't deserve to marry a man who would always be less than what she believed him to be. Because he would never be brave enough to tell her the truth. And what sort of life would they have then?

If he married, he'd want his wife to know

him, but baring his soul to Charlotte and seeing the look of disgust in her eyes when she realized he was a monster would be intolerable. The very idea made him nauseous. Within the short time they'd known each other, her opinion of him had become important. He couldn't stand the thought of her seeing his true self – a man who ought to hang for the crime he'd committed. Instead, he remained in hiding, too fearful of facing the punishment he deserved.

He scoffed. The world might look at Blayne MacNeil and think him strong because of how he appeared on the outside. The reality, however, was that he lacked the courage to tell Charlotte the truth.

Doing so would be pointless anyway. It made no sense to ruin the limited time they had left together by dredging up the past. She'd no reason to know since he had no intention of marrying her. And by God, he needed to keep every memory of her pure and untarnished – a haven for him to revisit whenever the darkness crept in and threatened his soul. In those moments, he'd hold on to her, to the kisses they'd shared and the smiles that lit up her face each time she saw him.

In Charlotte's eyes he was good – the best possible version of himself – a man he actually liked for a change. He couldn't risk losing that for any reason. Not even for the sake of being honorable.

CHAPTER TEN

WHEN CHARLOTTE RETURNED home after her outing with Blayne, she learned that Mr. Cooper was waiting for her in the parlor along with her parents. Charlotte thanked the butler for letting her know, exchanged an apprehensive look with Daisy who took Charlotte's bonnet and gloves, and went to discover why Mr. Cooper had come to call. Until now, he'd only joined her for afternoon tea, but it was too early for that – luncheon time in fact – which was an odd hour to stop by unless he'd been invited. And why were her parents here when they'd both had plans to be gone for most of the day?

Steeling herself, she entered the room. Her father was speaking with Mr. Cooper, his tone firm and his face more grave than usual. She instinctively froze as a chill swept the length of her spine. Something wasn't right.

"Ah. There you are," Mama said when she noticed her arrival. Papa and Mr. Cooper halted their discussion and stood. As soon as she found a seat, they reclaimed theirs. "We've been waiting for you for almost one hour. Where have you been?"

"Not with Mr. Wright, I hope," Papa said, his gaze narrowed at her in studious assessment.

"I, um…" Charlotte cleared her throat. Her heart beat faster. "I visited a bookshop. With Daisy. On our way home we stopped by the park for a walk."

"So you've not seen Mr. Wright today?" Papa asked.

Unsure why Papa suddenly seemed so opposed to Blayne whom he'd actually said he liked last night after the ball, Charlotte shook her head. "No. Why do you ask?"

"Because it has come to my attention that he's not the gentleman he has been claiming to be." Papa leaned forward. "As it turns out, he's not even called Mr. Wright. His real name is Mr. MacNeil, which makes him a dangerous criminal."

Charlotte swallowed. Oh dear. She glanced at her mother whose eyes were filled with concern before dropping her gaze to the table and wishing there were something for her to imbibe besides tea. Since there wasn't, she began preparing a cup if for no other reason than to busy herself with something.

"Did you know?" Papa's voice was like a whip against her guilty conscience.

"Surely you must be mistaken," Charlotte said, attempting to sidestep the question so she could avoid yet another lie. "No criminal could ever be as cultivated as Mr. Wright. Clearly he comes from a very good family."

"And do you perchance have any idea which family that might be?" Papa asked.

"A Scottish one, I suspect," Charlotte quipped.

"Charlotte," Mama implored while Papa appeared to seethe with controlled fury. "This is not the right time to jest. Mr. Cooper had the foresight to do what we should have done from the start when *Mr. MacNeil*, a man we knew nothing about, informed us of his intention to marry our daughter."

"*I* informed you of his intention to do so, Mama."

"Regardless," Mama continued as if Charlotte's factual reminder was of no significance whatsoever, "the point remains the same. Mr. MacNeil fooled us all with a clever scheme, one we might never have discovered had it not been for Mr. Cooper's efforts to have him investigated."

"What?" Charlotte's head spun around to face the man who'd decided to meddle in her affairs. "When?"

"Last night," he said, not looking the least bit apologetic. "I paid one of the Coventry servants to follow him home from the ball. Turns out, he lives in a slum and goes by a different name. More than that, he has ties to an outlaw known as Carlton Guthrie."

"Carlton Guthrie is now the Duke of Windham," Charlotte said. "His real name is Valentine Sterling and just so you know, he was cleared of any wrongdoing last year."

She'd been wary of Mr. Cooper's reaction, or

lack thereof, when he'd found her in the garden with Blayne last night at the ball. It hadn't made sense until now. As it turned out, the American businessman had elected not to force Charlotte into marriage with Blayne. By pretending indifference, he'd avoided a scandal while quietly gathering information against his opponent.

Apparently she'd underestimated Mr. Cooper. He was far more devious and scheming than he'd let on.

"Be that as it may, Windham is not the man we're discussing," Papa said. "Now, what I want to know is whether or not you were aware of Mr. MacNeil's true identity."

"He's a good man," Charlotte insisted. She'd not sit here and deny what she knew to be true. "The best I've ever met."

"I take that as a yes then." Papa's eyes were harder than flint. "And yet you brought him into our home. You allowed us to think he was worthy of keeping our company and, might I add, of marrying you!"

"He *is* worthy," Charlotte snapped. "Mr. MacNeil is kind and thoughtful. I feel safe when I'm with him and...I'm sure he's more than what he appears, even to me." A thought struck her. "Who did Lady Warwick say he reminded her of, Mama?"

Mama exchanged a cautious glance with her husband before saying, "Mr. Bruce Callanach."

"I've never heard of him," Charlotte said.

Mama pushed out a breath. "He used to be one of the richest men this side of The Channel."

"Used to be?"

"He died years ago. Not that it matters. Having met Callanach, I'd say the only thing Mr. MacNeil has in common with him, besides the height, is the fact that they're both Scottish."

"I see." Charlotte's hope of Mr. MacNeil somehow belonging to an upper-crust family dwindled. Not that it mattered. He could be the son of a murderer for all she cared, and she'd still stand by him. But it would have been nice to wield a connection to wealth and respectability as an additional weapon against this new assault on him. "Well. It doesn't change how I feel. Mr. MacNeil is the man I intend to marry and—"

"The hell you will," Papa snapped.

"Lord Elkins," Mama admonished.

"Forgive me," Papa said. He shot to his feet and crossed to the sideboard where he proceeded to pour a drink. "I'm afraid this matter has riled me more than what is deemed proper. My apologies, ladies. Mr. Cooper. Would anyone else like a brandy?"

When everyone declined, he returned to his chair with his own. Once seated, he took a long swallow before pinning Charlotte with a hard glare. "There will be no more talk of Mr. Mac-Neil. Is that clear? From this moment on it will be as though he never existed. It goes without saying that you're not to see him again."

"And if I refuse?" Charlotte asked while anger slid through her veins with increasing speed.

"Clearly we have been too lenient with

you, too distracted by your sisters' courtships, engagements and weddings these past few years to pay you much heed." Papa's voice was tight, his eyes blazing. "You seemed content to wait for the right man to come along. You weren't in the same kind of rush to wed as they were."

"I'm still not," Charlotte said. She couldn't allow this to go any further. Which meant it was time to be honest. "The fact is I don't actually want marriage. My dream is to write. That's what I'm passionate about."

"What a childish idea," Mama said with a shake of her head.

Charlotte fought the urge to rail at her. Instead she said, "I'm sure there are other women who feel the same, who do not wish to lose their independence to a husband. My plan is to purchase a cottage where we can live together."

"As spinsters." Her mother practically spat the word as if it tasted sour.

"And how exactly do you intend to fund this fairytale endeavor of yours?" her father asked.

She couldn't reveal that, so she simply said, "I have some savings."

Her father snorted in the sort of disbelieving manner that told her he didn't think she had an ounce of sense or any idea of how much a cottage would cost. As if to underline this sentiment, he gave his full attention to Mr. Cooper and said, "I must apologize to you for the manner in which I described my daughter, which now appears to have been highly exaggerated. Naturally, if you still wish to marry her, you have my full blessing."

"Besides that," Charlotte said, pressing on while her dreams crashed down around her, "I was hoping you would permit me to use my dowry."

Silence.

Papa and Mama shared a wary glance, the sort that gave Charlotte cause for concern. "Papa?"

Her father cleared his throat. "You have no dowry, Charlotte. I'm sorry."

"What?" Charlotte stared at him with growing unease. "What do you mean? Edwina and Melanie had vast sums settled on them so I don't understand why I wouldn't."

Papa took a deep breath, which he followed with a long swallow of brandy. "If you must know, I had some bad luck a few years ago when two of the companies I had invested in went bankrupt. Your dowry was used to buy shares in Mr. Cooper's business and for general expenses. Like the roof you have over your head."

Charlotte stared at him in outraged horror. Her dowry was gone. Spent. She glanced at Mr. Cooper, then back at her father. "So then?"

To his credit, her father did not pretend not to know what she asked. "You are a viscount's daughter, Charlotte, which makes you a prestigious match for a non-aristocrat. As the son of a simple tradesman, Mr. Cooper wishes to wed you in order to improve his social standing. In exchange, he will increase the returns on my investment by a multiple of ten."

The words sank in with explosive force. "So

what you are saying is that you have sold me?"

"Don't be crass," Papa blustered. "I'd never stoop so low."

And yet it seemed he had. "Papa. I—"

"Not another word, Charlotte." Her father stood and offered his hand to his wife. "Come now, my dear. I believe we should make ourselves scarce so these two can talk."

Gripping both armrests while clamping her jaw shut so tightly her teeth hurt, Charlotte watched with simmering fury while her parents exited the room. The door closed behind them with a click, leaving her completely alone with Mr. Cooper and without any doubt about what her parents meant to accomplish.

"I'm sorry," Mr. Cooper said after a brief moment had elapsed.

"No you're not." She forced her gaze to meet his with every piece of resentment she harbored. His answering smile incensed her all the more. "Judging by that look on your face, you're immensely pleased with how everything worked out."

"What can I say? I like winning. In fact, one might say I've made a sport of it."

"It's hardly a win when you don't play fair." She glared at him. "Are you always this underhanded?"

"Taking advantage of good opportunities isn't underhanded. It's smart."

"Even when you create those opportunities yourself?"

He sighed. "I didn't create anything, Miss

Russell. *You* did. It simply took me a while to figure it out. Now, I didn't expect it to be anywhere near as perfect as it is. Imagine my delight, though, when I discovered who Mr. MacNeil really is. I must confess I'm impressed with how well he cleans up and his general knowledge of all things." He gave a slight shrug. "Of course, that just proves he owns decent clothes – stolen, no doubt – and that he can read."

"You're horrid."

"I'm honest." When she sniffed in disagreement he said, "At least I'm not pretending to be someone I'm not. And if I am to be totally frank, I do feel some guilt over bringing the truth to light since I rather liked Mr. MacNeil. But considering your own appreciation for the man, I had no choice but to try and remove him from the running."

"You're mad if you think I'll consider marrying you instead."

"I prefer to think of myself as dedicated to my goals," he told her calmly, "I take great care in selecting what I want, whether it be a piece of land, my competitor's French chef, a mansion that's not for sale…or in this case, you. And once I do, I go after it until it's mine."

God help me.

Concern rose inside her. She'd grossly underestimated Mr. Cooper, which was most likely what he'd wanted. To trap her in a situation where he became the only option.

"You cannot force me." When he didn't comment, she said, "Drag me to the church if you want, but I won't say yes."

"You don't think?" He shook his head at her naiveté, stood, and strolled around the room, his attention seemingly on the various items kept on display. "I'm not the villain you wish to paint me, but neither did I take all this time from my busy schedule to cross the Atlantic simply to go back empty handed. You were promised to me by your father, Miss Russell, so if you refuse to accept my hand, I'll have no choice but to withdraw the offer I made him."

Which would in all likelihood bankrupt Papa.

Swallowing the bile in her throat, Charlotte reached for her tea and took a lengthy sip. Her choice was clear. She could either save her father from financial ruin and live a miserable life married to a man she did not like, or she could turn her back on her family and strive for the future she wanted. Although, to be fair, the second option wasn't feasible yet since she was still short on funding. So then, she only had one real choice. Unless she managed to reclaim her rights to *The Marquess's Unresolved Mysteries* and money began pouring in.

She set her teacup aside, raised her chin, and met Mr. Cooper's cunning blue eyes. "Let's make a deal."

Mr. Cooper gave her a curious look. "You're hardly in a position to bargain."

"You don't think?" Charlotte asked, throwing the words he'd spoken earlier right back at him. "Unless you want a difficult woman on your hands, I suggest you hear me out."

He looked oddly impressed. "As a strategist, doing so would not be in my favor, but as a businessman accustomed to negotiations, I feel obliged. Please, Miss Russell, proceed."

Charlotte breathed a sigh of relief. Mr. Cooper was no fool. Indeed, he was both clever and ruthless when it came to business. But he didn't strike her as cruel, which was something she meant to use to her advantage. "Give me a chance to find a solution we can both be satisfied with."

"What do you have in mind?"

"I don't know yet." She struggled to think. "What if I were to find another marital prospect for you?"

"Do you believe that's possible?"

"I need time to figure that out."

Mr. Cooper studied her. "How much time?"

"A month?"

"I'm afraid I can't give you that, Miss Russell. Considering it's already a month and a half since I left New York, I really need to be heading back soon. So the most I can spare is one week."

"One week? But that's hardly any time at all."

"It's the best I can do." He looked genuinely contrite. "However, if you are able to make me another offer within that timeframe, I shall consider it with the same degree of attention I give every business deal I'm presented with. You have my word on that."

"Thank you." It was all she could think to say.

"But if you fail, you'll marry me without causing a stir. Agreed?"

Charlotte swallowed. "Agreed."

He held her gaze. "To be clear, I came here in good faith and with the understanding that your father had explained the situation to you and gained your approval."

"He did not."

"No, and I mean to address that with him directly. However, I refuse to chalk this trip up to a wasted effort. I've invested valuable time and funds with every intention of using the Society wedding I believed would take place as a means of increasing my notoriety and expanding my business."

"You wished to make headlines?"

"Of course. The publicity would be tremendous, but more than that, marriage into the British peerage would increase my acceptance among the elite."

"I would have thought your accumulation of wealth would be enough for that in a country renowned for encouraging hard work and self-made success."

"Not if I'm to rub shoulders with powerful families like the Astors and the DuPonts."

Charlotte bit her lip. She'd never heard of these people. Judging from his tone, they were important, so she simply said, "I see your predicament."

He inclined his head. "If it's any consolation, I like you a great deal, Miss Russell. You've got a good head on your shoulders." He hesitated briefly, then gestured toward the door. "Shall we inform your parents of our agreement?"

"They are without doubt expecting us to announce our engagement."

"But we won't. Not yet at least." When Charlotte didn't move, he went to the door and opened it. "Ah, Lady Elkins."

The viscountess appeared so swiftly it was clear she'd been standing nearby, possibly eavesdropping. "My husband awaits you in his study."

Charlotte bristled. If only she'd been blessed with parents who loved her and respected her for who she was and what she wanted to be.

"When can we start planning the wedding?" Mama asked as soon as Mr. Cooper had left the room.

Charlotte stifled a groan. "We're not getting married, Mama."

"What? But you have to."

Not if Charlotte could help it. "I think I'll take my luncheon in my bedchamber. There's much for me to consider."

"But what about Mr. Cooper?"

"He is the reason I need time to think."

"Oh. I see." Her mother's hesitant tone was testament to her confusion, but she smiled nonetheless. "In that case, come find me when you're ready."

Charlotte gave a polite nod before heading upstairs. She moved slowly, desperately hiding the panic that tore its way through her like runaway horses. Once she was safe inside her room, Charlotte carefully shut the door and rang for Daisy. She'd no idea how to solve her predicament yet, but she was certain that whatever

she ended up doing, it would require her trustworthy maid's assistance.

Blayne stared at the neat brick façade of Number Two Berkley Square. When Charlotte hadn't
shown up at the agreed time, he'd decided to find
out why. So he'd gone to call on her directly,
only to be denied entry by the butler who'd told
him never to return again.

Something had obviously happened. But what?

He scratched the back of his head and turned
away. No sense in standing about on the pavement. Instead, he made his way back to The
Black Swan while wondering what had transpired. Was it possible Charlotte's parents had
figured out what she was up to? Could they have
learned he wasn't who he pretended to be?

Judging from the swift dismissal he'd just
received he believed that must be the case. Perhaps Lady Warwick's comment at the ball had
prompted the Russells to investigate him. But
he'd taken precautions in the event they did.
Guthrie had ensured that if they questioned
Lord Meyers, the home secretary, they would
receive a vague answer. And if they sought out
his place of business, they'd find a neat shop on
Bond Street. Of course, if they'd had him followed, they would have learned the truth soon
enough. It wouldn't have been too hard. He'd
just hoped his act was convincing enough to
prevent them from doing so.

The biggest question of all was where this left
Charlotte. Denied the income she'd been relying

on from her next book, her options were surely limited. Which meant she might have no choice but to do as her parents insisted and get herself married. And since he was now prevented from seeing her, Mr. Cooper was the only viable option when it came to potential husbands.

Not that Blayne had any intention of heading down the aisle with her himself. He just didn't want to see her unhappy.

He tensed at the thought of her marrying the American. The very idea of her in another man's arms made him want to punch holes through walls. He muttered a curse. There was no guarantee things were anywhere near as bad as he feared. His gut said otherwise, but he knew from experience he could not risk making a wrong assumption. For now, he'd send a couple of lads out to investigate matters further so he could get a better picture of the situation at hand. He wanted to know who came and went from that house and at which hour. Most especially, he needed to make sure Charlotte was all right.

CHAPTER ELEVEN

CAREFUL TO KEEP herself hidden by the creamy silk curtain flanking her window, Charlotte looked out onto the street below. Blayne stood there, frowning at her house as if it were some perplexing problem he wasn't sure how to solve. She'd heard him arrive and she'd also heard Everet's dry dismissal of him.

Her heart ached and a terrible knot squeezed her throat. She wanted nothing more than to open the window and call out to him, to offer an explanation so he would know it wasn't she who'd rejected him. He turned and began walking away, leaving her there, imprisoned in her own home.

After talking to Daisy, Charlotte had made up her mind. She would keep her appointment with Blayne and when she saw him, she'd tell him everything so he'd understand what was happening.

Unfortunately, she'd underestimated the awfulness of her current situation. Because when she'd tried to leave the house, Everet had stopped her.

"I'm sorry, miss," he'd said, "but your father insists you remain at home today. It is my understanding that he wishes to speak with you."

"Then he is here?"

"He has gone out but is due to return before luncheon."

"So I have until then," Charlotte had said. "Daisy and I shall take a walk. We shan't be long."

Everet had stepped in front of the door, blocking Charlotte's path. "Your father was adamant. He instructed me to tell you that should you decide to thwart his wishes, you would be putting my employment along with Daisy's in jeopardy."

Anger still rolled through Charlotte in waves, rising each time she recalled those words. She could scarcely wait for her father's return so she could give him a piece of her mind. This situation was not to be borne.

A soft knock sounded and then her door opened. Daisy stepped in. She'd brought a fresh pot of tea along with two cups, bless her. "How are you feeling, miss?"

"Wretched and furious." She watched Daisy set the tray down on top of her dresser. "They've taken the one thing I truly valued away from me. The ability to come and go as I please."

"I wouldn't be surprised if your father is trying to make sure the only man you see from now on is Mr. Cooper," Daisy said, her disdain for the viscount's machinations unmistakable. "You can't marry him."

"As I told you last night, I do not plan to."

"Good." Daisy handed Charlotte a cup and took one for herself. Once Charlotte had taken a seat on the stool in front of her vanity table, Daisy perched herself on the edge of Charlotte's bed. Charlotte couldn't help but smile. Somehow, Daisy had sensed she needed a friend right now more than a maid.

"What about Mr. MacNeil?"

Charlotte shrugged in a hopeless attempt to mask the pain that gripped her at the mere mention of his name. "You know the situation. I am forbidden from seeing him again."

"But you care for him." Daisy's probing gaze searched her face. "I know you do."

Of course she did.

"It doesn't matter." Charlotte took a sip of her tea and fought the sting in her eyes. "I'll just... I'll have to find a way to deliver the money I owe him."

Daisy shook her head. "I don't think he'll accept that."

"He has to."

"And what about your missing manuscript? Mr. MacNeil was trying to help you find it." Daisy huffed. "You can't give up now. Not when—"

"When what?" Charlotte set her teacup aside and stood. She felt as though she'd been pacing the room since yesterday. Her feet ached but once again, she had to move. "I am trapped, Daisy. Do you not understand? I cannot step outside on the pavement right now, let alone run around town with Mr. MacNeil for company. If someone sees us – if word gets back to my father, the situation would only get worse."

"How can it possibly get worse than this?"

"For one thing, Papa could choose to sack you, which would put you in a bind while leaving me without my confidante. And I need you, Daisy, now more than ever before. So I cannot afford to take any risks."

"You're right. Of course you are. I'm just so unbelievably angry on your behalf."

"Thank you." Charlotte gave her the best smile she could manage at the moment. "Your support means the world to me."

A frown creased Daisy's brow. "No one's stopping me from going out by myself."

"Daisy…"

"If you want, I could give Mr. MacNeil a message from you."

Emotion overtook Charlotte so forcefully, the tears she'd been fighting since yesterday finally spilled down her cheeks. She swiped them away and looked at her maid. "Thank you, Daisy. I did consider asking, but then I decided it would be selfish of me to do so. You're not comfortable venturing into that part of town. Certainly not on your own."

"I'll do it for you."

"Daisy, I—"

"Listen," Daisy said, her voice more firm than Charlotte had ever heard it. "Mr. MacNeil might not be the sort of man you ought to want, but—"

"I don't want any man, Daisy. Remember? I have no desire to form an attachment, get married, and lose my independence."

"Are you really going to keep telling yourself that?" When Charlotte stayed stubbornly quiet, Daisy softened her voice and added, "I might not be more than a maid, but I'm not blind or stupid. There's something between you and Mr. MacNeil — more than a passing flirtation. And while I know it's not my place to say this, I think you'd be better off with him than without. Miss, I know you've had a plan for years with a certain goal in mind, but maybe it's time for you to make a new goal — one that's better suited to the current situation."

"My parents will never give their approval."

"Probably not, but you're seven and twenty years old, so you don't really need it. Not legally, anyway."

"What you're proposing would lead to scandal. People would talk, Daisy. My parents, perhaps even my sisters, would suffer the consequence of such selfish action." Charlotte shook her head. "I won't allow that so please, let's not speak of it any further."

"All right, but my offer to give Mr. MacNeil a message on your behalf still stands."

At the very least, he might be able to keep on searching for the identity of the person who stole and then published her manuscript. Finding the thief would solve a great deal because then at least she'd be certain of an income with which she could help her father out of his bind so he'd

not need Mr. Cooper's help. Of course, even if
she managed to accomplish that, she would still
have to find Mr. Cooper another bride of equal
or better social standing, which would not be
the least bit simple. Certainly not within the
space of only one week. Charlotte took a deep
breath and decided it would be best to tackle one
problem at a time.

"Thank you, Daisy. If you're absolutely certain, I'd appreciate you giving Mr. MacNeil
the payment he is owed." Crossing to her desk,
she pulled out a crisp piece of paper, readied
her quill, and tried to think of what to write.
Uncertainty gave her pause. Blayne was more
than an employee, yet less than a fiancé. They
weren't really engaged, neither had a claim on
the other, so running to him felt wrong, like she
was asking him to commit to something he'd
told her he didn't want. But if he could help her
regain control of the manuscript, she would at
the very least have secured her income, which
would be an excellent start.

"So what do you think?"

Blayne blinked, bringing Guthrie back into
focus. The duke spoke from the corner of
Blayne's office, where he presently lounged in a
plush velvet armchair. "About what?"

Guthrie sighed. "Have you not heard a single
word I've just said? Christ almighty, Blayne, I've
been talking to you for a good ten minutes at
least."

"Sorry."

Guthrie frowned. "I want to know what you think of my idea to buy that vacant building I've been eyeing on Oxford Street, renovating it, and turning it into a tavern based on The Black Swan model. In my opinion the middle classes who frequent that part of town would appreciate a drinking hole. Right now, there's a gap in the market there. Everything's geared toward the wealthy Mayfair residents."

"Maybe there's a reason for that."

"Not one that makes any sense to me. After all, there are clerks and shopkeepers, servants even, who need a place to go without wasting precious time travelling to other parts of Town. And who knows? If the entertainment's right, we might even draw a few toffs. In any case, I want your help setting it up. You're the only person I can think of beside myself who knows what it takes to run a place like this while also having the skill required to straddle both worlds."

"Guthrie, I…" Blayne sighed. "Ye ken I'm trying to get out of London. Away from all this."

"And yet you're still here."

"Aye." It didn't seem like he was going anywhere anytime soon. "I just dinnae think I can run a tavern for ye on Oxford Street. The risk of me getting recognized is much greater there than it is here."

"And yet you took that risk for Miss Russell."

"I shouldnae have done so," Blayne said, his heart starting to struggle at the memory of the evening they'd shared at the Coventry ball and what it had led to. "It was foolish."

"Are you sure about that?'

The question caused an instant flare of anger, hot and sharp, to spear him. "Yes, damn it. Lady Warwick said I looked familiar – that I reminded her of someone she'd met in her youth. And while I didnae stay to hear the entire name of the man she wished to liken me to, I heard enough to know it was my father."

"That's hardly enough to start any speculations or rumors. Certainly not to have you chased down by the law."

"It's a start." He gave Guthrie a firm look. "If I'm smart, I'll steer clear of anyone who might be able to spot the connection from now on."

"That might prove harder than you think if you're still intent on winning Miss Russell. After all, she's firmly rooted in that world."

"Ye've got it all wrong. I was merely trying to help her and…" He shook his head. "She and I are just…"

Guthrie tilted his head. "Just what, Blayne?"

"Nothing." He ran his fingers through his hair. "I dinnae even ken why we're talking about her."

There was a long moment of silence, then Guthrie said, "I didn't think I was good enough for Regina either. In fact, I was convinced we'd never be able to have a future together. She was an earl's daughter after all."

"Yes, but ye were more than a criminal."

"And so are you."

"No. I'm not. My soul is more tainted than yers will ever be."

"You were just a lad."

"That's not an excuse." Blayne closed his eyes and forced out an agonized breath. "I've been looking over my shoulder all these years, afraid to accept my punishment. But maybe this is it. God knows a life without Charlotte will be the living hell I deserve."

"You're in love with her then."

Blayne opened his eyes, met Guthrie's, and decided to face the truth. "I dinnae ken when it happened, or how."

"It does tend to catch one by surprise," Guthrie mused.

A knock sounded at the door and Blayne called for whoever it was to enter.

It was Claus. "My apologies for the interruption, but I thought you'd want to know that Daisy is here."

A prickly sensation swept up the back of Blayne's neck. Stomach contracting and muscles tightening with anticipation, he stood. "Show her in."

Claus stepped aside and motioned for Charlotte's maid to enter. Her eyes widened when she spotted Guthrie – just enough to convey recognition – before landing on Blayne. Setting her jaw, she pushed her spine into rigid straightness, and approached him with determination.

"My mistress has asked me to give you this." Daisy handed him a letter.

With rising dread, Blayne stared at her outstretched hand and the folded piece of paper she held. His name was written upon it with elegant penmanship. His heart thudded against the confines of his ribs as he slowly reached out and took it. Holding the letter between his hands, he let his thumb stroke across Charlotte's seal. An involuntary smile caught the edge of his lips. The imprint in the blob of crimson wax depicted a quill. How appropriate.

Steeling himself, he tore the seal and unfolded the paper. Something fell out and floated toward the floor. Blayne crouched to pick it up, unease expanding within him at the sight of a promise note worth forty pounds. An unpleasant taste filled his mouth as he straightened himself and proceeded to read the few lines Charlotte had written.

My dearest Blayne,

An unexpected complication has kept me from our meeting this morning. I apologize for not being able to inform you of it sooner. Enclosed herein are the funds I owe you. Since there is no guarantee for when we shall meet again, I thought it best to have them delivered forthwith in case you need them.

As one last request, I ask that you do what you can to help me reacquire the rights to my book so I can receive payment.

Affectionately yours,

Charlotte W. Russell

Everything inside Blayne revolted at the words and what they suggested. Drawing breath became a challenge. He couldn't seem to get the air past the knot in his throat. A mixture of pain and anger assailed him. Her business-like words were like a betrayal − a denial of what they'd shared. The money she added was a goddamn insult.

He picked the promise note up and handed it to Daisy. "I dinnae want this."

"Miss Russell said you might refuse and that I should insist."

"Insisting willnae do any good." He shoved it into her hand and curled her fingers roughly around it. "Take it. Spend it on yerself if ye're too afraid to tell her I wouldnae accept it."

"I…I…I'm terribly sorry," Daisy sputtered.

"Are ye really," Blayne seethed while towering over the much smaller woman. Her expression was stricken, her body rigid as she began backing away.

"Blayne," Claus warned as he moved close to Daisy. "You're frightening her."

"Good." He glared at the maid as if she were the one who'd just taken an axe to his heart. "Ye need to leave. Right now. Go. And dinnae ever come back."

Daisy didn't budge. Instead she held his gaze like some martyr facing down a fire-breathing dragon.

"I said, get out," he roared, unleashing the tension that had been building inside him since he'd been turned away from Charlotte's house.

Daisy flinched, but to Blayne's amazement, she held her ground.

"That's enough," Claus said, his face etched in hard lines. Placing one arm around Daisy's shoulders he drew her against his side. "It's all right. He'll settle down in a moment or two."

The hell he would.

"May I see that letter?" The softly spoken words of calm came from Guthrie.

Blayne turned toward him, bringing the vibrantly clad man into his line of vision. For a moment, he'd quite forgotten his presence. Blayne gave him the letter. Fists clenched until his palms burned, he watched while the other man read.

"She obviously cares for you."

"Nae. I'm just a hired hand who needs to get paid."

Guthrie arched a brow. "Hmm…And yet you are her *dearest* while she remains *affectionately yours*. I hope she doesn't address all her male servants thus."

Blayne bristled. "What the hell are ye implying?"

"Merely that you need to clear your head." He set the letter aside on Blayne's desk and calmly crossed his arms. "You've twisted yourself into a chaotic mess over what she wrote in the middle because that's where she's pushing you away."

"Exactly," Blayne sneered. "She's pushing me away, Guthrie. Which obviously means she doesnae give a rats arse about—"

"Easy now," Guthrie told him sternly. "There's a woman present."

Muttering a curse beneath his breath Blayne swiped his hand across his brow and puffed out a hard breath. "Sorry, Daisy."

"It's quite all right." Her voice was weak with apprehension, but that didn't stop her from adding, "Miss Russell cares for you very deeply, Mr. MacNeil. It's not what you think. She's not adding distance because she wants to. It's…"

To Blayne's frustration, Daisy shook her head and fell silent. Frowning at her, he snatched the letter back and attempted to read it without allowing the implication of him being nothing more to Charlotte than a man in her employ give way to anger. His frown deepened. Apart from the warmth with which she'd opened and closed the letter, one sentence resonated with importance. *An unexpected complication has kept me from our meeting this morning.*

Her butler — no, her parents' butler — had informed him he wasn't welcome. Even in his confusion, while he'd walked away from her house that morning, Blayne had felt as though something was wrong. He'd even sent out scouts in the hope of discovering what had happened and to make sure Charlotte was all right.

But then he'd gotten word from her and instead of it being the cry for help he'd expected — the chance for him to come to her rescue and prove his regard — it had denoted the end of their relationship. It had felt like a thousand lashes across his back, the sting so acute he'd been blinded to the truth.

Determined to do better, he took a deep breath and strove for a more relaxed tone as he spoke to Daisy once more. "What happened?"

"I can't say." Distress marked her eyes.

"Cannae or willnae?" Blayne asked.

Daisy swallowed and reached for Claus's hand,

clasping it until her knuckles turned white. "She demanded I keep silent about it."

It took tremendous effort for Blayne to hide his irritation. Returning to the chair he'd vacated upon Daisy's arrival, he snatched up the half empty glass of brandy he'd left on his desk and downed the remainder.

"And you don't wish to betray her trust," Guthrie murmured. "I understand and I'm sure MacNeil does too. Isn't that right?"

"Aye." He set the empty glass aside. "Ye're loyal to yer mistress, Daisy, and I commend ye for that. But if she's in some kind of trouble, as I'm beginning to suspect she may be, then I'd like to help."

"She made me promise."

"Fair enough. I'll respect that." Even though he wanted to tear his own damn hair out in frustration. "If ye're certain of her well-being and ye're sure I shouldnae interfere, then I shall stay away as requested and let her handle things on her own."

A very fleeting look of doubt caught Daisy's eyes. She pressed her lips together and stared back at him, the wheels in her brain spinning so fast he could practically hear them clicking. "She doesn't want you to know what's going on."

"Because?"

"I don't think she believes you can do more than what she's already asked of you. And to my way of thinking, she doesn't want to give you more trouble."

"We may not be the pinnacles of respectability," Guthrie said, "but if your mistress needs help, she'll have not only Mr. MacNeil's assistance, but mine as well."

Blayne appreciated his stepping in. A duke always wielded more influence than a common man. When Daisy still refused to speak, however, he prepared to send her back to Charlotte with a note of his own. Opening his desk drawer, he grabbed a sheet of paper, then dipped his quill in the ink well and started to write.

My sweetest lass,

I cannot accept your money any more than you can accept my support. Whatever reason you have for putting a sudden end to our arrangement, please know that this past month has been—

"They know who you are," Daisy admitted in a whisper.

Blayne froze, unable to move as he stared down at his own writing. His pulse quickened. It was just as he feared then. Lady Warwick's comment had brought the truth to the surface and the Russells had chosen to take a closer look.

Needing to have her confirm it, he raised his head. "What do ye mean, Daisy?"

She knit her brow. "Lord and Lady Elkins know you're not the gentleman you've been posing as. Mr. Cooper had you followed. He told them about your true identity yesterday morning."

Blayne shared a quick look with Guthrie before giving his attention back to Daisy. His heart eased into a steadier rhythm. Not his true identity then. Just the one they believed to be true.

"So now they're refusing to let their daughter see me."

"No." When Blayne raised an eyebrow, Daisy stepped forward, away from Claus. "I mean yes."

"She cannae leave the house, can she?"

Daisy shook her head. "They've threatened to sack me and Everet if she does. But it's not just that. You see, they're now demanding she marry Mr. Cooper. According to what Miss Russell told me, her father has lost most of his fortune, including her dowry. Mr. Cooper is prepared to help him out of trouble though, in exchange for my mistress's hand."

Slowly and with a great deal of care, Blayne set his quill aside before he gave into temptation and snapped the thing in two.

"Blayne," Guthrie said, a clear note of warning in his voice.

Blayne scarcely heard him as blood rushed into his ears, continuing to the top of his head where it started to gather with forceful pressure. "The viscount is selling his daughter?"

"It's awful, I know, but at least Miss Russell was able to make a deal with Mr. Cooper." Daisy quickly explained the details. "It's not ideal, but it has bought her some time, useless though it may be when she's prevented from leaving the house."

Muscles straining across his back, Blayne fought for clarity. "A visit to the publisher is obviously in order. She's asked me to go there so naturally I'll do so. I'm just nae sure one week will be enough for me to prove she's the author and acquire the earnings she needs to fix her father's situation. I mean, if I were the publisher I'd nae take my word for it — I'd at the very least want to hear it from her." He glanced at Daisy. "I dinnae suppose she's willing to let Lord Elkins rot in hell?"

"Her sense of duty would never permit her to do so, no matter her father's wrongdoing."

"In that case, we've got to come up with something else — some other way in which to extricate Miss Russell from this hold Mr. Cooper has on her. In case her plan doesnae work."

"Just give me the word and I'll have him picked up," Guthrie said.

Blayne knit his brow. "Mr. Cooper isnae so different from ye, Guthrie. He made a bargain, that's all. Threatening him or worse wouldnae be right."

"Then what do you propose?"

"I'm nae sure. It would help if I knew how much Lord Elkins was hoping to make from this wretched agreement." Blayne looked at Daisy. "Any idea?"

Daisy gave a small nod. "Miss Russell mentioned two thousand pounds."

Blayne puffed out a breath. He'd feared as much. A hopeless laugh almost escaped him. "If I recall, Charlotte has two sisters, both of whom are married to wealthy men. Surely they can offer assistance."

"She has written to them both."

"As for acquiring a new fiancée for Mr. Cooper," Blayne went on, "there must be a woman of noble birth who would leap at the chance to marry a man as wealthy as he."

"Anything's possible," Guthrie said.

"I suggest we start with yer wife," Blayne said.

"What?" Guthrie sputtered.

Ignoring him for a moment, Blayne gave his attention to Claus. "Can ye please make sure Daisy gets back to Russell House safely?"

"It would be my pleasure," Claus said. He placed his arm around Daisy's shoulders and steered her out of the room.

The door closed and Guthrie crossed to the side table where he proceeded to pour a large glass of brandy. He took a deep swallow. "Now then. Why don't you tell me what your plan is and how Regina fits into it."

Blayne arched a brow. "She's connected socially, is she not?"

"She was before her father was hanged for murder and she decided to marry me."

"Does she not socialize with the other duchesses?"

"Occasionally," Guthrie confessed.

"Well, then. There you are."

"I don't quite follow."

Blayne let a smile slide into place. "I'm sure these ladies can find a fifth daughter of a Lord Somethingorother who would be happy to secure her future by marrying a rich American."

"I'll be sure to put Regina to the task as soon as I get home," Guthrie said. He grabbed his burgundy velvet top hat off a nearby table and donned it with a flourish. "We'll save Miss Russell. No doubt about that."

Blayne answered with a stiff nod. In spite of the odds against them, he had to believe success was possible.

CHAPTER TWELVE

FIVE DAYS LATER, Charlotte still hadn't solved her dilemma. And time to do so was swiftly running out. She sighed as she went to meet her parents for dinner. The last thing she felt like right now was being sociable, but neither did she want them to think she was sulking upstairs in her bedchamber. Having written her sisters, she'd hoped they might have been able to come to her aid financially, but she'd not yet heard back from either. As for finding a suitable candidate willing to marry Mr. Cooper on short notice, she was no closer to coming up with a viable option now than she had been when she'd made her bargain with him. And with only two days left, she was starting to see the hopelessness of her situation.

"I thought we might visit the modiste together tomorrow," Mama said when Charlotte met her parents in the parlor. "Mr. Cooper did suggest that he means to propose to you soon, and when it comes to ordering wedding gowns, there really is no time to waste."

"I've had a word with my secretary this afternoon," Papa said. "He will make sure invitations are prepared so they can be sent out as soon as you and Mr. Cooper settle on a date."

"Your father and I both agree that St. George's would be the best venue," Mama said.

"It's where anyone of consequence gets married," Papa said. "I'll meet with the vicar and find out which date suits best so I'm able to offer advice."

"Hopefully, before you send out invitations," Charlotte told him dryly.

"What?" Her father looked momentarily startled. And then he relaxed. "Oh yes. Right you are."

"Naturally, the wedding breakfast will be hosted here," her mother continued. "If the weather is good we can have a small reception outside in the garden. The flowers are lovely this time of year. It would be quite romantic."

"Indeed," Charlotte said. "Provided there will be a wedding."

Her mother frowned while squeezing her lips together in what looked like severe disgruntlement.

"Of course there will," Papa said. All agreeability had vanished from his face. "Mr. Cooper merely desires to give you time to recover from the MacNeil incident before taking over the role of your fiancé, which is mighty considerate of him."

"I agree," Charlotte said without bothering to hide her displeasure. "Which is why I am so overjoyed."

"There's no need for sarcasm," Mama chastised. "Rather, I would expect a bit more gratitude on your part."

Unwilling to argue, Charlotte kept quiet and did her best not to scream in frustration.

"Now," her father continued, "I was going to keep this a surprise, but maybe this is a good time to let you know that your mother and I plan to visit you in New York for Christmas. So it shan't be too long before you see us again – just a few months."

As things stood right now, Charlotte wouldn't mind never having to be in the same room with either of them ever again. She sighed and hoped dinner would be ready soon so she could drown herself in a large glass of wine.

A knock sounded and Everet entered. "Mr. Cooper is here."

What now? Charlotte wondered.

"Do show him in," Papa said. "It will be a pleasure to have him join us. We've much to discuss."

"I already made the suggestion, sir, but it would appear he wishes to speak with Miss Russell in private."

Charlotte blinked.

"Well don't keep the man waiting," Mama hissed. "I'm sure there's something very important he wants to ask you."

Charlotte sent her a glare, but got up and moved to the door. This couldn't be happening. Surely Mr. Cooper did not mean to deny her the last two days he'd promised. Apprehensive, she followed Everet to her father's study where Mr. Cooper stood waiting.

"Miss Russell." He dipped his head in greeting. "I thought it correct to speak with you first."

"About what?" she asked while her stomach proceeded to turn itself inside out.

"Apparently, I underestimated you."

"No more than I underestimated you, I'm sure," she said, more clueless than ever.

He grinned. "I should thank you though."

"Thank me?"

"For informing the Earl of Dervaine of my interest in finding a bride. His youngest daughter will suit me very well."

Charlotte stared at him while trying to grapple with what he was saying and what it meant. This was what she'd wanted, what she'd prayed for, but the chance of it actually happening had been so slim. In fact, it had been so thoroughly unlikely, it might as well have been totally impossible.

"Naturally, I won't be able to increase your father's return on investment like I'd initially promised, but as his friend, I'll be happy to advise him on how to increase his wealth." He grinned. "My company's not the only one with the promise of good returns."

"I...um..." Stunned, Charlotte wasn't sure what to say. She'd no idea how any of this had come about, but it did appear as though she was free from her attachment with him.

"Well. I just thought to let you know what the situation is before I speak with your father."

She collected herself and managed a smile. "Thank you, Mr. Cooper."

"If you could please ask him to come speak with me next?"

Charlotte nodded. It was the oddest thing, having a guest use her father's study to interview them each in turn. She quit the room on numb legs and returned to the parlor.

"Well?" Mama asked the moment Charlotte arrived.

"Um…" Charlotte glanced at both her parents before she focused on her father. "Mr. Cooper would like a word with you, Papa."

"To discuss the wedding details, no doubt." Papa crossed to the door. "Ladies, you must not wait for me with dinner. I shall join you as soon as I can."

Charlotte watched him go. With a rough idea of the conversation he was about to have, she dreaded his return.

"What did he say?" Mama asked.

"I think it might be best for us to wait for Papa before I tell you." Charlotte wrung her hands.

"Come now," Mama pushed. "At least tell me if he kissed you."

"He did not." Finally a question she could answer without hesitation.

"Well. Such things are overrated anyway," Mama said. "All that matters is that he is well situated and wealthy."

It took tremendous effort for Charlotte not to roll her eyes.

"Shall we?" Mama asked when dinner was

announced shortly after.

Charlotte nodded and followed her mother to the dining room. Food was served – a soup of some sort – and Charlotte ate while doing her best to engage in the subject her mother wished to discuss: her plan to redesign the garden in the spring.

They were almost halfway through the second course when Charlotte's father returned with a cross expression. He glanced at Charlotte, then at his wife. "The wedding is off."

Charlotte's heart made a joyful jump. Until this very moment, she'd not dared believe it.

Mama stared at Papa in wide-eyed dismay. "I beg your pardon?"

"Mr. Cooper will not be proposing to Charlotte after all," Papa said. He strode to his chair and lowered himself to the seat. "Instead, he means to marry the Earl of Dervaine's youngest daughter, Lady Fiona."

"But…" Charlotte's mother blinked in rapid succession. "He came here by *your* invitation and for the sole purpose of marrying Charlotte. He cannot just…just…change his mind."

"Clearly, he has." Papa poured himself a large glass of wine. "In fact, Mr. Cooper has made himself perfectly clear. An announcement declaring him engaged to Lady Fiona is due to appear in the paper tomorrow."

"But what about your agreement with him?" Mama asked. "I mean, you offered him Charlotte for a reason."

For the money, Charlotte was tempted to say.

She managed to hold her tongue though.

Papa took a deep swallow from his glass and sank against his seat. Incredulity lent a glassy appearance to his eyes. "He gave me a promise note worth one thousand pounds as a means of compensation."

Charlotte's mouth fell open. Mr. Cooper hadn't mentioned this to her.

"But that's extraordinary," Mama said.

"It's only half as much as I would have gained if Charlotte had wed him, but it is substantial enough to clear my debt and improve upon my financial situation."

Shocked by the startling turn of events the evening had provided, Charlotte tried to work out what had occurred. And failed. Until something Daisy had said when she'd returned from The Black Swan came into sudden focus.

Things have a way of turning out as they should. This won't be any different. I'm certain of it.

Charlotte frowned. This couldn't possibly be Blayne's doing. Could it? She pondered this possibility during the rest of dinner. She hadn't asked him for help with anything besides reacquiring the rights to her book – a task she'd received no progress information on yet.

But what if he'd realized she needed more help than she'd let on? Intent on getting answers as quickly as possible, Charlotte excused herself as soon as the meal was done, explaining she needed to gather her thoughts on top of the evening's shocking news.

"Of course," her mother said. "I'm sure Mr.

Cooper's decision to choose someone else must be quite a blow for you, dear."

Answering with a tight smile, Charlotte turned away and went to her room where she rang for Daisy.

"When you visited The Black Swan," Charlotte said once the maid arrived, "did you by any chance happen to mention the deal I made with Mr. Cooper?"

Daisy shifted her gaze to a spot somewhere off to the side so she didn't look straight at Charlotte. "You asked me not to."

"I did indeed."

"Mr. MacNeil suggested you might not be able to leave the house, so I explained the threat the viscount made about having me and Everet sacked."

Charlotte pinched the bridge of her nose. "You weren't supposed to tell him that."

"I know, miss. I'm sorry. It just slipped out and then…"

"And then?" Charlotte prompted.

Daisy wrung her hands together. "I may have mentioned the viscount's financial troubles and how Mr. Cooper was willing to help him as long as he married you."

"Daisy, you broke my confidence."

"I know, miss. My only excuse is that I was trying to help you, but I understand if that's not good enough. If you want to sack me, I'll not think less of you, miss. In fact, I knew I risked my position when I chose to confide in Mr. MacNeil."

"Which makes your decision all the more admirable." Charlotte waited until Daisy met her gaze, then said, "As ashamed as I am of Mr. MacNeil knowing what—"

"The Duke of Windham was there too," Daisy whispered. "So was Claus."

Charlotte sighed and started again. "As ashamed as I am of these men knowing my father was brought so low he saw no recourse but to use me to improve his own wealth, I cannot deny the relief I feel over not having to marry Mr. Cooper. That was your doing, Daisy, and I thank you for it."

"So you're not too angry?"

"I appreciate having a maid who's able to use good judgment. You were right to ignore my request for secrecy, Daisy. If it weren't for you, I'm not sure I'd have been able to get out of this mess in time. But that doesn't mean I approve of you lying to me. When I asked how your meeting with Mr. MacNeil had gone, you should have been honest."

"Yes, miss. I'm sorry."

"It's all right. I'll forgive you this once. Just don't ever do it again, Daisy. I need to know I can trust you. Do you understand?"

"Of course. And I truly am sorry."

Charlotte could tell she was from her pained expression. She'd taken a risk – one that could have cost her position. "I think you've apologized enough."

Daisy nodded. "What will you do now?"

It was a good question. Her parents would

probably expect everything to go back to the way they'd been four and a half weeks ago. Before her father announced Mr. Cooper's arrival and she'd introduced her parents to Blayne. But how could it? She still had the mystery of her stolen manuscript to solve, and her feelings for Blayne were such that she knew she couldn't forget him. And while she had no idea how he'd managed to help her, thanks were in order.

"I need to speak with Mr. MacNeil."

"Of course you do."

"Can you help me sneak out?"

Daisy looked very unsure. "It's awfully late, miss."

"I know," Charlotte agreed, "but it will be harder to do during the day."

"What about the viscount's threat?"

"Considering the turn of events, I doubt it applies any longer. Besides, Papa values Everet too much to sack him and as for you, I will always protect you, Daisy. You know that."

Daisy nodded. "Very well, miss. Just as long as you take that pistol of yours along for protection."

"I always do, Daisy."

Half an hour later, Charlotte exited through the servants' entrance at the back of the house. Dressed in a plain brown cotton dress and with the hood of her cloak pulled over her head, she kept to the darkest shadows while walking briskly up Davies Street, at the end of which she hailed a hackney.

"Are you sure, miss?" the driver asked when

she gave him directions.

"Quite," Charlotte answered crisply. She handed him a shilling. "You'll receive another once I reach my destination."

"Very good, miss." He pocketed the coin.

Charlotte climbed into the carriage and the horses were whipped into motion. She glanced out the window as they travelled the length of Oxford Street. It was almost midnight, so there weren't many people about, which wasn't surprising since the Season was almost over and social events reducing in number.

"Here you are," Charlotte told the driver once they'd arrived outside The Black Swan. She handed him the shilling she owed.

He took it and glanced at the tavern behind her. "Would you like me to wait?"

"That won't be necessary," she said just as two drunken men stumbled out through the door, one cursing loudly while the other one sang.

The coachman frowned. "You're sure?"

Charlotte nodded in spite of her racing heart. "Yes. Thank you."

He pressed his mouth into a firm line but nodded nonetheless. Charlotte turned away from the rattling sound of the carriage as it rolled down the street, only to find herself face to face with the two men she'd spotted. They were closer now – uncomfortably so – and studying her in a manner that caused the fine hair at the nape of her neck to stand on end.

CHAPTER THIRTEEN

CHARLOTTE REACHED INSIDE her reticule and withdrew her pistol. "Stay back. Both of you."

"Well, well, well. A bit o' muslin with a temperament." The tall fellow laughed. He appeared to be roughly her age with angular features and a nose that looked like it had been broken more than once. His shoulders weren't as broad as Blayne's, but he would still be strong enough to pick her up with one arm and carry her off into the night if he wished to.

"A lovely lady who's also feisty," the shorter man crooned. He seemed to be about the same age but with rounder features and thinner hair. "Let's give 'er some pleasure at our own leisure."

"Lay one hand on me and you'll be answering to Mr. MacNeil." She was glad her voice remained steady. Raising her chin, she tried to look as confident as she sounded.

Apprehension filled the shorter man's eyes, but the larger man simply leered at her as if he intended to find out exactly what she hid beneath her skirts. He dropped his gaze to the pistol she held. "MacNeil 'as no say over me."

Taking her by surprise, he grabbed her wrist, dislodged her weapon, and sent it flying through the air. It landed with a clank somewhere off to her right. Air rushed into her lungs on a deep inhale, but before she could scream he'd pulled her against him and clamped one hand over her mouth.

A thick stench of brandy, tobacco, and sweat overwhelmed her senses until she feared she'd cast up her accounts. Panic had swamped her brain seconds earlier and she fought now to gain control over it. If she was to extricate herself from this situation without getting hurt, then she had to think rationally.

Laughter rang through her ears. "You're finer than I thought. 'Ere, Georgie, 'ave a sniff. She's as sweet as a rose, this one."

The shorter man moved in closer and inhaled. "Oh yes. I could burry my nose in 'er for days."

Charlotte tried to recoil but the taller man at her back held her immobile.

He licked the side of her neck. "Tastes delicious too."

A shudder raked the length of her spine.

"Move your 'and, will ya, Felix, so I can sample 'er mouth."

No.

Wide eyed with fear, Charlotte watched Georgie step more immediately in front of her. He leaned in. Felix lifted his hand, and Charlotte screamed while bringing her knee up with as much force as she could manage.

A startled gasp left Georgie's mouth. His hand grabbed her shoulder as if for support as his legs gave way beneath him.

Not wasting one second, Charlotte bucked her hips backward hard, producing a curse followed by a deep groan. Felix's hold on her loosed and Charlotte tore herself free. Without looking back she ran up the steps and burst through the door leading into The Black Swan.

Heads spun toward her and several men smirked while giving her a head to toe assessment. The hood from her cloak had fallen back and she could feel hairpins starting to loosen. She scanned the room, searching for the one man she'd come to see.

The door opened behind her and two angry hands grabbed hold of her arms. "I think you need to be disciplined."

Felix's sneer made her insides curdle.

"Now wait one moment," a burley fellow said as he moved toward them. "Maybe the lady's not keen on the likes o' you."

Oh thank God. Someone decent was finally stepping in to help her.

"Maybe she'd rather 'ave someone else," the burley fellow continued. "Someone more like me."

Charlotte's heart sank. Other men started taking notice and moved in closer to see what was happening.

"I'll fight ya for 'er, Felix."

"Prepare to 'ave your teeth knocked out, Erwin."

Erwin grinned. "You're always welcome to dream."

He jutted his head to one side and Charlotte was shoved into the arms of someone else.

"'Ello, luv," a thick voice murmured. "'Ow about you and I sneak off together while these two idiots knock themselves out?"

Good lord. Was every man here a lecherous scoundrel? Clearly, the Black Swan's crowd was different by night than by day, no doubt on account of the drink they'd all had.

She struggled to free herself from the man's grasp and when that didn't work she tried the same move that had helped her escape Felix's clutches. But this man was fat, his belly the perfect buffer against her attempt to harm him. Eventually, she managed to step down hard on his foot, but that only caused him to laugh.

"Now, now. There's no need for you to be violent."

Felix's fist struck Erwin's cheek and the crowd erupted in cheers.

"Go on Erwin," someone shouted. "Deck 'im!"

Erwin pulled back his arm, prepared to do precisely that when a shrill whistle spliced the air like a carving knife. "What the blistering hell is happening here?"

Charlotte's pulse leapt with hope while air filled her frayed lungs with elation. "Blayne!"

The hulking Scotsman stepped into the melee as if every man around him were but a gnat he could easily squish between his fingers. Erwin stumbled in mind-punch while Felix took a step back and dropped both arms to his sides. A hush descended over the room and everyone froze while Blayne turned, searching the crowd until his gaze landed on Charlotte.

His jawline hardened and his eyes turned black. A vein pulsed at the side of his neck to further convey his fury. Tension had transformed his shoulders into rigid lines while the need to do violence was evident in his tightly clenched fists.

Charlotte's heart knocked about wildly. She'd never seen him like this, but it was suddenly very easy for her to imagine him wringing a man's neck. He'd told her he'd killed while working for Guthrie. He'd explained that he wasn't good company for a gently bred woman like her – certainly not the sort of man she ought to be kissing.

She hadn't listened, perhaps because she'd not wanted to think of him in that way or maybe because it had been impossible for her to do so when he'd shown no hint of the violence when he was with her. But now, in this moment, Charlotte saw that he was a man who could make the devil himself tremble in his boots. Strong and fierce, he looked ready to do bloody murder, and something about his harsh gaze made her worry she might be the first one to feel his wrath.

A shiver of apprehension rushed through her along with a contrasting pull. Even though much of his anger was likely directed at her and even though she should probably wish she'd never come here, seeing him like this only made her want to pull him into a private room and kiss him.

A muscle moved at the side of his jaw as he glared past her right shoulder. And then, with slow and very precise words, he quietly said, "I suggest ye release my woman before I knock yer block off."

Charlotte sucked in a breath, then released it just as quickly when the man who'd been holding her dropped his hands.

His woman?

A funny hum buzzed through her veins, filling them with delicious warmth.

"Now wait one minute," Felix grumbled. "I saw 'er first."

Blayne spun toward him and grabbed him by the throat. Felix yelped and clasped hold of his hands, trying to pry away Blayne's fingers. It was no use. Blayne was determined and with three long strides he'd marched Felix to the door, flung it wide, and given the man a rough shove that sent him stumbling out into the night.

"Who else laid a hand on her?" Blayne asked.

Fingers quickly pointed at Georgie who earned a punch to the eye before he too was tossed out on his ass.

"If either of ye comes back here again, I'll break yer bloody bones," Blayne called after them. He slammed the door shut and turned. "Erwin?"

Erwin gulped. "Yes, Mr. MacNeil?"

"Did ye touch her as well?"

"N...no, sir. Never even crossed my mind."

"Miss Russell?" Blayne gave her a questioning look.

She swallowed and tried not to appear as shaky as she felt. "He didn't touch me, but he was trying to win me. That's why he and Felix were fighting."

"Why, you little conniving who—"

Blayne's knuckles connected with bone, silencing Erwin with a loud crack. "Grab yer friend and go," he told the fat man who'd been holding Charlotte. "Ye'd best pray I never set eyes on either of ye again. Is that clear?"

The fat man gave a quick nod before pulling Erwin to his feet and escorting him out of the tavern. Blayne waited until they were both out of sight before glancing around. "As for the rest of ye, ye're welcome to stay until closing as long as ye dinnae cause trouble."

The crowd instantly scattered with men returning to their drinks and card games as if no altercation had taken place. Blayne grabbed Charlotte's hand hard and dragged her toward the stairs, not breaking his stride even as she stumbled along behind him, doing her best to keep up. He was like a thundercloud racing across the sky, seeking the right place in which to explode. They reached the landing and Charlotte tripped. A gasp tore through her as she lost her footing, yanking her arm against its socket.

If Blayne cared about her discomfort, he didn't show it. Instead, he threw open a door and shoved her into a sparsely furnished room in which rows of potted plants lined the window sills. The door slammed shut right next to Charlotte's ear, jarring her senses, and then she was thrust up against the wall by the same large hands that had thrown four men from the tavern a few short minutes ago.

"What the hell do ye think ye're doing?" he seethed, his eyes like granite and his mouth a hard line of disapproval. "Have ye nae common sense at all?"

The unease she'd felt since leaving home transformed into sudden anger. She set her jaw and glared back at him. "I came to see *you*."

"In the middle of the night and all by yerself? Christ, woman. Are ye mad? My God, I ought to have ye committed for being a danger to yer own safety." His eyes darkened even further while her anger grew. "What the devil do ye think would have happened if I'd nae been there to stop those randy bastards from taking what they wanted?"

It wasn't a question she dared consider, so although she knew she'd been lucky, she ignored it. After all, everything had turned out well in the end. "I won't do it again. I promise."

"Ye're bloody well right ye won't do it again." His fingers curled into her shoulders while rough breaths escaped his mouth. She had an inkling he wanted to shake her. Instead he just held her in place. "I need to know ye're smart enough not to place yerself in danger."

"I did bring my pistol," she countered so he'd not think her a completely naïve moron.

"Of course ye did. So how come ye didnae

use it?"

"I, um…I tried. Felix managed to disarm me though."

Blayne dropped his gaze and muttered a curse so fowl Charlotte's cheeks grew hot. "I'm starting to see why yer father insisted ye marry Mr. Cooper. And I'm also beginning to comprehend his wish to keep ye locked up until the wedding. Jesus Christ. I didnae notice before because I was tangled up so tight with ye I just couldnae see, but the truth is ye're too bloody reckless."

The anger inside her shifted once more, turning to pain. "Don't you dare suggest Mr. Cooper might have been good for me, Blayne, or that my father was right to do what he did." A sob tore up her throat. It was one thing to deal with the criticism of others, but she could not handle his. Having Blayne's disapproval was like a stab to her heart and with everything else she'd endured in the last few days, it was too much for her to bear. She punched his chest while her vision blurred and tears began falling against her cheeks. "You…You were all I could think of. I needed to see you. Don't tell me I came here for nothing, don't try and pretend you don't care or that—"

"Ye misunderstand me, lass." His voice was rough as he swiped one tear from her cheek with his callused thumb.

She gulped down a breath in an effort to regain a bit of composure. "You could have sent me straight home the last time I came here. But you didn't. Did you? So don't place all the blame on me now when you were just as happy to break the rules."

"Christ, Charlotte. Do ye not understand?" His forehead pressed against hers and he quietly murmured, "It would kill me if ye got hurt."

She blinked. It was the closest he'd ever come to revealing his feelings. Her heart leapt. Could he possibly care for her just as much as she cared for him? She drew a tremulous breath. "I know you helped end things between me and Mr. Cooper."

There was a brief moment of silence. And then...

"Daisy told me of yer father's arrangement with him," Blayne said, his voice thick with emotion. Easing back, he released her from his grasp and took a deep breath. "She also mentioned the deal ye made in an effort to find a solution."

"How did you get him to walk away?"

"By making a different match for him."

"Yes, but how? How did you convince the Earl of Dervaine to marry his daughter off to a man who's in trade?"

Blayne took a step back. Shoving his hands in his pockets, he crossed to the window, and all she could think was how much she missed his nearness – how even a few feet of distance between them was much too great.

"I asked the Duchess of Windham to get together with a few other peeresses. Together, they drew up a list of ladies for whom a rich American gentleman might be ideal. The list consisted mostly of younger daughters who'd made unsuccessful debuts or who'd somehow been linked to scandal."

"Women who stood little chance of making good matches for themselves here in England."

"Precisely." He glanced at her. "All Mr. Cooper cared about was the connection with a title."

Charlotte gazed back at him. "So to him it made no difference that Lady Fiona has a tongue as sharp as a whip or that she tossed her wine in the Marquess of Narwhol's face last season."

"If anything, Mr. Cooper seemed to appreciate her gumption," Blayne said with a smirk. "And he most certainly approved of her being styled *Lady* Fiona."

"An earl's daughter is more desirable than a mere viscount's," Charlotte agreed.

"To some, perhaps, but nae to me."

She held his gaze a moment while letting his words infuse her with warmth. "But finding Mr. Cooper an alternate bride only solved one part of the problem. How did you convince him to give papa a thousand pounds in compensation?"

Blayne gave his attention back to the window and raised one shoulder in a careless shrug. "It wasnae too hard, lass."

An incredulous laugh escaped her. "Not too hard? From my point of view you worked a miracle for me." When he refrained from responding she said, "I'm grateful to you for getting involved. If you hadn't, I honestly don't know what I'd have done."

Stepping away from the wall, she moved

toward him. It had been an emotional evening and all she really wanted right now was for him to offer assurance. She needed to know he'd forgive her for coming and that all would be well between them. And yet, when she reached him, she lost her courage. He was still so rigid, she didn't quite dare wrap her arms around him for fear he might push her away. So she simply found a spot close to his side and asked the first question that came to mind as she studied the long row of plants before her. "What are you growing?"

"Some chives, mint, and parsley for the most part. This here, as ye can see, is cucumber." He plucked one of the larger fruits from the vine, bit away half of it and handed the remainder to her. "Ye can try it, if ye like."

She did so without hesitation. Blayne's smile of approval instantly soothed the remainder of her agitated nerves. His anger with her had dissipated and they were finally getting back to where they were meant to be.

"I was trying to grow tomatoes over here," he added, indicating a few pots at the end, "but as ye can see, I havenae been very successful."

"They might need to be outside."

"Hmm. I suppose that's true for all the plants. It's part of the reason why I've been looking to buy a place for myself in the country. Nothing big mind ye, just a small house somewhere with a decent-sized piece of land to go with it."

Disliking the sadness the thought of him moving away stirred in her breast, Charlotte did her best to ignore it by aiming for levity. "Do you know, I never would have pegged you for a farmer."

He grinned. "Not a farmer, lass, but a leisure gardener of sorts. I love watching plants grow and if I can benefit from them, then all the better. It's why I took the job ye offered, because it would have helped me reach my goal a lot quicker."

"Yet you refused to accept the money."

"Only because it feels wrong to do so now. After everything we've shared, I'd hate for ye to think it was still about the money. God forbid ye should wonder about my reasons for kissing ye, Charlotte." He shook his head. "I cannae let ye pay me."

"I'm sorry."

"Dinnae be." His arms came around her shoulders, drawing her into his warmth. Turning her slightly, he brushed his fingers under her chin, tipping it upward until their eyes met. "I'm certainly not."

Dipping his head, he brushed his lips over hers. The caress was soft and sweet, conveying a depth of emotion no words would ever be capable of expressing. He did it again, and then a third time before giving in to more. And when he finally did, it was with an unrestrained passion that made her feel like she was caught in a storm.

His mouth devoured as if he were starved while his hands grabbed her tightly, pressing her to him with such force it felt like their bodies would meld. All Charlotte could do was hold on. Her fingers gripped the back of his neck and curled into his solid shoulders.

"My God," he murmured as he gave the ribbon securing her cloak a hard tug and pushed the garment away. His jaw scraped her cheek as his lips sought her neck, the unshaven stubble causing a series of tremors to dart through her body. "I could feast on ye like this forever."

She smiled with contentment and arched up against him. "I wouldn't mind that one bit."

A guttural sound left his throat as he leaned in to nuzzle the spot where her neck met her shoulder. "Charlotte, luv. Ye'll be my undoing."

"I think that's only fair since I'm already quite undone by you."

His fingers, which had begun tracing the edge of her neckline, stilled. Charlotte's heart hammered wildly against her breast while Blayne's hot breath swept over her skin. "What are ye saying?"

Fighting for courage, she speared her fingers through his hair and nudged him back slightly so their eyes could meet. Slowly, she brought her other hand up to cup his cheek, her thumb gently stroking along the edge of his jawline.

He turned his head slightly and pressed a soft kiss to her palm, the yearning etched in his features so fierce she had no choice but to say what was in her heart.

"I love you, Blayne."

He took a deep breath and exhaled it. "No."

"No?" Her stomach began to twist while a

sharp pain drove through her soul. She'd not expected him to reciprocate the sentiment, but neither had she thought he'd refute what she felt.

"Ye cannae be in love with me, lass. Yer mind's just a wee bit muddled because of the way I make ye feel when we're together like this. But that's just lust. Nothing more."

Clamping her mouth shut, Charlotte tried to pull air into her lungs as the pain his denial caused collided with anger. "Yes, Blayne. That must be it. I'm just a foolish woman who can't differentiate between love and infatuation."

"Charlotte. I didnae mean to imply ye dinnae feel something for me. It's just that—"

"It can't be love?" When he didn't answer she huffed a frustrated breath. "Don't tell me what I can or cannot feel, Blayne. These are my emotions and when it comes to you, they're so overwhelmingly strong they terrify me half the time. And when they're not doing that, they're making me wish we could somehow be more to each other than this. Whatever *this* even is anymore, because frankly I'm no longer sure. But you must feel something too. I mean, you said I was your woman, which is a pretty possessive statement to make."

A nerve ticked at the edge of his jaw. "I merely said it because I knew all those men would leave ye alone if they thought ye were already spoken for by me."

She shook her head. "You're lying."

"I cannae marry ye, Charlotte," he told her firmly, "so if that's where this conversation is heading, ye need to stop."

"I'm not suggesting we wed." Was she? For years she'd lived with the dream of building a life on her own without a husband and yet, whenever Blayne spoke of his own disinterest in marriage, she wished he would reconsider – that he would suggest she change her goal to one that included him.

She stared at him, at his almost hostile posture and the way he refused to look at her. Disheartened and unsure of what else to say, she bent to retrieve her cloak. Nothing about this evening was turning out as she'd expected. "You're a good man. No matter what you've done in the past, the person I know you to be is kind, helpful, and protective. You've supported me when no one else would, applauded my achievements even though most people would think them scandalous. You accept me for who I am and when I'm with you, I feel strong, safe, and complete."

He closed his eyes against her words as if they pained him. "Charlotte. Ye dinnae ken what ye're saying."

"Stop telling me that." She had a good mind to punch him. If he'd been of a smaller size she would have given him a good shake, but he was too massive compared with her. She'd not even make him budge.

"Charlotte," he whispered. "Ye cannae truly love someone unless ye ken all their flaws and accept them. Those qualities ye just mentioned may be good, but they cannae overshadow the bad. And trust me when I tell ye, ye dinnae want to ken how bad it really is."

She shook her head. "I don't believe you."

Shock registered in his eyes. "What?"

"I don't believe you," she repeated. "I know you, Blayne. You could never do something truly awful. Those men you told me you killed while working with Guthrie threatened your life and the lives of others. You rescued women and children from monsters. You fought to stay alive and while your actions might not have been legal, I still think you did the right thing. In my mind, protecting those who cannot protect themselves is heroic, Blayne. I admire you for it and don't think of it as a blemish upon your soul, because it's not."

"I'm nae speaking of that," he gritted as if it hurt him to talk. "I'm speaking of the life I had before Guthrie."

"Tell me about it."

"I cannae do that. Not ever. Ye just need to trust me on this."

She hated his stubbornness and the rift it was causing between them. Knowing he wouldn't budge, however, she grudgingly accepted defeat and gave a swift nod. They stared back at each other a moment before she asked, "When you went to the publisher about my book, what did they say?"

"I wasnae able to get past the clerk. The man didnae seem inclined to believe my story. He told me that if it were indeed true, I had to return with the author."

"I suppose that does make sense." Charlotte straightened her spine. "Will you escort me there tomorrow afternoon?"

"I probably shouldnae."

Fearing her voice would break if she spoke too quickly, she took a moment to gather her composure. "Please don't end our relationship like this. At least help me finish what we started."

"Very well. If that is what ye wish."

The resignation with which he spoke broke her already fragile heart. Pressing her lips together to stop her tears from falling, Charlotte flung her cloak over her shoulders, secured it with a bow, and pulled the hood up over her head. "Meet me at our designated spot. Four o'clock."

"Allow me to see ye home."

"There's really no need. If you could just—"

"Charlotte. I'm nae letting ye out of my sight until I'm sure ye're safely inside Russell House. Is that clear?"

His curt remark instilled both joy and misery in her bones. He cared, more than he was willing to admit, she'd wager. But what good did it do when he was determined to fight it – to walk away from her without a backward glance?

She tamped down the panic she felt at the thought of them parting ways soon. For now, there was still tomorrow, and she was determined to savor each second the day allowed her to spend in his company.

CHAPTER FOURTEEN

AFTER LAST NIGHT, there was no longer any doubt in Blayne's mind. He had to cut ties with Charlotte before this powerful pull between them led her into additional danger. It was the right thing to do. Especially since he could promise no future.

Sitting across from her in the hackney as they headed over to P. Agerson Publishing on Charring Cross Road in Whitehall, Blayne studied the woman he'd fallen hopelessly in love with. She was wearing a pretty pink dress today with a short sleeved shamrock green spencer. It had intricate pleats down the front and on the sleeves. To finish off the ensemble, she had on a straw bonnet, tied beneath her chin with a voluminous white ribbon.

He would never tell her how he felt. To do so would only cause her additional pain when he finally pushed her away for good. At least if she didn't believe his feelings matched hers, it might be easier for her to walk away without looking back.

Clenching his jaw, he struggled to calm his

breaths and steady his thundering heart. Never in his life had he wanted something as badly as he wanted her. It crushed him to keep all that bottled up inside, to not fall on his knees and pledge himself to her forever.

Giving his attention to the window, he forced himself to do what he always tried to avoid, which was to think back on the terrible crime he'd committed. His mother's wide eyes filled with fear and his father's large hands at her throat. His own useless attempt to pull his father away. The candelabra. An innate need to stop what was happening.

"What have ye done, lad?" His uncle's outrage filled the bedchamber. Blood stained the floor. "Christ have mercy, I think he's dead."

Wincing with pure disgust, Blayne blocked out the rest once more. It hadn't just been the murder charges he'd tried to escape, it had also been his uncle. The control that man would have had over Blayne after what he'd witnessed would have been intolerable.

"Mr. MacNeil?" Charlotte's voice was as blunt as it had been when she'd greeted him earlier. "We've arrived. Perhaps you can step down and help me alight?"

Bristling, he did as she asked without complaint. He knew she was punishing him out of pain and anger – that what she most likely needed was a good fight. Maybe later, when they were back in the carriage again with only Daisy to witness what would without doubt be an ugly display, he'd allow it. But for now, he had to make sure they both behaved with decorum. Especially if they were to accomplish what they'd come for.

Without saying a word, he climbed from the hackney and turned to offer his hand. She took it, then slowly met his gaze. Blayne's heart stumbled. Gone was the carefully schooled indifference she'd put on display thus far. In its place was the sort of turbulent anguish he wished he could turn away from. Her eyes glistened and for a brief moment Blayne feared she might cry, because he had no idea how he would deal with that.

But then, as if donning a thick piece of armor, she set her jaw and hardened her features, banking every emotion she'd just revealed.

"Thank you," she said as she stepped down onto the pavement.

Unable to resist, Blayne tightened his hold on her fingers before he released them. With emptiness and regret swooping in to replace the warmth of her touch, he turned away so he could offer assistance to Daisy as well.

They entered the building, which was far more spacious and impressive than the one occupied by Avery Carlisle. The same clerk Blayne had met before sat behind a desk near the front of the room. He peered at them from behind the spectacles perched on the bridge of his nose. His gaze zeroed in on Blayne. "I see you've returned."

"This time with the author I mentioned."

"Indeed." The clerk did not look or sound the least bit convinced.

Charlotte stepped forward. "If I may, I would like to speak with Mr. Agerson. It's in regard to the latest Cunningham novel."

"I see."

"If ye'll recall," Blayne said, "I mentioned it being published by an imposter."

"Hmm…" The clerk tilted his head and seemed to study Charlotte for a moment. "Perhaps if you make an appointment Mr. Finley can accommodate you within a reasonable time frame."

"And who, may I ask, is he?" Charlotte asked.

"One of our sales assistants. If he can verify your claim then I'm sure the matter can be reviewed by someone higher up. Eventually."

Charlotte gave the clerk a tight smile. "Mr. Agerson is the man with whom I wish to speak. He is the owner of this business, is he not?"

"Indeed he is, but—"

"In that case, I do believe he's the only one who can help me."

"I see. Well, um…I'm afraid Mr. Agerson has a full schedule today. Perhaps next week." The clerk began flipping through what looked to be an appointment book.

Charlotte frowned, her aggravation so clear it looked like smoke might start rising from the top of her head unless someone did something to calm her. Blayne stepped a bit closer to her and placed the palm of his hand against her back. She tried to shake him off and eventually gave him a glare when that didn't work.

"Surely you must be able to understand how

distressing it has been for this lady to enter a bookshop and find her stolen manuscript printed, bound, and available for sale." As he'd done while keeping company with Charlotte's parents and Mr. Cooper, Blayne abandoned his brogue in favor of the upper crust English he'd learned to speak as a boy, hoping it would earn them a bit more respect. "Aside from the obvious injustice, there's also the lack of revenue to consider. Money she should be receiving is going to a thief instead. And your company is playing a part in that. Now, you can either show us through to Mr. Agerson right this second so we can attempt to resolve the issue, or I can ask my solicitor to call on you later today with some papers demanding we meet in court. Now, what's it going to be?"

The clerk blanched. "I. Um. Well." He gulped. "What did you say your names were?"

"We didn't." Blayne stared back at him while doing his damnedest to affect aristocratic arrogance. "I am Mr....Wright and this is Miss Russell."

"Very good." The clerk nodded and went to knock on a door at the far end of the room.

As soon as he disappeared inside the office, Charlotte rounded on him. "I didn't need for you to step in."

"Really?" He'd thought she would thank him. Instead she seemed keen on confrontation. "And how were ye planning to gain that man's cooperation if I'd said nothing?"

"I would have figured it out eventually," she

told him with a stubborn tilt to her chin.

"He was two seconds away from turning us out, Charlotte, and ye ken it." She said nothing to this. Arms crossed, she just stood there, her eyes fixed on a point in the distance. Blayne sighed. "I'm sorry. I was just trying to help."

"And you did," she mumbled after a long stretch of silence. "My apologies. I should have thanked you, I just… I cannot keep relying on you for help when…"

When you'll soon be gone from my life.

Her unspoken words seemed to shake the floor beneath his feet.

Before he could answer, she added, "It's one thing for you to escort me and make sure I'm safe, but I have to be able to fight my own battles."

"I just wanted to make things easier for ye."

"And so you have, it would seem. I can't say I'm not appreciative since that would be a lie, but it makes me feel weak and dependent, which is something I cannot afford if I'm to survive this."

"Fair enough. I'll try not to interfere further." He couldn't begrudge her for feeling as she did, and he certainly harbored no resentment toward her because of it. If there was any ill will at all, it was directed at himself and the terrible choice he'd once made. Because it now meant he couldn't have her.

Doing his best to forget about that for the moment, he quietly told her, "Ye're the strongest woman I've ever met, Charlotte, and ye can do anything ye set yer mind to."

Her gaze met his with unguarded appreciation. "I wish—"

"Miss Russell," the clerk said, cutting her off,
"and Mr. Wright. This way, if you please."

Charlotte asked Daisy to stay behind and wait
while she and Blayne followed the clerk. In a way
Blayne was glad she'd been interrupted since he
wasn't sure he could take more emotional talk at
the moment. He certainly had no desire to hear
her tell him about her wishes when he wasn't in
a position to make them come true.

"Good morning," Mr. Agerson said when
they were shown into his office. A slim man of
medium height and roughly fifty years of age,
he wore an exhausted look suggestive of the sort
of man who lived for his work. "Mr. Mulberry
tells me you've come here regarding the theft of
a manuscript we've supposedly printed. Please,
do have a seat."

Charlotte lowered herself to a chair upholstered in dark brown leather, after which Blayne
and Mr. Agerson sat as well.

"My manuscript was stolen from Carlisle &
Co. about four weeks ago during a robbery
there," Charlotte explained. "Mr. Wright and I
have since attempted to track down the thief,
only to come up short. Until I walked into a
bookshop last week and found it in print."

"I see," Mr. Agerson said. "And how did you
know it was your book. I mean surely—"

"The title hadn't been changed and neither

had my name."

"Well, I'm not sure what to say really." Mr. Agerson frowned. "Nothing goes to print without me signing off on it. Now, you claim this book of yours was printed by us with your name on it, but I don't see how that's possible when I've not come across the name Russell before."

Charlotte fought the urge to roll her eyes. "Mr. Agerson," she said, drawing on every bit of patience she had in her possession, "When I told you it carried my name, I didn't mean my *actual* name."

"Oh. Of course." Mr. Agerson glanced at Blayne as if hoping he'd jump in and help. When he remained silent, Mr. Agerson gave his attention back to Charlotte and said, "It would be helpful if you could offer more details, like the book's title, for instance, and the actual author name on it. Better yet, if you have a copy of the book in question so I can verify that it was indeed printed by us, perhaps I can be of greater assistance."

Charlotte reached underneath the cloth covering of a small basket she'd brought along. Retrieving the book they'd been discussing, she handed it over to Mr. Agerson. "I hope I can count on your full discretion."

A snort of disbelief left him. His eyes met hers while the book remained suspended between his fingers. "This is the latest Cunningham novel."

"So it is," Charlotte said.

Bewilderment and, to some extent outrage, filled Mr. Agerson's features. "Miss Russell," he said as if fighting the urge to toss her through the nearest window, "are you trying to tell me you're Charles Cunningham?"

"That is exactly what I am telling you, sir. And someone — some charlatan — stole my manuscript from my publisher, brought it to you, and convinced you they were me. Whoever it is, is taking credit for something they didn't write while pocketing funds that are rightfully mine."

Mr. Agerson sighed. He considered Blayne once more. "Can you please explain to me why you believe this woman?"

Charlotte sat up straighter. "Mr. Agerson. Are you implying I—"

She clamped her mouth shut when he sent her a stern look. When she kept quiet, he shifted his attention back to Blayne. "Please proceed."

"I was there when she found out her publisher, Carlisle & Co, had been robbed, as well as when she spotted her book at Lee & Jones."

"The bookshop on Borough High Street?"

"Precisely." Blayne made a small move with his hand as if meaning to reach for hers, only to let it fall back in his lap. "She was most distressed."

"As she should be, if she is who she claims to be."

"Mr. Agerson," Charlotte exclaimed. "I would not lie about such a thing."

"Perhaps not, Miss Russell, but since I have only just met you, I have no way in which to be certain of that. What I do know," he added, raising a finger to halt her interruption, "is that

I've a client – a man – who introduced himself as Mr. Charles Cunningham and presented me with a manuscript carrying that name. Now, having read it, I must confess I struggle to believe a woman could have penned such a book, but since I don't wish to have any part in stealing from anyone, I shall do my best to resolve this matter."

Charlotte blew out a deep breath of gratitude. "Thank you, Mr. Agerson. Please tell me how you intend to proceed."

"Well, for starters, we need to figure out who's telling the truth. Or at least I do. Therefore, I propose a meeting between all parties involved. If you have an address at which I can reach you, I will let you know when such a meeting has been arranged."

"But…" Charlotte forced a smile even though it was a struggle. "Surely we can determine a time now and simply inform the other person of when to show up?"

"I'm afraid Mr. Cunningham—"

"The charlatan," Charlotte supplied.

"Must be treated with respect until I know more," Mr. Agerson finished with a pointed look at Charlotte. "The best I can do is send a letter requesting he join us for a meeting at his convenience."

"Or," Blayne said, speaking up for the first time in a while, "you could give us his address so we can pay him a visit ourselves."

"Absolutely not," Mr. Agerson said. "I would never hand out information about a client."

"Not even a counterfeit one?"

"He is only a fraud according to you." Mr. Agerson scowled. "Forgive me, but I have never met either of you before today. You've offered no substantial proof to back up your accusation, so the only reason I am even willing to investigate your claim is because I would hate to make a mistake – to not have acted with prudence when I had the chance to do so.

"But do not suppose for one minute that I trust either of you any more than I do the man who brought me a manuscript he claims he wrote. So if you want my help resolving this issue which, I will remind you, wasn't an issue until you showed up, then we shall do so on my terms or not at all. Is that clear?"

Knowing this was the best she would get, Charlotte gave a curt nod. "Perfectly so, Mr. Agerson. And in terms of proof, I can bring along the notes I made in preparation for writing the book, when next we meet." She ought to have done so today, but she'd been so distraught after last night's altercation at The Black Swan, she'd not managed to use a clear head.

"An excellent idea," Mr. Agerson said. "Now if you will please give me an address where you may be reached."

Charlotte promptly gave her address which he wrote down. "Thank you for your time, sir. I am extremely glad you agreed to meet with me."

"Of course, Miss Russell." His features eased a fraction as he stood to say farewell. "I will be in touch with you soon."

"Well," Charlotte said once she and Blayne were back in the carriage with Daisy. "That didn't exactly go as well as I'd hoped, but I suppose it could have gone a lot worse."

"Ye handled yerself perfectly in there," Blayne said. "I'm proud of ye, Miss Russell. Most women in yer position would have had a fit of hysterics."

Heat filled Charlotte's cheeks. "Thank you, Mr. MacNeil. Staying calm wasn't easy, but Mr. Agerson had a fair point. He doesn't have any reason to trust us over the man who gave himself out to be me."

"True. But we have no reason to trust Mr. Agerson either."

"Perhaps not, but we've little other choice."

Blayne didn't look pleased. "Doesnae mean I have to like it."

Charlotte chuckled. There was something so charming about him when he was eager to help but didn't know how. She loved him all the more for it – for caring even though he insisted he didn't. They were heading toward the intersection on Oxford Street where he would be dropped off before she continued onward to her home. While their outing had gone well, it wasn't enough. She wanted more – more time with him – another chance to find a way toward a shared future.

Recalling how adamant he'd been about cutting ties with her when they'd spoken last night, she opened the window and called out, "Driver, we'd like to change course, please. Take us to

Parker's Lane instead."

"Aye, miss," the driver noted.

"What are ye doing?" Blayne asked when she leaned back inside the carriage and shut the window. He shot a slightly panicked look at Daisy before meeting Charlotte's gaze. "Ye cannae be meaning to come back to The Black Swan with me."

"That is precisely what I mean to do," Charlotte told him firmly. "You and I need to talk."

"I thought we did enough of that last night," he grumbled.

"You certainly made every effort to push me away."

"For good reason. Charlotte..." He glanced at Daisy once more and cleared his throat. Exasperation puckered his brow as he blew out a breath. "Miss Russell. I hold ye in the highest regard, but ye and I are from two different worlds and—"

"You said I didn't know all there was to know about you. You told me you were worse than I could possibly imagine – that you've done something so terrible it would prevent me from loving you if I knew." She stared at him, her heart pounding for the man she wanted and the possibilities he threatened to throw away for reasons she didn't understand. "So tell me. Tell me what it is and let me choose for myself."

He crossed his arms and averted his gaze. A muscle ticked at the edge of his jaw. "Have ye no respect for my privacy?"

"Not when it concerns my future and the one

chance I have of being truly happy."

Closing his eyes, he expelled a breath through his nose. When he spoke again, his voice was soft and even. "Before ye met me, ye believed happiness hinged on a cottage somewhere in the countryside, in a place where ye could build a retreat for like-minded women. If I recall, ye said this had been yer dream for years. It's why ye saved every penny ye earned on yer books, and yet now, within the span of a few weeks, ye wish to abandon yer plans in order to what? Marry me and live happily ever after somewhere? Well it's nae going to happen. I willnae marry, ye, Miss Russell."

"So you've said," she snapped and crossed her arms.

"And yet ye've gotten it into yer head that ye're able to change my mind. Is that it?"

"I just don't see why you won't consider a more permanent attachment to me."

"Because," he said, leaning forward with flint in his eyes, "I dinnae love ye."

Daisy gasped and Charlotte instinctively placed a steadying hand on her arm for fear she might interfere. The words cut deep, of course they did, though not nearly as much as his decision to make her believe she was nothing more to him than a bit of fun he could simply move on from.

Straightening her spine, she narrowed her gaze. "You're lying to me again."

Anger and something else – something wrought with pain and fear – flashed in his eyes. "Nae," he said, his voice a harsh murmur, "I'd never do that."

"Tell me what you're hiding," Charlotte insisted. "Tell me what it is you don't want me to know."

The carriage drew to a halt. They'd arrived and she hadn't learned one additional thing.

As if he couldn't wait to quit her company, Blayne flung the carriage door open and leapt out. Turning, he told her fiercely, "Ye go too far, Miss Russell. Further than I am willing to allow. If ye still require a man's protection when ye're out and about, I'll see to it that ye get it. But it willnae be from me. Ye and I are done."

The door slammed shut in Charlotte's face, prompting her to jump. She glared at it for a good long minute before she made up her mind. "I can't let him do this. I won't."

"Miss?"

"Daisy," Charlotte told her maid firmly. "Do me a favor and don't fall in love."

"What?"

"It makes you do foolish things." She opened the door and stepped down. "Please excuse me while I go after that bull-headed man."

"Miss Russell. Should I—"

Charlotte didn't listen. She was too vexed and far too determined to let anyone or anything stand in her way anymore. Whatever it was Blayne had done, she'd forgive him. Why on earth could he not see that?

Well, she meant to make him see. She meant to prove to him that her love trumped all. Good lord, she would lay down her life for that man, live in sin with him if that was all he'd allow. The only existence she couldn't accept was one in which they lived apart. Knowing he was out there, unwilling even to try, was what would slowly kill her.

So she entered The Black Swan and ignored those who glanced her way. Instead, she kept her gaze firmly trained on the far end of the tavern as she marched forward.

"Miss Russell," she heard Claus call. "You shouldn't be here."

Charlotte ignored him. She just kept going until she reached the door to Blayne's office. Without knocking, she pushed it open and instantly spotted Blayne. He was standing by the sideboard to her left, pouring a drink. His eyes widened the moment he saw her, and then his lips parted as if he meant to say something.

Whatever it was, it would have to wait. She was tired of fighting, of trying to climb the wall he'd erected between them. It was time to just knock it down.

"Charlotte," he said, turning toward her and shifting his gaze to a spot behind her right shoulder while she closed the distance between them. "You should—"

She flung her arms around his neck, rose up onto her toes, and pressed her mouth to his in a kiss so fierce it seared her own lips. It didn't matter if he only stood there. She didn't care if he didn't immediately wind his arms around her and kiss her back. All that mattered was what she was saying with her caress. It was a simple declaration – one which words would only complicate.

This way, through this kiss, he would know. There could be no doubt left in his mind. He was hers and she was his. They belonged to each other and—

Someone cleared their throat. Not her and not Blayne.

Charlotte went utterly still, and then Blayne was easing her back, setting her carefully on her feet. Instead of desire, torment filled his eyes. "I'm so sorry. Ye shouldnae have followed me, lass. I…"

"Miss Russell?" a masculine voice inquired.

Charlotte turned, searching for the man to whom it belonged. Slim, with thinning blonde hair, piercing blue eyes, and a curiousness about him that put her on edge, he'd just risen from one of the armchairs located to the right of the door, so she'd not noticed him when she'd entered the office. Her mind had been fixed on solely one goal. She'd not bothered to check the room's occupancy and besides that, it hadn't occurred to her Blayne wouldn't be alone when he'd only left her outside a few minutes prior.

Pasting a smile on her face, she considered denying her true identity, then changed her mind since the man clearly knew who she was. So she straightened her spine and gave a quick nod instead. "Yes. And you are?"

He took a step forward and gave her a short bow. "Mr. Edmund Hallibrand, from the *Mayfair Chronicle*."

Dear God.

It took every ounce of control Charlotte possessed for her to stay calm, to not panic, to simply stand there and pretend all would be well. "I see."

"Mr. Hallibrand came to ask a few questions of me," Blayne said. He crossed to the man and handed him the glass of brandy he'd been pouring when Charlotte arrived. Glancing at her, he asked, "Would ye like one too?"

"Yes. Yes, please." She needed all the fortification she could get. How was Blayne able to look so calm? Well, perhaps not calm. Heavens, he looked more resigned than anything else. Good lord. What had she done?

"I couldn't help overhearing your father a few days ago when he conversed with friends during luncheon at Mivart's. According to him, your engagement to the American businessman, Mr. Cooper, was imminent. Then this morning, the Earl of Dervaine's butler stopped by my office to place an announcement in the paper. Apparently Mr. Cooper will be marrying Dervaine's youngest daughter, Lady Fiona. To be frank, I actually thought you were forming an attachment with Mr. MacNeil after spotting the two of you together around Town." Amusement flickered in Mr. Hallibrand's eyes. "I'm guessing your parents didn't approve and attempted to foist you off on Mr. Cooper instead. Figured I'd start looking into it in case there might be a story. That's why I'm here."

A shiver raked Charlotte's spine. She couldn't

believe he'd seen her in Blayne's company or that the manner in which they'd interacted had prompted the journalist to suspect a budding romance between them. How careless of her.

"Apparently, Mr. Cooper changed his mind with regard to marrying me," Charlotte told Mr. Hallibrand stiffly. "He was my father's choice. Our marriage was to be a practical arrangement intended to see me comfortably settled. But then Mr. Cooper found a better option and as a businessman, he chose to take it. There's not really much more to say, I'm afraid."

"Judging from the manner in which you just greeted Mr. MacNeil, I have to disagree." Mr. Hallibrand sipped his drink, his assessing gaze never straying from Charlotte's face. Her stomach churned and her heart felt as though it was being squeezed by a vice. "Now, I'm not a gossip columnist, but that doesn't mean I'm about to pass up the chance to write a compelling piece. In fact, I think your situation could serve as an excellent example for change. These marriages of convenience prohibiting people from different classes from following their hearts are unsustainable. With more and more people coming from low income backgrounds and prospering through trade, I predict the lines will blur with higher frequency in the future."

"Perhaps," Charlotte agreed, "as long as each party's financial situation is similar. But I doubt an aristocrat's daughter will ever marry a chimney sweep, Mr. Hallibrand."

"Be that as it may, Mr. MacNeil is hardly a

chimney sweep. Is he?" A smirk pulled at Mr. Hallibrand's lips. "I wonder. Do you know Mr. Cooper was raised in the slums of New York? His father was an Irish factory worker, his mother a Polish cleaning woman at a Manhattan hospital. The pair barely had enough funds to afford a small room to let, never mind enough to give their son an education. Which does make his accomplishments admirable, as long as one turns a blind eye to the questionable men who helped him get where he is today."

"How do you know all of this?" Charlotte asked. She couldn't believe this stranger was able to provide such information when her own father had failed to uncover it. Perhaps he'd just been too blinded by Mr. Cooper's wealth to consider his background. Or maybe he hadn't cared, which would make his firm dismissal of Blayne incredibly hypocritical.

"I'm a journalist, Miss Russell. I follow the news with the same dedication a gambler follows the races."

Speaking of journalism...

"I hope you don't mean to reveal my presence here this evening, Mr. Hallibrand."

"Forgive me, Miss Russell, but that is like asking a hungry dog to ignore a fresh morsel of roast beef."

A chill rushed through Charlotte's veins. "Please. You can't do this to us. You—"

"It's all right," Blayne said as his arm came around her midsection. He pulled her firmly against him and kissed the top of her head. "It's nae the announcement we'd hoped for, but if Mr. Hallibrand is determined...well then, we cannae stand in his way."

"What are you—" Charlotte began, only to be interrupted as Hallibrand asked, "What announcement would that be, Mr. MacNeil?"

"Being the clever journalist ye are, I'm surprised ye've nae figured it out," Blayne said. "Ye see, the real reason Mr. Cooper cannae marry Miss Russell, is because she promised herself to me before his arrival."

CHAPTER FIFTEEN

THE TENSION IN Charlotte's shoulders could not be ignored. Even though it was her fault he now had no choice but to do the honorable thing, she clearly wasn't pleased with how the situation had come about. Neither was he, but he was man enough to accept what was done and to face the repercussions.

Christ have mercy.

"So you never had an agreement with Mr. Cooper?" Mr. Hallibrand asked Charlotte with wide-eyed dismay. "In spite of your father's insistence to the contrary?"

Blayne squeezed her gently until she shook her head. "No."

"Incredible." Mr. Hallibrand downed the rest of his brandy and set the glass aside. "This is precisely the sort of thing that needs to end, these attempts at forced unions that—"

"Very good," Blayne cut in. "Now if ye dinnae mind, I'd like some time alone with my fiancée. If there's anything else, ye're welcome to drop by again tomorrow."

"Yes. Of course. I'll see myself out."

"Oh, and Mr. Hallibrand?" Blayne added, halting the man in mid-stride. "I'd like to read yer story before it goes to print."

"That's not how this works, I'm afraid," Mr. Hallibrand said.

"It is how it will work on this one occasion," Blayne told him with a deliberate edge to his words. "I'll nae have Miss Russell slandered. Is that understood?"

Mr. Hallibrand swallowed as Blayne's meaning sank in. "Of course. I'll be fair and discreet. And I'll let you see it before I show it to anyone else."

"Very good," Blayne said.

Mr. Hallibrand responded with a curt nod, and then he was gone.

Blayne blew out a breath, released his hold on Charlotte, and scrubbed his hand across his jaw. "Bloody hell."

Charlotte stared at the door through which Mr. Hallibrand had departed. As if recalling the glass of brandy he'd given her earlier, she raised it to her lips and downed the contents. She wheezed slightly, then seemed to recover. "Blayne...I...God, I'm so sorry."

"Aye, lass. Me too. Ye dinnae deserve to be saddled with me, but I didnae ken what else to say in the moment." It was the truth. Either she was to be his wife or Mr. Hallibrand would presume she was his mistress, which would be just as bad as calling her his whore.

"You have nothing to apologize for." She stared at him as if in amazement, then set the glass aside. "I came in here, intent on proving my love, and instead I trapped you in the exact situation you told me you wished to avoid. It was stupidly impulsive of me and not at all how I wanted things to turn out. I just thought if you understood how deep my feelings for you truly are, you would know there is nothing you could tell me to make me walk away. But I was a fool. I didn't see Mr. Hallibrand when I arrived and I didn't pause long enough to give you a chance to explain. And now you have sacrificed your own freedom for me. Blayne, listen, we can find a way out of this, surely."

"Not without making things worse."

"But—"

"Mr. Hallibrand will write about what he saw here today. All I can do without issuing threats, which I am nae prepared to attempt when the man is simply doing his job, is to ensure his honesty — that there's nae disparaging language or wording deliberately meant to encourage outrage or create a scandal."

"A scandal will be unavoidable if he mentions me being here, the fact that I came unchaperoned, and that I kissed you as if we'd been married for years and you'd just returned from war." She pinched the bridge of her nose. "There has to be a way out of this mess."

Blayne studied her for a moment. The anguish in her features was so palpable it made his heart hurt. "I dinnae believe there is, lass. At least not one in which ye and yer family willnae suffer ramifications."

Her eyes glistened with unshed tears. "You do not want to marry me."

"Have I ever told ye that?"

She blinked with confusion. "You certainly implied it when you said we could have no future – when you told me you don't want marriage."

"Ye told me the same thing, I believe." Reaching up, he cupped her cheek with his hand and gently brushed his thumb across her soft skin. "There's a big difference between not wanting something and choosing to walk away from it because the person ye care about deserves better. The fact is, I've nae been honest with ye about how I feel."

"So then?"

He was the worst sort of scoundrel – a murderous villain who would one day burn in hell for the crime he'd committed, but until then, he would pledge himself to her, to serve and protect, to love and adore. It was what she wanted, for some unfathomable reason he couldn't quite grasp. And he would make damn sure she would never regret choosing him as her husband.

"I love ye, Charlotte, and nothing would please me more than to wake up beside ye every day for the rest of my life." If he was lucky, the demons he'd feared for so long would quit hounding him so he could be happy as well.

"Are you sure?"

"Aye. I'm sorry I gave ye reason to doubt, luv. I only wanted what was best for ye." He brushed aside her tears, smoothing them lovingly over her cheeks. Leaning in, he kissed her before she could overthink what he'd said, before she insisted he tell her what he might have done that was so very awful. Now that the future had been decided, it was best if she never knew. He'd carry that burden himself, until the day he died.

To his relief, she simply sighed and accepted the kiss he offered. It was sweet, less tempestuous than the previous ones they'd shared – a declaration of the bond they intended to foster.

He brushed his lips over each of her cheeks, then placed a kiss on the tip of her nose before resting his forehead against hers. "I will escort ye home now, Charlotte. It's time for us to speak with yer father."

"Do we have to?"

He chuckled in response to her reluctance. "Aye. We most certainly do. Dinnae lose yer courage now, lass. Ye've faced much greater dangers than Lord Elkins, and ye mustnae forget that I'll be there by yer side."

A little over half an hour later, Blayne and Charlotte entered Lord Elkins's study after being granted entrance. The viscount stood, back straight, chin up, and hands clasped behind him as if prepared to inspect a regiment. All hints of pleasure were so far removed from his features, Blayne would not have thought the man capable of smiling if it weren't for the fact that he'd seen him do so before.

"I believe I made it perfectly clear," Lord Elkins said with a scowl directed at Charlotte. "That man is not welcome here anymore."

"Then neither am I," Charlotte said with such fierce determination Blayne had to bite his cheek in order to stop from grinning. "You see, Mr. MacNeil and I will be getting married."

"The devil you will," Lord Elkins barked. "If you think for one moment I'll let a criminal drag my daughter down into the slum he crawled out of then—"

"You will not speak of him like that in my presence," Charlotte said. She grasped Blayne's hand and held on so tightly he could feel her nails digging into his skin. "Now, if you would please cease being a pompous prig for one moment so I may explain, I think you'll agree there's no longer a choice. Not that I would want it any other way, I should add."

Her father gave Blayne a quick glare, then gestured toward the two chairs facing his from the opposite side of his desk. "Go ahead."

Charlotte expelled a hard breath and accepted the invitation to sit. She waited for Blayne and her father to do the same before saying, "Something has come about. You won't like it but—"

"I already hate it," Lord Elkins grumbled with marked discontentment.

"And that is your prerogative," Charlotte informed him in a manner that made Blayne incredibly proud. "However, the thing is that Mr. MacNeil and I were caught in a rather compromising situation this afternoon by a *Mayfair Chronicle* journalist at The Black Swan."

Her father blanched. "Good God."

"Precisely," Charlotte murmured. "So you

see—"

"What was his name?" Lord Elkins asked.

"I beg your pardon?" Charlotte said.

"The journalist's name," Lord Elkins clarified. "Tell me who he is and I'll meet with him straight away so I can get ahead of this catastrophe. I'm sure he and I can agree on a sum that can—"

"Papa." Charlotte clasped Blayne's hand tighter. "Mr. MacNeil has already done what he could in order to make sure the event this man witnessed will not be related in sordid detail. Now, imagine how much worse it will be if my father attempts to bribe him. Do you honestly believe for one moment he will not print that?"

"Mr. MacNeil has nothing to offer, you daft girl!"

Blayne hadn't meant to speak up until Charlotte was done convincing her father, but he certainly wasn't about to sit there while the man insulted them both. Without bothering to hide his brogue this time, he said, "Yer daughter is the most brilliant woman I know, Lord Elkins. She is courageous, smart, practical, kind, and forgiving, so I'll not let ye call her daft. And as for yer other point about me having nothing to offer, it is true that I dinnae have much, but I've enough to make sure she'll not suffer any hardship. I shall love her with all that I am, sir. Ye have my word on that."

Lord Elkins snorted. "And where do you see yourselves living? In a room above that tavern of yours in one of this city's filthiest and most crime-infested neighborhoods?"

"Of course not. Our intention is to find lodgings for rent in a more agreeable part of town while we work on increasing our savings. In time we'll hopefully manage to purchase a property of our own if we combine our funds." He knew he was making suggestions he'd not had a chance to discuss with Charlotte yet, so he gave her a quick glance to gauge her reaction and was instantly put at ease by the brilliant smile she gave him.

"I think that's an excellent plan," she whispered.

He rather agreed. They both wanted to live somewhere in the countryside, but neither could afford it on their own. Together, however, he was sure they would be able to do so in a few years considering she was as hardworking as he. Yet another benefit of getting married to this remarkable woman, the other one being the days he would spend in her company and the nights they'd enjoy in bed.

"And if I protest?" Lord Elkins asked in a low tone.

Blayne's muscles tightened with sudden swiftness, not because he cared one whit for Lord Elkins's blessing, but because of the hurt he saw in Charlotte's eyes. It infuriated him that anyone should make her feel less deserving than she was, that this man would dare to cause her additional pain when he had to know the situation was already difficult enough as it was.

Before he could say as much however, she

spoke up. "You have the right to withhold your blessing. I certainly cannot prevent you from doing so. But what would be the point, except to show displeasure? I would still have to marry Mr. MacNeil in order to lessen the scandal that's bound to arise when the *Mayfair Chronicle* journalist prints his story. So, if this is the course you wish to take, then understand this: I shall never forgive you for being so hateful and you will never see me again after today, which means you'll have no relationship with the grandchildren I may give you."

Stunned by the length to which she meant to go if her father didn't support their union, Blayne held his tongue and waited to see how the viscount would respond. It was all he could do without undermining her threat.

Instead of addressing his daughter, however, Lord Elkins gave Blayne a stare intended to strip the meat from a man's bones. "This is your doing, you good for nothing cur. I'd like to run you through with my sword until—"

"Right," Charlotte said, her voice clipped. She stood, forcing Blayne and her father out of their seats. "You clearly have no intention of trying to welcome Mr. MacNeil into the family or of wishing us happy."

"You were always my most practical daughter, Charlotte. How the hell could you let this happen?"

She managed a wan smile and said, "It was rather simple really. I fell in love."

Turning away, she started toward the door.

The pull of her hand on Blayne's forced him to follow her out, which he did with a swift, "Good day, sir," directed at Lord Elkins.

"I need to gather some things," Charlotte said when they returned to the foyer. Her voice shook.

"Are ye sure this is how ye wish to proceed, lass?"

She gave a tight nod. "If Papa can't accept you or give his support, then I don't see how he and I can ever hope to have a cordial relationship again."

"Ye're hurting, Charlotte, and that's normal, but cutting ties with yer family is—"

"Not with my family, Blayne, just with him."

"Nevertheless. Once ye step over that threshold it's hard to come back."

"I know, which is why it's so bloody hard, but I cannot love you as much as I do and also accept his lack of approval. Blayne, he tried to sell me to Mr. Cooper and now he's withholding his blessing out of spite. What sort of man does that to his daughter?"

"I suppose ye do have a point."

"Yes, I rather believe I do."

Ignoring the butler who'd arrived while they'd been speaking, Blayne wrapped one arm around Charlotte's waist, pulled her flush up against him, and gave her a thorough kiss. "Do ye ken how terrifying ye can be when ye're angry?"

She kissed him back. "Not enough to frighten you away, I hope."

"Never," he murmured, and kissed her again

before adding respectable distance once more. "I'm going to have Guthrie send one of his carriages over along with a couple of footmen to help."

"That really isn't—"

He silenced her with a finger to her lips. "Ye'll nae leave here by hackney, Charlotte. From now on, we do things properly, which means ye'll be visiting with the Windhams until ye and I are properly wed."

"But they've no idea I'll be coming, Blayne. We cannot impose on them like this. I'm really not comfortable with it."

"Would ye rather stay here?"

"No. I would rather go back to The Black Swan with you."

"And so ye shall. As Mrs. MacNeil. Not a moment sooner." When she frowned, he told her, "Ye've nae need to worry. Regina's a lovely lass."

"I know. I've met her on a few occasions."

"And Guthrie's not so bad himself. The important thing is they'll welcome ye with open arms. Of that I can assure ye."

Blayne wasn't wrong. When Charlotte arrived at Windham house later that day, Regina met her with a warm smile.

"Your Grace," Charlotte said once she'd handed over her outerwear garments, and she had been shown into the parlor. "Thank you so much for allowing me to visit on such short notice. I'm terribly grateful."

"I appreciate the company," the duchess told her. She gestured for Charlotte to take a seat on a sofa in front of a low table where a tea service stood at the ready. "And really, you must call me Regina. You and I have known each other long enough to allow for such informality, especially if you and Blayne are to be married. He's practically family, so it would be odd for me to be on familiar terms with him and not with you. As long as you do not mind, of course."

"No," Charlotte said with a laugh of relief, "I do not mind at all. I'd be happy for you to call me Charlotte."

"Excellent." Regina proceeded to pour two cups of steaming hot tea.

"From what I gather, I owe you a debt of gratitude for finding another suitable bride for Mr. Cooper."

Regina handed Charlotte her cup. "Think nothing of it. Lady Fiona was getting desperate and as an earl's daughter, she does make an agreeable option for an untitled foreigner."

"I hope she and Mr. Cooper will be happy together."

"I'm sure their expectations shall be met." Regina smiled. "You've chosen well for yourself, you know. Of course there will be those who won't understand what a gentlewoman can possibly see in a St. Giles ruffian, just like they still cannot fathom how an earl's daughter could marry a crime lord, even though he may now be a duke. Such people are fools, of course. They only see what's on the surface while subscribing to what the papers and gossips tell them. For as with my husband, a heart of gold beats beneath Blayne's coarse exterior, and although he may have the sort of dark past the law would protest, he is honorable and noble in a way few people are."

"I understand he helped save you from a terrible danger once?" Charlotte took a sip of her tea. "Forgive me if I'm being too forward by bringing it up, it is only that Blayne hasn't told me much about the life he led before. When he and your husband worked together, that is."

"It's quite all right. You may ask me anything you like. If there is ever a question I do not wish to answer, I will let you know." Regina leaned back in her chair. "Are you aware of how Carlton and I met?"

"I've heard you ran away from an unwanted marriage and ended up living with him at The Black Swan for a while."

"Yes, that is true. My behavior was rather scandalous, I'm afraid. Some ladies still cross the street when they see me coming in order to avoid having to greet me."

"How dreadful."

"Is it really?" Regina chuckled. "Such women are poor company to begin with, and I am better off without having to waste precious minutes conversing with them about the weather. Instead, I consider myself immensely fortunate to be the wife of a man who is principled, though I must confess I would like to see him wear a superfine coat for a change instead of the velvet he always favors. But that is an inconsequential detail and I am getting away from your question. You see, there are some terrible people in the world, and I was unfortunate enough to meet some of them during my time in St. Giles. I was kidnapped together with several other women, girls even, as young as eight."

"Dear God, that's awful." A chill raked Charlotte's spine. "What did you do?"

"I was trapped. Restrained. There wasn't much I could do, besides pray for Carlton to find me before it was too late."

"Too late?"

"We were to be auctioned off to men so awful not even your worst kind of nightmare would manage to conjure such evil creatures." Regina's eyes dimmed, losing some of their brightness as she related the horrid ordeal. "Luckily Carlton and Blayne came to find us with the rest of the crew. They rescued us. I've no regret about the men they killed in the process."

"No," Charlotte murmured. "Of course not. I'm glad those men weren't just arrested and forced to face trial."

"Actually, several of them did, including the man who kidnapped me since I prevented Carlton from killing him." When Charlotte frowned, Regina explained. "Things had calmed down. The fighting had ceased and those involved had been apprehended, so that man's death would have been outright murder at that point. I just couldn't allow Carlton to risk his soul like that."

"I understand."

"My husband still doesn't," Regina said. "He maintains that I should have let him mete out his own kind of justice. I disagree. So the subject remains one of contention between us."

"And the villains?" Charlotte quietly asked.

"Oh. They were all hanged by their necks outside the Old Bailey a few days later."

Expelling a sigh of relief, Charlotte sank back against her seat and drank some tea. As gory as the account might have been, it didn't put her off at all. Instead, it made her wish Blayne was there so she could hug him and kiss him for selflessly risking his life in order to save the innocent.

"Forgive me if this next question may sound a bit foolish," Charlotte said, "but what exactly should I call your husband? I mean, you refer to him as Carlton, but I know that's not his real name, so I'm not quite sure which to use."

Regina chuckled. "It's not easy, I'll grant you. Even I had trouble figuring that out for a while but in the end we decided that Carlton Guthrie, while assumed, is the name he's become accustomed to after using it most of his life. He only ever uses Valentine Sterling, Duke of Windham, when he's out among his fellow peers or introducing himself to someone for the first time. But here in this house he is either Carlton or Guthrie. He won't mind which part of the name you choose to refer to him by."

"I think I shall call him Guthrie, then," Charlotte said. "According to what you have told me, I do believe I'll like him a great deal."

Regina offered Charlotte a biscuit. "I think

you will find that the men who once ruled St. Giles are the most likeable ones in existence."

After enjoying a late luncheon with Regina, Charlotte took her time settling in, reflecting on her current situation, and penning a letter to her mother. Her only regret was the rift she had with her father. She wished he'd been more understanding, more supportive, and simply more able to ignore the social strictures for once. Of course, she realized it was a lot to ask, but she was his daughter for heaven's sake. She did not need to have children of her own yet to know she would do anything in the world to secure their happiness.

Folding the letter she'd written, she set it aside and after enjoying a lovely bath, dressed for dinner. Daisy, who'd accompanied her to Windham House, helped. Charlotte knew she would soon have to make new arrangements for the loyal servant since she wasn't sure she would be able to keep on paying her salary. At least not if she and Blayne were to put every penny they owned toward the countryside home they wanted.

Deciding to mull over the matter at greater length before making a decision, Charlotte thanked Daisy for her assistance and went to meet her hosts in the parlor. She entered the room and sucked in a breath when she spotted Blayne. He sat on the sofa across from Regina and Guthrie, while a third gentleman Charlotte had not yet met occupied an armchair.

Blayne's eyes shifted toward her, brightening

the moment their gazes met. A smile touched his lips as he quickly stood and came toward her.

"Ach, luv," he murmured, not breaking his stride until they were so close she'd be in his arms if she took a step forward. "Ye look bonnie this evening."

Bowing his head, he placed a kiss against her cheek, so achingly tender and slow it burned its way under her skin. Fearing her legs might buckle, she instinctively grabbed his arm.

"Steady now." His low chuckle rumbled through her, stirring to life every yearning she'd pushed aside while dealing with more practical matters. "Yer swooning will have to wait until later when we're alone."

"Devilish scoundrel," she muttered under her breath while mortification heated her cheeks.

"Aye. I cannae deny what I am," Blayne whispered against her ear while steering her toward the rest of the group. "And I must confess I look forward to showing ye just how devilish I can be once we're married. But first," he added, raising his voice while Charlotte did her best not to go up in flames, "I must introduce ye to Regina's brother, Mr. Marcus Berkly. From what I gather, the two of ye havenae yet met."

Mr. Berkly gave a short bow. "It is a pleasure to make your acquaintance, Miss Russell."

"Likewise, Mr. Berkly."

"Do call me Marcus. Everyone else here does and once you marry that hulking Scotsman by your side, we'll practically be related. Isn't that so, Guthrie?"

"Indeed," Guthrie said. "No other man has ever been more like a brother to me than Blayne. I am immensely pleased to see him get settled and very happy to welcome you to our family, Charlotte."

Warmth spread through Charlotte's veins on account of the welcome she was receiving. Foregoing titles in favor of given names lent an intimate closeness she'd never experienced with her own family. It undid her in a way, filling her with endless amounts of gratitude for these people who'd gone to remarkable lengths for her when her own parents hadn't been willing to act.

"Thank you," she said. "For everything. Your hospitality and generosity are without compare."

Much to Charlotte's relief, Guthrie seemed to appreciate the compliment. He was a strange sort of man – the kind she could never quite read. His gaze often scrutinized while his expression refused to give away even the tiniest hint of what he was thinking. It put her slightly on edge, so she was glad Blayne was there to help ease her nerves.

"Tell me, Charlotte," Marcus said once dinner had been announced and they'd taken their seats at the dining room table. "I do hope you don't mind me calling you Charlotte. If I recall, you never gave me leave to do so."

"It's quite all right," she said. "And expected if I am to use your given name."

"Nevertheless, a gentleman ought to ask for permission." Marcus smiled. "What I was going to ask is whether you've settled on a date for the wedding?"

"Oh. Um…" Charlotte hadn't even spared it one thought yet. She glanced at Blayne, seeking guidance.

"Charlotte and I havenae had a chance to discuss any dates yet," Blayne said. "But since our attachment will soon be described in the papers, I think it best to act with haste, which is why I spent several hours today securing a special license."

He placed his hand over Charlotte's, adding strength and warmth. Her heart fluttered in response, not only because of his touch but because of his words and what they implied. "We could marry tomorrow if we wish?"

"Aye. Provided we're able to find a vicar who's free to perform the service."

"That won't be a problem," Guthrie said. "Just leave it to me."

"Would tomorrow be too soon?" Charlotte asked Blayne while trying to block out everyone else. After all the resistance they'd faced so far, she wanted to seal their union as quickly as possible, before her father came up with some other plan to prevent it.

"Not for me, lass. I'd wed ye right now, if I could. My only regret would be denying ye the grand Society wedding ye deserve."

"You must know I don't care about that. The only thing of any importance to me is becoming your wife. As quickly as possible."

Blayne smiled and told Marcus. "It seems we've settled on tomorrow."

"Oh, how exciting," Regina said. "I will speak with Cook immediately after dinner so we can arrange a wedding breakfast for you along with a cake."

The butler, a brawny looking fellow whose jacket stretched a bit too tightly across his chest, entered. "Forgive the interruption, but your parents are here to see you, Miss Russell. I've shown then into the parlor."

Unease latched hold of Charlotte's ribs and squeezed her chest. She did not wish to see either of them right now, least of all her father. Why were they here, anyway? The only explanation she could think of was that they wanted to try and convince her to come home.

Squaring her shoulders, she thanked the butler and told him she would be there shortly. She would not return home or give up on Blayne. If it was a scandal they feared, she would assure them the wedding would be a small affair and that she would quietly slip from Society without any fuss.

"Allow me to come with ye," Blayne said, rising along with the rest of the men as soon as she stood. "I willnae interfere. I'll just offer support."

Charlotte appreciated the offer. He was her strength – the rock she knew she could lean on. She was glad he would be there to help her through this, so she took the arm he offered, made her excuses to everyone else, and allowed him to lead her into the parlor where her parents waited.

CHAPTER SIXTEEN

SCHOOLING HIS FEATURES to the best of his ability, Blayne waited for Charlotte to greet her parents, then spoke a succinct, "Good evening," himself.

It wouldn't do to appear hostile, no matter how much he wanted to toss Lord Elkins out for all the grief he'd caused his daughter. Charlotte didn't deserve the ill-treatment, and for Lady Elkins to try and pretend he was acting in her best interest was pure hogwash at this point.

"Why are you here?" Charlotte asked in the sort of detached tone that would have shattered Blayne if she'd been speaking to him.

"Your father told me what happened," Lady Elkins said. Her face was contorted in what looked like genuine pain. "We've come to see if amends are possible."

Blayne caught a momentary hint of remorse in Charlotte's eyes before she banked the emotion once more. Jaw tight, she said, "Papa made himself perfectly clear when he denied us his blessing."

"He was in shock," Lady Elkins said. She

swung back to face her husband, addressing him with surprising sternness. "Well, say something, will you?"

Lord Elkins gave his wife a hesitant look before expelling a deep breath. "I hope you can both accept my sincere apology for the manner in which I behaved. While I cannot pretend to be overjoyed by—"

"Edmund," his wife hissed.

Lord Elkins cleared his throat. "I believe I may have spoken too hastily this afternoon. If you would be so kind as to stop by my home tomorrow, Mr. MacNeil, we can see to the marriage settlement while Charlotte takes tea with her mother."

"I thought you said my dowry was gone," Charlotte said. "In which case I see no point in a settlement."

"While I cannot spare much," Lord Elkins said with embarrassment hanging off every word, "the funds I received from Mr. Cooper will enable me to bestow a small sum upon you. About two hundred pounds, which will be transferred to you upon your marriage to Mr. MacNeil."

"We'd like to help plan a wedding," Lady Elkins added.

"Thank you." Charlotte's posture and voice remained stiff. "I appreciate the offer but Blayne and I intend to marry tomorrow by special license. You may attend, if you wish."

"But what about your trousseau?"

"I am sure I can manage with the same things

I have gotten by with until now."

"Do you not want a wedding gown, Charlotte? We could order one from La Belle Anglaise. For a reasonable sum," Lady Elkins added when her husband winced.

"That really isn't necessary, Mama."

"And of course," Lady Elkins said, "there is the added benefit of diminishing talk by not rushing into matrimony."

"She does have a point," Blayne murmured. Initially, he'd wanted to get the whole business over and done with quickly before Mr. Halli-brand's story went to print. But as long as he and Charlotte were officially engaged and her parents showed their support of the match, the kiss the journalist had witnessed wouldn't be overly scandalous. In fact, a hasty wedding would only make people wonder if they might have done something more than just kiss.

By allowing more time, he would also have a better sense of whether or not the life he hoped for would be possible. A few additional weeks would give his uncle plenty of time to hear of his nephew's reappearance and for Blayne to learn if the man would leave him in peace.

His heart gave a hard thump. He'd no idea what he would do if the bastard suddenly showed. Or rather, he didn't want to accept what he'd have to do since that would mean giving up Char-lotte. Torn between the desire to bind her to him forever as soon as possible and taking the time required to assess the danger he might be placing her in if they married, he simply stood there, attempting to breathe.

There was a different kind of danger if they didn't marry of course – one in which her reputation could easily be destroyed.

Christ, what a mess!

He wanted to punch something, tear his own bloody hair out. How the devil could he have let this happen? The answer to that was all too simple – she'd crept under his skin, taken up residence in his heart, and tempted him with a dream he never should have allowed.

And now it was too late. They were both in too deep.

All he could do was pray their upcoming nuptials wouldn't be mentioned alongside a sketch of them in a Scottish paper, and that his uncle would overlook it if it were.

"Let's have the bans cried," Blayne heard himself say.

Charlotte blinked as she gazed at him through watery eyes. "I suppose the urgency has been slightly diminished now that we have my parents' support. But are you certain this is what you want?"

More uncertain than ever before, he forced out a confident, "Yes."

"It's settled then," Lady Elkins said with a smile so wide it stretched across her entire face. "Charlotte, your staying here with the Windhams is perfectly fine with us if you wish to continue your visit, but you should know that we would be happy to have you home again. And of course, it will make all the arrangements easier."

"I shall return tomorrow, Mama," Charlotte said. She glanced at her father who seemed to be doing his utmost to tamp down whatever opinions he might be having. "Hopefully, in time, we can put the recent weeks behind us."

Lord Elkins knit his brow and for a moment Blayne feared he would say something to earn a punch in the face, but then the frown eased and he slowly nodded. "I've wronged you, Charlotte. I see that now. I'm ashamed to confess my decisions were based on a mixture of stubborn blindness and greed."

"I appreciate your saying so," Charlotte told him.

The Elkinses took their leave and Blayne turned to Charlotte. "Are ye all right?"

"A little shaken to be perfectly honest, but I will be fine." She gave him a wobbly smile. "I'm glad they came to see me. The discord we've shared in recent weeks made me most uneasy. Being back on more cordial terms is a relief."

"Good, because I cannae bear for ye to be unhappy in any way, Charlotte." He cupped her cheek with his palm, tucked a stray strand of hair behind her ear – anything to simply touch her – before allowing his fingers to trail down the side of her neck and across her shoulder. "We should probably rejoin the others before they start on dessert."

"I quite agree," she said, though not before rising up on her toes and pressing a kiss to his lips.

Of course he wanted more, but he also had

no desire to let them get carried away in the Windham parlor while three other people sat in the next room. So he let the caress remain chaste and instead told her slyly while walking her back to the dining room, "There is one downside to a delayed wedding."

"And what would that be, I wonder?"

Her flirtatious tone made him chuckle. "I've a niggling feeling ye're well aware, Miss Russell, but just in case ye cannae figure it out, I'd best inform ye that it does involve a bed and fewer clothes than what ye're currently wearing."

He opened the door to the dining room before she had a chance to respond, effectively stopping their conversation from getting too out of hand. As it was, he could not recall the last time he'd lain with a woman, so with their future as husband and wife now decided, he was more than eager to make her his.

Delighting in the flood of color pinkening her skin, Blayne discreetly slid his hand over her lower back while helping her into her seat. She sucked in a breath, alerting him to her keen responsiveness.

God, how he longed to get her out of her dress and underthings so he could taste every glorious inch of her body. Aware such provocative thoughts would only lead to discomfort and possible embarrassment, Blayne forced himself to listen to Marcus who was speaking of his newly developed plans to travel to Edinburgh in pursuit of the medical education he wanted.

"But you will be so far away from us if you go

there," Regina said. "Can you not take the same courses here in London?"

"Edinburgh has the best medical schooling," Marcus said. "If I'm serious about it, then that is where I must go."

"Are you acquainted with the Duke of Redding and Mrs. Henry Lowell, the former Duchess of Tremaine?" Guthrie asked.

"Only vaguely," Marcus confessed. "I know they run St. Agatha's Hospital but I've never actually met either one."

"I can make the introduction if you like," Guthrie said. "Redding should prove especially helpful as a trained surgeon. I'm sure he'd be happy to answer any questions you may have."

"Thank you," Marcus said. "I appreciate that."

The rest of the dinner progressed with talk of Charlotte's and Blayne's decision to delay their wedding, which somehow morphed into a most peculiar debate about fabric and shoes.

"Are you sure postponing is wise?" Guthrie asked Blayne later that evening when they were alone.

The hour was getting late. Marcus had already retired a short while ago, and Blayne himself was beginning to think about heading home. His intention was to go find Charlotte so he could bid her farewell before taking his leave.

He met Guthrie's gaze head on. "I dinnae ken."

Guthrie nodded with pensive slowness. "Have you told her of your fear?"

"Nae."

"Maybe you should."

"For what purpose?" Blayne shook his head. "What can telling her possibly accomplish at this point? We have to marry in order to safeguard her reputation."

"And if your uncle decides to put in an appearance?"

"Then I'll figure something out." He took a long sip of his drink and prayed he'd know what to do if Seamus showed up, because at the moment, he'd no bloody clue.

CHAPTER SEVENTEEN

W HEN CHARLOTTE SET off from home
five days later, she did so with purpose.
Since returning to Russell House, her days had
been impossibly busy, filled with back and forth
conversations regarding wedding-related topics.
At least today, she would get to see Blayne again.

After sending him a note the previous afternoon, he'd agreed to visit for tea. Considering
how much time they'd spent in each other's company prior to their real engagement, she missed
him dreadfully. To Charlotte's relief, her mother
had agreed to give her a reprieve from planning
the wedding, which probably had more to do
with the viscountess's own prior engagements
than anything else.

So with only a couple of hours to spare before
Blayne arrived, Charlotte made her way along
the fashionable side-streets immediately behind
Oxford Street with Daisy in tow. As they
approached Bond Street, a gentleman exited a
shop up ahead and stepped onto the pavement.

"Mr. Cooper?" Charlotte quickened her step.
She'd been hoping to meet him again before he

left England, but with her own daily schedule now packed to the brim, she'd not known if it were possible.

He halted in response to his name and turned. "Miss Russell. How perfectly serendipitous that I should find you here. I've been meaning to call – or at the very least send a note – to congratulate you on your recent engagement. I saw the announcement in the paper a few days ago but I must confess, I've been a bit busy, what with my wedding tomorrow and the ensuing journey back to New York. Please forgive me."

"Of course." Charlotte drew closer, until he was able to fall into step beside her. "I've been meaning to call on you for similar reasons, but have been unable to spare the time. This is my first day off from all the wedding frenzy."

"And I'm sure you've only been allowed it because your mother had other plans."

"I believe there was a charity meeting she could not possibly miss." Charlotte allowed a brief moment of silence to settle between them before she said, "You've made an excellent match for yourself and I just want to tell you that I wish you every happiness."

"No hard feelings?"

"None at all." Charlotte smiled. "Considering what you came here for, I'd say Lady Fiona is much better suited to be your wife than I ever was. She'll make an excellent Society hostess without going off-script, as it were, whereas I'm a lot more unpredictable."

"So I learned," he said, dropping a glance in

her direction. "I'm still impressed by your nego-
tiating skills."

"And I am immensely grateful to you for
agreeing to make a new deal with me."

"I never pass on a good opportunity, Miss
Russell, and in the end I did snag myself a better
wife. If you'll excuse me for saying so."

"You also offered Papa compensation." Having
almost reached the end of the street, Charlotte
drew to a halt and waited for Mr. Cooper to
do the same. "Had you not done so, my father
would still be in financial trouble and not nearly
as forgiving of me as he has been. And since you
had no need to do so, I feel I owe you a huge
debt of gratitude."

Mr. Cooper frowned. He took a deep breath,
expelled it, and Charlotte realized he looked
extremely uncomfortable all of a sudden – like
his clothes were starting to itch.

He cleared his throat. "I did promise Mr.
MacNeil I wouldn't say anything, but I've never
been one to take credit for something I haven't
done. It feels wrong – deceitful – even if I've
been asked to do so."

"What are you talking about?"

"I didn't offer compensation to your father.
To do so would have gone against my principles
since you were the one who broke the initial
agreement."

"So then?"

"You may want to ask your fiancé about the
part he played in all of this." Retrieving his
pocket watch, Mr. Cooper glanced at the time.

"Please excuse me, Miss Russell, but I really must run. I'm due at the Earl of Dervaine's residence in fifteen minutes."

"Of course. Good luck with the wedding."

Mr. Cooper tipped his hat before striding away. Baffled by what he'd told her, Charlotte stood utterly still for a moment while trying to gather her wits. The promissory note her father received was from Blayne? She hadn't considered the possibility because... Well, for one thing Mr. Cooper had been the one to deliver it and for another, she'd not imagined Blayne had the means to provide such a sum unless he'd taken out a loan or...or... Good grief, one thousand pounds would surely be a staggering amount for a man in his position.

"Are you all right, miss?"

Charlotte flinched in response to Daisy's voice. "Not quite. Let's purchase that plant we came to buy so we can get back to the house."

Later that day, Charlotte told the butler she would receive Blayne in the garden when he arrived. The weather was pleasant – warm with a gentle breeze – and she had a need to be out of doors where the air was less confining.

"Charlotte." Blayne's voice whispered close to her ear, sending lovely shivers across her skin. Somehow, in spite of his size, he'd managed to sneak up behind her as she stood admiring the roses. She turned and was instantly in his arms. His mouth settled firmly on hers, kissing her with a wonderful blend of love and longing. "I've missed ye."

She smiled against his lips. "I've missed you too. So much I'm starting to regret not taking advantage of that special license you procured."

Laughter rumbled through him, filling her heart with warmth. He stepped back a little, just enough to add an appropriate amount of distance and to allow Charlotte a glimpse of Daisy and another maid, named Jane, who both looked remarkably interested in the branches of a nearby tree.

Heat flared in Charlotte's cheeks. She pressed her lips together. It was so easy for her to forget herself when she was with Blayne. His eyes twinkled with roguish humor – enough to prompt her to give him a playful slap on the arm.

"Do you prefer tea or lemonade?" she asked him.

"Is coffee an option?"

"Certainly." Charlotte tore her gaze away from his and asked Jane to bring two pots – one with coffee and one with tea – along with some biscuits. As soon as she was gone, Charlotte turned to Daisy. "I'm sure you would enjoy the view of the garden more from the bench over there."

Daisy bobbed a quick curtsey and retreated to the spot Charlotte indicated. It was within respectable distance of the table where Charlotte intended to sit with Blayne, yet far enough away for Daisy not to hear their conversation.

"There's something I must ask you," Charlotte said once she and Blayne were seated and their drinks had been served. She knit her brow. "I ran into Mr. Cooper this morning."

"Oh? And how is he?"

"Happy with his new bride, it seems." She sipped her tea while he drank his coffee. "Would you care for a biscuit? The ginger flavor is quite tasty."

Blayne picked one off the plate she offered and bit into it. A sound of approval followed. "These are good, but I feel like ye're stalling. What is it ye wish to ken?"

Charlotte had been trying to figure out how to ask him about the money he'd given her father and the possible state of his finances. It wasn't easy since such matters were generally considered taboo, but they were getting married, so she ought to know if he'd put himself in debt by helping her out. Right?

She cleared her throat. Took another sip of her tea. "When I attempted to thank Mr. Cooper for the promise note he gave Papa, Mr. Cooper informed me that it hadn't come from him but rather from you. Which does pose several questions since I would not have thought you were in possession of one thousand pounds." When Blayne said nothing, she had to ask, "Did you borrow the money from Guthrie?"

"No, lass. I didnae do that."

"Then where did the money come from?"

"Well, I didnae steal it, if that's what ye're thinking."

"Of course not," she hissed with sudden annoyance. "But considering how thrilled you were with earning five pounds a week when we first met, I know you're not exactly rich."

"Is that an issue for ye?"

"No. I love you for who you are, not for the amount of money you have."

"Then I cannae see the problem."

Gritting her teeth, Charlotte leaned forward. "The problem, Blayne, is that I want honesty in my marriage. So tell me, how did you manage to come up with one thousand pounds?"

He blew out a breath. "Ye willnae let this go, will ye?"

"Not likely. No."

"Very well. If ye must ken, I had the money in my account at the bank." When Charlotte said nothing, he eventually added, "I may not be more than a tavern keep, but that doesnae mean I'm financially irresponsible."

"I never suggested you were," Charlotte said so he'd not think less of her. "But one thousand pounds is no small sum."

"Ye're right. It's taken me almost twenty years to accumulate."

Air whooshed out of Charlotte's lungs. It felt like her heart ceased beating for a second while lead formed in her stomach. She blinked as reality bore down upon her. "Those were your life savings."

He shrugged as if this were completely inconsequential.

Charlotte's eyes began to sting. Her throat drew tight and Blayne transformed into a blurry image. "You gave my father all the money you put aside for your future."

"Of course I did." His voice was so soft and

gentle it only made Charlotte cry harder. A sob shook her and then, somehow, he was there, crouching beside her chair while stroking away her tears with his fingers. "Balanced against yer happiness, it was an easy choice to make."

"You love me that much?"

"Of course I do. And I reckoned it would only be a temporary problem since ye'll be raking in money as soon as we fix the publishing issue relating to yer latest book."

"Had I known, I never would have allowed you to do this."

Pensiveness stole into his eyes. "Ye have regrets?"

"No. Not with regard to getting engaged with you at least. I just wish you hadn't had to give up so much."

Blayne brushed his lips against hers. "Let's just be glad yer father wasnae in need of a larger sum, or I'm nae sure everything would have worked out as well."

"I would have married you anyway. No matter the possible scandal or the risk of getting cut off from my family, you and I would have spoken our vows. But I am glad it didn't come to that, and I swear to you, Blayne, I'll do what I can to pay you back."

"There's nae need for that, luv. My plans for the future have changed now, and while I may not have as much money as I once did, I can still afford to rent a decent place for us, just like I promised yer father."

Unsure if her heart could handle loving him

more than she already did, Charlotte kissed him with fervor. He'd given up everything he'd worked toward for the last nineteen years, just so she could have peace with her father. It was beyond remarkable.

"I have something for you," she said when Blayne returned to his chair. "It's not much, but I do think you'll like it."

"There's no chance of me not doing so if it's from ye."

Steeling herself for his reaction, Charlotte reached down and picked up the plant she'd bought that morning. She set it on the table and waited for him to unwrap it.

"A lemon tree?"

"From what I gather, they require a great deal of attention, but I wanted to give you something different that can also survive and produce fruit indoors."

"It's perfect." Blayne gazed at the small tree in mesmerized silence for a while before shifting his gaze back to Charlotte. "Ye are perfect, in every conceivable way."

Overjoyed, she grinned at him while hoping the next two weeks would fly by, because as far as she was concerned, their wedding day couldn't come soon enough.

It seemed like forever before his wedding day arrived. Blayne knew Charlotte had been busy in recent weeks but so had he. Perhaps if they'd seen each other more often, the time would have flown by quicker, but between finding a house to rent and all the practicalities related to that, plus having a new set of clothes ordered for himself, it had been hard to manage. At least now, there were only a couple of hours left before he and Charlotte would be pronounced husband and wife.

Excitement and relief rippled through him. He'd not heard from his uncle, which meant his marriage had either escaped his notice, that he'd not realized Blayne MacNeil and James Callanach were one and the same, or that he no longer cared about apprehending his nephew. Whatever the case, it would allow Blayne to move on and build the future he so dearly wanted with Charlotte by his side.

Dressed in black with a red and gold brocade waistcoat, which were both brightened by his white shirt and cravat, Blayne set off for the church. He'd had a clean shave and a fresh haircut as soon as he'd risen, after which he'd taken a bath before eating breakfast. Since he'd not hired any servants, Claus had assisted as makeshift valet. The younger man strode alongside him now, keeping pace as they made their way toward St. George's.

"I've a feeling ye'll be seeing more of Daisy once her mistress and I are wed," Blayne said. His mood was as bright as the sun in the sky. Nothing would please him more than to see other men as happy as he. "Maybe ye can have a future with her."

"I do like her lot," Claus said after a few more paces.

"And she clearly likes ye."

"Do you think so?"

"Aye. It's blatantly obvious, lad. If ye want her to be yers, I reckon she will be."

"I have been wondering about asking her out for a stroll or maybe to luncheon if she can spare the time one day. Except ladies' maids don't get much time off so—"

"Leave it with me, Claus. I'll make sure Miss Russell can manage without her on occasion."

Claus answered with a broad smile. "Thank you, Blayne. I appreciate that."

"Think nothing of it." They arrived at the church where the vicar stood waiting. Guthrie and Regina had also arrived together with Marcus and a few other people.

"Are you ready?" Guthrie asked once Blayne had finished greeting everyone and they'd headed inside. "Or is your stomach one big knot the way mine was when I waited here for my bride?"

"I must confess I feel like a tangled mess inside."

Guthrie grinned and gave him a slap on the back as they moved toward the altar where they would await Charlotte's arrival. "It will ease the moment you see her step through those doors. Mark my word."

Blayne answered with a stiff nod and took his position with Guthrie by his side. He dipped his head occasionally in acknowledgement of guests arriving and was surprised by how many peers showed up. The Dukes of Huntley, Coventry, and Redding were all in attendance together with their wives, as was Redding's brother, Mr. Lowell and his wife, the former Duchess of Tremaine. Besides them, Blayne spotted the Earl of Fielding who sat with his wife a bit further back. And then there were the Earl and Countess of Warwick along with a slew of other people Blayne didn't know. Charlotte's parents must have invited them all, which had to mean they'd truly changed their minds about him or else they'd have favored a more discreet event.

Blayne straightened his spine and scanned the pews for that one face he hoped not to see. He couldn't help it. After looking over his shoulder for almost twenty years, he had to be certain his uncle would not leap from the shadows at the last second and ruin everything. Blayne's stomach tightened. If they could just get through the next hour, he and Charlotte could slip away quietly into obscurity.

"Take a deep breath," Guthrie said with a chuckle. "You look like you're getting strangled by your cravat."

It did feel a bit snug. Blayne fought the urge to reach up and give it a tug. And then the organ began to play and a choir started to sing and he simply forgot all about it. Because, there she was, stunning as ever in simple ivory silk. A veil pinned to her bonnet gave the illusion of misty clouds swirling around her luminous face.

Blayne's heart stumbled in response to her ethereal beauty, but then his world righted itself and the anxiety he'd experienced earlier dissipated just as Guthrie had said it would. Everyone else faded away, disappearing into the background. The only person who existed for him in that moment was Charlotte. Love shone in her eyes and happiness drew her lips into a wide smile.

"I barely slept one wink last night," she whispered as soon as she reached him. "Thank goodness we're finally here."

"I couldnae agree with ye more," he murmured as he took her arm. Turning, he guided her forward a couple of steps so they could face the vicar together.

"Dearly beloved," the vicar intoned, "we are gathered together here in the sight of God, and in the face of this congregation, to join together this man and this woman in holy matrimony."

Blayne did his best to stay perfectly still so as not to look too impatient while the vicar continued. He spoke of marriage being rooted in the church, of its sanctity, and how one should enter the sacred institution for the right reasons.

"Therefore," the vicar said in even tones, "if any man can show any just cause why they may not lawfully be joined together, let him now speak, or else hereafter forever hold his peace."

A deliberate pause followed. Blayne held his breath. And expelled it as soon as the vicar turned the page in his book of scripture.

"I require," the vicar continued, "to—"

"Objection!"

Blayne's blood froze in response to that voice. He couldn't move, could only stand there, helpless, while the world crashed down around him.

The vicar gave him a questioning glance. At his side, Blayne could sense Charlotte's shock.

"Proceed." Guthrie's firm voice sounded from somewhere nearby.

"If ye do this, James," Seamus said, his voice echoing through the church, "yer wife will have to endure the ensuing scandal and the burden of yer sins. Is that what ye want?"

Slowly, so as not to shatter if he moved too quickly, Blayne turned to face the bastard from whom he'd been hiding for most of his life.

"Who is James?" someone asked amid additional whispers.

Blayne stared down his uncle who stood near the exit. The years had whitened his hair and his beard. They'd also transformed the large and dangerous highlander Blayne remembered into a much smaller man who looked almost frail. He'd not come alone though. Blayne knew the chief magistrate well enough by sight now to recognize him immediately.

So. This was it then. He'd been defeated at the last second.

Resigned, he turned to Charlotte, the one person he cared for and to whom he owed more than any apology could convey. Her eyes were wide and imploring. Tears clung to her lashes. "I'm sorry, lass, but I cannae do this to ye."

"What do you mean?"

"Marrying ye would be wrong. It always was but then there was Mr. Hallibrand and the threat of scandal and I could see nae way out."

"Listen to me," she told him firmly. "I don't

care what that man has to say about you. All I know is that I love you and that I intend to spend the rest of my life with you, no matter what."

"Ach, luv. If it were so simple, I'd wed ye in a heartbeat. But ye see, what I failed to tell ye because I feared yer reaction was that I'm wanted for murder." He watched her flinch and decided to add, "I killed my father in cold blood and as much as I've tried to escape it, the time has come for me to face the consequence."

When all she did was stare at him, Blayne turned away and went to meet his uncle while gasps and horrified chatter erupted around him.

It was difficult to fathom how swiftly one's happiness could be stolen. Only seconds ago Charlotte had been overjoyed with the prospect of building a life for herself with Blayne – a life destined to start a few minutes later once they were pronounced husband and wife. Now, she struggled to hold back tears while the congregation transformed into a chorus of unkind comments and outraged remarks.

She'd been jilted by a man who'd just been declared a criminal worthy of hanging. It didn't seem possible. In fact, it felt completely surreal.

"Come," Regina said, her hand gently settling on Charlotte's arm. "You could probably do with some fresh air and a drink. Guthrie has a flask of brandy in the carriage. I suggest we go and find it."

Numb, Charlotte forced one foot in front of the other while doing her best to block out the voices around her.

"My God," her father exclaimed as he bore down upon her. "I knew I shouldn't trust him and now look at what has happened. It's deplorable, beyond the pale, utterly ruinous."

"Please, Lord Elkins," Regina said while steering Charlotte past him. "You're not helping."

"What would you have me do?" he asked.

"Accept the situation for what it is," Regina said, "and support your daughter. Lord knows she faces a difficult time ahead after what just happened."

Charlotte didn't doubt it and with Regina being the daughter of a condemned murderer, she surely knew a thing or two about it. Her friendship was a consolation.

"Here," Regina said a few minutes later when she and Charlotte were comfortably seated inside the Windham carriage. They'd closed the curtains to block out the world. It was an illusion, of course, but a welcome one at the moment.

Charlotte accepted the flask Regina offered and took a long sip. The spicy brandy slid down her throat to heat her insides. A wonderful sense of calm followed. Charlotte's head cleared. She pondered the recent events, what that awful man had said and how he'd called Blayne by another name. James. It felt off.

Dismissing Blayne's possible false identity for a moment, Charlotte thought back on her previous interactions with him and the conversations they'd shared. He'd told her he wouldn't marry because of his past – that he'd once done something much worse than anything he'd revealed to her. And yet, the man she knew him to be was generous, loving, and kind beyond compare. His personality didn't square with that of a cold-blooded killer.

Something wasn't right.

She took another sip from the flask before handing it back to Regina. "I need to speak with your husband."

"What are you planning?"

"To find out as much as I can about Blayne's past." Because nothing seemed to add up. In spite of Blayne's own assertion of guilt, Charlotte was certain he'd not murdered his father for no good reason. And if that were the case, if there were even the slimmest chance he could be acquitted, she would move heaven and earth in order to find it.

"I must say," Guthrie drawled when Charlotte voiced her intention to him later, "I'm quite impressed by your willingness to stand by him through this."

"Blayne has offered me more support these past two months than I have received from anyone, including my own family, for my entire life. Of course I intend to stand by him. And damn anyone who dares to get in my way."

"Brava," Marcus said from his position in a nearby armchair.

After informing her parents she'd be home later, Charlotte had returned to Windham House for what she hoped would prove an informative discussion. She'd ignored her father's protests completely.

"So," Charlotte said, her eyes focused on Guthrie, "why does Blayne believe he's guilty of killing his father, and who on earth was the man who stopped us from speaking our vows?"

"In answer to your first question, Blayne believes he killed his father because he did. The man you refer to is his uncle, Mr. Seamus Callanach."

Guthrie's calm voice put Charlotte at ease in spite of the damning words he'd just spoken. "Tell me what happened, as precisely as you can."

"According to what Blayne has told me, he was seventeen years of age when it happened. Apparently, he was woken one night by piercing screams, so he rushed to see what was going on. The noise came from his mother's bedchamber. When he arrived there he found her pinned against the wall by his father, her expression one of pure terror." Guthrie knit his brow. "Her lover was on the bed, covered in blood."

"Dear God," Charlotte muttered.

"Blayne tried to get his father away from his mother, but he wasn't strong enough. When Callanach went for his wife's throat and it became clear he'd not let up until she, too, met her maker, Blayne grabbed a candelabra and struck him over the head with it as hard as he could, effectively killing him on the spot."

"So then, he saved his mother's life."

"Yes, but that's not how he sees it."

"I don't understand why he wouldn't. It doesn't

sound as though his action was worse than when he worked for you, and he seems at peace with those deaths."

"There's a world of difference between striking down a rapist who's nothing but scum, and taking your father's life. No matter how awful your father may be or the sins he might have committed, he's a relation. And you must consider Blayne's age as well. He was barely more than a child – a timid lad according to his own words. When his uncle arrived on the scene and said he'd hang for murder, Blayne panicked and ran. Which was probably a wise choice since Blayne insists Seamus always hated him."

"But surely Blayne's mother would have come to his defense," Charlotte said. "In fact, it disturbs me greatly to think the woman never attempted to find her son after he left."

"It's not always easy to know why people behave as they do," Regina said. "Families often have secrets they keep well hidden behind closed doors. What you see when they're out in public is oftentimes a façade."

"There was disharmony between our parents," Marcus murmured, "but neither of us was aware of it until Guthrie brought the past to light. I still have trouble believing my father killed his on account of jealousy."

"How did Blayne's uncle even know it was his nephew who was getting married?" Regina asked. "I mean, if Blayne's real name is James Callanach and the announcement mentioned Blayne MacNeil, I don't see how Seamus would have figured out his true identity."

"I agree there's a mystery there," Guthrie said. "Perhaps someone recognized him as he feared they would if he ventured out in public, and the person informed his uncle of his reappearance."

"Lady Warwick noted the similarity between Blayne and Bruce Callanach during the Coventry Ball weeks ago," Charlotte said. She held Guthrie's penetrating gaze. "Do you suppose she might have written Seamus?"

"Possibly," Guthrie said. "I certainly wouldn't put it past her since I've never encountered a woman more meddlesome than she. Nor one who takes greater pleasure in bringing scandals to light."

"Regardless of how Blayne's identity was revealed, I intend to help clear his name."

"Any idea on how to do that?" Marcus asked.

"Getting his mother to serve as witness would be useful," Charlotte said, "provided the woman is still alive, that is. Guthrie, do you not have some sway over the chief magistrate? As a duke, can you not have him put off an eventual trial until we're able to gather more information?"

"I might have been able to if it were up to him, but since the crime was committed in Scotland, I believe Blayne will have to stand trial there, and I very much fear a powerful family like the Callanachs will have more sway over the legal system there than I ever would."

"Right." Charlotte didn't like the sound of this one bit, but neither was she about to give up on account of a geographical snag. "In that case,

I suggest we find out if a trial will occur, where it will occur, and when it will occur. Once these facts are in place, it will be easier for us to make a plan. Either way, I fully intend to travel to Scotland so I can meet with Blayne's mother. Perhaps some servants can be stirred up as well, but since Blayne's mother was part of the whole ordeal, she will be the key witness."

"He's lucky to have you," Guthrie murmured. "Your dedication to him is most impressive."

"I was about to marry him a few hours ago," Charlotte said. "Just because I never managed to say my vows doesn't mean I don't take *for better or worse* seriously."

"You should escort her," Regina told Guthrie.

"I was actually thinking of sending Marcus in my stead. It will give him a chance to visit Edinburgh University and speak with the professors Redding recommended he get in touch with. And besides," Guthrie said, his eyes twinkling as he regarded his wife with affection, "I'm not so keen on leaving you at the moment, my love."

Regina blushed. She gave Charlotte and Marcus an almost shy smile. "I suppose we might as well tell you both that we've recently learned I'm expecting."

"Goodness," Charlotte said. "That's wonderful news."

"Congratulations," Marcus said with a grin. "I've been looking forward to becoming an uncle. Lord knows I'm going to spoil that child."

"Getting back to the subject at hand," Guthrie said a few moments later, "I will head over to Bow Street right now in order to figure out what's going on."

"I'll join you," Charlotte said. To her relief, Guthrie did not protest.

Two hours later, after learning Blayne had left London at least four hours earlier, Charlotte located Daisy and informed her parents she would be heading north.

"But you can't," Mama said. "Tell her, Lord Elkins. She'll only make matters worse."

"I'm not sure she cares," Papa said.

Charlotte rounded on them both. "Just so you know, Blayne was the one who helped you out of financial ruin, not Mr. Cooper. He's the best man I know and right now he needs help, which I intend to provide."

"If you do this, you forfeit the two hundred pounds I was prepared to give you in dowry."

"Fine," she countered. "We'll make do without it."

"Charlotte, please be reasonable," Mama pressed.

Everet entered the parlor before Charlotte had a chance to respond. "A letter for you, Miss Russell."

Doing her best not to take her frustration out on the butler, Charlotte thanked him and took the letter from the salver he held toward her. She tore the seal and scanned the contents.

Dear Miss Russell,

You are invited to participate in a meeting between myself and the man who submitted the manuscript you claim was stolen. Please be at my office at nine

o'clock on August twenty-second. Hopefully, the mat-
ter you've brought before me can be cleared up then.
  Sincerely,
  Mr. P. Agerson

Apparently when it rained it poured. The date
Mr. P. Agerson suggested was in two days. Charlotte closed her eyes for a brief moment while
aligning herself with the fact that her chance of
reacquiring her rights to the manuscript would
in all likelihood slip through her fingers. Because
when it came to a matter of choice, there was
only one – Blayne needed her and nothing was
going to stop her from doing all she could in
order to save him. Which meant she would have
to miss the meeting with the publisher.

Jaw set, Charlotte pocketed the letter and faced
her parents. "I'll see you both when I return."

"If you leave this house right now to chase
after that good for nothing gutter rat, you'll
never be welcome here again," Papa sputtered.

Mama gasped and proceeded to plea with her
husband to not be so cruel. "She's our daughter,
my lord. Please be reasonable."

"In my opinion, I've been more than reasonable where she's concerned. God's teeth, the chit
should have married Mr. Cooper when she had
the chance."

Fuming, Charlotte left the house she'd grown
up in without any further goodbyes, and climbed
into the recently arrived Windham carriage
where Marcus waited.

"Trouble with the parents?" he inquired once
Charlotte and Daisy had taken the opposite

bench.

"You have no idea," Charlotte grumbled.

Marcus chuckled. "Never mind them. If all goes well you'll get Blayne acquitted and marry him over an anvil."

Allowing a smile in response to his jovial tone, Charlotte settled herself against the squabs and said, "That sounds like an excellent plan to me."

CHAPTER EIGHTEEN

THE SITUATION WAS worse than Blayne had feared. For one delusional second he'd let himself imagine Guthrie would work his magic and get him released. He might not be able to marry Charlotte or even go back to the life he'd known at The Black Swan, but he'd be alive, which was always something.

Instead, he now sat opposite his uncle in a carriage bound for Edinburgh. Two rough looking fellows Seamus had brought along for protection and for the purpose of keeping an eye on Blayne accompanied them.

"I'm guessing ye came to find me after seeing the wedding announcement in the paper?" Blayne willed himself to look Seamus straight in the eye. "I'm just nae sure how ye knew I was Blayne MacNeil."

Seamus snorted. "Yer wedding announcement has nothing to do with me showing up in London. I came on account of a letter I received from an old friend."

Blayne thought on that for a moment. "The Countess of Warwick by any chance?"

"Aye. She saw the resemblance between ye and yer da when she met ye and decided to reach out to me."

"How considerate of her."

"I think so." When Blayne shifted his gaze toward the window, Seamus said, "Ye killed a man – my brother, as it happens. I'll nae let ye get away with that. In fact, I've every intention of seeing justice served on his behalf."

"He murdered Mr. Roberts. I saw the blood. It was everywhere. And he would have killed Mama too had I not acted."

"Perhaps, but that doesnae mean I'm any keener to forgive ye for what ye did. I loved Bruce, ye ken?"

"He was a madman."

"Don't. Say. That."

"I still have scars on my back from all the times he whipped me." Blayne had been but five years old the first time his father had meted out discipline. And Seamus had simply stood there and watched. To say there was no love lost between them would be an understatement.

"Ye were weak and in need of toughening up."

"It seems like it worked then, wouldnae ye say?"

When Seamus said nothing, Blayne resolved to ignore him as much as possible during the four days he expected the ride to take. There was little for them to discuss. Blayne knew he'd acted abominably when he'd struck down his father. He should have called for help instead, or at the very least hit Bruce somewhere less likely to harm him. And the fact was that if Bruce had lived, he probably would have gotten away with killing Mr. Roberts. After all, the man had been in his wife's bed, completely naked, from what Blayne recalled. Considering Bruce's status and connections, the incident would in all likelihood have been swept under a rug, never to be spoken of again.

Blayne tried to place himself in Seamus's position for a moment. Would he have behaved in a similar fashion had their roles been reversed? Unlikely, but in a strange way Blayne understood the man. He could not fault him for looking up to his older brother, or for trying to avenge his death. It was just damned inconvenient for Blayne – destructive to his plans for the future. In all likelihood it would be his end.

Blindly, he watched the countryside roll by. If only he'd come clean with Charlotte sooner. At least then she'd know his side of the story. He dared not even consider what she might be thinking. Not that it mattered. She was much better off without him and that was an undeniable fact.

It was extraordinarily difficult for Charlotte to quiet her nerves. She was agitated, worried, and very convinced the carriage was not moving nearly as fast as it could. In fact, she was beginning to contemplate the idea of hiring a horse for herself at the next posting inn so she could tear along the road at full speed. At least then, she might stand a chance of catching up with a carriage that had gained a six hour advantage by the time she'd been ready for departure.

An involuntary chuckle vibrated through her at the thought of what she would look like riding astride with her skirts bunched around her legs. Somehow, since meeting Blayne for the very first time, her life had strayed with greater degree from what was considered proper and taken on a guise more suited to one of her stories. Good grief! She'd hired a man whom she'd promptly turned into a fake fiancé, made a deal with a businessman, gotten compromised, engaged, and jilted by a would-be murderer whom she now intended to save. It was too fantastical a tale by half. If she penned it, people would call it ridiculous.

"What's so amusing?" Marcus asked.

She shook her head, glanced at Daisy who slept by her side, and said, "Things don't always turn out as one would expect, do they?"

"Not at all," he murmured. "I certainly never imagined being stripped of my title and becoming a social pariah. We peers are raised in such comfort, we don't even know how to appreciate what we have."

"I'm sorry. I did not mean to remind you of all you have lost."

The edge of his mouth curved. "In a way, it's been a blessing. Not the part about my father, mind you, but rather being forced to make my own way in the world. Inheriting wealth is easy – accumulating it on your own, that's something to be admired."

"So you respect the working class?"

"I respect anyone who can improve their situation through honest means." Marcus stretched out his legs and leaned back against his own corner. "That's not to say every tradesman or laborer deserves respect, but then again, neither does every peer. If I've learnt anything in recent years, it's that even those who walk among us as if they're beyond reproach can be guilty of horrible crimes."

"You refer to your father?"

"Who else? Unlike Blayne who killed his father by accident while attempting to save his mother, my father went to Windham House with every intention of killing the duke. Most of the staff was at church that day, but an unfortunate maid perished too. Guthrie himself barely escaped after my father set the place ablaze in an effort to cover up what he'd done."

"I can't even fathom such cruelty."

"Of course you can't, because you're a good and decent person."

"A good and decent person who'd like to run Blayne's uncle through with a sword."

Marcus grinned. "There's nothing wrong with having bloodthirsty thoughts as long as you don't follow through on them."

"Of course." Charlotte bit her lip while contemplating their journey and the goal they hoped to accomplish. They would soon have to stop for the night. After that, they would have three more days of travel before they reached their destination. "I do hope Blayne's mother is still alive."

"There's no guarantee after nearly twenty years, but let's stay positive."

"Right now, the one thing working in our favor is surprise. Seamus doesn't know we're coming or that we plan on defending Blayne." After arguing back and forth with Guthrie, Charlotte had eventually accepted the funds he'd provided for legal representation. As he'd pointed out, now was not the time to be prideful. Of course, he'd been completely correct.

"I'm thinking Seamus will be living at the family home," Charlotte said when they stopped four days later on the city's outskirts. Due to their late departure from London, it had taken them one day longer than she'd have liked to reach their destination. Stretching her legs while trying to gather her thoughts in preparation for battle, Charlotte paced about while Marcus leaned one shoulder against a nearby tree. "According to Guthrie's account of what happened, he lived there when the incident took place, so it makes sense for him to still be in residence."

"Unless he was merely visiting. Or the house has since been sold. Or—"

"Yes, yes, there are other alternatives, of course. I just don't want to show up and come face to face with him, that's all."

"So what's your plan?"

"According to what I know, Stockbridge is the most affluent neighborhood – Edinburgh's Mayfair, if you like. My intention is, therefore, to knock on doors and make inquiries until I learn where Mrs. Callanach might be residing. If gossip works as effectively here as it does in London, the information shouldn't be too hard to come by."

What Charlotte did not count on was being turned away the moment she mentioned Mrs. Callanach's name. Nobody cared who Charlotte was or why she had come. As soon as she made her inquiry, gazes grew shuttered and she was promptly asked to leave. She never even made it past the butlers.

"This is so frustrating," she muttered when she returned to the carriage after her fifth attempt.

"You mustn't lose hope, miss." Daisy's voice had that soothing softness intended to reassure, but it didn't quite work.

"I think a change of strategy is in order," Marcus said. "Surely there must be a place nearby where we can happen upon a few ladies and gentlemen who aren't being so ferociously guarded?"

"A park would be perfect." Charlotte glanced around, then went to address their coachman. "You've been to Edinburgh before. Any idea if there's a park somewhere nearby where the upper-class might go for strolls?"

"Mr. Guthrie and his wife visited the Royal Botanical Garden when they were last here."

"Excellent. Please take us there."

Ten minutes later the carriage pulled up next to the pavement, and Marcus jumped out so he could help Charlotte alight. Arm in arm, they entered the garden and proceeded along one of the pathways while Daisy followed behind.

"I almost wish we were here for leisure," Charlotte said when they'd walked for a while. "There are so many wonderful plants and flowers, it would be lovely if we could take our time to enjoy them."

"Maybe you can return here with Blayne before heading back to London?"

"Now there's an idea worth hoping for," Charlotte agreed. "Come, I think we'll try approaching that couple over there. Excuse me! I'm sorry to trouble you on your walk, but I'm hoping you might be able to help us."

The couple, a lady who looked to be in her fifties and a gentleman who appeared slightly older, stopped and turned more fully in Charlotte and Marcus's direction.

"Yes?" the gentleman inquired.

"We've travelled here from London and aren't too familiar with the area, so we'd be most obliged if you could lend your assistance with some directions." Charlotte added a smile and prayed the couple would not be as standoffish as the butlers she'd met with earlier.

"Certainly, Mrs..?" the gentleman inquired.

"Miss Russell," Charlotte supplied. When the gentleman frowned Charlotte decided a lie might serve her best, so she hastily added, "And this is my brother-in-law, Mr. Davies, who has been kind enough to accompany me on this journey. My mother is unwell, you see, and has tasked me with finding a long lost friend of hers."

"Indeed." The gentleman's expression eased a little. "And who might ye be seeking?"

Charlotte took a deep breath and prayed for success. "Mrs. Shannon Callanach."

Every muscle in the gentleman's face grew taut. "Her name isn't spoken in polite Society, Miss Russell. Not after her lover and husband were both murdered by her son. She's an outcast and ye'd do well to tell yer poor mother she'd best forget all about her. Good day."

"But I've a message for her I have sworn I'd deliver."

The gentleman huffed a breath. Pity shone in his wife's eyes.

"Surely there's no harm in telling them where they can find her?" the lady gently suggested.

"Fine," her husband grumbled. "Last I heard, Mrs. Callanach was living in a modest town-house on George Street. That's all I know."

"I trust then that her brother-in-law resides at Callanach House?" Marcus asked.

The gentleman snorted. "Aye. That man could not become the lord of the manor fast enough. Never met a more arrogant fellow in all my life. I didnae care for his brother either, but that doesnae mean he deserved to be bludgeoned to death. Now, if ye'll both excuse us, we'd like to continue our walk."

"Of course," Charlotte said. "And thank you."

"Mr. Davies?" Marcus quizzed as soon as they were alone again.

Charlotte shrugged. "Seemed better than using your actual name and them having heard of you."

"True." They started back toward the carriage. "I suppose we're off to George Street now?"

"Yes. Let's hope it's not too far. It would be nice to find the right house without much trouble."

Two hours later, after the coachman had figured out how to locate George Street and they'd made a few inquiries themselves, Charlotte and Marcus were shown into Mrs. Callanach's tiny drawing room by a maid. The lady of the house herself stood upon their arrival, and gestured for them to sit. To Charlotte's surprise, the maid — an older woman with graying hair — took a seat at the table with them.

"Mrs. Callanach does nae speak," the maid explained, as if sensing Charlotte's curiosity over the unusual etiquette. "I'll answer any questions ye may have to the best of my ability and for the sake of efficiency since she would otherwise have to write her responses."

Taken aback, Charlotte glanced at Blayne's mother, then back at the maid. "Why won't she talk?"

"Because she cannae, miss. Her larynx was crushed years ago. She never recovered her voice."

"Dear God." The situation was worse than Charlotte had imagined. Most likely more severe than Blayne even realized since there had been no reference to such an injury before. Surely if he'd known, he would have mentioned it to Guthrie? "I'm terribly sorry."

Mrs. Callanach gave a slight shake of her head as if to convey it was quite all right.

"Losing her son was much worse than losing her voice."

Charlotte's heart clenched. "I cannot even begin to imagine the pain she must have endured."

"Ye said ye had information about him?" The maid proceeded to pour everyone a hot cup of tea. "Mrs. Callanach is hoping ye ken where he might be buried so she can visit the site."

"Buried?" Charlotte blinked. "She thinks her son is dead?"

The maid went utterly still. "That is what Seamus told her. James fell off his horse while attempting to flee and broke his neck. The horrid man refused to tell Mrs. Callanach anything more. As ye can imagine, it has been the source of great distress for her, not knowing what happened to her dear boy."

Charlotte could only stare at the woman in dumbfounded silence.

Marcus eventually cleared his throat. "I believe Mrs. Callanach may have been severely misled by her brother-in-law."

The maid stilled. "What are ye saying?"

Charlotte and Marcus shared a glance before Charlotte carefully said, "James Callanach is still alive."

Mrs. Callanach's teacup and saucer clattered to the floor.

The maid rushed to clean up the mess. "Ye mustnae say such things unless ye are certain."

"I am," Charlotte said.

Mrs. Callanach snatched up a notepad and pencil, wrote with jerky movements, then showed Charlotte her question. *How?*

"I met him in St. Giles a little over two months ago. He was running a tavern there and, as I would later learn, living in hiding. The two of us were about to get married when Seamus showed up to ruin it all."

Tears filled Mrs. Callanach's eyes and her lips began to tremble. She pressed her hand to her mouth to stifle a sob. Charlotte averted her gaze to allow the woman a moment of privacy. Learning the son she'd thought dead for nineteen years was, in fact, very much alive must be overwhelming. Blayne had stayed away out of fear, but in that moment Charlotte wished he had found a way to inform his mother of his well-being. It wasn't right that she should have suffered such grief when it could have been prevented.

"Where is James now?" the maid asked while Mrs. Callanch gathered her composure.

"I'm not sure exactly. He went with Seamus willingly, partly out of resignation I imagine, and partly to save me from marrying a murderer." When outrage hardened Mrs. Callanach's eyes and she looked like she meant to try speaking in spite of her handicap, Charlotte hastened to say, "I know his situation is not what it seems. While Blayne – James, that is – believes himself to be guilty, I think his memory of the events that took place are so fuzzy and distorted he's turned himself into a monster. But based on what I have learned, I believe he acted to defend you from a man who clearly would have strangled you to death had he not been stopped.

"The true murderer was your husband, whose crime Seamus also pinned on James."

Mrs. Callanach made another note. *I never tried to fight it. How could I without a voice? As an adulteress, my reputation was in tatters. No one would have listened.*

"I know."

A brief silence passed before Marcus asked, "Why did you take a lover?"

"That is a highly inappropriate question," Charlotte said and immediately apologized to Mrs. Callanach.

"The answer could be helpful," Marcus argued. "If there's some way for her to gain compassion from the public, her testimony would probably get more traction."

"Nevertheless," Charlotte said, "we have no right to—"

Mrs. Callanach snapped her fingers to draw attention. She held up her hand, motioning for them to wait, then proceeded to write. When she was done, she handed her note to Charlotte, who proceeded to read.

"My marriage was one of convenience, completely devoid of love. Bruce Callanach was a violent man who had no qualms about striking others. He whipped my son..." Charlotte swallowed hard in an effort to tamp down her rising fury. "And he would often strike me for the slightest offense. Since he had his own lovers, I saw no reason not to seek comfort in the arms of another. In retrospect, it was foolish. I played a dangerous game with my husband – one in which a man was killed."

"A good solicitor might be able to use this to gain some sympathy for you," Marcus said. "Especially if there were witnesses to your abuse."

"I saw the master strike her on numerous occasions," the maid said. "So did the butler."

"What about James?" Charlotte asked. She couldn't believe he wouldn't have done some-thing sooner to try and help them both out of such an awful life. Of course, she reminded her-self, he'd only been a boy and not a very tough one either, until circumstance had forced him to change.

Mrs. Callanach shook her head. She wrote another note. *I did my best to protect him from the truth. It's possible he viewed me as a weak woman who lacked the strength to stop her husband from beat-ing her son, but the truth is, I tried, and was always punished as a result.*

The image Mrs. Callanach painted of a home ruled by tyranny, caused Charlotte's heart to ache. "And Seamus?"

"He idolized his brother," the maid responded. "And did his best to absolve him posthumously by pinning the murder of Mr. Hollander on James. As soon as Master James ran, Mr. Cal-lanach ordered Mrs. Callanach removed from the premises immediately. After applying to her brother for help, she was set up in this house."

Charlotte drew a tight breath. "And her brother?"

"Has since passed away. Her nephew manages the rent, but makes sure to keep his distance so as to avoid tarnishing his own reputation by association."

"I see." Charlotte sipped her tea which had now grown tepid. She set the cup aside and folded her hands in her lap. "Do you know where Seamus might have taken James?"

"Possibly to the Police Court in the Lawnmarket," the maid suggested. "He'll want the constables there to help with James's arrest and imprisonment until a trial can be held."

Mrs. Callanach nodded.

"Thank you." Charlotte glanced at Marcus to see if he had anything further to add. When he kept quiet, she said, "We'll head over there straight away to see if he's there. And then we'll acquire a solicitor to help in his defense."

"Would a barrister not be better?" the maid asked after sharing a hesitant look with her mistress.

"I'm hoping one won't be required, seeing as I intend to prevent a trial. Which I suspect would also be in Seamus's best interest. Let's not forget that stirring up the past in a public forum would not be beneficial to his reputation either."

"No, but it could secure his position as his brother's heir, which is likely why he's doing this," Marcus said. "And money might matter more to him than public opinion."

"In any event," Charlotte said, "we shall be in touch with you both as soon as we know more."

Mrs. Callanach made a new note. *I'd like to see him.*

"And I am certain he'll want to see you as well." Charlotte smiled at the woman she hoped would become her mother-in-law. "Rest assured, I will do all I can to ensure your son's acquittal."

When Charlotte was back in the carriage, she turned to Marcus. "That poor woman. Can you imagine the hell she has been through, first in her marriage, then as a widow?"

"I almost wish her husband would rise from the dead so I can kill him," Marcus said.

"She cannot speak because of him and then, as if that weren't enough, she was told her son had died. Never mind the damage done to her reputation because she decided to take a lover. Which I'll allow is not a commendable choice, but given the fact that her husband did the same and beat her, I really can't blame her for trying to find a few moments of happiness for herself."

"Neither can I." Marcus gave her a grim look. "Mrs. Callanach's situation is to be pitied, not criticized."

"I'm sure Seamus had a hand in branding her the worst sort of harlot while turning his brother into a saint. And she could not even speak in her own defense." Charlotte cast her gaze out the window as the carriage tumbled along the cobble-stoned streets toward the Lawnmarket. She could not wait to come face to face with Seamus

Callanach, because she was very determined to give that man a piece of her mind.

CHAPTER NINETEEN

SEATED ON A rickety wooden bench in his cell at the Police Court, Blayne pondered the events that had brought him so low. His uncle had clearly been threatened by Blayne's reappearance. He'd referenced the notion of Blayne attempting to come back and claim what belonged to Seamus on more than one occasion. Blayne hadn't argued. He'd not seen the point when he knew the law was against him. So he'd accepted his fate – the one that had been chasing him for so many years – and walked into the Police Court without the slightest resistance two days earlier.

"Mr. Callanach," a clipped tone spoke from beyond the bars. "Ye've two visitors."

With the weariness of a man well into his eighties, Blayne stood. It would probably be his uncle's prosecutor with his clerk, although he'd not expected either to arrive until later. He snorted. The speed with which they'd shown up was a testament to how eager Seamus was to put an end to things.

Sighing, he approached the bars and waited. Still dressed in the clothes he'd put on six days ago when he'd gone to get married, he felt like hell. There had been no chance to bathe along the way, no opportunity for privacy. He'd slept in the same room as the two men his uncle had hired to guard him, which meant he'd barely slept at all.

A soft feminine tread accompanied by the firm clip of men's boots approached. Blayne shrugged. He supposed the prosecutor's clerk could be a woman. But when Charlotte's lovely face materialized before him, he was forced to blink several times just to make sure she was real. It wasn't possible, yet there she was with Marcus by her side. Her smile was brittle, but it held as she reached out and clasped his hand through between the bars.

"It is so good to see you again," she whispered, her voice thick with emotion. Stepping closer, she pressed up against the bars so she could kiss him. "I've been so terribly worried and concerned for your wellbeing, Blayne."

His heart thrummed in response to her sweet caress. "Ye ken now that's not my name, lass."

"It always will be to me." She took a step back. "Unless you prefer I call you James."

He shook his head. "Why are ye here?"

"To get you out of this mess so you and I can get on with our plans."

A startled laugh escaped him. "I'm going to hang for murder. My God, Marcus, whatever were ye thinking, bringing her all the way to Scotland?"

"It was actually she who brought me," Marcus

said.

"I tried to bring Guthrie," Charlotte said, "but he and Regina have recently learned they're expecting, so he was reluctant to leave her side. Besides, Marcus has been meaning to travel to Scotland anyway in order to visit the university. This seemed like a good opportunity."

"Naturally, my intention is to help you first," Marcus said. "The rest can be handled once we've seen to your release."

"Guthrie's going to be a father?" Blayne found the notion strangely amusing.

"Never mind that. Right now, we need to focus on stopping your uncle from accomplishing his nefarious goal." Charlotte raised her chin. "We've spoken to your mother from whom we've learnt a great deal – things I'm sure you are not aware of."

Baffled by her expediency, Blayne could only stare at Charlotte in wonder while she continued to tell him all manner of things, like how his mother could no longer speak after what had happened, how his father used to beat her, and how she'd been denied any chance at defending herself or Blayne.

"I am convinced a competent solicitor can have this entire case torn to pieces before it's even launched," Charlotte continued. "After all, your father was the one who murdered Mr. Hollander. You yourself only struck your father with the candelabra as a last resort, and you did so in order to save your mother's life. The fact that her larynx was crushed just proves she would have died had you not interfered when you did."

"I can scarcely credit the lengths ye're willing to go to on my behalf," Blayne murmured as tears crept into his eyes. He did not want her to see him weak, but it couldn't really be helped. She'd completely undone him.

"Would you not do the same for me?" she asked with a wry smile that knocked his heart into higher gear.

"Of course I would, lass, but—"

"Well, there you are then." She squeezed his hand. "I love you, and in spite of all the concerns you must have had over me discovering all of this, it doesn't change how I feel. If anything, it makes me furious on your behalf and on your mother's as well. What the two of you had to endure because of those two horrid men is beyond the pale."

"I never knew Papa hit her, although I suppose I should have realized the sort of man who'd whip his son would have no trouble with laying his hand on his wife."

"My only reproach against you, Blayne, is that you never wrote her. All these years, she thought you were dead."

"I never knew that, but ye're right, I should have sent word. I was just so afraid my uncle would intercept my letter and track me down." He'd known Seamus would stop at nothing and as it turned out, he hadn't. Even after nineteen years, Blayne remained an obsession to him – an opponent who had to be gotten rid of.

"I know, and I do believe she'll forgive you for

that reason. I certainly will."

"When we arrived here," Marcus said, "we were fortunate enough to overhear a conversation between a couple of gentlemen. One was clearly a solicitor and since he sounded like a competent fellow, I asked him for his card. We'll head to his office as soon as we've finished speaking with you."

Against his better judgment, hope bloomed in Blayne's chest. Winning in a battle against Seamus would be no easy task. He could not allow himself to believe it possible until it actually happened. All the same, he pulled Charlotte closer so he could kiss her again. "Thank ye, lass. I'll never forget what ye've done for me."

"I'd do it again a thousand times over," she promised. "No man gets to ruin my wedding without facing the consequence."

Blayne grinned and kissed her one last time before she and Marcus left.

Mr. Richmond was an older gentleman with a grave disposition – the sort who looked like he'd scowl in response to a joke rather than laugh. He was precisely the sort of thoughtful person Charlotte wanted in Blayne's corner.

"Tell me all you know," Mr. Richmond said once they were seated in his office. His voice was slightly gruff, but lacked the distinctive brogue Charlotte had grown accustomed to from the Scotts. "Don't leave anything out. Remember, even a seemingly insignificant detail can prove useful."

Charlotte began. She related how she and Blayne had met, who he'd pretended to be for most of his life, why he'd taken a false identity, how and why he'd killed his father, and his uncle's subsequent lies absolving his brother of all wrongdoing. "Seamus Callanach insisted James was dead."

"Indeed." Mr. Richmond made several notes before raising his gaze to Charlotte. "Killing a man is a serious offense, Miss Russell, regardless of the reasoning. And while I will agree Mr. Callanach may have deserved his fate, if he did indeed murder Mr. Hollander as you describe, there is no proof this is what happened."

"Mrs. Callanach witnessed it with her own eyes," Charlotte protested. "She may not be able to speak, but she can write a statement."

Mr. Richmond's grim expression was not a good source for optimism. "Her reputation has been torn to shreds by what happened. No one will take her at her word. Certainly not after all these years. Which makes any testimony she might be willing to give as good as useless."

"Mr. Callanach lied," Charlotte insisted. "He told the world his nephew had been so enraged when he'd learnt of his mother's infidelity that he'd murdered Mr. Hollander, then struck down his father when he'd tried to restrain him. Mr. Callanach said James Callanach died when he fell from his horse while fleeing, and that he had him buried in an unmarked grave as punishment for his sin."

"And therein lies the defense."

Charlotte blinked. "I beg your pardon?"

"Earlier, you referred to the man who has been imprisoned by Seamus Callanach as Mr. Blayne MacNeil. And yet, you have spoken of Seamus' nephew – the lad who's reputed to have committed murder – as James Callanach." Mr. Richmond steepled his fingers. "Are you in fact quite certain the two are one and the same? And I suggest you take a moment to consider your answer carefully, Miss Russell."

Charlotte sat back.

"Maybe," Marcus said in a slow drawl, "Mr. Seamus Callanach has been mistaken."

"That is what I am thinking," Mr. Richmond said.

"After all," Marcus added, "One cannot bury someone and then resurrect them two decades later. Can one?"

"It does seem unlikely," Mr. Richmond agreed.

"So…" Charlotte said, warming to the idea she was being presented with, "Mr. Seamus Callanach has accused an innocent man to whom he's not related?"

"He has certainly accused a man known as Blayne MacNeil of being someone whom it would be impossible for him to be when Seamus himself has said that person is dead." Mr. Richmond frowned as if in thought. "And on what grounds? An old woman's suggestion that Mr. MacNeil might bear some resemblance to Bruce Callanach? That's hardly a solid basis for an arrest, never mind a trial. Plus, you've also said your mother, Lady Elkins, saw little resemblance either, besides them both being Scottish and tall."

Charlotte considered this. Denying Blayne was James would be the simplest way forward – so simple in fact it surprised her she'd not thought of it herself, or that Blayne hadn't used it in his defense. Perhaps he'd believed in his own guilt so much he'd simply accepted his fate when Seamus showed up in the church and accused him.

Of course, insisting Seamus was mistaken – that he'd wrongfully blamed a different man – would lead to another problem, namely Blayne losing out on whatever inheritance might be his due. There could be thousands of pounds in the Callanach coffers, money that would forever after belong to Seamus if Blayne denied his true identity. But considering the alternative, which would be a lengthy trial with an unpredictable outcome, it might be an option worth taking. Indeed, it might be the *only* option if he wished to live.

And yet…

"Since any attempt we make to defend Mr. MacNeil will have a direct impact on him," Charlotte said, "I believe it would be best if you were to meet with him, Mr. Richmond, in order to present him with his options so he can decide how to proceed."

"I'll do so tomorrow," Mr. Richmond assured her. "If he agrees to let me help him, I'll meet with the Chief Judiciary afterward so we can resolve the matter as quickly as possible."

Pleased with Mr. Richmond's solid advice and efficiency, Charlotte paid his fee and offered her thanks. Having forfeited her dowry when she departed for Scotland, her chance of regaining rights over her manuscript as good as lost, and Blayne sacrificing his savings to help out her father, she wasn't sure how they would ever afford the life they'd hoped for.

She shook her head and chastised herself for worrying over such things. All that mattered was that they'd be together, and if that meant living at a St. Giles tavern for a while, then so be it. At least they wouldn't be homeless.

Hope filled Blayne to the brim as he listened to Mr. Richmond. He'd not dared believe he actually stood a chance of acquittal, and yet, the solicitor had found a cunning way to beat his uncle. Provided Blayne was willing to make one last sacrifice.

Unfortunately, as luck would have it, the solicitor returned the following morning with unwelcome news.

"I was denied a meeting with the Chief Judiciary," Mr. Richmond informed Blayne with regret. "In other words, I was unable to issue a plea to have you released on grounds of unjust imprisonment. To make matters worse, a trial has been scheduled for Thursday next week at the High Court of Justiciary. I'm sorry."

Blayne could only stare at him while an unwelcome sense of defeat crawled through him. "Sounds like I'll be needing a barrister then."

"Indeed. I've already spoken with a colleague of mine. Mr. Walsh is the finest defense barrister you'll find this side of Hadrian's Wall. After explaining your situation, he believes you could have a chance of winning."

"Thank ye, Mr. Roberts. If ye dinnae mind, as one last request, I'd like ye to ask Miss Russell to come and see me again." It surprised Blayne a bit that she hadn't been back yet. He missed her.

"Right." Mr. Roberts shifted his feet. "Turns out the prosecutor has barred you from receiving visitors."

"What?"

"I thought you'd been informed."

No one had told him a bloody word. Blayne scowled. "Perhaps ye can pass on a message then?"

"Of course."

"Just tell her I love her and that I'm prepared to do all I can to end this nightmare."

Mr. Roberts pressed his lips together and nodded. "I'll be sure to let her know."

As soon as Mr. Roberts was gone, Blayne slumped back onto the bench in his cell and lowered his head to his hands. He'd hoped to avoid a public spectacle where he'd be questioned about the past while a crowd of onlookers watched. Already, the papers would probably be in the process of notifying the public. *Bruce Callanach's murderous son returns to stand trial.*

Blayne scoffed and tried to think of Charlotte – of her lovely smiles and the welcoming warmth of her embrace. The kisses they'd shared and her stalwart support. Her declarations of love.

His heart beat soundly against his chest. He'd give up whatever he had to for her – deny his true identity and walk away from the right to his inheritance. It was the only way in which he could be assured a future with her – the only way to avoid being charged with murder and hanged. And besides, what did a manor and some coin matter anyway? He'd lived without all of that this long, he'd easily continue to do so in years to come.

The only thing of any importance to him was her, so if remaining Blayne MacNeil for the rest of his days was what was needed in order for them to marry, then there was nothing more for him to consider.

Satisfied with the decision he'd made, he entered the courtroom on the appointed day with his head held high. Murmurs raced from corner to corner. Blayne ignored it all and sought out the one person who could provide him with reassurance.

Charlotte's gaze snared his, a slight – almost imperceptible – nod followed. Blayne's chest expanded in response to her support. It felt as though an invisible thread existed between them, binding them as one – a joint force against the rest of the world.

Forced to turn away from her in order to take his place before the judges, Blayne caught a glimpse of his uncle. A smug smile pulled at the man's mouth. Clearly, Seamus finally had Blayne precisely where he wanted him.

"Let's keep this brief," the prosecutor, introduced by the clerk as Mr. Shedwell, intoned. "Ye've all heard the charges against the man ye see before ye. Mr. James Callanach murdered two men. Stabbed one to death and struck down the other. I'm sure many of ye recall the brutal event." Murmurs of agreement followed this statement. "But rather than face the consequence of his actions, the coward ran."

Blayne forced his gaze back to Charlotte in search of calm. She raised her chin and smiled, offering him a much needed reprieve from the accusations laid against him and the anger he harbored toward himself.

"Now, he's back. And I say we see him punished so his poor uncle can finally have the justice he deserves." Mr. Shedwell gestured toward his right while cheers of agreement erupted throughout the room. "Mrs. Archer. If ye'd be so kind as to give the court yer testimony."

"Silence," one of the judges, introduced as MacNally, shouted when the cheers continued. "If ye would, Mrs. Archer."

Blayne steeled himself for what the former housekeeper would say. "That night, when it happened, one of the footmen alerted me to some right awful goings on upstairs. The poor boy – Mr. Dunn, was his name – could barely speak on account of the horror he'd seen. When I arrived at the scene, all I could see was blood. There was so much of it, it registered before I noticed the bodies."

"Do ye ken who committed the crime?" Mr.

Shedwell asked.

"Aye. It had to have been Master James, didn't it? After all, he was the only one who was missing. It's hard to believe an innocent person would run."

"I quite agree," Mr. Shedwell said. He motioned for the next witness, and then the one after that, until five testimonies had been provided.

In Blayne's opinion, none proved a thing, but then again, they didn't have to. According to the law, it was up to him to show the court that there was no basis behind the charges and to prove his own innocence. He waited calmly for Mr. Walsh's turn.

The barrister eventually stood. He took a moment to study those present, then said, "As I understand it, Mr. James Callanach has been charged with stabbing his mother's lover to death, after which he apparently struck down his father with the use of a candelabra. Is that correct?"

"I dinnae ken where ye're going with this, Mr. Walsh," Judge MacNally said. "I trust ye're not wasting our time?"

"On the contrary," Mr. Walsh said.

Judge MacNally grunted and indicated the clerk who'd read the charges. "Ye may answer the question."

"Aye, that's correct," the clerk said.

"Well, in that case," Mr. Walsh said, "I suggest we end this farce of a trial before it goes any further, because according to Mr. Seamus

Callanach's own testimony, which I've located a record of"—he produced a piece of paper which he handed to Judge MacNally—"Mr. James Callanach has been dead and buried these past nineteen years."

Gasps of outrage filled the courtroom.

"That's a damned lie," Seamus shouted while pointing an angry finger at Blayne.

"In fact," Mr. Walsh persisted, his voice rising amid the noise, "the man sitting there, wrongfully accused, is Mr. Blayne MacNeil, a London tavern owner with nae connection at all to the Callanachs beside the fact that he happens to come from the same country."

"Ach, for Christ sake," Judge MacNally muttered. He handed the piece of paper over to the other two judges so they could see it as well. "Did no one think to confirm the accused man's identity?"

"I took Mr. Callanach at his word," Mr. Shedwell said, his voice dripping with annoyance.

"Mr. MacNeil," Judge MacNally said, directing his gaze on Blayne, "Can ye prove who ye are?"

Blayne nodded. "Aye." He reached inside his jacket pocket and retrieved the gift he'd intended to give Charlotte after their wedding. For the first time in several days, he was glad he still wore the same set of clothes. "Here ye go."

Judge MacNally accepted the piece of paper Blayne gave him and studied it for a moment before holding it up and saying, "This is a deed to The Black Swan tavern, transferring half the

ownership of said tavern from Mr. Blayne Mac-
Neil to his wife, Mrs. Charlotte MacNeil, upon
the day of their marriage."

Blayne watched as Charlotte's eyes began to
glisten.

"Now, with this added piece of evidence taken
into account," Judge MacNally said, "I really
dinnae see how this man can be anyone other
than who he claims to be. Case dismissed."

"Ye'll nae get away with this," Seamus shouted.
"I'll nae let my brother's killer go unpunished!"

"Bailiffs," Judge MacNally said, "please have
Mr. Callanach escorted out before he makes
a bigger mockery of this court. Mr. MacNeil,
ye're free to go."

Blayne could scarcely credit his good fortune.
Charlotte had done it. By some miracle, she'd
managed to get him released. Without hesitation, he went to her and pulled her fiercely into
his arms.

"Thank God this is over," she whispered
while he wound his arms around her in a tight
embrace. "These past few days have been the
worst of my life."

"I cannae disagree with ye there, lass." He
kissed the top of her head before easing away
and adding a bit more respectable distance. His
gaze shifted to Marcus who stood by her side.
"Thank ye both for yer efforts. I'm truly grateful."

"It was mostly Miss Russell's doing," Marcus
said. Blayne nodded.

"I can't believe you planned to give me half

of your business," Charlotte said while gazing at him with wondrous eyes.

He smiled at her. "I've little else left to offer, and I wanted to give ye something."

"You know you're all I need. Right?"

"I do." A thought struck. "How will my mother fit into all of this?"

"She's not your mother," Charlotte murmured. "She can't be. But she can be a woman on whom I have taken pity after hearing her story. I would suggest we invite her to return to England with us. If you agree and she wishes to come."

"Aye," Blayne said. "I think that's a grand idea."

"Shall we go see her then?"

Blayne could scarcely wait. He and his mother had not been especially close, but he'd still loved her. The thought of seeing her again after all this time instilled in him a mixture of nervousness and excitement. She'd been severely wounded when they'd last parted and even though he'd not realized as much at the time, he'd still left her with two dead men and an unkind brother-in-law. Blayne hoped she'd forgive him.

Taking Charlotte's arm, Blayne escorted her through the front door of the High Court of Justiciary and out onto the pavement beyond. The sun shone from a clear blue sky, bathing him in its warmth. Intent on telling Charlotte he loved her, he turned toward her as gunfire shattered the calm.

Screams engulfed the air.

"Get her back inside, Marcus." Blayne pushed

Charlotte behind him and scanned the street. People were running, seeking shelter. Blayne stayed where he was until he spotted a rough looking fellow on the opposite corner.

The shooter turned and started hurrying away, so Blayne gave chase. It was one thing to try and kill him, but to make the attempt while he was with Charlotte was not to be borne. Not to mention there were other people about, any one of whom could have gotten between Blayne and the lead ball no doubt meant for his chest.

Charging forward, Blayne barreled straight into the would-be assassin's back and felled him. The man cried out in pain as he hit the ground.

"Who ordered ye to murder me?" Blayne asked even though he already knew the answer. Only one person was mad enough to go this far. Seamus wanted vengeance on behalf of his brother. He'd not accept letting Blayne walk away. Considering the threat he'd made when the case had been dismissed, Blayne should have realized as much, but he'd been too overcome by relief to notice the danger Seamus still posed.

"I dinnae ken what ye're on about."

Blayne slammed his fist into the man's face. Cartilage crunched beneath his knuckles. Blood spurted from the man's nose. He cried out in pain. "Give me a name."

"I cannae."

"Ye'll do so soon enough, I wager." Blayne disarmed the fellow, then hauled him to his feet by his jacket collar and marched him back to the courthouse. Two constables who'd come to see what was going on met him when he arrived. "This gunman just tried to kill me. I suggest ye charge him and figure out who he's working for."

"We'll get it done right away," one of the constables said as Blayne handed the man over to their care.

"And see to it that the man behind this attack gets what he deserves."

The constables nodded and marched the gunman away.

Blayne took a deep breath. His hands were shaking, not so much on account of the danger he himself had faced, but rather because he'd feared for Charlotte's life in a way that had nearly crippled him. Lord have mercy, it was hard to love someone so fiercely.

Forcing himself to be calm for her sake, he followed the constables back inside the building only to learn that the fear he'd experienced seconds earlier was nothing compared with the gut-wrenching panic that ripped through his body when he saw blood pooling at the front of Charlotte's spencer.

"I believe I was shot," she said, her voice weak as he hurried toward the bench where she sat. Marcus held her in a propped position while a constable kneeled on the floor nearby with medical supplies he apparently had no clue what to do with.

"Jesus."

"I don't think it's as bad as it seems," Charlotte said while Blayne did his best not to fall apart.

He had to remain cool-headed. He could not allow himself to panic.

"Where's the nearest hospital?" he asked.

"A mile or so away," the constable said.

"Well then, let's go."

"I really don't think there's a need for that," Charlotte countered. "I'm sure it's just a scratch. In fact, I barely feel it at all."

She would once the surgeon began extracting the lead ball. "Hand me the compress ye've got there."

The constable placed a thick cotton wad in Blayne's hand. Blayne placed it firmly over the spot on Charlotte's shoulder and pressed down hard.

"Ow!"

Ignoring her discomfort, Blayne swept her up in his arms. "Would someone please get a carriage ready."

"I'm on it," Marcus assured him.

"And make sure that damn gunman tells ye who was behind this," Blayne yelled. "I want his head on a bloody pike!"

Chest tight and very aware that all he cared for in this world could be lost if they didn't make haste, Blayne held Charlotte in his lap while the police carriage they rode in charged through the streets with reassuring speed.

What had begun as a dull ache in her shoulder had since transformed into burning pain. Charlotte did her best to hide it so as not to worry Blayne, but it was difficult not to wince when he shifted her in his arms.

"We'll be there soon, lass." His voice swept the top of her head, the low tones of his brogue a soothing comfort that put her at ease. "Ye'll be right as rain before ye ken it."

She nodded against the solid wall of his chest while breathing him in. Her hand clutched the front of his jacket, but it was becoming harder and harder for her to hold on. Lightheadedness overwhelmed her. She became aware of Marcus saying something but couldn't quite make out the words. Other sounds followed, all of them unfamiliar, and she felt herself getting jostled about. She heard herself groan. A spicy liquid with a hint of bitterness slid down her throat.

"That's it," Blayne said from somewhere far away. "Drink as much as ye can."

Charlotte did her best to swallow the strange concoction. She felt an odd pull and tug sensation accompanied by a wonderful weightlessness as every sound faded into the background. And then, there was nothing but glorious silence.

"She was incredibly lucky."

The unfamiliar voice pulled her out of the deep water she'd been swimming in. It was a sunny day, so she and Blayne had found a lovely lake to bathe in.

"The lead ball missed all major veins and muscle."

Who was this man and what on earth was he talking about?

"So she'll be fine?"

Ah. Blayne. Oh, how she loved him. They'd

have a picnic when they were done swimming. Only, she wasn't in the water anymore and…she felt like she was lying down. How strange.

"She'll be sore for a few days and will require much rest, but yes, she will be fine."

"Thank Christ."

"Blayne?" She couldn't make sense of the world right now but at least he was there.

A large hand swiftly clasped hers. "I'm right here, lass."

"You sound funny." His voice was rougher than usual and slightly thicker as well.

"I'm just mighty relieved to ken ye'll be staying with me," he murmured.

In spite of the drowsiness trying to pull her back down, Charlotte forced her eyes open so she could gaze up at his handsome face. "Your eyes are wet."

"Aye," he said with a grin. He gave the tears a quick swipe, then pressed a kiss to her forehead. "Ye very nearly stopped my heart today."

"What happened?" She glanced to the side and frowned. "We were at the lake together but now we're in a small room. I don't understand."

"The lake must have been a dream. Ye've been asleep for at least two hours." His hand stroked over the top of her head. "Someone tried to kill me, but they shot ye instead by mistake."

"Oh. Good."

"Good?" He sounded appalled.

"Better me than you."

"Ach, lass. I've got to disagree with ye there."

She chuckled and instantly regretted it when

she felt an answering soreness in her shoulder. "The gunman?"

"He's been apprehended. The constables at the Police Court are questioning him, which I'm hoping will lead to an order for Seamus to be arrested."

"You think he was behind it?"

"Aye. I've nae doubt about it."

Charlotte closed her eyes. She could feel her grip on consciousness slipping.

Blayne squeezed her hand. "Get as much rest as ye need. I'll be here when ye wake."

With this assurance, Charlotte sank further into oblivion.

When she woke again, she was starving. "I feel like I haven't eaten in years."

Blayne smiled. "I'll order some food for ye right away."

"Where's Marcus?" Charlotte asked when Blayne returned to her bedside.

"Chatting with one of the doctors, I believe. Learning as much as he can about his profession of choice before he goes to visit the university."

"We probably should encourage him to do so now that you've been released. I think you and I can manage well enough on our own from now on. Don't you?"

"I do."

A nurse arrived with a tray filled mostly with fruit and a few slices of ham. Bread and wine accompanied the dish and Charlotte dug in with gusto. She stopped mid-bite when she caught Blayne grinning. "What?"

"It's just grand to see ye show such enthusiasm for food."

"Would you like some?"

"Nae. I'll grab another bite to eat later when ye've gone back to sleep."

His comment gave her pause. "How many meals have you had while I've been here?"

"Three, if ye count my breakfast this morning. There's a decent inn just down the road. Marcus and I spent the night there."

"The night?"

"Aye." He laughed when she kept on staring at him. "Ye were shot yesterday afternoon. After ye went back to sleep ye were out for twelve solid hours"

"I see." She had no sense of time at all, but it did explain his change of clothes.

"According to the doctor and the surgeon who operated on ye, ye'll be ready to leave the hospital tomorrow. We'll see how ye do from there, aye?"

"Aye," she agreed, and bit into a crunchy apple slice.

CHAPTER TWENTY

AS EXPECTED, CHARLOTTE was discharged from the hospital the following afternoon with instructions to keep her wound clean by gently washing it and re-applying fresh bandages twice daily. She was to return immediately at the first sign of infection.

"Will this do for now?" Blayne asked when he showed Charlotte to the room he'd acquired for her and Daisy. The maid looked like she might throw herself into her mistress's arms, though she did manage to restrain herself. Blayne couldn't help but smile. He knew precisely how Daisy felt.

"It's perfect," Charlotte assured him. She reached out and took Daisy's hand. "It's good to see you again."

"I can't tell you how relieved I am to see you looking so well, miss. You gave me a right awful fright."

"Me too," Blayne said. "But our Charlotte is made of stern stuff. I'll let ye get settled. When ye're ready, ye can meet me downstairs in one of the supper rooms. Daisy, ye can escort her, right?"

"Of course. I'll not let her out of my sight."

"Good to know." Blayne left the two women and went to drop his new hat and gloves in his own bedchamber before heading downstairs. He wished he and Charlotte could share a room so he could look after her himself, but since they weren't married yet and Daisy was here, he had no excuse to dismiss propriety in such a way. But it was one of the subjects he meant to discuss with Charlotte, so he launched straight into it as soon as she arrived by asking, "After everything that has happened and all ye've learned about me these last few days, do ye still want to be my wife?"

"Yes, Blayne. Marrying you is the only thing I want at the moment."

Seated beside her, he leaned closer so he could kiss her. "Thank God, for I dinnae ken how I'd survive if ye walked away from me now."

"I'll never leave you, no matter what. But there's something you should know. My father said he would withhold my dowry if I followed you to Scotland, so we won't be able to count on that money."

It didn't really seem fair since the money had been Blayne's to begin with. He wondered if Charlotte had mentioned this to her father, but decided it didn't matter. No sense in bringing up something that wouldn't be able to help them.

Closing his eyes, he placed his forehead against hers while holding her hand. "Our lives willnae be as easy as we had hoped. We'll have to give up the townhouse I rented. Unless ye were able to reacquire the rights to yer book before coming after me."

She stiffened. "About that…"

Leaning back, Blayne met her gaze. "What is it?"

"I received a letter from Mr. Agerson right before departing for Scotland."

"And?"

"He invited me to meet with him and the imposter in order to sort out the mess, but if I chose to do so, I would have had to delay coming after you." She shrugged her shoulders. "It's just a book, Blayne. I can always write another."

Undone by the sacrifice she'd made for him, Blayne drew her against him with careful movements so he could kiss her as thoroughly as she deserved. "It's nae just a book, Charlotte. It's *yer* book and ye deserve to get paid for it."

"I agree, but you are still more important to me than any book I'll ever write."

By all that was holy, he wasn't sure what he'd done to deserve a woman who loved him with such devotion. "We'll get it back. Mark my word, lass, I'll make certain of it."

She smiled against his mouth as she kissed him, and blushed all the way to her hairline when a serving girl cleared her throat. The servant had arrived without either of them taking notice and was ready for their order.

"What would ye recommend?" Blayne asked, while Charlotte kept her gaze on his chest.

"We've a suckling pig this evening. It's been

roasting since morning."

"Two portions of that then," Blayne said, "along with two tankards of ale. And please make sure Miss Russell's maid receives some as well."

As soon as the serving girl was gone, Blayne returned his attention to Charlotte, "Now then. Let's figure out when we ought to get married."

"As soon as possible." Charlotte's cheeks turned an even deeper shade of pink, but she did not shy away from looking at him while she spoke. "After you've met with your mother."

"And after yer wound has completely healed," he added.

"But that could take several more days."

"It probably will, but I'd like ye to be completely recovered for our wedding night."

"Goodness."

He grinned and placed a swift kiss on her cheek. "We'll start with my mother tomorrow and take it from there. Besides, this may be Scotland, but I still intend to wed ye in a church in front of a vicar, not over an anvil like some eloped couple with scandal nipping at their heels."

She snorted. "I'd say we met scandal face to face and gave it a run for its money."

"True enough, lass. True enough."

In the end it took four days to arrange the wedding, at which point Charlotte's wound was healed, but still a tad sore. Blayne's reunion with his mother a few days prior had gone remarkably well, but he'd been in a dim mood when they'd left. His guilt over what had happened and the subsequent choices he'd made still dogged him. Charlotte could only hope the weight he carried deep in his heart would ease with time and that bringing his mother to live with them would help in this regard.

Dressed in a pale pink day dress she'd packed for her journey, and accompanied by Daisy, Charlotte went to meet Blayne by the inn's front door. He was joined by Marcus with whom he appeared to be deep in conversation until he registered her arrival.

Eyes sparkling with unabashed pleasure, he turned more fully toward her. "Are ye ready?"

"More so than ever before."

Blayne offered Charlotte his arm. It was a short walk to the church and the weather was pleasant, so they'd chosen not to bother with taking the carriage.

"How's your plan to become a doctor coming along?" Charlotte asked Marcus when they'd gone a few paces.

"Well, I imagine. I'm to meet with the admissions board tomorrow to learn if they'll accept me."

"They will," Blayne said. To Charlotte he added, "He's received letters of recommendation from the Duke of Redding as well as from two physicians who work at the hospital where you were treated."

"Impressive. When would you be scheduled to start?"

"The academic year begins in ten days, on

September twenty-first."

"I'm excited for you," Charlotte said. They'd reached the church. "I trust you will write to let us know how it goes?"

"I still have to be admitted."

"You will be," Charlotte said, echoing Blayne's sentiment.

They entered the church and greeted Blayne's mother who'd come with her maid. The vicar came to bid them all welcome. "If ye're ready, we can proceed."

Charlotte took a deep breath and smiled at Blayne. "Shall we?"

"Absolutely," he murmured and led her toward the altar.

Not a single word was spoken this time when the vicar asked if there was cause for Blayne and Charlotte not to be joined in holy matrimony. She breathed a sigh of relief and glanced at Blayne. His smiling eyes met hers and instantly warmed her heart while he promised to love her, comfort her, honor, and keep her in sickness and in health, forsaking all other,

And then it was her turn, to make the same pledge. Speaking clearly, she said, "I will."

They gave their troth to each other next and then Blayne placed a thin gold band upon her finger. "With this ring I thee wed, with my body I thee worship, and with all my worldly goods I thee endow: In the Name of the Father, and of the Son, and of the Holy Ghost. Amen."

A prayer followed and after that a blessing and a psalm. Charlotte scarcely heard another word.

All she could focus on was that it had been done. She was finally Blayne's wife and as such, she could not wait for them to be done with the wedding so they could begin their life together. And then, more suddenly than she'd expected, Blayne swept her into his arms for a kiss so thorough it made her dizzy.

"Congratulations to you both," Marcus said.

"I'm so incredibly happy for you, miss," Daisy added with a beaming smile.

Mrs. Callanach drew Charlotte into her arms for a tight embrace.

"She's grateful to ye," said Mrs. Callanach's maid, whose name turned out to be Hannah. "Ye brought her son back and saved him from his uncle."

Since Blayne's release Seamus had been arrested for attempted murder, and while he would not be sentenced until he'd been heard in court, it was clear his actions would lead to severe consequences. The news had made the headline in the previous day's paper.

"Shall we go and see about our wedding breakfast, Wife?" Blayne asked with a twinkle in his eyes. The inn where they were staying would provide it in one of their supper rooms.

Charlotte grinned. "Indeed we shall, Husband."

"Ach, I do like the sound of that word," he said as they set off together, arm in arm.

The wedding breakfast was a small affair, hardly worth mentioning at all by Mayfair standards. In Charlotte's opinion, it was perfect.

Devoid of nosy gossips and those who *had* to be invited because of their rank, it consisted only of the people who truly cared about Charlotte's and Blayne's well-being. There was no judgment to be found here, no condescension or shocked dismay over a viscount's daughter marrying a St. Giles tavern keep who'd been accused of murder. Only happiness reigned, and it was wonderful.

"My mistress would like to offer ye both a wedding gift," Hannah said when Mrs. Callanach nudged her after dessert.

"That's generous, Mama, but there's really nae need," Blayne said. He looked slightly uncomfortable all of a sudden, so Charlotte placed her hand over his to offer support.

"Ye're her son," Hannah said. "Her only child. And she is yer only parent, so if she feels the need, ye ought to accept it with grace."

Mrs. Callanach nodded her agreement, then handed a piece of paper to Blayne. After unfolding it, he proceeded to read. His eyes widened. "This is too much. We cannae possibly accept."

His mother handed him another piece of paper and smiled as only a mother could when faced with a stubborn child. Blayne frowned. "I knew ye'd say that," he read, "but I insist."

"What is the gift?" Charlotte asked, her curiosity mounting with each passing second.

"Read for yerself." Blayne handed her the letter, then told his mother, "I really dinnae deserve this."

Another note crossed the table. "It's not just for ye. It's also for yer wife and…" Blayne's voice faltered slightly before he managed to add, "my grandchildren."

With heat creeping into her cheeks, Charlotte tried to focus on her own reading while Blayne and Hannah exchanged a few words. And now Marcus was adding his opinion and Daisy too. Doing her best to block them all out, Charlotte fixed her gaze on the neatly penned words before her.

With no inheritance to speak of and having sacrificed your own hard-earned savings in order to free the woman you love from a disagreeable union, your future is not as secure as it ought to have been. I'm sorry for this. The events that took place so long ago and forced you to flee are largely my fault, and while I cannot change the past, I hope to have some influence over the future. As such, I wish to bestow upon you and your wife the sum of four thousand pounds.

Charlotte sucked in a breath.

The funds are the remainder of my inheritance from my father. He always believed a woman should have her own means by which to support herself. Just in case.

Smart fellow. Charlotte wished she could have met him.

She folded the letter and met Mrs. Callanach's gaze. "Thank you. This truly is most magnanimous of you." To Blayne she said, "I'll let you decide what to do, but consider the following first. We have invited your mother and Hannah to live with us. Children will follow if things take their natural course. So maybe that cottage we had in mind, or something slightly bigger, would not be the worst idea. Provided we can afford it?"

He took a deep breath while pressing his lips together in obvious disapproval. "It's a huge sum, Charlotte."

"Agreed." Lowering her voice, Charlotte told him softly. "I'm happy to stay at The Black Swan if you prefer, but I think it would please your mother to know she was able to help you in some way."

"I suppose the countryside would be a better spot for us to raise a family," he grumbled.

"And you can plant as many crops as you like."

"That would *nae* be my reason for accepting this."

"No. Of course not. But you have to admit it's an added benefit." She gave him a wry smile. "But the fact is, we'll still need an income. Of course I'll keep writing, but with a decent piece of land, you could earn a living too from the very thing you dream of doing. We could in fact end up getting exactly what we've both wanted for so long much quicker than if we were to refuse your mother's kindness."

"I dunno." He glanced at his mother.

"I can just see you managing a shop full of plants on some village high-street," Charlotte murmured. "Say yes, and give her your thanks."

He promptly did as she asked. The edge of his mouth twitched. He shook his head as laughter seeped into his eyes. "Am I to be managed by ye in this way for the rest of my days now?"

"Not at all," Charlotte quipped as she leaned

in and kissed his cheek. "I promise never to try and sway your opinion on Sundays."

Everyone laughed in response to that swift rejoinder, then raised their glasses in celebration of the newly married couple. It was later agreed Blayne and Charlotte would leave for London five days later together with Mrs. Callanach, Hannah, and Daisy, since this would allow Marcus the time he needed to learn if he would be staying in Edinburgh or not.

"Have I ever told ye how stunning ye are?" Blayne asked Charlotte when they retreated to his bedchamber later. Leaning against the door, he watched her move around the room with a restless energy. "I remember the very first moment I saw ye, sitting at a table at The Black Swan. Ye were the bonniest lass I'd ever laid eyes on, but it bothered the hell out of me that I couldnae discern the length of yer hair."

She stopped at that and turned toward him, her expression one of puzzlement. "How curious."

"It was hidden beneath yer bonnet." He pushed away from the door and moved toward her. "The next day, when I came to yer home, I learned yer hair must be quite long and thick to produce the voluminous knot at the nape of yer neck. Now, I finally get to discover how long it really is and how it feels between my fingers."

Her cheeks turned a lovely shade of pink as she gazed back at him with endless wonder. Lips parted, he could not resist. He closed the distance and captured her mouth with his while pulling her flush up against him. God, she tasted divine, and the way she wound her slim arms around his neck until she clung to him for support was enough to drive him mad with longing.

His hand stole its way up her back until his fingers connected with the first hairpin. Pulling it free he sought out another, and another, and the one after that, until her lustrous black locks fell over her shoulders.

"Christ, ye're divine," he told her when he managed to get a good look at her. "I want ye like this every day from now on."

"It really wouldn't be proper," she said with a shy smile that urged him to kiss her once more.

"It will when we're alone together," he told her while pulling her back in his arms. "And just so ye ken, lass, I plan on that happening a lot."

She answered him with a kiss of her own and as he deepened the caress, he lost himself completely in her warmth, her scent, and her flavor. She was perfect in every way and he craved her – craved the nearness they'd have without all this fabric between them, and the bond they would share once they joined their bodies together.

Eager to progress to that point, Blayne popped the first button at the top of her gown and proceeded from there. He kissed his way along the side of her jaw while easing the sleeves down over her arms, then along the length of her neck as he went to work on the laces holding her stays. His mouth traced the curve of her shoulder, eliciting lovely mewls from deep in her throat. And she was no passive bystander either. Her deft hands had already pulled his shirt free from his trousers and snuck their way underneath. The effect was so provocative, he struggled to think straight.

"Blayne?" Her voice was a sensual murmur of pure enticement.

"Hmm?" he purred against her skin.

"Take off your jacket, waistcoat, and shirt."

How could he deny her? Without hesitation he shucked his jacket and tossed it aside. His waistcoat and shirt swiftly followed.

"You're stunning too," she whispered with so much awe he felt like Zeus himself. And then she reached out and trailed the pads of her fingers across his chest, over his arm, and toward his back.

Blayne stiffened in response to her intake of breath. Lord help him, he knew he wasn't perfect. He'd also known his wife would see the ugly welts crisscrossing his flesh. Perhaps he should have better prepared her so she'd not be put off?

"Your father did this?" Her fingers carefully traced the scars.

"Aye." There was no denying his past any longer. No matter the shame.

"I don't think I've ever hated anyone more. Not even Seamus." Her voice cracked. "Perhaps I'm awful for saying this, but I'm glad your father's dead." She pressed a hot kiss to his back.

Pleasure ignited within every cell of his body. A groan rumbled through him. He turned, and caught her in his arms. "Charlotte."

A smug smile of pure satisfaction curled her lips. "Feel good?"

"Aye."

As if emboldened, she leaned in and kissed him again, right over his heart. Blayne wrapped his arms more fully around her and hugged her close for a moment, until her hands slid to his waist and dipped inside his trousers. At which point he lost all reason.

Her clothes were completely removed in seconds, the rest of his own discarded immediately after, and then they were on the bed, his skin against hers.

Blayne kissed her deeply while letting his hands explore every glorious curve she possessed. He reveled in her own attempts to familiarize herself with his body. This was what he'd dreamed of, unguarded vulnerability made possible due to their love. In the end, it was good she knew all there was to know about him, because this – this connection they could now share – was more honest and open than it would have been if he'd managed to keep his past secret.

Lord, he'd been wrong to think doing so would be right. He planted a series of kisses along the length of her torso while sliding one hand up over her hip. Thank God she'd been wiser than he. Thank God she'd chased after him all the way here. And thank God she still loved him in spite of what she now knew. It was miraculous, and he loved her all the more for it.

"Blayne," she gasped when he settled himself between her thighs a short while later and nudged his way forward.

"Aye?" Heaven have mercy, she felt incredible. Taking a deep calming breath, he braced himself above her and tried to keep in check the vigor with which instinct told him to take her. Charlotte deserved to be bedded with gentle movements. She would need time to adjust and acquaint herself with this new activity.

Her fingertips curled into his shoulder and her legs wound around his hips. "I love you."

"I love ye to," he managed to say while gritting his teeth. She really was testing his sanity and his control.

"Then make me yours, Blayne. I promise I'm ready."

"Are ye sure?"

"Yes."

He needed no more incentive. Lowering his head, he kissed her to distract her from the sharp pain he knew she might feel. And then he continued to kiss her. Because he could, because she was his, and because he loved her beyond all reason.

CHAPTER TWENTY ONE

"YOUR FRIEND, MISS Avery Carlisle, is here to see you," Daisy said when she located Charlotte in Blayne's study at The Black Swan. After returning from Scotland two days earlier, Blayne had made temporary arrangements for everyone to stay at the tavern until he and Charlotte found the right property to purchase. They'd begun making inquiries the previous morning.

Surprised, Charlotte shared a quick glance with Blayne before addressing Daisy. "Please show her in."

Avery entered the room a moment later, her somber expression cause for instant concern. Following in her wake, his face downcast, was Albert. Charlotte stood and greeted them both. Blayne followed suit.

"I'm so glad we've finally found you," Avery said. "When we went to your house, or rather your parents' house, they gave us no clue at all of your whereabouts. But then a footman chased us down the street as we walked away. He said you'd gone off to Scotland and gotten married

– felicitations to you both, by the way – and we learned you moved here upon your return."

"Daisy, would you be kind enough to bring us some tea?" Charlotte asked. The rush of words pouring from Avery's mouth suggested they'd all need a fortifying cup very soon. To their guests she said, "Please, come have a seat. You look like you've run all the way here and need a rest."

Avery pushed out a heavy breath and sat in one of the proffered chairs. Charlotte noted her hands were trembling. She cast a look in Blayne's direction and saw that he'd noted this too. Contrary to his sister, Albert appeared more angry than anything else, which was curious.

"Mr. and Miss Carlisle," Blayne said, his calm voice easing the agitated atmosphere Avery and Albert had created. "It's good to see ye both again. I trust yer business has recovered from the break-in ye suffered?"

Avery responded with a tight nod while Albert's expression tightened.

"Did ye ever figure out who was behind it?"

A gulp was the only sound Avery managed in response to that question. She promptly burst into tears.

"Now look what you've done," Albert said while glaring at Blayne.

Baffled by Albert's clipped manner, Charlotte stared at him for a moment in dumbfounded silence before she managed to collect herself. She turned her attention to his sister. "Avery. Whatever is the matter?"

"I'm so sorry," Avery sobbed. "I should have

known. I should have realized what was going on sooner."

Daisy arrived with a tea tray and quickly distributed cups which she then proceeded to fill.

"Take a deep breath, Avery," Charlotte instructed. She turned to Albert. "Do you have a handkerchief you can give her?"

When he shook his head, Blayne retrieved one from his jacket pocket and handed it over.

"Now then," Charlotte said once Daisy had gone and Avery had finished dabbing her eyes. "Why don't you have some tea and tell us why you're so distraught?"

Avery pressed her lips together and gave a tight nod. She drank the tea as instructed, which thankfully seemed to soothe her. "As it turns out, the robbery wasn't random at all. Nor was it carried out by strangers, but rather by my very own brother."

The bitter words shook, as did Avery's teacup and saucer. Charlotte quickly removed them from her hands and set them on Blayne's desk before they could fall to the floor and shatter. She returned to her chair and stared at Albert. "You broke into your sister's office and stole my manuscript?"

"Can you believe it?" Avery's eyes hardened against the tears. "It is the worst sort of betrayal."

Indeed it was. Charlotte glanced at Blayne whose furious glower ought to make Albert regret ever coming here. She could not imagine he'd wrong his sister in such a way. Or her, for that matter. He'd always been so pleasant. "How could you?"

When all he did was shrug, Blayne crossed to where he sat, grabbed him by his cravat, and hauled him upward until he gasped. "Answer the question."

Albert fell back in his seat and coughed. He turned to his sister. "Will you really let that brute treat me like that without protest?"

"Call my husband a brute once more," Charlotte warned Albert, "and you'll have more reason to fear me than him. Now answer the question."

Albert scowled. "It's unjust how hard we struggle to make ends meet when all you have to do is write a ridiculous story."

"My ridiculous story," Charlotte said with mounting anger, "required a lot of hard work. You'd no right to steal it or to reap the reward of my labor."

"My suspicion regarding Albert's involvement," Avery said, "was first raised when I learned of the extravagant purchases he'd begun making. There were new clothes, a gold pocket watch. He even moved out of the rooms we'd been sharing and rented a place for himself on Bond Street. When he turned up to work one morning with an expensive looking new bonnet for me, I had to ask how he could afford it."

"Bloody hell, Avery," Albert snapped. "You're a damn fool when it comes to business. The contracts you offer your authors give them too great an advantage without leaving you with a big enough profit. Especially with regard to someone as successful as *Charles Cunningham*. My God! I had to do something or we'll end up in the poorhouse once the last of our inheritance gets depleted."

"Nothing can justify what you did," Charlotte murmured. "I thought you were my friend, Albert."

He answered with a snort. "Friends don't tease each other with promises of something more."

Charlotte sat back. "I never did any such thing."

"He fancies himself in love with ye," Blayne said. Addressing Albert, he asked, "Am I right?"

"She's too good for the likes of you," Albert seethed. To Charlotte he said, "You broke my heart when you told me you meant to marry that man."

Charlotte shook her head. She'd never considered Albert's interest in her as more than a passing infatuation. "So you decided to punish me? Is that it?"

When Albert didn't respond, Blayne said, "I'm thinking I'd like Mr. Carlisle to be my opponent in the upcoming match this evening."

Albert straightened. "What match would that be?"

"The sort where I get to punch ye in the face," Blayne informed him. When Albert blanched, Blayne tilted his head. "Unless ye convince me of how sorry ye are and give my wife the money ye owe her right now."

"Unfortunately," Avery cut in, "there's no way for you to be reimbursed in full since Albert already spent much of the money he received for the manuscript. But Albert and I have recently visited P. Agerson Publishing to inform them of the situation."

"Surely they'll want to press charges," Blayne said.

"I think Mr. Agerson took pity on me. We agreed it had all been a big misunderstanding, provided Albert quits the publishing business entirely. Mr. Agerson has assured me further payments for the publication of *The Marquess's Unresolved Mysteries* will go to you once you've met with him in order to make the necessary arrangements."

"Thank you, Avery." Charlotte turned to Albert and stared him down. Most of the confidence he'd shown upon his arrival had vanished. Instead, he now looked like a weak man cowering in his chair. "Well?"

He gave Blayne a hasty glance. When Blayne flexed his hands Albert met Charlotte's gaze. "I'm sorry for what I did. It was wrong of me."

"While I appreciate that," Charlotte said, "I think it would be wrong of me to let you walk away unpunished."

Albert's eyes widened while Blayne turned toward her with unmistakable surprise. Apparently he'd thought she'd be soft and lenient. She smirked. Not after all the trouble Albert had put her through.

"Considering you're now out of work, Albert, and my husband requires a new dishwasher, I expect you to show up here every morning for a full day's work until the money you owe me has been paid off."

Outrage filled Albert's eyes while Blayne quietly chuckled. "You want me to slave away for free?"

"I'm thinking it will dissuade you from ever doing something like this again."

"I told you we shouldn't have come here," Albert said to Avery.

His sister scoffed at him. "Shut up, Albert, and face the consequence like a man."

"I'm sorry this happened to you," Charlotte said when she and Blayne escorted Avery to the door a few minutes later while Claus showed Albert the kitchen. "But I am glad you were able to help. *The Marquess's Unresolved Mysteries* will probably have to remain with P. Agerson Publications, but maybe the next novel I write can be published through you again?"

"Would you really trust me with another contract?"

"You've proven yourself to be a loyal friend, Avery. The blame for what happened lies exclusively with Albert."

"And if yer brother is correct with regard to yer contracts leaning too far in the author's favor," Blayne said, "I'd be happy to help ye out from a business standpoint."

"Oh." Avery smiled for the first time since she'd arrived, then frowned. "But that might not be in your wife's best interest."

"We like to think of ourselves as fair-minded people," Charlotte said. "I do not want to take advantage of you any more than you would want to do so of me."

"In that case, I would be happy to accept any help you're willing to offer. Thank you both."

Charlotte pulled her friend into a hug. "We'll be in touch." As soon as she was gone Charlotte turned to Blayne. "Poor woman."

"Indeed." He drew Charlotte into his arms. "This victory does have a sting to it."

"I still can't believe Albert did this."

"He wanted ye for himself, lass, and when he realized that wouldnae happen, he sought to hurt ye."

"And his sister."

"A man in love doesnae always ken how to use his brain." He tilted her chin up and lowered his mouth to hers. "How else can ye explain why I let ye transform me into yer fake fiancé?"

"That happened the day after we'd just met," Charlotte said while gazing into his brown eyes. "You cannot mean to tell me you'd already fallen in love with me then."

"Not completely, perhaps, but I was at least one tenth in love with ye when I realized ye'd pulled yer pistol on Mr. Evans after he dared touch ye."

She chuckled. "And the rest?"

"Yer willingness to fight for what ye want. Yer fondness for Mr. Cunningham. *Being* Mr. Cunningham. Renegotiating with Mr. Cooper. Believing in me when no one else did. Following me all the way to Scotland. Reuniting me with my mother. Setting me free. Showing me every second how much ye love me in return. All yer sweet kisses. That's more than enough for one hundred percent and I'm just getting started."

"I love you too," Charlotte whispered while tears stole into her eyes and her vision blurred. "For saving me when you weren't obligated to do so, for helping me out of my bind with Mr. Cooper. For showing me how to live and for always offering help whenever I needed it. You risked your freedom – your life – to save my reputation."

"Instead, I ruined it."

"Not that I mind." She raked her fingers up through his hair. "I would gladly risk scandal and ruination a thousand times over as long as it means I'll be yours."

"Ye'll always be mine, lass. This I swear." He captured her mouth once more, cementing the certainty of his words with a kiss so thorough it left Charlotte breathless.

Not that she minded. She kissed him right back with equal fervor while joy swam through her veins. She loved this man for countless more reasons, and as long as they had each other, nothing else mattered.

CHAPTER TWENTY TWO

The Windham ballroom, seven years later.

STANDING OFF TO one side, Marcus casually sipped the brandy he favored over the bubbly champagne being passed around by the footmen. A white marble pillar to his left allowed him to savor the music in peace. He loved the classical pieces being played but hated the idea of having to meet with the peers who had been invited to celebrate Regina's birthday. She'd insisted he be there of course, so he was, without revealing his presence.

The brandy slid down his throat, its spicy flavor heating a path straight to his stomach. Later, when all the guests had gone home, he would meet in private with Guthrie and the other dukes for a game of cards – an activity he always relished because they treated him as their equal.

"Supper is ready," the butler intoned once the last piece of music had faded.

Chatter ensued as guests began moving toward the adjoining room. Marcus waited for the subsequent silence, then stepped out from behind the pillar and crossed to the terrace. There was plenty of time to enjoy a bit of fresh air before the guests returned.

He pushed through the French doors and took a deep breath, inhaling the sweet scent of jasmine that clung to a nearby arbor. And froze as soon as he realized he wasn't alone.

"If only he would pay more attention to me," said the lady who stood a few paces away. "But what would ever compel him to?"

Marcus peered through the darkness. The lady stood alone, a little off to one side. He glanced around. There was no one else.

"Do you have any idea?"

Marcus paused. She must have heard him arrive and probably thought him a friend of hers. He began to retreat. The last thing he needed right now was to offer romantic advice to a woman who loved a man whose interest clearly lay elsewhere.

"Oh, if only you would speak."

Halting, Marcus cleared his throat. "Forgive me. I believe you must have mistaken me for someone else."

The lady spun around so fast she nearly lost her balance. "Who are you?"

He stared at her. "Apparently not the person you believed you were addressing."

"No. I…um…" She looked askance.

"Riiiibiiiit."

Marcus frowned. "Were you conversing with a frog?"

"Not at all," the lady said at the exact same

moment as a fat toad hopped out from behind her. It paused for a moment before continuing onto the grass beyond the terrace. She sighed. "Maybe."

Marcus chuckled. "How unusual."

"It wasn't very helpful."

"Not with its advice perhaps, but maybe by lending an ear." He tilted his head in thought. "Do toads even have ears? I'm sure they must."

The lady gave him a hesitant smile. "I should probably go back inside. Being out here alone was all right until you joined me. Now it would be improper."

She moved toward the French doors behind him. He would not stop her from leaving. To do so would be wrong, possibly ruinous for her if she were found keeping his company. A pity, since he'd enjoyed their brief encounter.

Marcus turned to watch her go as an older gentleman exited onto the terrace. His gaze immediately settled on the young lady. "Louise. What are you doing out here?"

"I was merely taking a small reprieve," Louise replied in a more timid tone than the one she'd used with Marcus.

"Go and find your mother. She's in the supper room waiting for you."

"Yes, Papa."

The young lady offered Marcus a swift smile in parting, and then she was gone. Her father, however, remained. His dark expression focused solely on Marcus. "I know who you are, Mr. Berkly, and as such, I demand you stay away from my daughter."

"With whom do I have the honor of speaking?" Marcus asked. He'd never met this man before, which clearly put him at a disadvantage.

"The Earl of Grasmere."

Marcus held the man's gaze. "A pleasure, my lord."

"A pity I can't say the same," Grasmere said. He snorted with visible disdain, then walked away.

Raising his glass to his lips, Marcus polished off the rest of his brandy. There had been a time when men like Grasmere would have thought him a fine catch for their daughter. But that was a long time ago, before his father's crimes had come to light, before he'd been hanged for murder, before the title the Berkly family had held for nine generations had been absolved.

Expelling a sigh, Marcus went back inside, crossed the ballroom to the hallway beyond, and made his way to the exit. Remaining for the sake of the music alone was no longer enough. What he wanted now – what he wished for most – was a chance to dance with Lady Louise so he could find out why she spoke to toads. And since that would never happen, he found no reason to stay.

THANK YOU SO much for taking the time to read *Her Scottish Scoundrel*. If you enjoyed this novel, you'll also enjoy the sequel! Order your copy of *The Dishonored Viscount* today so you can read Marcus's story too!

Or if you haven't read the previous books in my *Diamonds In The Rough* series, you might consider starting at the very beginning with *A Most Unlikely Duke* where bare-knuckle boxer, Raphe Matthews, unexpectedly inherits a duke's title. Figuring out how to navigate Society won't be easy, but receiving advice from the lady next door may just be worth it.

You can find out more about my new releases, backlist deals and giveaways by signing up for my newsletter here: *www.sophiebarnes.com*

And don't forget to follow me on Facebook for even more updates and fun book related posts.

Once again, I thank you for your interest in my books. Please take a moment to leave a review since this can help other readers discover books they'll love. And please continue reading for an excerpt from *The Dishonored Viscount*.

GET A SNEAK PEEK OF THE SEQUEL!

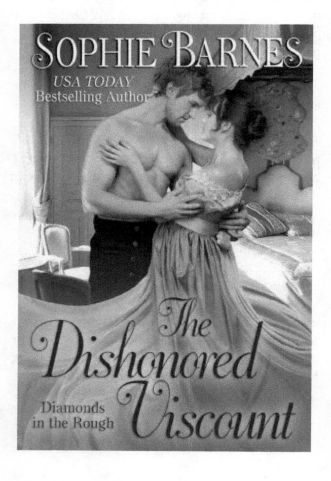

CHAPTER ONE

London, 1828

THERE WAS NOTHING worse than living in fear, Louise mused while sticking comfortably to the edge of the ballroom. And yet, this was precisely what she'd been doing for most of her life.

Every day when she woke, she prepared to face the possibility of drawing attention for the wrong reason, of being mocked for her inferiority, and of having to recognize she was a failure. All of which were directly tied to her greatest terror of all – of one day waking and not being able to see. And of the pain this would lead to, not just emotionally, but physically as well.

Because she remembered.

Even though she wished she didn't, since not remembering might have allowed her to live a more normal life – one in which she'd not be burdened by constant anxiety. But she had been seven the first time her eyes were couched by a doctor in order to fix the blurry vision she'd had since birth. At thirteen, the procedure was repeated. Then again when she was seventeen.

Apparently there was no guarantee the result would last.

A shudder raked her spine at the memory of it. No one wanted to sit still while a doctor inserted a needle into one's eye so he could push the ruined lens out of the way. It was unbearably painful. So much so she'd decided never to have another operation unless it was absolutely necessary. Consequently, she'd not told her parents when she'd lost her sight on the right eye at the age of sixteen. It had happened during a game of shuttlecock when the hard end of the birdie had struck the side of her head. Although the effect had been immediate, she'd told everyone she was fine. After all, she'd still been able to see with her left eye, provided she used her spectacles. Unfortunately, her reprieve from surgery had been short-lived. When her left lens had unexpectedly shifted a few months later, she'd had both eyes couched again. As luck would have it, she now faced the same risk once more since her right eye had failed her again a few weeks earlier.

Thus the fear. Not just of the pain and discomfort, but of when and where disaster might strike.

Last time, she'd been at a musicale. Her least favorite people in the world, Miss Rebecca Bowes, Miss Nicole Frazier, and Lady Deidre Brackenbridge, had been in attendance as well and as usual, they'd sought her out for the purpose of telling her something unkind. In this case, it had pertained to the spots on her fore-head. They'd been a nuisance for her at that age.

"You look rather blotchy this evening," Lady Deidre said while Miss Bowes and Miss Frazier both snickered. "I do hope you're not ill."

Of course, the three awful women were blessed with perfect complexions. Life was unfair that way.

Determined to hide her mortification so she wouldn't look weak, Louise had raised her chin and forced a smile. "Perhaps you should keep your distance from me then. Just to be safe."

Lady Deidre had grimaced. "Poor thing. It can't be easy knowing you've no chance of mar-rying well."

The remark prompted Louise to glance across at Mr. Nigel Fairbanks, a handsome gentleman she'd taken a fancy to last year when he'd asked her to dance at her coming out ball. Since then, her feelings for him had been steadily growing. Unfortunately, nothing escaped Lady Deidre's notice. She'd instantly laughed. "Good heavens. You really do aim for the impossible, don't you?"

"Well, it's better than...than..." Unable to think of anything clever to add, Louise had clamped her mouth shut and glared at Lady Deidre before turning away. Her intention had been to locate her seat, but then her eyesight had failed and she'd tripped over something. One second later she'd been sprawled on the floor while laughter echoed behind her. Apparently, Lady Deidre and her friends had found the inci-dent very amusing.

Since then, Louise stayed close to her family during social functions – particularly to her siblings. All were older than she and happily married. Albert, Viscount Linton, to Diana Winterly, Kimberly to Viscount Laringsby, and Helen to the Earl of Crofton.

Presently, Louise stood with her sisters and surveyed the Redding Ballroom. It was filled to capacity by London's elite, all dressed in their evening finery. Gowns cut from silk shimmered in response to the candlelight while gemstones sparkled and crystal beads winked. Louise herself had elected to wear one of her favorite dresses. Fashioned from a watery turquoise, it complimented her dark brown hair and eyes. A nearby refreshment table offered iced cakes and trays piled high with triangular sandwiches. Musicians placed on the opposite side of the room slid their bows across the strings of their violins, filling the air with harmonious notes in accompaniment of the quadrille currently underway.

"He's dancing at the moment," Kimberly told her.

"Who is?" Louise asked with every intention of feigning ignorance.

Kimberly snorted and shook her head. "The same man you look for at every social function. Mr. Fairbanks, of course."

"Why don't you go and talk to him?" Helen asked.

Louise sighed. "Because whenever I am in Mr. Fairbanks' presence, I either forget how to speak or say something foolish." When he'd helped her up at the musicale three years earlier, she'd forgotten to thank him. Instead she'd remarked on his scent, since this had been the first clue she'd had of the man who'd come to her aid. He'd chuckled and voiced his appreciation, but her mortification had been complete.

"Didn't he ask you to dance at your coming out ball?" Helen asked.

"He did," Louise admitted, her heart fluttering slightly at the memory. The dance had brought him to her attention, but it was the help he'd given her when she'd been in distress that had caused her to fall completely in love with him.

"Well there you are," Kimberly said. "I'm sure he'd treat you kindly if you were to strike up a conversation with him."

Louise's stomach twisted in that nervous way it always did whenever she thought of stepping out of her element. "I don't believe he thinks of me in the same way I think of him. If he did, he'd surely have asked me to dance again since."

"Do you honestly think so?" Helen asked. "After you've not danced in years?"

Her sister did have a point. After the musicale incident, Louise was wary of walking onto a dance floor because what if she suddenly lost her sight again in the midst of a reel? What if she crashed into other dancers or tripped and fell to the floor? She'd make an even bigger spectacle of herself then — the sort she feared she'd never live down.

"If you want to marry," Kimberly said, "you'll have to accept the attentions of men."

"You make it sound so simple," Louise murmured while taking an instinctive step backward. She'd still not forgotten the comment Lady Deidre had made. Worst of all, Louise didn't think she'd been wrong to question Louise's ability to make a good match.

Yet another reason for hesitation.

"And if the man you choose to marry cares for you, he'll overlook your need for spectacles," Helen added.

Louise shook her head. "No man will want to saddle himself with a woman who might lose her sight at any second. I'd be a danger to his reputation."

Kimberly placed a calming hand on Louise's arm. "Your condition is fixable, Louise. And every time your sight is restored, it lasts for years."

"There's no guarantee it will though. If I lose my sight again, the procedure might only last a day, a week, or a month. I've been incredibly fortunate so far to have it last in such long increments, but it might not keep doing so."

"I still think you should talk to Mr. Fairbanks," Helen said. "You've been in love with him for so long the very idea of him marrying anyone else would be highly unpleasant."

Louise smiled on account of her sister's kindness. "You're a romantic, Helen. Of course you'd say that. But that doesn't mean Mr. Fairbanks deserves to be burdened by me."

"Stop it," Kimberly admonished. "You're a wonderful catch for any gentleman lucky enough to get to know you."

"Only if I'm able to keep my eyesight." A horrible thought struck. "Can you imagine if I were to lose it while walking up the aisle on our wedding? I'd likely trip and get tangled in my gown. It would be disastrous."

"I suppose that is a legitimate concern," Helen said.

"Agreed." Kimberly gave Louise's arm a squeeze before letting go. "I'd be worried about that too if I were in your position."

"And it's not just that," Louise told her sisters. "It could happen while I'm hosting a dinner, or during a ride, or while I'm watching our children."

"You probably ought to refrain from riding," Helen said in a pensive tone.

Louise cut her a glance. "I already do."

A pause in the conversation followed while chatter ensued around them. The music guiding the dance Mr. Fairbanks had been participating in began to fade, and Louise invariably sought him out as he bowed to his partner. A flutter fanned out within her breast as she watched him step off the dance floor. Impeccably dressed and with almost black hair and classically handsome features, he cut a striking figure in his evening attire.

"No risk, no gain," Kimberly whispered near Louise's ear.

Heat filled her cheeks. She swallowed. "Quite right."

"Then talk to him," Helen urged. "We can

come with you, if you like."

"No." That would only make her feel more like a coward. If she was going to do this, she'd do it alone. Because in spite of her fears, her sisters did have a point. If she wanted to marry, she needed to make a match sooner rather than later. At twenty years of age, her chance to do so would soon be gone, and she could only use her eye surgeries as an excuse for so long. Plus, Mr. Fairbanks had proved himself to be a good man. He wouldn't laugh at her or treat her cruelly if she approached him. She was certain of it.

"I'll just inquire about his wellbeing," she said, more to herself than to anyone else.

"And we'll be waiting for you right here," Kimberly said, her voice full of encouragement. "Take as long as you need."

Grateful for the support, Louise made her way through the crowd toward the man she'd been dreaming of since he'd saved her from being overlooked. Her stomach tightened as she drew nearer, and then he was suddenly there, his attention focused upon…

Louise sucked in a breath and prayed she might turn invisible. She seriously pondered the idea of taking a sharp left turn to avoid Mr. Fairbanks completely. Because the last thing she wanted was to have to greet him while Lady Deidre gazed at him as if he were some magical creature who'd promised to make all her wishes come true.

And then, as if things couldn't possibly get any worse, Lady Deidre's gaze swept toward Louise.

A smile curled her lips.

"Lady Louise," Lady Deidre said, obliterating whatever hope she'd had of being ignored so she could escape back into the crowd and pretend her life wasn't one long series of awful moments. "It's so good to see you again."

Louise froze. She stared at Lady Deidre, balled her hands into fists, and straightened her spine. She did her best to offer a smile in return. "Likewise."

A pause followed, during which Louise could feel heat creeping up the back of her neck. She could think of nothing else to say, so she glanced at Mr. Fairbanks, who took this as his cue to ask, "Are you enjoying the ball?"

"Yes," Louise said. "And you?"

"To be honest I found it rather dull until I encountered Lady Deidre. She told me the most incredible tale earlier." He smiled at Lady Deidre who promptly chuckled as if abashed. It was nauseating to watch. "Perhaps you would care to repeat it for Lady Louise's benefit?"

"Of course I'd be delighted to do so," Lady Deidre said, "though it is a rather long story and our set is sadly about to begin. Shall we proceed, Mr. Fairbanks?"

"Indeed." He offered Lady Deidre his arm, which she latched onto like a leech. "Perhaps—"

"Mr. Fairbanks," Lady Deidre purred while turning him away from Louise, "the other couples are already taking their places. We really must hurry if we're to find a good spot on the floor."

"Of course," Mr. Fairbanks said while Lady Deidre proceeded to lead him away. "Please excuse us, Lady Louise."

Humiliation burned the tips of Louise's ears as Lady Deidre glanced back at her with a vindictive grin. The woman had known of Louise's affection for Mr. Fairbanks for three long years, and had clearly chosen to turn this knowledge into a weapon.

Swallowing her anger, the frustration it wrought on her nerves, and the keen awareness that every poke Lady Deidre dealt her just chipped away at whatever confidence she still possessed, Louise glanced toward the terrace doors with longing. Kimberly and Helen had said they would wait for her return, but right now, all Louise wanted was to be alone. So she swept through the crowd with determined steps, leaving behind the buoyant music, the lively chatter and laughter, the dazzling atmosphere filling the ballroom to claustrophobic capacity, and Lady Deidre's hatefulness.

Fresh air filled her lungs the moment she stepped outside, its coolness washing her skin of the heat she'd experienced indoors. She breathed in the sweet scent of jasmine that wafted toward her on the breeze and savored the stillness. Much to her surprise and pleasure, no one else was out here. For once, it would seem, something had worked in her favor.

She moved slowly toward the stone railing, closer to the spot where steps led down to a torch-lit garden. Overhead, the ink-black sky stretched in every direction, as if it wished to encompass the world. Stars – tiny flecks of sparkling silver – twinkled like sun-kissed diamonds. A smile caught Louise's lips. The world had so much beauty to offer, if one would but take the time to pause and look.

"Riii—bit."

Louise dropped her gaze. It took her a moment to locate the toad – a fat creature perched upon the top step. Her smile broadened – not because she cared for any form of reptile, but because it occurred to her that a toad's presence was much preferred to Lady Deidre's.

This thought brought her mind back to Mr. Fairbanks. "If only he would pay more attention to me," she said, addressing the toad, "but what would ever compel him to? Do you have any idea?" When the toad continued to sit there, motionless and silent, Louise sighed. "Oh, if only you would speak."

Someone cleared their throat behind her, and then a man said, "Forgive me. I believe you must have mistaken me for someone else."

Startled, Louise spun around and nearly lost her footing in the process. Of course someone had to witness her talking to a toad. That was simply how her life worked. She stared at the stranger – a handsome gentleman with an inquisitive gleam in his eyes. "Who are you?"

He studied her for a moment. "Apparently not the person you believed you were addressing."

"No. I…um…" She looked askance. Perhaps she could tell him something more socially acceptable than the truth?

"Riii—bit."

Louise bit her lip. *Drat!*

The stranger frowned. His appearance was different from Mr. Fairbanks's, whom she'd always thought the handsomest man in the world. By contrast, this man possessed fair hair, his jaw was more angular too – less delicate in appearance – while his mouth seemed on the verge of smiling, without actually doing so. The effect lent a jovial air of mischievousness to him that Mr. Fairbanks, who either smiled with complete abandon or not at all, lacked.

"Were you conversing with a frog?" asked the stranger, his casual tone not the least bit condemning.

"No," Louise tried as the toad hopped out from behind her. It paused for a moment before continuing down the steps toward the grass beyond the terrace. She huffed a breath and chose to accept defeat. "Maybe."

A low chuckle resonated between them. "How unusual."

She knit her brow. "It wasn't very helpful."

"Not with its advice perhaps, but maybe by lending an ear." The stranger tilted his head in thought. "Do toads even have ears? I'm sure they must."

Louise instinctively smiled. There was comfort to be found in this man's company, which was odd since she'd no idea who he was. And since they'd not been formally introduced… "I should probably go back inside. Being out here alone was all right until you joined me. Now it would be improper."

She started toward the French doors behind him while he tracked her steps in silence. A pity she could not stay when instinct suggested she'd like conversing with him at greater length. She was almost at the doors when one side swung open and her father stepped onto the terrace. "Louise. What are you doing out here?"

She took a fortifying breath and prayed he'd stay calm. "I was merely taking a small reprieve."

He held her gaze. "Go and find your mother. She's in the supper room, waiting for you."

"Yes, Papa." What else could she say? He was her father and she'd always done as he'd asked. Glancing toward the stranger, she gave him a swift smile in parting before she returned inside, resigned to the idea of not being able to leave the ball any time soon.

"The man you met on the terrace," Papa began once Louise and her parents were finally heading home in their carriage three hours later. "You're never to speak with him again. Is that clear?"

Curious about her father's apparent dislike of a person she'd thought to be rather pleasant, she asked, "Who was he?"

"If he approaches you, you're to walk away immediately," Papa said, ignoring her question. "To be seen in his company will most assuredly lead to ruin. Mark my word."

"Goodness," Mama said with a gasp. "You really must be careful, Louise. Listen to your

father and protect your reputation at all cost."
The fact that she believed it was the only asset
Louise had left besides her increasingly large
dowry was heavily implied.

"I gather he's a rake then?" Louise said, since
this was the sort of man her parents had always
warned her against.

"I've no idea," Papa said, then hastily added,
"but it wouldn't surprise me if he were."

"Hmm…" Louise frowned. She found her
father's vagueness, his reluctance to mention the
man's name, peculiar.

"Cast him from your mind," Papa said. "He's
not worth sparing a thought."

"Instead," Mama said, "I would suggest you
make more of an effort to be seen by the eligible
gentlemen looking to marry. If you continue to
hide in various corners, they'll forget all about
you."

"I'm not hiding in corners," Louise grumbled.

"You're not making an effort either," Mama
said.

"I spoke to Mr. Fairbanks," Louise blurted,
her intention being to win this frustrating argument.

She instantly regretted it when Mama said, "I
believe he's enamored by Lady Deidre."

"He hasn't announced an engagement yet,"
Papa said. "Louise could still win him."

"Yes," Mama agreed in a tone devoid of conviction. "I suppose she could."

Louise sighed. She knew she had to do better,
try harder, be more assertive. If only fear didn't

always lurch at the back of her mind, it would be so much easier.

To her surprise, her musings on the subject led her thoughts straight back to the stranger she'd met on the terrace. Gazing out the carriage window at the dark streets beyond, she went over their conversation while picturing him in her mind's eye. Would she ever meet him again, she wondered. More to the point, who on earth was he?

Order your copy today!
https://books2read.com/u/38RlP6

ACKNOWLEDGMENTS

I WOULD LIKE TO thank the Killion Group for their incredible help with the editing and cover design for this book.

And to my friends and family, thank you for your constant support and for believing in me. I would be lost without you!

ABOUT THE AUTHOR

BORN IN DENMARK, USA TODAY best-selling author Sophie has spent her youth traveling with her parents to wonderful places around the world. She's lived in five different countries, on three different continents, has studied design in Paris and New York, and speaks Danish, English, French, Spanish, and Romanian with varying degrees of fluency. But most impressive of all - she's been married to the same man three times, in three different countries and in three different dresses.

While living in Africa, Sophie turned to her lifelong passion - writing. When she's not busy dreaming up her next romance novel, Sophie enjoys spending time with her family, swimming, cooking, gardening, watching romantic comedies and, of course, reading. She currently lives on the East Coast.

You can contact her through her website at
www.sophiebarnes.com
And please consider leaving a review for this book.
Every review is greatly appreciated!

CPSIA information can be obtained
at www.ICGtesting.com
Printed in the USA
LVHW041459220721
693425LV00001B/50